The
TESTIMONıᴠM

MW01064104

To Alice,
a fellow lover of
ancient things —
enjoy the story!

[signature]

" Quid est veritas?"

The
TESTIMONIVM

Lewis Ben Smith

eLectio Publishing
Little Elm, TX
www.eLectioPublishing.com
Join the conversation:
http://bit.ly/Testimonium

The Testimonium

By Lewis Ben Smith

Copyright 2014 by Lewis Ben Smith

Cover Design by eLectio Publishing, LLC

ISBN-13: 978-1-63213-044-0

Published by eLectio Publishing, LLC

Little Elm, Texas

http://www.eLectioPublishing.com

Printed in the United States of America

Without limiting the rights under copyright reserved above, no part of this publication may be reproduced, stored in or introduced into a retrieval system, or transmitted, in any form, or by any means (electronic, mechanical, photocopying, recording, or otherwise), without the prior written permission of both the copyright owner and the above publisher of this book.

If you purchased this book without a cover, you should be aware that this book is stolen property. It was reported as "unsold and destroyed" to the publisher and neither the author nor the publisher has received any payment for the "stripped book."

The scanning, uploading, and distribution of this book via the Internet or via any other means without the permission of the publisher is illegal and punishable by law. Please purchase only authorized electronic editions, and do not participate in or encourage electronic piracy of copyrighted materials. Your support of the author's rights is appreciated.

Publisher's Note

This is a work of fiction. Names, characters, places, and incidents either are the product of the author's imagination or are used fictitiously, and any resemblance to actual persons, living or dead, business establishments, events, or locales is entirely coincidental.

The publisher does not have any control over and does not assume any responsibility for author or third-party websites or their content.

THIS BOOK IS DEDICATED TO:

My wife, Patty, who has spent many an evening watching TV alone while I hunched over the keyboard creating this opus

My dear friend, Ellie, who read it chapter by chapter as I wrote it and furnished many, many insightful comments and suggestions

AND the GCS Senior Class of 2014, who quickly learned that asking me about my progress was a great way to get out of a history lecture – and many of whose names I used for minor (and not so minor) characters herein

I actually did it, guys!

"And that these things did happen, you can ascertain from the Acts of Pontius Pilate."

— Justin Martyr,
writing to Emperor Antoninus Pius, circa 150 AD

PROLOGUE – Jerusalem, 33 AD

The Roman prefect eased his weary frame onto a stone bench, the folds of his toga bunching up around him. His exhausted body finally relaxed, but his mind remained full of turmoil. What was any civilized man to make of the behavior of barbarians? And was there any tribe, nation, or tongue in all of the *gens humana* more maddeningly barbaric than the Jews? Forever carping about how their unnamable, unknowable, invisible God was going to take offense at this or that. "Chosen people," indeed! What god in his right mind would choose them? But for all their insufferable self-righteousness, they could be as vicious as a hyena if anyone threatened to upset their *mos maorum*—or, as they referred to it, the "traditions of their elders." The governor was still not sure which god he had offended to merit such a disgraceful posting, although he knew why the vindictive Emperor Tiberius had sent him there. Judea, the armpit of the Empire!

His body ached for a good massage and a long nap, but he knew that he should record the events of the entire week while they were still fresh in his mind, lest he forget important details. He did not know what to make of the matter himself, at this point, and if any further unpleasantness came of this whole sordid affair—Jupiter! They might report him to Caesar—again! He had to record it all now, then. Sleep would have to wait. So, rubbing his eyes, Lucius Pontius Pilate called for his scribe.

EARTHQUAKE STRIKES ITALIAN COAST

(AP) A moderate earthquake, measuring about 6.3 on the Richter scale, struck the coast of Italy last night, according to the Italian Geological Bureau. The epicenter of the quake was approximately a mile off the coast of the scenic Isle of Capri, once a resort of Roman emperors, and now a popular tourist destination. No tsunami warnings were issued, and only minor damage has been reported thus far. No injuries have been reported.

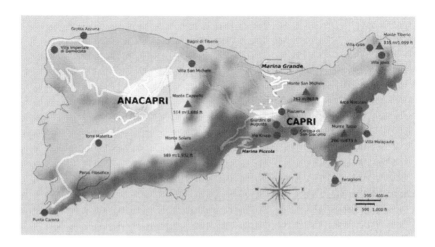

CHAPTER ONE

Giuseppe Rossini looked sadly at the floor of his study before reaching for the broom and dustpan. The lovely Etruscan vase that had decorated his bookshelf for years had been knocked off by the tremor and lay in a hundred pieces at his feet. Several of his books had also tumbled to the floor, but the broken crockery was a safety concern, so he slipped on a pair of sandals to protect his feet. The vase was only a replica—a conscientious archeologist, Rossini did not collect real artifacts other than a few common items that he used as part of his teaching presentations on Capri's Roman era. But it was a high-quality replica that had cost him a good many lira, back when Italy still used the lira, and it would be hard to replace. On the other hand, though, his roof was still attached, and the spiderweb cracks in his wall plaster were more aesthetically than structurally damaging. Some of his neighbors were not as lucky—one house had a collapsed balcony, and the local market had suffered some serious damage. At least, since the quake had struck at 3 AM, no one was inside the building to be hurt. All in all, it could have been much worse.

It took him the better part of an hour to go through his house and pick up all the debitage of the quake. Overall, he had fared quite well— the vase was the most expensive loss, although several picture frames had fallen from the wall, and there was broken glass where they landed. Earthquakes were not uncommon in parts of Italy, although this was the first one to strike Capri since he had moved there a number of years before. By midmorning he was done cleaning up his house and finished getting dressed. He pulled on some sturdy hiking boots and donned his hat, as the early spring day was already warm and he had a good hike ahead of him. He did not think the massive stones of the Villa Jovis would have taken much damage, but as the on-site curator of the ancient ruin, he knew that he would have to go see for himself. At least it was a beautiful Sunday morning for a stroll—and he had not planned on attending Easter Mass anyway.

On his way out the door, he grabbed his walking stick. His limp was almost indiscernible these days, but the hike up the steep Via Tiberio always made his leg ache. Once an active field archeologist, he had taken a bad fall fifteen years ago while conducting an excavation near Herculaneum. He suffered a severe compound fracture of the left femur, and that leg was now a full half inch shorter than the other. It had taken him several weeks in traction and a year of physical therapy to recover his mobility, and the pain never left completely. The Bureau of Antiquities had assigned him as an on-site curator and docent once he was able to return to work. He spent several years giving tours and lecturing students at Pompeii and Herculaneum before being posted to Capri. Capri was a less popular site than the two volcano-ravaged ancient cities, but Giuseppe had come to love the island over time. The folk were friendly, and the tourists were more likely to be serious students of history and not just the gawkers who had seen an article on Pompeii somewhere. He missed the thrill of discovery and the hard physical labor of excavation, but at sixty-two, he realized that those days were past him.

The Via Tiberio was built over an ancient Roman road, but it was still fairly steep. The view from the top was always worth the hike, though. Covering over an acre of land on the second highest point of the entire island, the former villa of the Emperor Tiberius must have been one of the most beautiful buildings in the Empire during its heyday. It was here that the reclusive Emperor had retired from Rome in 26 AD, leaving his corrupt henchman Sejanus to govern the Empire for him. According to Suetonius, a second-century historian, Tiberius had given free rein to his most twisted baser instincts at this luxurious retreat, engaging in wanton pedophilia with children from surrounding villages, and lavishly rewarding those who pleased him, while ordering those who did not flung from the island's steepest cliffs to the rocks below. Personally, Giuseppe thought that Suetonius was a gossipy old busybody who had no way of knowing what went on at Tiberius' villa a hundred years earlier, and thus decided to make up whatever salacious details would sell the most books. After all, journalism couldn't have changed that much in two thousand years!

It took about forty-five minutes to hike up the narrow lane from Capri village to the ruins of Villa Jovis. As Giuseppe walked the steep trail, he was distressed to see signs that the quake had indeed slightly damaged the slopes of Mount Tiberio. Here and there were rockslides, and at one point a fissure cut across the road—only a few inches wide, but deep and black, showing that even the face of the mountain was not immune to the forces of nature. He began to worry that the magnificent ruin might have been damaged by the quake.

As he topped the rise, his initial reaction was a sigh of relief. The sprawling ruins seemed to be undamaged. But as he mounted the steps to the Emperor's receiving hall, he saw that was not entirely correct. One of the remaining Corinthian columns had been toppled, and here and there new cracks and fissures showed where the ancient marble and limestone had split under the force of the violent tremor. Overall, though, the damage did not look too severe. He moved through the complex, checking all the remaining walls and staircases for further damage and finding none. He was almost done when he saw it.

Coming down the last staircase, he saw a scatter of masonry sprawled across the limestone floor of the level below, right alongside the stairs. Rounding the corner, he saw that a portion of the wall that held up the staircase had collapsed, leaving a gap about four feet tall and two feet wide. More than just a gap, in fact—there was a void beyond the wall revealed by the collapse, a blackness that even the noonday sun could not illuminate. Some sort of sealed chamber had been revealed by the collapsing wall!

As Giuseppe drew closer, he smelled a distinct aroma coming from the ancient chamber. It was the smell of dry, musty parchment, of dust and rat droppings and decay, the smell of ancient wood dried beyond the point of rot, the smell of air that had been sealed up on itself for centuries. It was the smell of history. He eased a small flashlight out of his jacket pocket and shone it inside the chamber, then let out a low gasp. He reached into his shirt pocket for his cell phone and hit speed dial.

"Bureau of Antiquities, how may I direct your call?" said the voice on the other end.

"Dr. Isabella Sforza," he replied. "It's urgent."

* * *

Dr. Joshua Parker folded his long legs under him and settled into the pew after the last song ended. He picked up his well-worn New American Standard Bible and smiled as his father, Benjamin Parker, walked up to the pulpit. "Brother Ben," as Baptists in one tri-state area referred to his father, was a towering man in his early seventies with a deep booming voice and an accent that had never left the Ozark ridges where he had been born at the end of the Great Depression. It was Easter Sunday, and Josh smiled at the thought that Dad's new church was about to hear his signature sermon for the very first time. This message lay at the core of everything his father had believed and taught over a ministry that stretched nearly fifty years. Josh had heard the sermon many times growing up, and every year his father polished it a bit, updating the pop culture references to fit his current congregation before he let them have it on Easter Sunday.

"This morning I want to talk to you about one of my favorite passages of Scripture," he began. "But it isn't because it is my favorite that I want to tell you about it. It's because I consider it to be the MOST important passage in all the New Testament—arguably the most important passage in all of Scripture." As Brother Ben's golden tones resonated throughout the crowded auditorium, the audience shifted its attention slightly. Some leaned forward; others redirected their gaze from the people around them to the tall figure in the pulpit. Obviously the new pastor, whom they had already come to respect and admire, had something important to say.

Casting his piercing gaze around the room, Parker smiled, then lowered his eyes to the large-print Bible before him. Although his father could quote this passage from memory, Josh knew he preferred to read verbatim: "From the Book of First Corinthians, Chapter Fifteen, beginning in Verse One: 'Now I make known to you, brethren, the gospel which I preached to you, which also you received, in which also you stand, by which also you are saved, if you hold fast the word which I preached to you, unless you believed in vain. For I delivered to you as of first importance what I also received, that Christ died for our sins according to the Scriptures, and that He was buried, and that He was raised on the third day according to the Scriptures, and that He appeared to Cephas, then to the twelve. After that He appeared to more than five hundred brethren at one time, most of whom remain until now, but some have fallen asleep; then He appeared to James, then to all the apostles; and last of all, as to one untimely born, He appeared to me also. For I am the least of the apostles, and not fit to be called an apostle, because I persecuted the church of God.'"

Looking up, he posed a question: "Why is this so important? Simple. It is, first of all, the earliest written account we have of those who actually saw the Risen Christ. Most scholars think the crucifixion was in 33 AD. Paul wrote these lines in 54 AD—twenty-one years later, and about ten years before Matthew, Mark, and Luke began composing their gospels. Obviously, he placed great weight on these words, because he described them 'as of first importance.' This simple account of the Resurrection was foundational to everything Paul taught the churches throughout his ministry. Now let me draw your attention to an odd phrase here: 'I delivered to you . . . what I also received.' What does Paul mean? Well, when rabbis used that phrase, it was to indicate that the teaching they were about to impart was something they themselves had been taught earlier. The list of witnesses that followed is arranged in simple Greek verse form so it could be easily memorized. This wasn't just a random bit of trivia that someone taught to Paul: it appears to be one of the very first catechisms composed by the early Church. So when would Paul have learned these lines about how many people witnessed the Resurrection? What opportunity did he have to meet the disciples who were there in Jerusalem that first Easter morning? The answer can be found in Paul's first letter, which we call The Book of Galatians, written about 48 AD. In his account of his conversion, Paul explains: 'Three years later'—that is, after his conversion on the Damascus road—'I went up to Jerusalem to become acquainted with Cephas, and stayed with him fifteen days.' Now of course, Cephas is the Greek form of Simon Peter. What makes this so critical? The timing, my friends. Paul was converted only a few years—maybe two or three at most—after the Crucifixion. And three years after that, he is in Jerusalem, visiting Simon Peter. That would place this visit about five or six years after Jesus was crucified. Nearly all the eyewitnesses were still alive at this point! And not just the friendly eyewitnesses either. The men who crucified Jesus were still present, and most of them still in power. The members of the angry mob that arrested him were still around, as would have been some of the soldiers who guarded the tomb."

Parker paused, gathering steam. From his pew, Josh watched with interest. His dad had them now. Every eye in the place was on the pulpit. This was not just another tame old Easter sermon; this was thought-provoking stuff! The elder Parker continued: "Now, we have grown up in the church, most of us. We have had the Easter story recited to us every year since we were toddlers. And most of us have never questioned it. So the incredible import of what Paul is telling us here is easy to miss! Let me put it to you this way: suppose that, around the summer of 1969 or 1970, I showed up in Dealey Plaza down in Dallas and climbed up on a soapbox and began to talk about what had happened there just six years earlier. Suppose I said: 'Yes, my friends, it was right here that President Kennedy's motorcade passed through town. And three shots rang out, one of which pierced his brain and took his life. And he was buried in a lavish tomb in Arlington National Cemetery that Monday, as all the world looked on. Then, three days later, he rose from the dead, and he appeared—first to Bobby, then to the Cabinet. After that he appeared to LBJ, alone, then to the cabinet again, and then to over five hundred witnesses at the same time—most of whom are still alive today! Last of all, I saw him myself, right on I-30 between here and Texarkana!' How do you think THAT would go over?" he thundered.

The audience was trying to process this. Some of the younger ones laughed out loud, while many older ones scowled at the pastor, wondering what he was getting at. Josh, who had heard this illustration many times before, was nonetheless moved by it all over again. His father's voice crackled across the assembly: "They'd start measuring me for a rubber room, wouldn't they? Because they understood a fundamental truth in Dallas in 1970, just the same as they understood it in Jerusalem in 40 AD—dead people STAY dead!"

Now they got it. Many in the audience began to nod; others looked stunned as they processed what they were being told. The church was absolutely silent. Josh saw that his father's words had made a visible impact on them. As his father read the next passage from Corinthians Josh began to reflect on the many churches that had heard this message before. Josh had been born in 1980, while his father was pastoring in Denton, Texas. His earliest memories were of scorching hot summers and mild winters, of church fellowships and youth rallies, and of the fascination with the past that his father had shared with him. They had scoured creek beds for fossilized shark's teeth and arrowheads, and read and discussed biographies of presidents and kings long dead. They had gone to see every traveling exhibit of ancient artifacts from foreign cultures that came through the museums in nearby Dallas.

When he was ten, his father had been called to a church in Spiro, Oklahoma, and Josh had listened with wonder to old-timers talk about the amazing Indian mounds that had stood there before treasure hunters looted them during the Depression. One time, an elderly archeologist who had been there in those days had come to town and described how the central burial mound at Spiro contained a vaulted chamber with a ten-foot ceiling, stacked high with rare and perishable artifacts never seen in any American site: feather capes still perfectly preserved, shell gorgets, wooden burial masks plated in copper, and thousands of turquoise beads. It was at that lecture that young Josh had made up his mind to become an archeologist—to discover and excavate ancient treasures, to see them properly written up and curated, preserved so that future generations could gaze at them.

As he grew older, Josh became disgusted with the state of American archeology—politics had forced the science to pander shamelessly to Native American demands, so that beautiful and scientifically valuable relics were required by law to be put back into the ground, never to be seen again by anyone. He then decided that, while his love of archeology was unchanged, his focus was not going to be the flint chips and pottery shards the Native Americans had left behind. His faith was drawing him toward the Middle East, to the place where Christianity had been born, where traces of its origins could still be found today, proving that the Biblical record was more than just myth and legend. Josh believed that Christianity was rooted in real, irrefutable history. So he got his degree and then his doctorate in Biblical archeology, and participated in excavations at Qumran, Capernaum, and most recently Ephesus, where he had helped discover the remains of a fourth-century church built on the reputed burial place of the Apostle John. Now he was home on a brief sabbatical before returning to Ephesus to finish cataloguing and publishing his finds there.

His father was reading the final passage of the day as he returned his attention to the sermon: "'For if the dead are not raised, not even Christ has been raised; and if Christ has not been raised, your faith is worthless; you are still in your sins. Then those also who have fallen asleep in Christ have perished. If we have hoped in Christ in this life only, we are of all men most to be pitied.'"

Brother Ben looked slowly around the room. "I put it to you today, my friends, that Paul got it absolutely right. The world has been doing its best to put Jesus back in that tomb for two thousand years because they understand what many Christians forget: that if Jesus did not rise from the dead, our faith is based on a lie. Our belief is not in a risen Savior, but a desiccated corpse. If Jesus did not rise from the dead on the third day, we might as well tear down the church and build a bowling alley, for all the good we are doing anyone!" He paused for the last time. "But that isn't the case, is it? We serve a living, risen Lord! And because He was powerful enough to conquer the grave two thousand years ago, He is powerful enough to handle whatever you are struggling with today! He holds out His hand to you this morning, offering to take your burden, to forgive your sin, to cleanse your life, and to make you a new creature! All you have to do—is TAKE IT!"

The organ swelled, and the choir began singing the old hymn: "I serve a risen Savior; He's in the world today. I know that He is living, whatever men may say!" The congregation rose and sang along, and Josh joined them, his clear baritone ringing from the rafters.

* * *

Isabella Sforza could not believe it. She knew and respected Giuseppe Rossini, but what he was describing seemed impossible. "You realize that the ruins of Villa Jovis have been excavated dozens of times?" she asked.

"Of course," replied Dr. Rossini's voice from Capri. "Starting in the 1300s! I assisted on one of the most recent digs here, back in the 1980s. But I am telling you, from my brief glimpse, this chamber has never been breached since it was sealed—and I am sure that it is Roman in age, possibly from the time of Tiberius himself. You need to get over here!"

Isabella thought for a moment. "I have a class tomorrow evening, but my graduate assistant can cover that if need be. There's an Antiquities Board meeting tomorrow afternoon, but they can certainly carry on without me. I'm the most junior board member anyway. It looks like this was well timed for me to come help—my schedule is pretty light all this week. All right, first things first. Close the ruins to tourism till further notice—put a barricade across the road if you have to. Go speak to the monks at the old church and warn them to stay away from the site, and cover the entrance of the chamber. I'll see if I can pull a few strings and catch a chopper to Capri this afternoon. I'll give you a call as soon as I can make arrangements."

Rossini laughed. "Still full of fire, my dear! I always liked that about you. I look forward to seeing you in a couple of hours, then. And don't worry—I won't leave the chamber entrance unguarded."

"Good," she replied. "I will be there as soon as I can. And Giuseppe!"

"Yes?"

"Don't enter the chamber till I get there!"

He chuckled again. "Don't worry, Isabella. I am aflame with curiosity, but using a cane for these last fifteen years has also made me cautious. *Ciao!*"

Dr. Sforza went to the cabinet in the corner of her office and quickly gathered her field gear—khakis, a backpack with bottled water, digital camera, energy bars, chalk, measuring tape, twine, and a variety of brushes and small picks for cleaning away matrix, dirt, and dust from ancient artifacts. She was a slender woman of thirty-one years who looked a good deal younger. She was born Isabella Verdi, to a family that had lived and farmed on the same land for generations. Precocious as a child, she had been fascinated with Italy's history—the family farm in Tuscany featured the ruins of a Roman military camp and an ancient Greek temple, where she frequently found bronze arrowheads and the occasional badly corroded ancient coin. Earning excellent marks in school, she had already decided by age ten that archeology would be her life's work. The arrival of puberty and the subsequent discovery of boys had never dampened her passion for history, and she had decided early on that men were more trouble than they were worth. She finished secondary school early, entered college at the age of sixteen, and by age twenty she had her degree in archeology and was in graduate school, with neither a boyfriend nor fiancé in the picture to complicate her plans.

That is, until she met Marc Antony Sforza. Their shared passion for Roman history and archeology flamed into passion for each other. They married after a short courtship, finishing graduate school as husband and wife. She went on to finish her doctorate by age twenty-six, while Marc had worked for two summers on excavations at the ancient port of Ostia. The marriage was mutually fulfilling and happy until Marc died in a plane crash five years before. Devastated, Isabella had buried herself in her career ever since, ignoring the many admiring glances she received from colleagues and strangers as she divided her time between archeological sites and the museums and laboratories where she studied and analyzed her finds. Logically, she knew that her husband was dead, and at some point, she should try to find another man to share her life with, but no one she met could ever measure up to the delightful man she had loved and lost. The fact that most men, seeing her for the first time, were more interested in what was in her blouse than what was on her mind did not help. While Isabella objectively knew that she was a well-built and attractive woman, she had no use for someone who put the physical ahead of the intellectual. She understood that physical beauty is fleeting and shallow, while the achievements of the mind would last forever. Her goal was to make such a name for herself that scholars around the world would remember her for the discoveries she made and the papers she published, not because she looked good in a set of khakis. She had been flattered to be offered a position on the Board of Antiquities at the age of thirty; however, she also knew that the promotion was due more to the government's desire to appear friendly to women than to her merits as a scientist, and that bothered her a great deal. She wanted to earn her position!

The problem with that goal was that, so far, she had made no remarkable discoveries. Italy had one of the richest historical and archeological heritages in the whole world, but so many scholars and treasure hunters had dug and excavated there for so long that remarkable discoveries were now few and far between. Like nearly all Italian archeologists, she had spent some time in the ongoing excavations at Pompeii and Herculaneum—nearly two hundred years after their discovery, these two buried cities were still being slowly uncovered. She also helped excavate and study an ancient temple of Minerva discovered during street work in the city of Rome, but it had been leveled and built over in the ancient past, so that the foundations and flooring were just about all that remained. Despite all this, her professional reputation was solid—just not remarkable.

She hoped the discovery on Capri would change all that. Tiberius was the second emperor of Rome, the adopted son and heir of Augustus Caesar himself, and had ruled during the life and times of Jesus of Nazareth and his apostles. She reviewed her knowledge of Tiberius from her college classes and personal readings. His mother was Livia Drusilla, and his father was Tiberius Claudius Nero. When he was a child she had divorced her first husband, a cruel and vain man, in order to marry Caesar Octavianus, subsequently named Augustus by the Senate when he became the first Emperor of Rome. Tiberius was already in his late fifties when he became emperor in 14 AD after Augustus died. He had been forced to divorce Vipsania, the woman he loved, in order to marry Julia, the daughter of Augustus by one of his earlier marriages. It was a miserable marriage, and Julia had publicly shamed him by taking many lovers. Tiberius hated Rome and despised the Senate, and after only a few years as Emperor had retired to the Island of Capri, where he owned twelve villas, of which the Villa Jovis was the largest and best preserved.

Could Rossini have actually found a chamber from Tiberius' day, sealed for nearly two thousand years? The odds seemed remarkably long, but stranger things had happened. She was glad that it was Giuseppe Rossini who had made the discovery. He had been one of her early mentors, and by all accounts a tremendous field archeologist before his crippling injury. Unfortunately, she had only gotten the chance to go on a dig with him once, as a teenage volunteer. But he had become a close and trusted friend during her college years, and had been a great comfort to her when she lost Marc, and then her father, within a few months of each other. She knew how badly it chafed Rossini to be unable to lead digs as he used to, and decided that whatever it was that he had found, he would get full credit as the discoverer. As Isabella called various people and made arrangements to fly to Capri that afternoon, she wondered more and more if this could be the excavation that finally earned her the fame and acclamation she had sought for so long. It was all she could do not to get her hopes too high.

Lucius Pontius Pilate, Senior Legate, Prefect, and Proconsul of Judea, to Tiberius Julius Caesar Augustus, Princeps and Imperator of Rome, Greetings.

Your Excellency, you know that it is the duty of every governor to keep you informed of events in the provinces that may in some way affect the well-being of the Empire. While I am loath to disturb your important daily work with a matter that may seem trivial at first, upon further reflection, and especially in light of subsequent developments, I find myself convinced that recent events in Judea merit your attention. And I would be telling an untruth if I were not to say that I am concerned that other accounts of these happenings may reach your ears which are not just unfavorable but frankly slanderous of my actions and motives. The situation was one of unusual difficulty and complexity, and hard decisions were called for. As always, I tried to make the decisions that I felt would most lend themselves to a peaceful and harmonious outcome for the citizens of the Republic and the people of Judea. But local passions in this case were so strong, and so diametrically opposed to each other, that it may be there simply was no completely correct choice to make. I leave that to your judgment.

CHAPTER TWO

Dr. Rossini sat in a folding chair, notebook open, sketching the dark opening in the ancient wall before him. He was tired and his leg was throbbing slightly—a couple of Tylenol had relieved his pain somewhat, but not entirely. However, he had managed to get a great deal done in the three hours since his conversation with Dr. Sforza. The police chief of Capri village had closed the Via Tiberio leading up the side of the mountain with barricades informing tourists that the ancient road was not safe due to earthquake damage. Rossini had talked to the friars at the Church of Santa Maria Del Soccorso, informing them that the ruins adjacent to their church had been damaged and were not safe for foot traffic. There were only three elderly clerics tending the Medieval-era chapel these days, so he doubted they would come poking around anyway, but better to cover all bases, as his American friend Dr. Luke Martens used to say. Rossini thought it was an American football term, but was not sure. Sports had never been of much interest to him. The friars had also loaned him a folding chair and filled his flask with excellent brandy, which had made his wait on the mountaintop much more comfortable.

True to his word, he had not set foot inside the tiny chamber yet. But he had carefully walked around the entire staircase, and compared its height, width, and other measurements to the other staircases in the ruin. Then he had picked up and looked at each of the scattered blocks knocked loose by the quake, mentally restacking them and seeing how they had fit together to form a solid wall covering the ancient chamber. He wanted to cover the entrance, but there was nothing on the site that would serve as a drapery or tarp, so instead he just guarded the ancient opening until Isabella could arrive with proper supplies. Last of all, standing outside, he had shone his light into the void, mentally marking its approximate dimensions and shape. He thought that perhaps this staircase had rested on a solid pile of stone, like the others, and that whoever built the chamber had simply removed some of the stones from the pile, inserted braces to support the weight of the stairs, and then ordered some of the original blocks replaced when they decided to seal up the chamber. Certainly there was no visible arch or framing stonework for an ancient doorway; the stones that had finally fallen outward to reveal the entrance looked no different from the stones all around them, or the stones of the other staircases in the old villa. The secrecy and cleverness of the design were about right for the deeply paranoid and suspicious character of Tiberius Caesar, the island's most famous inhabitant.

As for what was in the chamber—he tried very hard not to think about that. Everything was coated with a deep, solid layer of powdery stone dust from twenty centuries of feet tramping up and down the stairs, but he could tell that, from what he could see, the space was not empty. What those tantalizing shapes he had glimpsed actually were, he could not say with any certainty. But he definitely felt that he was not wasting Isabella's time.

As if on cue, he heard the sound of a helicopter approaching in the distance. He carefully closed his sketch book, took one last sip of brandy, and watched as an Italian government helicopter slowly lowered itself over the largest extant floor of the ancient villa, which had once been Tiberius' audience chamber, on the level above the chamber he had found. The small chopper delicately touched down, and Isabella hopped out, grabbing a heavy backpack and some notebooks, and then waved them off. Rossini walked up the steps to greet her with a smile.

"Isabella! So good to see you again! When are you going to put aside your widow's weeds and make me a happy man?" his strong Italian voice boomed over the fading sound of the rotors.

Dr. Sforza threw her head back and laughed. Rossini was thirty years older than she, and a widower for the last ten years, but even when his beloved wife was still alive he had always flirted with her shamelessly—

and harmlessly. "As soon as you lose thirty years and thirty kilos!" she shot back. "Now let's see your great discovery."

"All business with you young people these days!" he laughed. "In my time we would have celebrated the discovery of a chamber like this with three days of music and dancing before we thought about going inside!" Of course that was not true, but Rossini was enormously fond of Isabella. Although he had not spent much time with her since her husband's death, he still thought of her as his adopted daughter.

Bantering back and forth, the two archeologists descended the steps toward the collapsed section of wall. Isabella already had her camera out, snapping pictures of the scene. Then she carefully measured the opening, and stepped back for a wide-angle shot of the entire staircase. She jotted down a few lines in her field notebook, then closed it and put it in her pocket. She reached inside her backpack and pulled out a powerful, battery-powered halogen lamp. She set it just outside the opening, shining in, and switched her digital camera over to video mode to record her first impressions of the chamber.

"April 8, 1630 hours. Preliminary investigation of chamber inside Villa Jovis, Capri, exposed by this morning's earthquake. The chamber is hidden beneath a large staircase, revealed when a section of its exterior wall fell outward. Chamber is roughly triangular in shape; maximum height is about two and a half meters, sloping sharply downwards towards the rear. Floor and walls appear to be undressed stone. Contents of chamber are all heavily shrouded in stone dust from the stairs above. Clearly visible are a small, low table with several indeterminate objects on it, a backless stool resembling the 'curule chairs' favored by Roman magistrates, and some sort of rectangular box or cabinet that is wedged into the angle formed by the descending ceiling and floor of the chamber. Switching over for still shots." As she spoke, Isabella had carefully filmed the entire chamber—each wall and object, as well as the floor—holding the camera in one hand and the halogen lamp in the other. Now she carefully photographed the entire chamber, recording the original position of every visible object. Only when she had photographed everything and double checked on her camera's image viewer to make sure that the pictures were clear and sharp, did she turn to Rossini. "Professor, this is your discovery. By all rights you should be the first to enter and see what it is you have found."

Rossini reached down to pick up a small brush from her assortment. "Are we in agreement that we can remove some of the overburden of dust at this point to see what is beneath it?" he asked.

"Yes," she said. "I suggest we start with the small table near the door. And, of course, bag samples of all the dust we remove for pollen residue analysis."

"Don't teach your grandmother to knit, girl," he growled in mock irritation; although he admired her thoroughness. One thing every archeologist lived in horror of was having a find's authenticity called into question due to sloppy field technique. He shone the light on the floor of the chamber to make sure that he was not stepping on anything but dust, and then eased his way in until he was standing over the table, which was a little over a meter in height. The curule chair had been pushed almost underneath it, so there was room for both of them to stand over the table, albeit very close to one another. Isabella handed him a plastic bag with a zippered top; very similar to commercial food storage bags, except these were a bit larger and manufactured to be acid-free. The largest object on the table, a lump about two inches across and three inches high, was as good a starting point as any. With deft, gentle strokes, he began clearing the dust off of it and brushing it into the bag—although not without sending plumes of atomized stone and mortar into the air, which set him coughing in a matter of moments. Isabella handed him a painter's dust mask and he donned it before continuing. She was already wearing a similar mask.

Within a few minutes he could recognize the object he was uncovering. It was a small bottle or jar, made of ancient greenish glass or porcelain. The bottommost layer of dust was very stubborn, especially along the top edges of the jar, where it clung to the surface as if it had been glued—leaving that area of the jar much darker than the outside, almost black. But then, as he cleaned his way around the outside surface, he saw a long streak of the black stain running down one side of the jar. Frowning, he teased the dust away from that part of the table. Suddenly he laughed out loud. "*Bravissimo*, Isabella!" he exclaimed. "It's an inkwell! And look at this—it was actually used at this very table!" As he cleaned around the base of the glass, several dark spots of ink showed on the ancient lacquered tabletop.

Isabella's lustrous brown eyes lit up as she pondered this. "Could this be a writing nook or chamber of some sort?" she wondered out loud. "Or did someone just store their writing table here when they were done?"

He looked over her head, at the wall above the door, and gave a start. "Look above you, my dear!" he said. "That's not only a lamp niche, there appears to be a lamp still in it!" The depression in the wall had been barely visible from the outside, but from this angle he could see an odd-shaped, dust-covered object that could only be a small oil lamp. Isabella asked him to pause while she snapped some more pictures of the new discovery.

"That lamp looks placed to illuminate this table pretty well," he said. "That and the position of the table and chair make me think that this is a writing nook, not just a storage space."

"You're right!" she said. "It's a bit cramped, but for someone who enjoys privacy and isn't claustrophobic, it would not have been uncomfortable."

Rossini turned from her and resumed dusting the objects on the tabletop, and collecting the fine powder in a series of the acid-free bags. Little by little the dust of centuries disappeared, and the objects became recognizable. "We have a red candle, laid down horizontally," he said after a few moments. "And here is a golden candleholder. I wonder . . ." He looked at the two items for a moment.

"What?" asked Isabella.

"Sealing wax, perhaps?" he said. "We know that it was widely used in Roman times."

"That is possible," she replied. "Good God, Giuseppe, what have you found? These are the kind of things that are never preserved!" Her pulse was quickening as she thought of what this find might be. Calm down, girl, she thought. It could be so many things . . . the workspace of a servant, of a low-level clerk, a household steward. But here—in the Villa Jovis—just a few yards from where the Emperor had slept. Could it be . . . ?

Rossini sensed her excitement and smiled. "Let's not get too excited, my dear," he said. "It could just be the den of some medieval cleric who wanted to get away from the monastery while he wrote down the shopping list!" Then he turned back to the writing table and readied another bag. "But there's only one way to find out. Let's see. How about this one next?" He took his brush to a small round lump near the edge of the table and began whisking away at it. Seconds later he gave a low whistle of amazement. Isabella crowded in to see what he was staring at, and then grabbed his shoulder for support as her knees went weak.

"Oh, Giuseppe!" she gasped.

It was a ring—a man's ring, from the look of it, large and heavy, and glimmering in the torchlight with the unmistakable sheen of gold. But it was not the precious metal that made her lose her breath—it was the shape and size. This was clearly a signet ring used for sealing documents. And the stamp on its wide, flat working surface was one she had seen before, on denarii and other Roman coins from the first century AD. But never had she seen an example this perfectly preserved, lacking the wear, scratches, and corrosion of the ages. Sealed in this chamber, the ring had sat on this table for twenty centuries, accumulating no damage and no wear—only dust. The letters on the ring were reversed, of course, so that they would be legible when stamped into the bright scarlet wax used to seal official documents. But the Roman eagle was unmistakable, and so were the Latin letters—TIB CAES PRINC IMPER—the abbreviation for "Tiberius Caesar, *Princeps Imperator.*" Tiberius Caesar, First Citizen and Emperor of Rome.

Rossini stared a long time at this unprecedented find. The personal sealing ring of a Roman Emperor—and not just any Roman Emperor, but only the second man to bear that title! The man who had conquered much of Germany as a general, the man who succeeded Augustus, the Emperor during whose reign Christianity had been born.

"Isabella," he finally said. "We need to proceed very, very carefully. This may be the most important discovery in classical archeology since Heinrich Schliemann discovered the ruins of Troy! The site will have to be completely secured and guarded round the clock. We need to call Bernardo at the Bureau immediately and let him know what we have found, and have proper equipment delivered on-site for the preservation and removal of these artifacts."

"Completely correct," she said, glancing outside. "We have about three more hours of daylight left. I am going to suggest that we finish cleaning off the items on top of this writing table and photographing them, then begin securing the site and informing the authorities. I am a woman, after all—you know I can't leave an item of furniture half dusted!" She laughed to cover her eagerness. The actual writing table used by an Emperor of Rome! Never in her wildest dreams had she thought that she might find something of this nature.

20

Rossini looked at her long and hard. He wasn't sure he approved of her haste, but he shared her enthusiasm. "I will finish this last object," he said. "I want to leave at least some of the dust undisturbed for later comparison." He leaned over the table and began cleaning off an oblong lump near the center, whisking the dust into another baggie. In seconds the lump became a long, skinny cylinder with a few spiky filaments poking out of each side. "A quill!" he said. "By God, girl! He got up, put his pen down, and sealed the chamber!"

Isabella did not say a word. She was staring at the quill—no, not at the quill. Past it. At what it was lying on. "Giuseppe!" she said. "It's not lying on the desk at all!"

"What?" He looked past the ring for the first time and saw what she was referring to. The top of the table was nearly black in the places he had uncovered it—it had obviously been richly lacquered at one time, probably being made of teakwood. But the ring was resting on a dirty, pale yellow surface that had no sheen or luster to it. It looked for all the world like a dirty piece of—"Papyrus!" he said. "Isabella! The quill is lying on top of—Mother of God, could it be?"

Completely forgetting the time, or the need to secure the site, he began quickly whisking, exercising great care as he slowly cleared away the centuries of dust. This time he took much longer, because of the wider surface area and the delicate nature of what he was uncovering. He was vaguely aware that Isabella had switched back from camera to video mode and was narrating in a low voice as he slowly uncovered the document lying on the desktop—a rectangular piece of parchment about the size of a yellow legal sheet. The parchment was not blank, either—as he very carefully whisked the brush back and forth, thin spidery letters began to swim up from the paper. Latin letters. Letters that were shaky and poorly formed; the writing of an old man with trembling hands. Rossini was too excited, and the letters too badly squiggled, to read in the glaring halogen light—till he uncovered the bottom of the page. There the hand was a bit bolder, a bit firmer, and the writing a bit larger. There could be no doubt about what it said. "Tiberius Julius Caesar Augustus" was scrawled boldly across the bottom of the ancient letter. They were looking at the signature of the second Emperor of Rome.

* * *

Bernardo Guioccini was stunned. "You've found WHAT?" he barked into the cell phone. In his three-year tenure as the Chief

Archeologist of the Italian Bureau of Antiquities—indeed in his entire thirty-year career as a classical archeologist—this was the most outrageous claim he had ever heard. At the same time, he knew and respected Isabella Sforza as a consummate professional without a sensationalist bone in her body. For her to make a claim like this, it had to be legitimate. The half of him rooted in classical history was thrilled; the half of him that dealt with the public was wary of the media circus that was sure to ensue when word of this discovery became public.

"We have not moved anything except dust," Sforza was saying. "Every step has been chronicled with digital photography and video, and is stored in encrypted files on my laptop. We need tents, a very small and select field crew, and a mobile lab on-site, and probably some security as well. This location is going to be very hard to keep secret. Dr. Rossini is collaborating with local authorities to close the mountain to tourism for the next few days. It may be . . ." She paused a moment.

"What are you thinking?" Guioccini asked. At the moment, he was open to any insight or ideas she might have.

"The chamber is very small, and it appears that there are only a very few items in it. Once we clean the dust away, it may be that we can simply relocate all the artifacts to a secure lab for study, and then carefully document the chamber itself. We could then potentially reseal it, or perhaps even open it to the public for tourism."

"That is a bit unorthodox, but not unprecedented," said the senior archeologist. "Indeed, given the very public nature of the site, that may well be the most practical solution. But we will have to wait and see exactly what the chamber contains, and how safely the artifacts can be relocated. For now, secure the site overnight and I will be there first thing in the morning."

"Very well, Dr. Guioccini," said Isabella. "We will be here waiting."

Even as she was dialing the Bureau of Antiquities, Rossini had been talking to the chief of police in Capri village. Alfonse Rosario had come to the island about the same time he had, when the old police chief had been removed after being indicted in a corruption scandal. As the community's two newcomers and outsiders, both had been regarded with a bit of suspicion at first. This resulted in each of them discovering a friend and kindred spirit in the other. Rossini had always been fascinated with police work, and Rosario had a strong layman's interest in archeology. As each of them had gradually been accepted as part of the little island community, their circle of friends had widened—but never to the exclusion of each other. Rossini knew he could count on the police chief for discretion and logistical support.

"Alfonse? This is Giuseppe. Listen, I am going to need your help this evening," he said as soon as they were connected.

"By all means," said the chief. "What are you up to in those old ruins, that you need back-up?"

"I'm not at complete liberty to say," replied Rossini. "But what we require at the moment is to be undisturbed for a few days. On a practical level, a more permanent roadblock at the base of the mountain, and some food and drink for the evening would do for starters. A couple of tents and sleeping bags, because I don't think we will be coming down off this mountain tonight—and the fewer people that know something is going on, the better."

"Hmm, I am guessing you must have found something important, my friend! Did the tremor shake something out of the mountainside?" asked the policeman.

"You are fishing, Chief Rosario!" laughed Rossini. "All I can say is, as soon as I am at liberty to divulge it; you will be the first person I tell. But for now, the quieter we keep it, the sooner I can tell you what we've found."

"All right," said the chief. "I'll play by your rules, and I'll have a couple of tents up there, along with some bedding and food, within the hour. Then we'll barricade the old road and leave you alone with your infernal secrets!"

After he hung up, Rossini walked to the edge of the villa and looked to the west, with the length of the island of Capri stretched out toward the setting sun. He wondered how the view would have looked two thousand years before, as old Tiberius stood on the same marble floor, staring off across the body of water the Romans called *Mare Nostrum*— "Our Sea." He had always been fascinated by the titans who had struggled for power during the last days of the Republic—Gaius Marius, the wealthy commoner who had become Rome's greatest general and been elected consul seven times; Lucius Cornelius Sulla, the ruthless patrician who had purged the Senate of plebeian influence by a series of bloody proscriptions; and the one who surpassed them both—Gaius Julius Caesar, the soldier, writer, statesman, and reformer who had, depending on who you listened to, either destroyed the Republic in a

23

mad fit of pride or been goaded into a needless war by his fanatical, idiotic enemies in the Senate. It had been Caesar's great-nephew and adopted heir Augustus who built the Villa Jovis as a quiet retreat from Rome. He had, in turn, bequeathed it to his stepson and heir, the reclusive general Tiberius, who had turned it into his primary residence after leaving the city of Rome. And it was Tiberius that Rossini pondered now, the cruel, unpopular tyrant who had ruled a quarter of the earth's population from this gem of an island off the coast of Italy. Was he the twisted monster Suetonius had portrayed in his histories, or was he a misunderstood old man who simply wanted to escape from the madness and noise of the imperial city?

Giuseppe was so caught up in his reverie that he did not hear Isabella come up behind him until she lightly placed one hand on his shoulder. "We did it," she said softly. "Or, more truthfully, you did it. You made the discovery that will ensure that archeologists a hundred years from now will have to learn our names!"

Rossini laughed and kissed her young hand. For a moment, he wished he were thirty years old again. How beautiful she was! But his affection for her, for all of his banter, was more like the love of a doting father for a daughter who made him very proud. "Dear child," he said. "There is no one on earth I would rather share this discovery with. To think that you and I were the first in two millennia to see the signature of the man who was the adopted child of Augustus himself! I've always wondered how Howard Carter felt when he poked his head through that hole into the tomb of Tutankhamen, or Heinrich Schliemann when he held the golden mask of Agamemnon for the first time. Now I know." The two archeologists stood in silence and watched the sun drop into the Mediterranean.

In order to understand the choices that were thrust upon me during the Jewish festival of Passover this year, Caesar, I must acquaint you with the events over the last three years that led up to it. As I am sure you are aware, the Jews' rather odd religion has for centuries prophesied about the coming of a savior they call the Messiah—Christos in Greek—who would redeem them from their slavery and restore the great kingdom that was theirs at one time. This belief makes them particularly vulnerable to the machinations of various charlatans and lunatics who pop up from time to time claiming to be this Messiah. Such men invariably spell trouble for whoever is currently holding the Jews on a leash— be it the Assyrians, the Greeks, or we Romans.

However, most of these men in the past were quickly exposed as the frauds that they were. For all their protestations of holiness and religious fervor, the House of Zadok which controls the high priesthood is quite comfortable with the mutual arrangement they enjoy with Rome. Indeed, since Pompey the Great added this troublesome province to the Empire nearly a hundred years ago, the Priests have been Rome's staunchest allies, and an invaluable aid in keeping the peace. So when rumors began to circulate of a new would-be Messiah rising up in Galilee, I figured they would take care of him soon enough.

CHAPTER THREE

Bernardo Guioccini had hardly slept that night, after he made the travel arrangements and ordered the necessary supplies for the excavation on the mountaintop. The potential significance of this discovery was enormous, and he did not want to make any mistakes. He would be flying out on an Italian army helicopter early the next morning, but even as he lay in bed, he was reviewing the choices he had made the evening before.

The mobile lab was actually quite easy to arrange—the Israelis had created the perfect example during their lengthy excavations at Qumran, where the Essenes had copied thousands of scrolls and stored them in the caves near the Dead Sea. Ancient parchment and papyrus manuscripts required careful handling and treatment in order to keep them from simply crumbling away once unearthed. The large trailer he had requisitioned had a small stockroom full of chemicals for treating and preserving ancient parchment, papyrus, wood, and fabric. It also had several stainless steel tables and benches, flat, sealed cabinet drawers for storing whatever was found, plexiglass rehydration tanks, state of the art computer systems, and several microscopes of varying degrees of power and illumination. There was even a small cookstove and a cappuccino machine. No need to live like complete barbarians while on-site!

As for the crew—he had put long thought into it before deciding who to call in. Father Duncan MacDonald was a no-brainer—any excavation from the early Christian era needed at least one representative from the Vatican present, or at least, that had been Guioccini's policy from the moment he became director. He did not believe that archeology should pander to faith, but when the two worlds of faith and history intersected, as they frequently did in Italy, it was foolish to needlessly antagonize the world's—and Italy's—largest Christian denomination. And MacDonald made that kind of liaison much easier for the scientists involved, because he was a first-rate Biblical archeologist who never let religious bias get in the way of his quest for truth. Of course, as a Catholic clergyman, he also firmly believed that the historical record, when accurately interpreted and analyzed, would back up the claims of the Church—which, more often than not, it did. MacDonald was a master at treating and preserving ancient documents. After years of experimentation with various polymers, he had developed a preservative formula that could easily be sprayed onto any ancient document. With it, he could take a papyrus manuscript that was completely falling apart and stabilize it in a matter of hours; making it strong enough to handle and study without damage.

Dr. Simone Apriceno was another natural choice. A paleobotanist, she specialized in analyzing pollens and spores from ancient sites, and had been instrumental in debunking a number of purported "Holy Relics" by showing they contained traces of plant life that did not exist at the time and place they supposedly originated. If anyone could determine whether or not the materials in the chamber had truly been there since the time of Tiberius, she could. Nearly sixty years of age and built like a fireplug, she had the strength, stamina, and enthusiasm of a woman half her age. She was also a remarkable chef in her spare time, whose knowledge of ancient herb-lore enabled her to come up with dishes whose flavors had to be tasted to be believed.

The third team member, however, was one of the reasons that Guioccini was having trouble sleeping. He had wanted to include his American friend, Dr. Luke Martens, a widely respected historian and archeologist specializing in the early Roman Empire. However, when he called him, he was crushed to find out that Dr. Martens was in traction following a ski accident. The professor had recently married a woman named Alicia, some fifteen years his junior, who apparently was a bit of an adrenaline junkie. Her latest winter vacation idea had landed her husband in the hospital. "She does keep me young, Bernardo," laughed Martens as he explained his predicament. "When she is not trying to kill me, that is!" The Italian archeologist had heard an outraged female voice in the background, and chuckled. His own wife would not be caught dead on a ski lift. But Martens' injury made a journey to Capri out of the question for another week or two at least.

"But I do have a replacement in mind," said the American, "if you are willing to accept my judgment. He is young, but he is very sharp and trained under the best. I've been supervising his work at Ephesus, and he is very enthusiastic, but also a hundred percent professional. He's on sabbatical right now, getting ready to return to Ephesus to write up the work he's done there. But honestly, the other folks on the dig can handle that end of it just as well, and it sounds like you could use some youthful energy on this project. Also, he's a pretty staunch Christian, so anything from the first century will hold particular interest for him. He did an excellent doctoral dissertation on the impact of the Emperor Domitian on the early church, and backed it up with some marvelous research and scholarship. Believe me, Joshua Parker will be a better asset to your team than I could."

Not wanting to disappoint, Guioccini had accepted, but he was a bit ambivalent about inviting someone onto the team that he had never met before. Still, it wouldn't hurt to have some Protestant input to balance out the Catholic presence, and if the boy was half the field archeologist that Martens claimed he was, he could serve well. All in all, he decided, he had done the best he could in the short time available. He just hoped that Dr. Parker would call him back soon; he needed the team to be complete as soon as possible. Finally, about 1 AM, he closed his eyes and began to drift off. That was when his phone rang.

* * *

Back at the Villa Jovis, Isabella and Giuseppe had gotten their tents set up pretty quickly. Chief Rosario had brought the supplies up the steep trail on an ATV just before sunset, about an hour previously, and they had met him at the lower end of the ruin, where the trail head was located—and out of sight of the ancient chamber. He had a sturdy Army issue cot for each of them, with sleeping bag and pillow to go on it, two pup tents, and a grocery bag from which the wonderful aroma of fresh baked bread, butter, and garlic was issuing. Isabella thanked him, then grabbed her gear and headed back up the trail, leaving the two friends to chat a moment.

"Giuseppe, you old fool!" said the Chief. "If you had let me know who you were sharing the mountaintop with tonight, I could have brought one tent—by mistake, of course!"

Rossini growled back: "You know I am too old for that sort of thing, my friend—although I will agree, she carries that first-rate mind of hers inside a first-rate package! I've known Isabella since she was a teen, though—even if I was so inclined, it would not feel right. Not to mention I'm sure she's had better offers than this old carcass of mine."

The Chief sensed he had offended, so he changed topics. "Any chance of getting a small glimpse of what you have found?"

Rossini smiled sadly. "I would love nothing better than to give you the grand tour, but it is just not possible yet. We'll have some VIPs here in the morning. After we talk to them, maybe I'll be able to tell you a bit more." After a bit more conversation, he saw the police chief off and walked up the steps to the level where the chamber was. Isabella already had her tent mostly up, and he began pitching his own a few yards away.

29

Before he was half done, hers was finished and she joined him. There were two small folding chairs inside the bag with the tents, so when they were finished setting up camp, they sat companionably beside each other and shared the delicious stromboli and bread that he found inside the grocery bags, washing them down with the last of the brandy from the old monks.

"Well, we have a writing table, a manuscript, a curule chair, and some implements so far," he said. "Then there is the lamp up in the niche on the wall. What else do you think we will find?"

"I must admit, I am very curious about that large boxlike item at the back of the chamber," Isabella replied. "What do you think it could be?"

"Placement, size, and shape would argue for a cabinet of some sort, or a storage chest. But will there be anything in it?" wondered Rossini.

"That is the real question, isn't it?" she replied. "What we have found is truly remarkable, but I cannot help but wish for more. I don't know that I will be able to sleep tonight!"

They chatted pleasantly for another hour or so as the stars came out and the moon began to sink in the west. Isabella caught Rossini up on her most recent work, and after a while began to speak, a bit hesitantly, about the loss of her husband five years before. Rossini had spent a good bit of time with her shortly after the loss, and had tried to comfort her as best he could, but it had been several years since they spent any time together. This troubled him, because Isabella had gone to some lengths to comfort him when Carlotta, his wife of forty years, had died a decade before. He thought of the raw, aching grief he had felt for weeks afterward, and was sad for his beautiful young friend, who had barely had time to fall in love with her gentle young husband before he was cruelly taken from her. Giuseppe could tell by the raw tone of her voice as she tried to talk about those awful days after the crash that she was still missing Marc terribly, and that the loss of her father had compounded that sorrow. He found himself hoping that, before her grief made her old and bitter, she would someday find another man to love.

After a while, her voice trailed off and he began to speak in turn. He spoke of his son, a career Italian army officer currently on duty in Sicily, and his only daughter, the wife of a rising young politician currently serving in the civic government of Turin. He did not see his children as frequently as he would have liked, but they were both fine young people and he was glad that they still enjoyed a close relationship. Whenever possible, he explained, he emailed them every night and kept them caught up on his life.

Soon, however, their talk turned back to archeology and history, their mutual passion, and before long the moon had set and the stars blazed out in full glory. Then they both headed off to bed, still feeling wide awake.

Surprisingly, though, the excitement of the day had left both of them drained and ready for slumber. Within a half hour of climbing onto their separate cots, the two archeologists were sound asleep, and did not wake until the first rays of the sun began to illuminate the eastern sky beyond the ruins of the ancient villa.

* * *

Josh Parker cast his line out with an ease born of long practice, watching the lead sinker and the hook with a half-frozen shrimp on it go arcing out over the gently rippling waters of Lake Hugo before hitting the surface and sinking straight for the bottom about fifty feet from his father's boat. He fed the line out until he felt the sinker hit the bottom, then flipped the bar of his reel over and turned the crank until he felt the line tighten. His dad already had two rods cast out by the time he got his own fully set—but then, Ben Parker had been fishing for about thirty years longer than his son. Josh kept one finger on the line, feeling the drift of the boat slowly pull the sinker across the clay and rock twenty feet below them. Before long, the channel catfish that loved this big, muddy lake in southeastern Oklahoma would smell the shrimp being dragged through their watery home and come out to investigate. He hoped.

"Well, Dad, that was a real stem-winder you preached yesterday," he said.

"And how many times have you heard me go on about that passage?" his dad asked with a smile.

"Oh, just a few," Josh said. "But it's an important truth, and too many people forget how foundational it is to our faith. That message drives it home in a way that few of them will forget anytime soon."

"You must need help paying off your student loan or something," his father said with a laugh. "You normally are picking my sermons apart, verse by verse and illustration by illustration!"

31

"I'm doing fine, Dad," said Josh. "I guess it's just that—well, I've missed you. It was good to listen to you preach again." His voice caught a bit—he was incredibly fond of his dad, but it was hard for him to express it in words sometimes.

"It is good to have you home again, son," his father said. "Now, did you hear the one about the small-town preacher who looked just like Conway Twitty?" His father was about halfway through the joke—which Josh had heard before, but he would never admit it because he loved his dad's lively comic nature—when he felt a tug on the line. Two light taps at first, then a hard jerk as the hungry fish grabbed the shrimp and ran with it. He jerked back on the rod hard and clean, and felt the hook set. Then it was off to the races. The panicked fish lunged and swam as Josh slowly reeled him toward the top. His rod bent nearly double as the fish tried to return to the deep water, but each time it gave up as he kept a steady pressure on the line, taking up a few feet of slack every time the fish changed direction.

"Stay with him, bud!" his father shouted, reaching for the dip net. After a struggle of nearly ten minutes, Josh caught his first glimpse of his aquatic quarry—a flash of white belly reflecting the morning sun as the fish rolled in about four feet of water and dove for the bottom again. It was a big one, all right. He played it a moment or two longer, then his quarry ran for the surface and breached the ripples, scattering spray in all directions. No channel cat was this! It had the unmistakable color and high dorsal fin of a blue catfish, or a "high fin blue" as the local anglers called them. He let it run one more time, and then began cranking the reel to bring it to the surface. Ben Parker held the dip net ready. But the wily fish was not out of tricks yet—it shot straight out of the water, spinning in midair, and as it dove again, snapped the fifteen-pound test line it had wrapped around its body. A single flash of its white belly, and it was off to the depths to digest its hard-won shrimp breakfast.

"*Quod sugit et facit me vis iactare!!*" shouted Josh. He had taught himself to swear in Latin long ago, so that on the rare occasion when he felt the need to say something profane, he would not embarrass his father by saying something vulgar—or at least, not something his father would understand.

Ben Parker was not going to have it though. "And what does that little gem phrase mean?" he asked his son.

Josh sighed. "Nothing too bad," he said. "It's Latin for 'That sucks and it makes me want to throw up!'"

His dad threw back his head and laughed. "Well," he said, "I guess losing a twenty-pound blue does merit some sort of expletive. I wonder if I said that in front of my deacons whether or not they would bother to look it up?"

At that moment Josh's cell phone rang. He debated whether or not to answer, but the LED indicator showed that the call was from his mentor Dr. Martens, so he looked at his dad as if to say "What else do you do?" and answered.

"Josh!" boomed the voice of his former thesis advisor. "Hope I didn't wake you from some dreamy vacation nap!"

"Hello, Dr. Martens," Josh replied. "Has Alicia managed to put you in the hospital yet?" Like most of the grad students in the Biblical Archeology Department at Tulane, he had been shocked when the graying, bearded professor of Biblical Archeology had married a Marine Biology grad student fifteen years his junior. But the attraction between them was real, and after the amazement wore off, Josh could tell the two were good for each other.

"Funny you should mention that," Martens chuckled. "I'm, well, kind of recovering from a ski accident at the moment."

"Wow!" Josh said. "I was only kidding! What did she do, talk you into some sort of extreme ski jump competition?" Alicia's fascination with high-risk acrobatics was a subject of some campus gossip long before she and Professor Martens had married.

"If you must know, I swerved to avoid an eight-year-old on the bunny slope and hit a tree," growled his old mentor. "But I think I'll tell your version from now on!" Josh laughed at this sally, but then Dr. Martens' voice grew more serious. "Look, Josh, my disability may turn into a major professional opportunity for you if you are interested," he said. "Are you still up on your first-century Latin and Greek?"

Josh was all ears. "Been reading Cassius Dio in my spare time," he said. "Now tell me what's going on."

"I don't know a lot of the details," said Martens, "but it appears that they have made what may be a major document discovery at the Villa Jovis on Capri. Some documents, or at least one document, dating to the reign of Tiberius Caesar—maybe even written by Tiberius Caesar! They need a first-century Latin specialist with a strong background in New

Testament archeology. I praised you to the high heavens when the Director of the Italian Bureau of Antiquities called me a couple of hours ago, and he has agreed to include you on the team that will excavate and study the ruins if you are up for it."

Josh was excited beyond words. "When do I need to leave?" he asked.

Martens said: "The sooner the better, but I don't know the details. I have Dr. Guioccini's number here. Got a pen?"

"I'm in the middle of Lake Hugo holding a rod and reel," said Josh. "Can you text me the number?"

"Sure," said the professor. "But don't waste any time before calling. He's trying to get this team assembled and on-site ASAP. Good to talk to you again. Now get over to Italy and make me proud!"

Josh looked at his dad after he said goodbye to Dr. Martens and hung up. His father was already reeling up his first line, and Josh reached for the other rig and began reeling it in too. "Well," said Ben Parker, "looks like the fish are safe for now. So where are you off to this time?"

Before Josh could answer, his phone chirped to let him know the text had arrived.

* * *

Isabella Sforza stretched and yawned as the morning sun peeked over the stone staircase that had hidden the ancient writing nook for two thousand years. She had slept well enough, but the army cot was far from comfortable, and in her excitement the day before, she had forgotten to pack her toothbrush. Between the stromboli, the garlic bread, and the brandy, her mouth tasted like a homeless vampire had crawled in it to die. She had a small hairbrush in her purse, which she ran through her unruly black tresses a couple of times before giving up. She was an archeologist in the field, after all, not a schoolgirl going to a dance. She looked over to see Giuseppe Rossini limping toward her with a distinct grimace.

"You look like you could use some ibuprofen," she said. "I keep a small bottle in my purse."

"Some morphine, a bottle of Chianti, and an affectionate Swedish masseuse would be more like it," Rossini said in a croaking voice. "But ibuprofen will have to do."

She gave him a couple of the small brown pills and he swallowed them with a sip of bottled water. She looked at her watch and then began to carefully roll up her sleeping bag and pack up her few personal effects. "I imagine they will set the mobile lab up here on this level, next to the chamber," she said. "We'll need to get our tents out of the way. I can't wait to continue our work when they get here!"

Giuseppe joined her and they quickly broke down both tents and moved them, along with their other gear, over to the foot of the staircase that had concealed the writing nook for two thousand years. She had used the flat tarp that was meant to go under the tent to cover the entrance of the ancient chamber the night before. A better protective cover would be coming with the mobile lab, but in the meantime, she wanted to keep as much modern pollen and dust out as she could. They had used some of the original masonry blocks to weigh down the tarp at top and bottom—it was long enough to reach from the ground and lap over the top edge of the staircase, if they positioned it just right. They had barely finished stowing their gear when they heard the sound of the chopper approaching in the distance.

* * *

Bernardo Guioccini was feeling a good bit easier about his team as the chopper carried him across the deep blue waters that separated Capri from the Italian mainland. Josh Parker had called him at about one in the morning, and his quick answers and incisive questions made Guioccini realize why Dr. Martens had so much faith in the young academic. Clearly Parker had a strong working knowledge in his field, combined with a practical streak and a sense of humor as well. He was supposed to be arriving later that day, having reserved a seat on a flight to Italy that would be landing about the same time Guioccini and his team arrived at Capri.

Guioccini did not intend to stay on the island for long, once Parker arrived. "Too many cooks spoil the broth, and too many archeologists delay the dig," was an adage one of his professors had passed on years before, and it was true. Archeologists as a rule tended to be a pretty strong-willed, territorial bunch, and when several of them worked in close quarters it was easy for tempers to fly. He knew that Rossini and Sforza had a good mentor-student relationship, and that MacDonald was an easygoing fellow who had worked with Dr. Rossini before. Dr. Apriceno could be testy, but only when it came to her specialty. Aside

35

from her precious ancient spores, she was a warm and motherly figure. But with a find of this significance, even the most even-tempered professionals could develop hostile tendencies if their pet theories or field techniques clashed.

Dr. Simone Apriceno looked out the window intently, waiting to see the lovely island of Capri come into view. She had not been there in many years, but still harbored fond memories of the place, since she and her ex-husband had enjoyed a very happy honeymoon there thirty-five years before. Later on, events had come between them, and his infidelity had led to their divorce—but they had some awfully good years before then, and those years had started at Capri. In her mind, she tried to visualize the Villa Jovis as she remembered it from an afternoon hike they had taken during their stay, but she had been to so many old ruins in the years between that she was having a hard time picturing the place in her head.

Duncan MacDonald had no such difficulty—he had visited Capri many times, first as a student tourist during semester breaks, and later as a scholar of Roman history and archeology. The first century AD fascinated him, as did the late Roman Republic. It was not only one of the most important and influential eras in the history of the world, it was also the time in which the faith that he lived by had been born. He had studied the Gospels and the other books of the New Testament for years, and had also read and studied the works of the Apostolic Fathers, second-century Christians who had known the original Apostles or their disciples. He was familiar with (and somewhat contemptuous of) all of the Gnostic gospels as well—they were all composed in the second, third, and fourth centuries, although frequently attributed to the original apostles of Jesus. As a lot, they were so far inferior to the canonical gospels as to richly deserve the rejection the Church had dealt to them when they were written. It always amused him to see how various pop culture books or celebrities occasionally "discovered" the Gnostic works and tried to claim that they represented the "real" Christianity that the Church had covered up for 2,000 years. He wondered if any of these people had actually read and compared the two sets of works. If they had, he thought, then they were even more empty-headed than he had imagined. But his defense of the original Scriptures was just part of the Church's two-thousand-year struggle against heresy of all sorts. Why should this century be any different from all the previous ones?

All three scientists were ready to hop out of the chopper the moment it began to hover over the ruins, but before they could disembark, the mobile lab it had been carrying beneath it had to be lowered into place. The level on which the chamber had been discovered also featured a large, flat floor area that had been cut directly from the mountain beneath it—once covered over with expensive marble, no doubt, most of which had been removed centuries ago to decorate some wealthy medieval Italian home. The floor was just the right size to accommodate the lab, and the two archeologists on the ground helped guide the pilot to set it down. Once that was done and the cable disengaged and reeled in, the chopper touched down briefly on the higher level in order to let the three eager academics hop out and grab their equipment and luggage. The chopper would be back with some other living amenities later that afternoon, but for the moment, they could commence work.

As the helicopter lifted off, Rossini and Sforza mounted the steps to greet the arriving team. "Only two?" Isabella asked Dr. Guioccini. "Could Dr. Martens not make it?"

"Luke is recovering from an accident at the moment and cannot travel," he replied. "He is sending a surrogate, but Dr. Joshua Parker was on sabbatical in the U.S. and cannot arrive here until this afternoon. I've never met him, but Dr. Martens endorsed him with great enthusiasm."

"I've heard the name," Isabella said, "but that's all. This must be Dr. MacDonald, then?" she asked, looking at the man whose khaki shirt was topped with a clerical collar.

"Doctor, Father, 'that priest who calls himself an archeologist'—I'm like Gandalf in *The Lord of the Rings*: many are my names in many lands," returned the cleric in a soft Scottish burr. "Delighted to meet you, Dr. Sforza. I had the pleasure of speaking with your late husband at a conference in London eight years ago."

"I went to London with him," said Isabella, "but wound up not being able to attend the conference due to a nasty bout of food poisoning. No wonder the British used to rule half the world—if they can survive on English food, they are made of sterner stuff than most of us!"

He laughed. "Just come up to Scotland, lassie, and I can show you what TRULY terrible food tastes like! My mother's haggis is the main reason I haven't gone home in over twenty years!" He then turned to

Dr. Rossini. "Giuseppe, you old goat, I might have known I would find ye camping on an island with a beautiful young woman!"

"What is it about a clerical collar that automatically confers a dirty mind on those who wear them?" Rossini shot back. "I'll have you know, Father Duncan, that Dr. Sforza is a model of womanly virtue, as the two tents folded by yon wall should have shown you!"

"You poor dear," interjected Simone Apriceno. "Having to work alongside these two terrible old men for the next few weeks! Fear not, I shall protect you from their wicked ways!"

Isabella laughed. "I've known Giuseppe for years," she said. "He is all bark and no bite. Compared to some of the archeologists I've worked with, these two are choirboys! You must be Dr. Apriceno. We've never met, but I've studied some of your work. The debunking of the Veil of Magdalene was a nice bit of forensic science."

"The sisters were terribly disappointed to find out their most cherished relic was made in France in the 1300s," said the paleobotanist, "but the Mother Superior said it was better to know the truth than to pass on a myth. I respected her greatly for that."

"Now that we've all gotten acquainted," said Guioccini, "Isabella, why don't you show us what you and Giuseppe have found?"

"My pleasure," she replied. "Follow me down the steps, my colleagues—and back in time two thousand years!" The team descended the steps of the Villa Jovis together.

This particular would-be Messiah of the Jews was a former carpenter who apparently claimed descent from their ancient King David—founder of a dynasty that was toppled by the Babylonians over six centuries ago! I first heard the stories and asked the centurions whom I have stationed in the various cities of Judea to keep me informed if this fellow gave signs of making trouble. However, he seemed to have no interest whatsoever in politics. He wandered about with a small band of farmers and fisherman— and, oddly enough, one Jewish publicani who chose to renounce tax farming and join him. His activities seemed to focus on long, rambling sermons commanding people to love one another, and describing a "kingdom of God" that would rule over men's hearts rather than their bodies. Harmless mystical nonsense, it seemed to me. The other stories about him were so incredible that I ignored them at first, but they continued over so long a period that I eventually began to pay them heed. This man, Jesus of Nazareth, apparently had a remarkable power of healing that was widely witnessed. Indeed, one of my senior centurions told me that Jesus had healed a servant of his by merely saying a few words from miles away! I scoffed at that account, but he swore that it was true. But, as you will (I hope) agree, I saw nothing in this man that caused me any concern for the Empire or its control of Judea. However, the religious leaders of the Jews were adamantly opposed to this man's teachings—he claimed some sort of direct relationship to their God that they said was blasphemous. As governor, I saw no reason to involve myself in a minor religious dispute.

CHAPTER FOUR

"I first noticed the fallen masonry from the top of the staircase," said Rossini as the team approached the entrance. "When I reached the bottom and was able to view the entire wall, I saw this opening that had been revealed by the collapse. I had a pocket flashlight with me, and poking my head inside—being careful not to actually step into the chamber—I saw the very thick coating of stone dust, as well as the table and stool, plus the square object to the rear of the chamber. I immediately realized that this had the potential to be a find of some significance, so I backed out and called Dr. Sforza."

Isabella took up the narration from that point. "I arrived about four hours later. Giuseppe did not have a camera, but he had prepared detailed sketches of the staircase, the opening, and the shape of the chamber as much as he could see from the entrance. I immediately began taking pictures and video to document what we found as we went inside. Since it was Giuseppe's discovery, I let him begin to uncover the first artifacts while I filmed."

As she spoke, Rossini deftly removed the tarp Isabella had covered the entrance with. He stepped inside and illuminated the writing table with his flashlight. The others congregated at the entrance as she continued her narration. "The stone dust on top of the table was about a centimeter and a half deep, shrouding every object. We decided to start with the table as the easiest choice. The largest object on the tabletop proved to be this inkwell. As we uncovered it, it was apparent that some of the ink from it had dripped out and stained the tabletop—which led us to conclude that the inkwell was actually used on this table. We still had no idea how old it was or who may have used it, but it was Roman era glass. Next we found a red wax candle and a bronze candleholder. Again, obviously Roman in age—in fact, the candleholder was embossed with a Roman eagle and the SPQR of the Republic. That puts it squarely in the first century. But it was the next object that made us realize the true significance of the site."

Rossini had been using his pocket torch to illuminate the various objects as they were described, and now he brought it to bear on the golden ring. It had not been moved since they uncovered it, but the insignia was facing toward the door, so that the seal was plainly visible. As Isabella described it, the three archeologists leaned forward in fascination. "This sealing ring bears the name and title of Tiberius Julius

Augustus Caesar, Second Emperor of Rome. It is lying next to the sealing wax candle—and, when I enlarged the photos on my laptop, there actually appear to be remnants of sealing wax embedded between the embossed letters on the ring. Someone—most likely Tiberius himself—used this ring at this table two thousand years ago."

Father MacDonald let out a low whistle of amazement. "Amazing!" he said. "This is the first artifact ever uncovered that can be said with certainty to have belonged to a Roman Emperor of the first century."

Isabella smiled. "It gets better," she said. "I will add that at this point Dr. Rossini suggested that we cease uncovering artifacts and secure the site. It was my decision, and mine alone, to continue uncovering the items on top of this table. If it was the wrong decision, I want the record to reflect that. We did continue to record our progress both on film and with still shots, so that there would be no question of any tampering with the site or its artifacts. There was one object still visible on the tabletop, covered by the same thick layer of dust. We bagged up samples of the dust covering each artifact, by the way, Dr. Apriceno."

"Excellent!" the paleobotanist interjected.

"This time, we uncovered a quill pen, lying in the center of the desk. I was the one who realized that it was not, in fact, lying directly on the desk but on a sheet of papyrus completely concealed by the stone dust. Dr. Rossini very carefully proceeded to remove the dust from the sheet, which was covered with Latin writing. We did not take the time to decipher the handwriting, which was terribly shaky and rather small. We were a bit shaky ourselves by that point! But what we were able to read was a signature that was large enough and bold enough to be legible. It is the signature of Tiberius Caesar."

Although Bernardo had already been told what they found, actually looking at the ancient document took his breath away. The other two team members were too stunned to speak for a moment. Finally Father MacDonald spoke up. "This is an incredible find, but that papyrus needs to be stabilized immediately. The longer it is exposed to the air the harder it will be to preserve. May I step inside?"

Isabella stepped back a bit and let him in to look at the ancient text. He carefully studied it from every angle, then took a very fine-bladed pen knife and tried to insert it under one corner of the letter for the slightest fraction of an inch. Then he turned to the others. "I was afraid of this. The lacquer on the tabletop has bonded to the papyrus, and there is not going to be any easy way to detach the sheet from this table. I will have to move the whole thing to the lab and work on it there—which means that the other artifacts will have to be removed from the tabletop and all the stone dust cleared from it as well. Simone, I presume you will want to take some samples from the remaining undisturbed dust layer first?"

Apriceno stepped forward. "It looks like all their samples were carefully collected and labeled, but I am going to remove dust from the undisturbed areas of the tabletop to be certain. At that point you can remove the other items from the tabletop and carry them all to the mobile lab. Then I'll need to chase all of you out of here while I get samples from every other surface inside the chamber. Ideally, that dust should be identical in makeup to that which you removed from the tabletop, which will confirm the antiquity of the chamber and a lack of any tampering with the site."

Isabella nodded. "I don't see any problem with that," she said. "I think cleaning, cataloguing, and studying the other pieces will take up the next couple of days. Hopefully when Dr. Apriceno finishes collecting all her samples we can vacuum out the chamber and get a look at what lies under all this lovely ancient stone dust."

They stepped out of the chamber to let the pollen specialist collect her samples. For some time they discussed the site's potential, and the best means of curating what had been found so far. After some time Dr. Guioccini's phone buzzed, and he glanced at the incoming text message. "It seems Dr. Parker will arrive at Capodichino Airport in Naples at six PM. I've directed the chopper pilot who delivered us to pick him up there, so our team will be complete by the end of the day. So while we are waiting for Dr. Apriceno to complete her work, let's finish getting the mobile lab set up."

The four archeologists entered the lab. The equipment had all been secured for transport, and for the next hour or so they unbuckled straps, adjusted sensitive equipment, and opened various cabinets to check the instruments within. Rossini plugged the main power line into a small but powerful portable generator and started it up. MacDonald took a quick inventory of the chemicals he would need, and then lowered the viewing hood he would be using to study what they were already calling the "Tiberius manuscript." Guioccini walked around the small trailer, checking to see that everything they needed would be there, and listing the items that would have to be flown in. Once the mobile lab was set up, he asked the three to step outside.

"I will be leaving on the chopper that brings Dr. Parker in," he said. "For the time being I will be operating out of the Antiquities Bureau office in Naples. I want updates on any new discoveries, and any progress made with the ones already documented. Hopefully in a few days we can make some kind of public statement. This is already a remarkable find and has the potential to become even more so, depending on what else is in that chamber. MacDonald, I would like a rough translation of the Tiberius manuscript within the next forty-eight hours, if possible. Make sure that you and Dr. Parker agree on the translation before you forward it. The sealing ring, candle, quill, and everything else should be carefully analyzed, photographed, and documented so that I can present them to the Bureau before the week is out. Any questions?" There were none. He had chosen his team well.

"I've collected all necessary samples of the dust from on and around the table," Dr. Apriceno interrupted the briefing. "We can begin moving it from the chamber to the lab in a few moments. The table is not secured to the floor, but we will need to remove the other artifacts from the top of it before we transport it."

Guioccini nodded his agreement and dismissed the team. They waited outside the chamber while Giuseppe donned a pair of gloves. Moving carefully, Dr. Rossini reentered the chamber and used a pair of padded forceps to gingerly lift each object from the tabletop and place them in clear plastic boxes, which he then sealed with airtight lids before handing them to Isabella and Dr. MacDonald, who gingerly carried them to the lab. Once the inkwell, ring, candle, and candleholder were removed, Rossini asked MacDonald to take a careful look at the ancient document and the quill that rested on it. The Vatican archeologist very carefully prodded the quill with a long-handled pair of tweezers. It shifted easily, without any of the papyrus adhering to it. Breathing a sigh of relief, he gently placed it in an oblong plastic box and handed it out to Dr. Rossini. Then he carefully lifted the ancient stool that had sat under the writing desk for twenty centuries and carried it to the mobile lab as well, shielding it from direct sunlight with a thin sheet of opaque, acid-free plastic wrap. It was surprisingly light from dry rot, and he doubted that it would ever be able to bear a person's weight again. While it was an interesting and rare find, it could wait until after the ancient manuscript had been translated and analyzed.

Returning to the chamber, he carefully studied the writing table and the ancient document it held. He pulled a small tape measure out of his pocket and measured the width of the table itself, then the entrance of the chamber. He also measured the height of the table and compared it to the opening as well, frowning for a moment. "Dr. Rossini," he said, "is this block of stone removable?" He indicated a block that protruded near the bottom of the opening.

Rossini studied the projecting block for a moment, and gave it a gentle nudge with his foot. It shifted outward easily, so he gently pulled it from its resting place and laid it alongside the other blocks that had kept the chamber walled up for twenty centuries. MacDonald nodded his thanks, and then stepped out of the chamber to breathe some clean air and retrieve a large sheet of the acid-free plastic wrap. Coming back, he carefully stretched it over the entire tabletop and fixed it to each side of the table with a rubber-tipped pair of clamps.

"Dr. Sforza," he said. "You are young and sure-footed. I want you to very carefully lift the far side of this table out of the chamber, keeping it perfectly level the entire time. I will grasp the opposite side. Then we will carry it quickly across to the mobile lab. Ancient documents do NOT like sunlight, so we will expose it for the briefest period possible. Just please, don't trip!"

Isabella laughed nervously. "If I do, please don't fall after me!" she said, envisioning the priceless relic smashed between their falling bodies like a prop in a slapstick comedy movie. But they were both exceedingly careful, and covered the thirty feet between the mobile lab and the chamber entrance in a few seconds, while Dr. Rossini held the lab door open for them. In a moment the ancient teakwood table was positioned on a low workbench, and they both breathed a sigh of relief.

The sound of a helicopter began to grow in the distance. Guioccini smiled. "It looks like our final team member will be here just in time to help you get the real work started," he said. "Let's cover that entrance back up and go greet him, shall we?"

* * *

Josh knew he should be exhausted, but the events of the last twenty-four hours had him on such an adrenaline rush his body was feeling no fatigue. As soon as he got the call out on Lake Hugo, his father had headed for the boat ramp. Once the Bass Tracker was loaded up, Josh had dialed the number for Dr. Guioccini and gotten through. The Italian antiquarian sounded sleepy but responded to Josh's name very positively. He thanked Josh for calling back so quickly and then filled him in on the nature of the discovery and the need for a Latin historian and archeologist to assist in translating the document that had been found—and any more that might still be hidden in the chamber. As the reality of the discovery sunk in, Josh could hardly contain his excitement. At his father's house near Texarkana, he had thrown some clothes into his satchel, grabbed a handful of reference books for his carry-on, and been back out the door by the time his dad had gotten the boat unhooked and hosed out.

"Are you really going to fly to Italy smelling like dead shrimp?" his father asked him, and Josh looked down at his stained fishing pants and gave a laugh. He ducked back in the house, grabbed a clean change of clothes, and then showered and washed his hair in record time. The drive to D/FW International Airport had taken just over three hours, and Josh had used his phone to go online and find last-minute seats on a flight to London Heathrow, with a forty-five-minute layover before picking up the connecting flight to Naples. If all went as planned, Josh would arrive in Italy less than twenty-four hours after pulling his dad's boat out of the water in Oklahoma.

Josh had tried to immerse himself in the works of Cassius Dio during the trans-Atlantic flight, but not even the lively Latin narrative by the gossipy Roman consul who had served under the Emperor Commodus could keep him from speculating about what had been found on the island of Capri. He finally put the book down and tried to remember what he had learned about the reclusive emperor who had made the island famous. Tiberius was one of the least popular Roman emperors, mainly because he was portrayed as a sour, bitter old man who hated the city that was the capital of the Empire he governed from 14 to 37 AD. Following in the footsteps of his legendary stepfather, Augustus, he had always been jealous of the enormous popularity of his nephew and adopted son, Germanicus. Not long after Tiberius succeeded to the imperial throne, Germanicus had died under mysterious circumstances—many said he had been poisoned by order of the jealous emperor, a suspicion that was enhanced when the accused poisoner died before his trial. In an effort to dispel these suspicions, Tiberius had adopted Germanicus' young son Gaius as his own heir. Gaius was already known to the soldiers of his father's legions as "Caligula," or "Little Boots," because of the miniature general's uniform his father had loved to dress him up in. It was Caligula, grown into a deeply psychotic and perverted young adult, who had reportedly ordered Tiberius to be smothered with his own pillows when the old man's illness proved to be less fatal than Gaius had hoped. Caligula had reigned for four brief years before the Roman army had enough of his paranoia and rapidly accelerating lunacy, and he was murdered, along with his wife and infant daughter, by two generals who had been companions of his father.

Josh loved historical novels, and thought often about how Tiberius had been portrayed in popular works—a giggling, cruel, and paranoid old fool in the nearly pornographic movie *Caligula* (Josh had never admitted to his father that he had watched that film in college), a rather sweet and harmless old recluse in Lloyd C. Douglas' *The Robe*, and as a vindictive and calculating monster in Robert Graves' *I, Claudius*. He wondered which of the fictitious portrayals came closest to the real character of actual Tiberius, and found himself hoping the new discoveries on Capri would shed some light on them. There was one passage he had always found curious: according to Tertullian, a Christian apologist who wrote around the end of the second century AD, Tiberius had apparently heard of and been impressed with the teachings of Jesus, and had supposedly suggested to the Roman Senate that Christianity be recognized as a legitimate religion throughout the Empire, even suggesting that a statue of Jesus be erected in the Roman pantheon. Josh thought that last bit was probably wishful thinking on Tertullian's part, but he still found it fascinating to think that the Emperor of Rome might have actually heard about Jesus' ministry only a few years after the Resurrection.

Josh had finally gotten a few hours of light sleep before landing in London, and the flight from London to Naples had gone smoothly. He was tired and a bit jet-lagged, but eager to see what the fuss was about. At the airport he was met by a young Italian army lieutenant, who steered him toward a waiting helicopter. The sun had not yet set when Josh saw the ruins of the Villa Jovis coming into view. As the chopper closed in, he could make out the trailer housing the mobile lab, and in one of the stone walls near it, a tiny black dot that marked the entrance to the hidden chamber.

Isabella waited on the ancient marble flooring that had come to double as a helo deck for the Villa Jovis. Dr. Guioccini stood next to her, his travel bag in hand. "I am leaving you and Rossini in charge," he said. "If there are any problems with any of the team members, just let me know. Keep me updated on any finds you make, or any developments of importance. We hope to begin releasing this story to the press as soon as possible, but we want the information we release to be carefully controlled and double checked for accuracy. Let me know if the team has any further needs."

Sforza smiled back at him. "I will do so, sir," she said. "Thank you for expediting everything so quickly. This has been a very exciting twenty-four hours!"

Guioccini smiled back. "You have made a great discovery, Dr. Sforza. Moments like this are what every archeologist lives for. But as exciting as it is, remember procedure. The whole world will be reading your findings—and, more than likely, looking for an excuse to question them. We are in a cutthroat profession, so don't give your critics any ammunition if you can help it!"

He had to shout by the end of his declaration, for the helicopter was touching down in front of them. The cargo door slid back, and a tall, lanky, deeply tanned young man stepped out, carrying a heavy duffel bag. Shielding his head from the prop wash with one hand, he stepped forward, set down his duffel, and held out the other. "Dr. Guioccini, I presume?" he said.

"You are correct, Dr. Parker. Welcome to the isle of Capri, and the Villa Jovis! This is Dr. Isabella Sforza, who will be supervising your work here."

Josh was taken aback by the vision in khakis that stood before him. Dr. Sforza was, without exaggeration, the most beautiful woman he had ever met. Josh was a bit awkward around girls, even though most women found him attractive, a fact he was largely unaware of. In high school he had been obsessed with preserving his virginity until he found the wife that God intended for him, and then during his college years, he had been so turned off by the casual promiscuity of many of his classmates—many of them professing Christians—that he had never gotten around to looking for that special person. Instead, he had let his career dominate his passions, and tried to look the other way when he found himself staring at a woman and thinking inappropriate thoughts. But how could he ignore this vision of feminine beauty when he was going to be working with her for the next few weeks?

Suddenly he realized that Dr. Sforza was standing there with her hand out while he was staring at her. "I'm terribly sorry," he said, holding out his hand. "Dr. Josh Parker, at your service."

Isabella looked at the handsome young American and realized he was blushing deeply beneath his tan. Under other circumstances, she might have been somewhat offended, but there was something so sincere about his awkwardness that she found herself somewhat charmed by it. "Just call me Isabella," she said. "I understand that you have a strong background in first-century Latin and *koine* Greek?"

"Yes, ma'am," Josh replied. "I love reading history in its original language when I can. What have we found so far?"

We? Isabella wondered if he was trying to take credit for the work already done, or simply trying to think of himself as a member of the team. His manner seemed earnest and sincere enough, but she decided to keep an eye on him nonetheless. "So far we have one papyrus document," she said. "It is written on a single sheet and was left lying flat on the tabletop. The weight of the dust and sediment that built on top of it over the years has fused it to the lacquered finish that was on the table, so I don't know that we will be able to separate it. But, at the same time, the lacquer has also preserved it so that the writing is still quite legible. Dr. MacDonald is working to stabilize it as we speak. You and he should get along quite well—your specialties overlap."

Guioccini interrupted. "Isabella, I am heading back to the mainland. Keep me informed and good luck!" he shouted as he climbed into the chopper. Parker grabbed his bag and followed Sforza down the steps of the Villa Jovis to the mobile lab.

By the time of the most recent Passover, this Jesus of Nazareth had acquired a huge following, and the stories about him were becoming fanciful to the extreme. They said, just before Passover, that he had actually brought a man back to life who had been dead for FOUR days! It was after this story began circulating in the city that the Jewish leadership decided that Jesus must die. His followers now numbered in the thousands, and they feared an armed revolution. When he came to the city for the Passover feast, their plans for his demise were already cemented into place—even though he refused the offering of a crown that the enthusiastic mob made when he entered the city.

You may be wondering why I did not step in at this point. While I do have several informants who are seated on the Jewish Sanhedrin, during this time, the high priest and his cronies only met with a select few that did not include my agents. This small group bought off one of Jesus' disciples (that man has subsequently disappeared; rumors abound that he hung himself after the events that followed) and sent a large mob, accompanied by the Temple guard (and a single cohort of Legionaries whose centurion wisely saw the commotion and followed along to see what was going on and keep the peace if necessary). They proceeded to a quiet garden outside the city walls where the Nazarene was known to meet with his disciples. Jesus was arrested without any major incident—apparently he was with only a small group of followers, and only one of them even tried to defend him. Jesus was then interrogated before both the former High Priest, that evil old serpent named Annas, and the current holder of that office, Caiaphas. Finally, in the third hour past midnight, the enormous mob showed up, with a bloodied and battered Jesus, at the Praetorium, angrily demanding that I sentence him to death.

CHAPTER FIVE

Dr. MacDonald studied the ancient tabletop and the papyrus document that was fused to it carefully. Stabilizing and preserving ancient manuscripts was tricky work, but the unique circumstances of this find had made the work a good bit easier. Normally, ancient, desiccated papyrus had to be carefully rehydrated and unrolled before it could be read, but this piece had been left flat, and the weight of the stone dust over the centuries had pressed it deep into the waxy, lacquered surface of the table, which had impregnated the porous sheet with its waterproof coating—most likely a combination of beeswax and paraffin. His task was a matter of removing the most stubbornly clinging dust and grime from the surface of the paper, then coating it with a sealant to keep contaminants out and preserve the ancient writing permanently.

He took a sterilized cotton pad, moistened it slightly, and began gently blotting the ancient papyrus surface. It was a slow process, but he was surprised at how readily the accumulated stone dust adhered to the cotton. The spiky scribbles on the document became clearer and darker as he slowly worked over it.

"Whatever happens, we will have to read it where it lies," a calm voice interjected, interrupting his concentration. He had been so absorbed in the work that he had not heard the lab door open and close, but there stood Isabella and a tall young man in khakis. The American accent—somewhere in the South, by the sound of it—made him pretty sure who was speaking.

"Ah, you must be Dr. Parker," the priest said, turning and placing the cotton on the table before holding out his hand. "I am Duncan MacDonald, humble priest and renowned historian!"

Josh laughed. "Are you sure it's not the other way around?" he replied. "It is an honor to meet you. Your field manual on document preservation has a permanent place in my travel kit." The priest nodded at this acknowledgment of his work, and Josh went on. "Looks like this papyrus has solidly adhered to the tabletop," he commented. "Certainly makes the preservation easier, but I doubt we will ever be able to remove it—the thing would wind up like poor old King Tut!"

MacDonald nodded in agreement. It was not generally known outside the archeological community, but when Howard Carter opened the sarcophagus of Tutankhamen in 1924, he had found the mummy of the boy king completely fused to the bottom of the coffin. Apparently the burial had been somewhat rushed and the fluids used in the mummification process had not completely dried by the time the young Pharaoh was placed in his sarcophagus. Unwilling to try to dissolve the ancient unguents that had glued the boy king to his wooden coffin, the archeologists had simply torn the mummy apart, removing it in several pieces. MacDonald shuddered as he envisioned the precious manuscript crumbling to pieces as they tried to remove it from the tabletop where it had rested for twenty centuries.

"Have you thought about how to do carbon dating?" asked Josh.

"Yes, I have considered it," said MacDonald. "I tested one corner of the manuscript to see if it would move at all, and saw that it did nothing but start crumbling. Since that tiny corner is already loosened, it can be easily removed and sent to the main lab in Rome for testing. But the first priority is to finish cleaning and then read and photograph the manuscript. I am about two-thirds done."

"Very good," said Josh. "I will get my things settled, and then come back in a bit and see if I can be of any help."

Dr. Sforza led him outside. "Your tent will be over there by Dr. Rossini's," she said. "Once things are more settled up here, we will probably rent rooms at the small hotel in Capri village, but for now I want us all to stay on-site. Speaking of Giuseppe, I need to introduce you to him and to the other members of the team. Follow me!"

Over the next hour, Josh got to meet and visit with the other two archeologists. He found that he warmed to Dr. Apriceno immediately; she reminded him of many of the Southern matrons that had attended his dad's churches over the years—stout, strong, smart, and with a low tolerance for nonsense. Rossini, on the other hand, seemed a bit wary of the young American at first. It took a moment for Josh to see why—but then he noticed that the old man seemed jealous whenever Sforza got close to Josh or spoke to him. After the conversation continued for a few moments, Rossini seemed to lighten up a bit. Later on, as he got to know them both better, Josh realized that Rossini was very protective of the younger archeologist—in a fatherly way. Apparently he wasn't too sure of the young American's intentions!

After the round of introductions, Josh and Isabella headed back into the tent. MacDonald was carefully spraying the manuscript with a pungent aerosol. "This is a clear polymer that binds and seals papyrus, parchment, leather, or any other ancient, organic surface," he says. "It keeps out moisture, repels dust, and prevents the surface from crumbling. As soon as it sets we can study this document at our leisure."

Josh recognized the polymer as one he had read about but not tried yet in the field. "It's supposed to soak up and set in very quickly—does it?" he asked.

"In less than five minutes," said MacDonald. "In fact, I am about to move the viewer over the document so we can begin to decipher the writing. Why don't you grab pen and paper and parallel with me?" Parallel inscribing was a common way to double check the exact wording of ancient handwritten manuscripts. Two archeologists or historians would sit side by side, without exchanging a word, to copy and translate what they thought was the exact wording of the manuscript they were studying. Then they would compare notes and see what, if any, words or phrases they did not agree on. Josh took the proffered notebook and sat on a stool beside MacDonald, looking through the illuminated magnifying glass. The handwriting was small and a bit shaky, but not nearly as indecipherable now that the dust of the ages had been removed. After about ten minutes, MacDonald set his pen down. Joshua was done a moment later. "Read yours first," said MacDonald, so Josh complied, reading his rendition of the note from Tiberius Caesar:

Tiberius Caesar ad Mencius Marcellus, senescallus Villa Jovis

Ego sum Romam—aliquid iuravi numquam, sed politica relinquere me paulo electio. Occasio est nolle redire mihi—septuaginta octo sum tamen, et insolentia itineris. In procinctu reditus villam custodiendam et dimittere extra culinam virgam redde choros mittere domo mea ob parentum. Tu suscipe verba non revertar—videlicet quod mortuus fuit itineris mei—conscripsi cubiculum velit signa sua. Non opus puer serpens Gaius ad pawing per privatas litteras! Ut scilicet ponat in cubiculo Capsula—Proin transtulit ad annos funere imaginum, sed etiam usu congregem correspondentia nolo aliis legi. Illud in latere et caemento, ut omne tempus quieta foret! Tibi serviet mihi etiam amicum. Hoc mihi operae pretium et loculos a mensa. Deos ora pro nobis—redeo ad nidum serpentium!

Tiberius Julius Caesar Augustus

"Excellent!" said MacDonald. "I only have one word different—I had *'conscripsus'* instead of *'conscripsi.'* But looking at the original again, I think you got it right. So let me correct that, and then I will translate yours and you can translate mine. Hopefully we will agree just as fully."

The two scholars exchanged tablets and retreated to opposite ends of the mobile lab. Josh sat on a folding chair with the notebook balanced on his lap, while the Vatican archeologist sat on a small couch. Isabella satisfied herself with carefully examining the table on which the document had rested for so long. Something about it simply did not look right. She puzzled over it while the two translators worked. After a few moments she realized what she was seeing, but decided to wait until they were done to say anything.

Josh took his time, trying his best to match up the Latin words to their nearest possible English equivalent. Translation was always a bit of a tricky business, as the many different versions of the Bible from the Greek and Hebrew originals clearly demonstrated. After about thirty minutes, he looked up and found MacDonald looking at him serenely. "Why don't you read your version first, Father?" he asked.

"Fair enough, laddie," replied the priest. "This is what I came up with:

Tiberius Caesar to Mencius Marcellus, Steward of Villa Jovis

I am returning to Rome—something I swore never to do, but politics leave me little choice. There is a good chance that I will not return—I am seventy-eight, after all, and unaccustomed to travel. Keep the villa in readiness for my return, but dismiss the extra kitchen staff, and pay off the dancers and send them home, with my thanks to their parents. Should you receive word that I will not return—in other words, that I have died on my journey—please seal up my writing chamber and its contents. No need for that young serpent Gaius to go pawing through my private letters! Be sure to place the reliquary in the chamber as well—I transferred the funerary masks to a new cabinet years ago, but I still use it to store correspondence that I don't want others reading, and mementos that are mine alone. Brick it up and mortar it in, that it may be undisturbed for all time! You have served me well, old friend. Do me this last service, and take the purse from the table as payment. Entreat the gods on my behalf—I return to a nest of serpents!

Tiberius Julius Caesar Augustus

As the Scottish antiquarian read, Josh compared notes. He quickly realized that they had gotten the identical meaning from the passage, with only a few minor synonyms deviating in their translations. He noted that MacDonald had left the Latin "*Imaginum*" where he had gone ahead and translated it to "masks," but the meaning was clear. All noble Roman families kept a small cabinet of wax masks and wigs, made from the death masks of their famous ancestors, so that during their funeral rites, actors could be hired to march in the procession, impersonating those illustrious Romans and illustrating the high public standing of the deceased. These masks were usually kept in a portable wooden cabinet, or reliquary, along with other precious possessions, which could be moved from one villa to another.

After they had each read their translations, there was silence for a few moments. Then Father MacDonald let out a low laugh. "Dancers!" he said. "And all this time Suetonius would have us believe that Tiberius was luring children up here to take obscene advantage of their innocence!"

"Well, 'dancers' could be a euphemism," said Josh. "But I agree that the tone makes it sound a lot more innocent than those old histories did! But the cabinet—the reliquary he described—do you think he is referring to the box at the rear of the chamber?"

"Certainly could be," said MacDonald. "Which means if old Mincius Marcellus obeyed instructions, this may be the first of many documents we translate from this site!"

"Gentlemen, I hate to interrupt your work," said Isabella, "but I think I may have found something." They both looked at her with curiosity, since she had not left the lab the whole time they had been translating. She met their confused glances, and then laughed. "Not something else in the chamber," she said. "Something about this writing table."

"What?" they both said at the same time.

"Look," she said. "You have focused entirely on the top of the table, where the document was—have either of you ever looked underneath it?" A rueful glance between them showed that they had not. She gestured them over to the table. "See here," she said. "The tabletop is obviously solid all the way around, and there is about ten or twelve centimeters of ornately carved paneling directly underneath it on each side before the legs of the table begin. But there is a solid bottom here that is level with the tops of the table legs. That means that there must be a drawer or space beneath the tabletop!"

They carefully surveyed each side of the paneling. There was no visible handle or lock anywhere. The front side of the table that would have faced the writer had an ornately carved Roman eagle with "SPQR" on a small gold blazon across its breast, while the other sides simply had geometric designs carved into the solid wood.

"There is nothing that looks remotely like a keyhole or handle," said Isabella. "So the only thing left is—this!" She firmly pressed the golden blazon on the eagle with her index finger. It resisted briefly, and then sank in about a half inch or so. There was an audible click, and the entire front panel popped outward from the top down. The ancient hinges shrieked slightly as the weight of the panel gradually caused it to drop forward, revealing the hidden recess inside.

"Don't touch anything," Dr. Sforza said. "I want to get the rest of the team in here to document this." She left the Scottish antiquarian and the young archeologist staring at each other as she stepped out of the mobile lab and began calling the other two scientists. Moments later Rossini and Apriceno followed Dr. Sforza into the lab. She had her digital camera out and snapped several still shots of the table and the drawer, and then had Josh lift the front panel back up so she could photograph the eagle and the golden blazon that had unlocked the panel.

"I'm going to switch to video now," she said. "I want to record this discovery before we go any further." She began narrating again. "April 9, 19:30 hours: As Doctors MacDonald and Parker worked at translating the papyrus which is cemented to the top of the small writing table from inside the chamber, I began to record the dimensions of the table now that it was cleaned of dust and inside the mobile lab. As I did so, I noticed that there was a space between the top and bottom of the table approximately fifteen centimeters in height that could only be a drawer or storage nook of some sort. When they were done with their initial translation, I called their attention to the anomaly and we examined the table more closely. The only possible latch was the golden blazon on the Roman eagle decorating the paneling on the front of the table. I pressed it and the front panel dropped open to reveal a hidden drawer beneath the table. Now we are going to look inside the drawer and see if anything is stored inside it. Dr. Parker, would you shine the light inside for us?"

Josh moved closer and shone the powerful halogen light into the recess. It was not as dusty as the top of the table had been, but there were a few ancient cobwebs visible inside. There were two or three sheets of papyrus laid flat across the bottom of the drawer, and on top of them rested a small leather bag. It had a drawstring top, and was lying open with the mouth facing toward them. A small golden figure of a horse's head was sticking out of it.

Isabella continued her narration. "We appear to have a small leather purse with a drawstring top, partly open, containing a very small equine sculpture or toy which is facing towards us. It is lying on top of several sheets of papyrus. Dr. Parker, can you see any writing on the papyrus?"

Josh did his best to sound professional, although the discovery of this new treasure had him very excited. "I can only see part of the top sheet, but it appears to be clean and blank except for some staining around the leather," he said. "If the leather were oiled at one time to keep it supple, then there is a good chance that the oils soaked in as the purse dried out and stained all the papyrus in the drawer."

"Shall we try to remove these objects?" asked Rossini.

Isabella shook her head. "No," she finally said. "We have rushed a great deal already, and it has been a very long day. Dr. Apriceno, how are you progressing in the chamber with your sample collections?"

The archeobotanist coughed. "Well, I have taken copious samples with both my hands and my lungs," she said. "But I have collected dust from virtually every surface and item in the chamber. I have one or two small areas left to go, and then tomorrow I shall put every specimen under the microscope. My gut reaction, from what I have seen thus far, is that the chamber has been sealed tight for a very, very long time. I imagine my initial pollen analysis will confirm that. After that is done, I will send all my samples to the mainland for a more thorough analysis. However, once all the samples are collected, we can proceed with cleaning the dust from all the remaining objects and surfaces in the chamber so that the excavation can continue."

Dr. Sforza listened carefully. "Well, I know that our scholars have completed their initial translation of the Tiberius document—I'm going to be optimistic and say the FIRST Tiberius document. Dr. Apriceno, go ahead and finish collecting your last few samples and return them to the lab. Then you and Dr. Rossini can seal up the chamber for the night. Father MacDonald, you and Dr. Parker go ahead and begin pitching the tents. Once the public announcement has been made, we can begin staying down in the village at the inn, but in the meantime we are all up here on the mountaintop together—so hopefully no one snores TOO loudly!"

The group had a good laugh at that. "Once the tents are pitched and the chamber sealed up for the night, we can gather in the lab and listen as our linguists share their translation with the whole team," she continued. "And after that, supper!"

"Actually, I think supper had better come first," said Rossini. "I don't know about everyone else, but I am famished, and I told Signora Bustamante to have a supper for five ready this evening. Ancient Latin documents are always more entertaining on a full stomach."

"You know, I think you're right," she agreed. "Go ahead and call down as soon as you get the chamber sealed up."

The scholars all set about their appointed tasks as soon as she finished. Isabella started to follow Parker and MacDonald out the door, but paused for just a moment to shine the light into that drawer one more time. The tiny golden horse glittered in the glare of the halogen bulb, as bright as it had been when the Emperor of Rome had placed it there twenty centuries ago. Was it a toy that Caligula had once played with? Or an ornament that had graced the neck of some highborn Roman matron? The tiny mouth seemed twisted in a mysterious equine smile. Sforza shook her head and walked out of the lab. It was a mystery that could wait till tomorrow.

An hour later, the archeologists sat in a circle. Rossini had called down into the village earlier in the day and placed a supper order from the same delightful restaurant that had served him and Sforza the night before, and Chief Rosario had driven up the Via Tiberio in his golf cart to bring it to them. He wagged his head as Giuseppe had come down the trail to meet him. "From dinner for two to dinner for five?" he asked. "And helicopters coming and going all day? What on earth have you dug out of the old villa, my friend—the mummy of Tiberius himself?"

"You know I would tell you if I could," said Rossini. "But I am going to have to ask you to contain your curiosity a little while longer."

"Nonsense!" said the policeman. "This is just some plot you cooked up to impress that beautiful young scholar who you are up here hobnobbing with!"

Rossini laughed and shook his head as he waved goodbye to his friend. He saw the young American coming down the ancient trail toward him. "I thought you might need a little help carrying up the munchables," said Josh. "So I just followed my nose. Good grief, that stuff smells wonderful!"

"Jet travel always leaves one hungry, does it not?" asked Giuseppe. "Listen, my young friend, I would like a word with you before we rejoin the others."

"By all means," Josh replied. "What can I do for you?"

"Isabella is a remarkable woman in every way," replied the old scholar. "But she also lost someone she cared very deeply for when her husband died. I have watched her bury herself in her work for years now to avoid dealing with her grief. Now, today, I see her looking at you as she has not looked at any man in a very long time. I don't know you, other than your professional reputation, Dr. Parker. You seem a decent enough young man. But if you do anything to hurt her—well, you will have made a bitter and cunning enemy. So tread softly!"

Josh was stunned. *She* was looking at *him*? That simple statement blew his mind so thoroughly that it took him a minute to process the rest of what the older archeologist had said. But as the man's concern sunk in, he thought for a moment before replying. "Dr. Rossini— Giuseppe, if I may—you are quite right when you say you do not know me. And frankly, the way Americans are portrayed in pop culture probably doesn't give you much ground for trust. But I will tell you this—I was raised by a very devout Southern Baptist minister who taught me to live by the Golden Rule. And if I ever did anything dishonorable or unchristian to *any* young lady, he wouldn't leave enough hide on my bones for you to come after!"

Rossini threw his head back and laughed. "Someday you must introduce me to this father of yours," he said. "I think I would like him a great deal!"

An hour later, after a delicious meal of tortellini and chicken Marsala, the team listened as MacDonald and Parker shared their translation of the letter from the tabletop. There was a lively discussion of what impact this would have on the scholarship of the Tiberian era, but then Rossini picked up on the significance that Josh and Father MacDonald had already discussed. "The large square box at the back of the chamber—you think it is the reliquary, don't you?" he said.

"That seems the most logical assumption," said Parker. "And if that is indeed the case, we may well have a treasure trove of Imperial Roman correspondence from the first century AD. Dr. Apriceno, you are the only one who has ventured to the back of the chamber. Any observations on the objects you observed?"

"All I have done is removed a small core sample of dust from every wall, every part of the floor, and every object," she said. "The big square in the back of the chamber is very heavily coated—there are about six or eight centimeters of dust on top of it, and it was partially buried in a dirt slide long ago, so its dimensions are hard to determine with certainty. But I can confirm that it is made of wood, since I went all the way down to the original surface in collecting my sample. It will take several days to clean it off so we can actually see what it is."

At this point they all retired to their tents. Josh broke out his old journal—he still kept it the old-fashioned way, with pen and ink—and recorded his thoughts on the day's events. But despite the excitement of the discovery, his mind kept going back to what Rossini had said about Dr. Sforza. She was looking at him! With Isabella's face floating in his mind, it was a long time before he went to sleep.

This I was reluctant to do. First and foremost, I believed and still believe that the man was innocent of any offense against Roman law. The second reason is more personal, but you of all people should understand it. For each of the three previous nights, my wife had woken me with her screams. She was not entirely coherent, but one thing she said on each occasion was, 'Do not kill the Galilean! He is innocent! You will be damned forever if you do!' These statements troubled me deeply. Every Roman knows the story of how the noble Calpurnia sought to dissuade the Divus Julius from going to the forum on the Ides of March. Dreams are powerful things, and sometimes the gods use them to speak to us. Even as I stood before this angry mob, trying to make sense of their accusations, she sent me a note that read "Have nothing to do with the death of this innocent man." At this moment, I realized that Jesus was actually a subject of King Herod Antipas, since he was from Galilee rather than Judea, so I sent him to stand trial before Herod. Unfortunately, Herod was unwilling to pronounce judgment on him, and two hours later Jesus was brought before me once more. The only positive development from this incident was that Herod, who had been quite hostile to me for some time, has become friendlier ever since—although given his mercurial nature, I have no confidence the improvement in our relations will be permanent.

CHAPTER SIX

Josh rose early the next morning, his body still unsure exactly what time it was or when it was supposed to wake up. He had always been unable to sleep once the sun was up, so after rolling over several times in a vain attempt to recapture his slumber, he slowly stirred and stretched. He pulled on his shoes and got a clean khaki shirt out of his duffel bag, then stepped outside. The snores from the tent next to his told him that Dr. Rossini was still asleep, so he walked over to the mobile lab. Dr. Apriceno and Isabella were already there, and the rich smell of coffee brewing filled the trailer.

"Our American friend is an early riser," the older woman commented. "The other two men could learn a lesson from him!"

"Well, Simone," said Isabella, "I don't know MacDonald that well, but Giuseppe has been hard at work on this site ever since the earthquake! He's earned the right to sleep in a little, and it's not even seven AM yet."

"I'm only awake because my body is convinced it is mid-afternoon, or whatever time it is in Oklahoma," said Josh. "Well, that, and I have never been able to sleep once the sun comes over the horizon. It will take me a couple of days to catch up from my jet lag. Is that coffee ready?"

"Here you are," said Dr. Sforza, pouring him a cup. "We like it dark and sweet here in Italy, but I could probably find you some cream if you like."

"Honestly, I hate coffee on principle," said Josh. "Never even been inside a Starbucks. But I figured a cold Dr Pepper was too much to hope for in Italy. A Coke would be all right, too, I suppose. But for the moment, this nasty stuff will wake me up and get me going." He sipped the coffee and made a wry face.

Apriceno wrinkled her nose. "Dr Pepper? I had that stuff in the States one time. Tastes like prune juice!"

Josh raised an eyebrow and waggled his finger at her. "Dear lady," he said, "you may question my character, belittle my faith, deride my appearance, and record over my favorite DVDs—but *don't ever* insult the Elixir of Life!"

The two women laughed at this jibe, and Isabella said, "I must confess that I love your soft drink choice. It's hard to get Dr Pepper here in Italy, but perhaps we can order some from Naples before the week is out. In the meantime, I know the store down in Capri village has Coca-Cola and several other American drink brands. We'll try to have a coffee substitute up here tomorrow for you."

Dr. Apriceno walked back to the storage closet in one corner of the lab and pulled out a small metal vacuum cleaner. "I have taken all the dust and pollen samples I need from the chamber," she said. "Now I will begin clearing out the remainder of the dust, so that you all may begin your work inside. It will take a few hours, but I hope to have the chamber ready for excavation by the end of the day. So if you will excuse me, I will be off to work." They bid her a good day as she took the vacuum and several spare bags out the door.

"I've had to excavate all manner of ancient overburden, from Roman era privies to volcanic ash to rich Italian farm soil," said Isabella, "but I have never encountered a site that was coated with so much plain old dust!"

"I imagine she will save every one of those vacuum bags, too," Josh said. "That way there will be samples available for study to any archeological lab that wants to verify her findings."

Dr. Sforza sat down across from Josh at the small dining table, looking at him with a clear gaze that was piercing and a bit unsettling at the same time. It didn't help matters that she had the most beautiful green eyes he had ever seen. "So, Dr. Joshua Parker," she finally said. "Tell me a bit about yourself. How did you become an archeologist?"

Josh thought about it a moment. "I guess my dad gave me a big push in that direction," he said. "My father is a pastor, but he has a deep love of history, science, and nature. As a boy he took me all over North Texas collecting arrowheads and fossils, but he always made sure that I understood that they were more than just pretty rocks. He taught me to catalog each and every piece I found, so that their significance would be recorded and preserved. Then when we moved to Spiro, Oklahoma, I heard about and saw what had happened to the famous Indian mounds there. Have you ever heard of the Spiro mounds?"

"Isn't that the big ceremonial site that was largely destroyed by looters during the Depression?" she said. "I think I read an article about it once."

"That's the place," he replied. "When I was a kid I heard a famous Oklahoma archeologist talk about what happened there. It's hard to blame the looters—there were no antiquity laws in place then, and they were just poor men trying to feed their families in a desperate time. But as Dr. Bell described all the marvelous things that were found there, especially inside the largest mound, I made up my mind that I was going to be an archeologist myself. I dreamed of finding a site like Spiro, completely undisturbed, and being the first to excavate and study it. But as I got older and learned more about American archeology, I realized that science had been completely sold down the river in the name of political correctness. In my country, the Native American populations have the power of life and death over every archeological excavation. In Texas about ten years ago, they found a seventy-five-hundred-year-old cemetery site, the oldest mass burial ever found in the United States. There were artifacts there that had never been found in Texas before, bannerstones and ceremonial artifacts that are normally only found in the Ohio River valley. So what did they do? They excavated, photographed, and then turned everything back over to the Karankawa Indians—a tribe that lived in that region in historic times. And the Indians performed their religious rites and buried everything all over again. Artifacts, remains, the whole shebang, back in the ground! No one will ever be able to study them, or learn from them, or simply look at them and appreciate the artisanship that went into making them. And, worst of all, we have no way of knowing if the tribe we turned them over to are the descendants of those ancient skeletons or not. No DNA test required, no historical or archeological links, nothing. All a tribe has to do is claim an artifact as 'an object of cultural patrimony,' and the archeologist's hands are tied. It is sickening! That's one thing that led me away from American archeology."

Dr. Sforza was astonished—both at the ridiculous restrictions placed on science in the name of respecting aboriginal religious beliefs, and also at Josh's obvious anger at the policies he described. She nodded in agreement at his assessment, and then said: "You said that was one thing that led you away from American archeology. What is the other?"

He paused for a while. "It's a bit more personal," he said. "It's a matter of faith and science combined. My father is a Baptist minister, but he is also a serious student of history, as I said. He always told me that good science and solid archeology would never undermine Scripture. His idea is that, if the Scriptures seem to be telling us one thing, and the earth, or the historical record, seems to be telling us another, then we are not reading one or both of them correctly. And I must say, as far as the New Testament era goes, I have yet to find or read anything that proves him wrong. Time and again, skeptical scholars have tried to say that this discovery or that would debunk some aspect of the Biblical narrative—and yet, they haven't managed to disprove anything yet! And many of the discoveries made over the last century have confirmed the New Testament stories rather than disproved them. So I decided to come over here and do my work, my scholarship, in the land where my faith was born—the ancient Roman Empire. I've worked at Qumran, Ephesus, and Capernaum, excavating and studying. It has been an incredible experience, and so far everything I have found has strengthened my convictions that Christianity rests on a foundation of real, historical events. Thomas Huxley said 'Any doctrine that will not bear investigation is an unworthy tenant in the mind of an honest man.' I guess I have devoted my life thus far to investigating the doctrines I believe in."

Sforza was amazed. Genuine men of faith were almost unheard of in the sciences in general, especially in archeology. Like many of her colleagues, she had heard stories of the "brain-dead fundamentalists" who wielded so much power in American politics, but this young man seemed anything but the kind of zealot she had heard about. "A true believer," she said. "I have encountered a few in the Catholic Church— Father MacDonald, I know, is a man of real faith, and a solid scientist. But I will be honest; you don't look or sound anything like the fundamentalist American Christians I have heard of."

"That's because very little of what you hear is true," Josh replied. "Don't get me wrong—I have known some very unimaginative, ignorant, and prejudiced people in the churches my dad pastored over the years. I had one tell me once that he refused to believe dinosaurs existed because they were never mentioned in the Bible. This was right after Dad and I had discovered and excavated a mosasaur skull in the Sulphur River bed too, so what could I say?"

"So what did you tell him?" she asked.

"I told him to go read Job 41," replied Josh. "It's an ancient description of a huge sea beast called a Leviathan. I have no idea what God was describing to Job, honestly, but the description sure sounds like some sort of giant aquatic reptile. But here is the point I was going to make. Most of the images that people have of American Christianity come from one of three sources. It's either from Hollywood, which is largely populated by atheists, Buddhists, or lapsed Jews and Catholics who have a pretty hostile view of Protestants in general and evangelicals in particular. Then there is the American and international media, which is also made up largely of skeptics, agnostics, and atheists who have a rather harsh view of all religions. So every time they want to portray the state of religion in America, they go find some ignorant extremist like Fred Phelps or David Duke to interview, and thus affirm the worst stereotypes about people of faith. They never portray the good that is done by the American church because they are almost entirely unaware of it. Finally, sadly, there are the American televangelists. There are some good, doctrinally solid Christians among them, of course, but the ones that get the press are the con men and nut jobs. As a result, most of the world never really gets a good look at the real face of American evangelicalism—men like my dad, who has pastored over a dozen churches, has two master's degrees, and reads a book or two a week. Guys like him never get any publicity beyond the local newspapers, and so the world thinks that the face of American Christianity is some guy with a pompadour and a thousand-dollar suit who pronounces 'God' with about six syllables while bilking little old ladies out of their Social Security checks, or some radical lunatic waving a sign about how 'God Hates You'!"

He spoke with strong emotion, and Isabella found herself more and more intrigued by this young man. "So, do you think that these 'atheists and agnostics' are bad people?" she asked.

"Not at all." said Josh. "I've met quite a few of them in person, and dozens more in various online forums and chat groups. The vast majority of them are perfectly nice people. The problem is that many of them have never met an evangelical Christian, and have no clue how we think or what we believe. They just accept the stereotypes that have been created about us without question. It's very frustrating, because most of them I have met are genuinely surprised to find that I can actually read and that my knuckles don't drag the ground when I walk. No, they're not bad people—they're just, as my dad would say, 'lost as jaybirds.' I'm sorry, Dr. Sforza, you've got me going on one of my pet peeves." He paused a moment to calm himself down. Here he had a rare opportunity to have a private conversation with the most fascinating woman he had ever met, and he was ranting like a talk radio host. "Tell you what—I've told you about myself now. How about if we talk about you for a while?"

69

"Not a lot to say," she said. "I was born on a small farm near —" But before she could get any further, the trailer doors opened and Father MacDonald came in, followed by Dr. Rossini. "Good morning, gentlemen," said Isabella.

"*Bon journo*, Isabella." said Rossini. "The coffee smells wonderful! So what is our first order of business today?" he asked as he poured a cup and gave it a small dose of crème de menthe.

"Last night's discovery first," she said. "Father MacDonald, I want you and Josh to see if we can remove the items from the drawer without damaging them."

"I don't think I can do it without damaging meself until I have some coffee, lass," said the Scottish priest. Josh noticed that MacDonald's accent was always stronger when he was clowning around, while it became almost unnoticeable when he was serious. The Scottish priest poured himself a large mug of coffee; meanwhile, Rossini went over to a cabinet and opened it, pulling out a large covered tray that was full of pastries when he took the lid off of it.

"I told Signora Bustamante to send up a tray of breakfast items with our dinner last night," he said. "These are cold but still quite fresh—she baked them yesterday evening along with our meal."

The scientists dug in with gusto, snagging cinnamon rolls and strudels with abandon. Josh allowed himself two of the rolls, and then paused with his mouth full.

"We need to take some of these to Dr. Apriceno," he said. "Or at least tell her they are here. She's already working with nothing but a cup of coffee in her belly." He grabbed a large butter pecan Danish and laid it on a napkin, walking out of the trailer toward the alcove. The plastic shield that had replaced the makeshift tarp covered the entrance, but had a vertical zippered opening for the team to come and go. He could hear the high-pitched whirr of the vacuum going. The archeobotanist was still working near the entrance to the chamber, busily sucking up centuries of dust while being very careful not to vacuum up anything that wasn't stone dust. Josh called her name twice and finally tapped her shoulder. She started, then stood upright and shut off the small but powerful appliance. "I thought you might like some breakfast," Josh said.

"*Grazi*," she replied. "You are very considerate." She took a large bite of the Danish and gave a small groan of satisfaction. The town's restaurant was well known for its food, and the breakfast was outstanding.

"So have you found anything, now that the dust is being removed?" Josh asked.

"I've only uncovered the nearest part of the alcove, where the table and lamp were located," she said. "There appears to be some graffiti on the wall next to the desk." Joshua peeked in. Uncovered by the removal of centuries of dust, a crude drawing was revealed in the halogen light, about four feet off the ground—roughly head level for someone seated at the desk, he realized. The drawing had been made by a blade of some sort scratching into the masonry of the wall. There was a crude serpent wrapped around some buildings and people, with an evil grin on its fanged, humanoid face. Beneath it the words *"Gaius Caligula serpens Roma"* had been hacked in large crude Latin letters.

"Looks like Suetonius did get something right," said Josh. "He said in his chronicles that old Tiberius told his friends that he was 'raising up a viper for Rome' in the form of Caligula. Let me go tell Dr. Sforza about this—she will want to get some pictures."

After the new find in the chamber was photographed and recorded, the four team members met back in the lab, while Apriceno got back to her work. Father MacDonald carefully studied the objects inside the small drawer under the table, and then called Josh over for a quick consultation. After conferring for a few moments, they turned to the others.

"It appears the papyrus inside the drawer has not adhered to the wood of the drawer's bottom at all," said MacDonald. "Probably because the inside of the drawer was not lacquered, like the top of the desk, and also because there was not several centimeters of dust on top of the papyrus, pressing it into the wood. I think we can remove the papyrus and the leather purse on top of it all at the same time. The leather on the drawstring bag is completely stiffened, of course, so we will first X-ray it to see what is inside, and then begin rehydrating the leather so that we can open the bag without destroying it."

"How do you propose to remove it from the drawer?" asked Isabella.

"Simple," said Josh. He held up a small, thin, rigid square of plastic. "We trimmed this from an extra plexiglass container lid. It is very thin, but still quite rigid. We cut it to the exact width of the papyrus sheets inside the drawer, and made it a little longer than the drawer is deep. We are going to carefully slide it underneath the bottommost piece of papyrus all the way to the back of the drawer, then lift the entire stack onto this tray and carry it straight to the X-ray machine. We'll take a quick picture or two of the bag's contents, and then slide the tray into the rehydration tank. In twenty-four to forty-eight hours, the leather should be supple enough for us to tease the drawstrings open a bit and remove the contents. We should also be able to separate the purse from the papyrus sheets and see if we have anything other than a stack of blank writing paper here."

"Excellent description, Josh," said Father MacDonald. "You have very steady hands, so I will nominate you to do the actual removal when you are ready."

"All right, Professor," said Parker. "You hold the tray. The goal is to leave the drawer's contents unsupported for the least amount of time possible. Bring it over here to my right—that's good."

Rossini and Sforza leaned in to watch. This was the most delicate part of any archeological excavation—removing a fragile artifact from its original context. Done properly, it made a relic available for closer study and examination with no impact on its stability or condition. But if botched, the process could destroy a priceless piece of history in the blink of an eye. Both were holding their breath as Josh approached the tiny drawer that had remained hidden for two millennia.

He carefully laid the plexiglass sheet flat on the bottom of the drawer, then used a flat, spatula-like blade to slowly lift one corner of the bottommost sheet of papyrus. He slowly eased the plexiglass underneath that edge, then carefully moved the blade across, lifting the ancient writing paper one inch at a time until the plexiglass had slid under its entire width. Then he slowly moved the spatula back to the center, gently lifting the entire stack a fraction of an inch and sliding the sheet in a bit further. Back and forth, across the sheet of papyrus he went, slowly sliding the plastic further underneath it until it reached more than two inches underneath the stack. "That's as far as this tool can reach underneath without potentially tearing the edge of the papyrus," he said. "Now I will use the sheet itself to lever the stack upward and slide back." He set the spatula-like instrument aside, then carefully took the sheet and pressed down on the far end. The stack of papyrus, and the purse on top of it, slowly lifted up without resistance. He slid the sheet back an inch further, and then repeated the process until finally, the plexiglass bumped against the back of the drawer. The four archeologists breathed a collective sigh of relief.

"Now then," he said. "Stand by with that tray, Father MacDonald!" He took a deep breath and grabbed the plexiglass by each edge, slowly lifting and pulling it up and back. The stack of papyrus sheets and the leather drawstring bag on top of it emerged into the light with a tiny puff of dust and a few ancient cobwebs trailing behind them. The golden horse's head glittered under the lab's fluorescent lights, peeking out of the mouth of the purse as it had for so many centuries. Josh lifted it and looked at the jeweled eyes. "Time to tell us your story, little guy!" he said, and then placed the papyrus sheets onto the tray that Father MacDonald was holding. The priest/archeologist quickly placed the tray on a small rolling cart and wheeled it across the lab to the X-ray table. The XFA—or the Portable X-Ray Fluorescence Analyzer, to give it its proper name—was a small tabletop unit that put forth minimal radiation and was used in archeological field work all over the world. The images it produced were not nearly as refined as a large, laboratory-based X-Ray Analyzer, nor as clear as a CT-scan or MRI, but it was a very handy device for taking a quick look inside sealed containers, ancient wrappings, and mummified remains.

Once the tray was set in place, the group came to take a closer look, seeing the entire surface of the ancient papyrus for the first time. It was completely blank, except for a small ink mark at the top corner of the top sheet. There was a large, brown stain surrounding the ancient drawstring bag, darkest directly under it and fading like a corona until it ended, about an inch away from point of contact where the bag rested on the papyrus. There was nothing else resting on the papyrus other than the ancient purse. Moving deftly, MacDonald set the parameters on the XFA and drew the lead-lined curtain around the tabletop. "Stand back, my colleagues, you know the protocol," he said as he took the remote in hand. When everyone had scooted back the prescribed ten feet, he himself stepped back and pushed the buttons on the remote, adjusting the angle and taking several shots of the ancient coin purse. Then he stepped across the room to a monitor and they all waited as the images slowly downloaded onto the desktop file. Once the download was complete, he double-clicked on the file and pulled up the first image. Several objects showed on the first X-ray. A group of small metallic discs—most likely coins—were clumped together near the bottom of the purse. A narrow, pointed object lay on top of them, its wider end difficult to see from the angle of the shot.

But the small item with the horse's head on one end was at the opposite end of the small bag, apparently having been shoved in at the last possible moment. There was nothing overlapping or obscuring the unmistakable shape. Josh chuckled. "Well, that's one mystery solved!" he said.

"A key!" exclaimed Isabella.

"I just wonder what it opens?" asked Dr. Rossini.

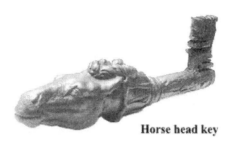

Horse head key

At this point, most excellent Tiberius, I felt that I could not proceed any further without at least trying to find out what this Galilean holy man had to say for himself. My Aramaic is not the best, so I sent one of my Centurions into the crowd to find an interpreter. He returned a few moments later with a terrified-looking youth of about twenty years of age, whom he described as one of the Galilean's disciples. I found myself admiring his courage, following a screaming mob that was howling for his master's blood! The young fellow did not speak Latin very well, but his Greek was quite passable. Although the mob outside and their religious leaders had voiced many charges against the bloodied figure before me, I asked him about the only one that really mattered to me as a Roman magistrate. "Are you the King of the Jews?" I demanded, nodding at the youth to translate.

My interpreter proved unnecessary. Jesus looked at me with a deep and curious gaze that I found quite unnerving, then spoke in clear, excellent Latin without a trace of an accent. "Do you say this of your own accord?" he asked. "Or did someone else tell you this about me?"

"Am I a Jew?" I asked, more harshly than I intended. His intense stare was throwing me off balance. "Your own people— your own priests—have delivered you up to me as an evildoer. What do you say for yourself?"

He was silent for a long moment, his lips moving as if he were speaking to someone I could not see. Finally, his eyes met mine again, and he spoke with incredible force and clarity. "My kingdom," he said, "is not of this world!"

CHAPTER SEVEN

"That's a good question," Duncan MacDonald said as he studied the white-on-black image on the screen. "A logical guess would be that it fits the reliquary that we have yet to uncover. We may get a chance to find out fairly soon, once Simone is done clearing the dust from the chamber. In the meantime, we will have to content ourselves with beginning the process that will let us remove the contents from this leather purse for a closer examination."

He pulled the lead-lined curtains back, and took the tray with the purse and papyrus sheets on it across the lab to a small tank that looked for all the world like a terrarium. He set the tray inside and pulled the plexiglass door down, sealing the gasket along the bottom so that the tank was airtight. Then he set a series of controls at the top and punched in some commands. "The humidity is set at seventy-five percent," he said. "A bit high for a papyrus document, but just about right for leather. There is enough antiseptic in the tank's atmosphere to prevent the growth of any mold whose spores may be embedded in the leather or the papyrus. It should take about twenty-four to forty-eight hours for the material to be rehydrated enough to flex without crumbling. Unless Simone uncovers more small items that can be removed, our next object of study will be the lamp from the niche above the door."

Isabella spoke up. "Then it appears we may be in for a lull of about twenty-four hours or more," she said. "Dr. Apriceno will not be done clearing the dust from the chamber till this evening, and then we will need to take a careful inventory of the chamber and any additional items uncovered by the removal of all the dust and debris. You and Dr. Parker are more than capable of doing that without me. I want to take Dr. Rossini back to Naples and confer with the Antiquities Bureau's Director and Dr. Guioccini. I also want to get some security on-site, so that you can take a break from the tents this evening and spend the night in more comfortable quarters. We will need one archeologist to stay on-site at all times, of course, but there is simply no need for all five of us to be up here twenty-four hours a day."

Rossini spoke up. "There are two small villas and one larger hotel in Capri village," he said. "However, I have a nice house with two large guest bedrooms, and plants in desperate need of watering! If you go down this evening, you are welcome to spend the night in my home—

provided, Joshua, that you can keep this intemperate Scot from drinking all my good wine!"

MacDonald guffawed and made a tippling gesture. Josh smiled and said, "Don't worry, sir, I'll make sure he only drinks the cheap stuff."

MacDonald replied, "Why not let Simone Apriceno go down with you, lad, and I'll take the first night shift? Then Giuseppe's precious wine cellar will be safe—for at least one more night."

"You can work that out among yourselves," said Isabella. "I need to make some calls, and I want to go through my laptop and make sure I have plenty of photographs and video to show to the Director and Dr. Guioccini. Hopefully we can have some security on-site here by mid-afternoon."

"I am going to walk down to my home and get a change of clothes," said Rossini. "Joshua, why don't you accompany me and I will show you where my house is?" Josh nodded his assent and the two of them headed out the door of the lab toward the Via Tiberio.

Dr. Sforza watched them leave with some affection. Giuseppe's place in her heart was permanent—he was a friend, a mentor, and in many ways, a father figure to her, especially since her own father had passed away not long after her husband had died. As for the young American—she was having a hard time sorting out her emotions about him. *Intrigued*, perhaps, was the best description of how she felt about him. He was so focused and passionate about his religious beliefs that she would have a hard time taking him seriously as a scientist—were it not for the fact that he obviously possessed a first-class intellect and some impressive academic skills. Physically—well, Isabella thought to herself, she might as well be honest with herself. She found him very attractive. To a small degree, he reminded her of her dear, departed husband—but only to a small degree. He was taller than Marc had been, and his eyes were a deep brown as opposed Marc's steady gray—but he was slender, powerfully built, and had a certain steadiness about him. You got the feeling that if the ground under you began to shake, he would be a solid anchor to cling to. She shook her head at the thought. She'd known him less than twenty-four hours, after all, and should be more focused on the ongoing excavation than on his considerable physical and emotional charms.

"I see you and Isabella have hit it off rather well," said Giuseppe as he and Josh began hiking down the trail toward Capri village.

"I hope so," admitted Josh. "Although I'll admit I'm not sure what she thinks of me. We were having a normal breakfast conversation one minute, the next minute she had me mounted on a hobby horse and riding like there was no tomorrow."

Giuseppe looked at the young American with a furrowed brow. Although his conversational English was quite proficient, it pained him to admit that he had no idea what a "hobby horse" was. However, his pride was such that he didn't really want to admit that to his companion. Josh saw his expression and chuckled. "Sorry, Professor," he said. "Your English is so good I forget that cultural idioms don't always translate smoothly. She asked me about a topic on which I have strong feelings— a 'pet peeve,' if you are familiar with that phrase. I became rather animated and fear I may have made a bit of a fool of myself."

"And what topic was that?" asked Rossini.

"The way Evangelical Christians are portrayed in the American media," replied Josh. "Every time I come to Europe I have to fight the stereotypes that have been fostered about us. But this time I found myself defending my beliefs to a person who I—" He paused and blushed, remembering Rossini's earlier warning.

The older man laughed. "Someone on whom you wish to make a good impression?" he asked. Josh nodded ruefully. "Listen, my young friend, Isabella is very dear to me, but I understand that she is beautiful, single, and very attractive. Nothing would make me happier than to see her wind up with a young man who would treasure her and love her as she deserves. I am not angry at you for being interested in her. I just was concerned that your interest might be—well, less than honorable. The more I get to know you, the more unlikely that seems."

Josh thought for a moment. "She fascinates me," he said. "But I don't want that fascination to get in the way of what we are doing here. This site, this find, is of tremendous significance, even if we find nothing beyond what we have already uncovered. But the potential is enormous. If we find the actual personal correspondence of a Roman emperor— not copies, but the original autographs—the whole history of the early Empire could be rewritten!"

"Not to mention the history of the Church." said Rossini. "You can't tell me it's not lurking in the back of your mind. Tiberius was Emperor during the actual life and ministry of Jesus of Nazareth. Any mention of Jesus, of the early Church, or early Christian doctrine would be the earliest such documentation ever found."

"You're right," said Joshua. "But how likely is it, after all? Tiberius died in 37 AD, only a few years after the crucifixion of Jesus. Christianity had not yet spread beyond Judea. The Apostle Paul had not even begun his ministry yet, and not a single book of the New Testament was written. I think that Christianity was still well below the Imperial radar at the time this chamber was sealed."

"You are probably right," said the older man. "You know, like most Italians, I was baptized and raised in the Catholic Church. I embraced my parents' faith as a young man, but I have moved away from it somewhat over the years. But I have always been curious as to whether the simple carpenter from Galilee was something more than just a mortal man. It would be nice to find out."

"Oh, I am certain He was more than a carpenter," said Josh. "I have analyzed the Gospel narratives thoroughly, and studied every ancient source available. I am just as convinced that Jesus of Nazareth really was the Son of God as I am convinced that Caesar Augustus was the first Emperor of Rome."

Rossini looked at him with curiosity. "Perhaps when I return from the mainland, you shall explain to me why you are so sure," he said. "But for now, here is my home up ahead. Let's go in and get it ready for guests."

For the next hour they busied themselves with straightening up some items that Giuseppe had not had time to fix before climbing up to the Villa Jovis three days before. Then he showed Josh the linen closet and asked him to make the beds in the guest rooms while he took a long shower and put on some clean clothes. When he emerged, Dr. Rossini told Josh to use the shower while he walked down the street to the excellent restaurant where their food had come from the night before. As he ordered a full meal for three delivered to his home for 7 PM, the police chief came ambling in for his lunch break.

"Giuseppe," he boomed. "Descending from the mountain like Moses! Did you leave the Ten Commandments at your house so you could have some of Mrs. Bustamante's excellent cooking?"

"No, you fool; I left them in the Ark of the Covenant where Indiana Jones could keep an eye on them," Rossini shot back. "Shouldn't you be out arresting criminals somewhere?"

"I have it on good authority that dangerous international terrorists are going to kidnap Mrs. Bustamante and force her to reveal her recipe for chicken Marsala," said the chief. "I am here as part of a complex sting operation to bring them to justice, and protect excellent cooking from scoundrels and evildoers."

"And to take shameless advantage of my discount for police officer lunches," said Antonia Bustamante over her shoulder as she bustled back into the kitchen. She was a middle-aged Spanish woman whose beauty had doubtless turned many heads in her day, and was still a handsome woman. Rossini had thought many times about asking her to go to the theater with him, but always held back at the last minute. She had been widowed for many years, far longer than him, but had never remarried. Every older, single man on the island had probably entertained the same thoughts that Giuseppe had about her at one time or another, but today he made up his mind that, when the business on top of the mountain was done, he would suck up his courage and invite her out for a night on the town in Naples.

"So," Chief Rosario said after the restaurant owner made her exit, "what of the excavation? What remarkable discovery have you made up there?"

Rossini sighed. He hated to keep his friend in the dark any longer, and the Bureau of Antiquities would probably be announcing the discovery soon. As police chief over the entire island, Rosario had a right to know something, surely. "Well, old friend, I cannot tell you everything—not yet. But I think I can tell you something, provided you keep it in utmost confidence until the Bureau issues a press release. The earthquake opened a hidden chamber in the Villa Jovis. Inside we have found a cache of artifacts that date all the way back to the time of Tiberius. We are still cleaning and removing them, but you can appreciate the magnitude of such a discovery."

The police chief let out a low whistle of amazement. "Congratulations, old friend. That is truly a great discovery. Now I understand why you were being so secretive. Fear not, I shall not mention it to a soul. But I still want a guided tour as soon as you can give me one. I am very proud for you, Giuseppe. May I buy your lunch?"

"Sadly, no, old friend. I am just gathering some personal effects and cleaning up so I can fly to the mainland in a little while. Isabella and I are meeting with our superiors to brief them on the discovery." Rossini stood and tipped his hat to Mrs. Bustamante, who had just come out with a steaming plate of manicotti for Chief Rosario. "By the way, two members of the team will be staying in my home tonight, so don't be surprised if you see the lights on this evening. *Bon journo*, Antonia."

He found Josh dressed and toweling his hair dry. "The last shower I took was in Oklahoma," Josh said. "You have no idea how good this feels. I just wish I'd brought my clean clothes down with me, but I'm going to change into them as soon as we get back to the Villa Jovis."

As they walked back up the mountain, Giuseppe asked Josh about his own homeland. Josh explained how he had grown up moving every few years, and described the scorching, flat plains of North Central Texas, the rolling prairies and granite heights of eastern Oklahoma, and the beautiful Ouachita Mountains that straddled the border between Oklahoma and Arkansas. Rossini had visited the northern states a few times, but never the southeast, and the two of them talked about fishing, fossils, and artifacts all the way up the side of the mountain.

Isabella had gotten on her cell phone right after Josh and Giuseppe began their walk down the mountain. Dr. Guioccini had answered in person. "Marvelous work on translating the document so quickly, Dr. Sforza." he said. "Your team seems to be working well together, and the new discovery sounds very promising."

"They are a first-rate group," she replied. "I would like to get some security up here on the peak so that they can actually stay in greater comfort down in the village at night. I also think that it is time for us to go public. We have shut down Capri's best known tourist attraction for three days now, and the longer we go, the more likely some curious tourists are to ignore the roadblock and come wandering right up into our excavation."

"I have been talking this over with the Bureau's Director," said Guioccini. "I think you are quite right, but we will need to have both some physical security as well as perhaps some docents who can direct the curious away from the dig while, at the same time, explaining enough of what we are doing to satisfy their curiosity. We will discuss it this afternoon. Would three o'clock give you adequate time to prepare?"

"Yes, sir," she said. "As I mentioned in my email this morning, we have hit a temporary lull in the excavation process that provides a window for us to meet with the board and share our findings. I am bringing Dr. Rossini over with me—as the discoverer, I think he deserves the honor of presenting the artifacts to Signor Castolfo. Dr. Apriceno is busily clearing the dust and debris from the chamber so that tomorrow we can finish our inventory of the contents and begin removing the remainder of the artifacts."

"Everything sounds in order," the chief archeologist said. "I shall look forward to seeing both of you in a few hours."

When Isabella got off the phone, she was surprised to see a rotund figure in a black robe carefully descending the stairs toward the site. She had almost forgotten about the friars in the Church of Santa Maria Del Soccorso. The one descending the steps was probably the youngest man there, but he was still at least seventy, and huffed and puffed as he descended the staircase. Isabella walked quickly up to meet him. "Father, is something wrong?" she said.

"Not in the least, my child," he responded. "But we were told three days ago that the ruins had been damaged by the earthquake, and we have seen helicopters come and go, and now there is a campsite and a trailer set up less than a kilometer from our church. We did not take a vow to renounce curiosity when we donned our robes, so my brothers delegated me to come down and see what it is you good people are up to in Tiberius' old playground."

Isabella laughed. The clerics from the old church were the last group she would have suspected to be the first intruders on her site. But, she thought, they would be the easiest to deal with. Their contact with the outside world was virtually nonexistent, and they were unlikely to have much interest in the artifacts besides a bit of natural, academic curiosity.

"The earthquake uncovered a small, hidden chamber in the Villa Jovis," she said, unconsciously using the same words Rossini would speak to Chief Rosario in Capri village an hour later. "There are a few artifacts in there dating to the time of Tiberius Caesar, and we are excavating them for further study."

"Fascinating," said the old monk. "Tiberius was a sad, lost soul, you know. The ancients portrayed him as a monster, but I always thought that he was more afraid than evil."

"I've always thought that the stories about him were exaggerated because he was so protective of his privacy," said Isabella. "Even in our own time, those who live as recluses have all sorts of rumors made up about them."

82

"A wise observation," said the old monk. "I don't suppose that I could take a peek at the things you've uncovered, could I?"

"Not yet," said Isabella. "They are fragile and still being stabilized for study. But, before long, I promise that you and your brothers will receive a guided tour of the site."

About this time Father MacDonald came out of the lab and spied them. He called out a greeting and came over to visit with his fellow cleric. Within a few moments they were chatting like old friends, and Isabella repaired to her tent to see if she could make herself a bit more presentable before heading out to the mainland. When she came out, the friar was almost out of sight, slowly climbing the steps back to his church, and the Scottish priest was waiting for her.

"What a delightful old man." he said. "Turns out that he knew my old divinity professor at the Tuscany Seminary. We really should go spend an hour or so visiting with them while we are engaged in this project. They don't receive many visitors, and would be delighted of our company."

Some time later, she saw that Rossini and Parker were making their way up the trail from town. They were enjoying an animated conversation, laughing and chatting like old friends. She felt a bit better about warming to Parker as quickly as she had, since Giuseppe was a very shrewd judge of character and had come to like the American as quickly as she had. They saw her standing by the tent and quickly crossed over to talk. "I've made arrangements for dinner to be served at my house this evening," said Rossini. "After we leave, they can go down and eat, then discuss who will return to spend the night up here at the site—assuming security can guard the place long enough for them to have a decent supper and clean up a bit."

"Dr. Guioccini is sending three professional security guards out in the helo that is picking us up," she replied. "That will make our job much easier, although I would like to have at least one of us spend each night up here. You and I, old friend, will have a decent dinner and an evening in Naples, and return in the morning."

Josh had ducked into his tent to put on clean clothes, and when he came out Isabella asked him to gather the whole team together for a quick consultation. Dr. Apriceno came out of the chamber, coated with chalky stone dust and wearing a white painter's mask. When she lowered it, she was smiling. "I'm over halfway to the back of the chamber now," she said. "If I keep it up at this pace, the place will be ready for further examination by tomorrow morning."

"Good," said Isabella. "Giuseppe and I should be back by then. In the meantime, I am leaving Father MacDonald in charge. Security should be here shortly to watch the site for us; all three of you can go down to Dr. Rossini's house for supper and a shower, and I will leave it to you to decide who shall return to the site to spend the night. I am planning on returning around nine AM. Duncan, I want you and Josh to go ahead and remove the lamp from the niche above the entryway and get it photographed and cataloged this afternoon. Anything else Dr. Apriceno uncovers will be left undisturbed in the chamber until Dr. Rossini and I return. We have gotten off to a great start."

The team was still standing in a loose circle, talking, when the sounds of the chopper intruded on their conversation. The Italian army helicopter landed on the level above the chamber, exactly where it had the day before, and Isabella and Giuseppe climbed the steps to meet it. Three figures in khaki climbed out of the chopper and conferred briefly with Dr. Sforza before heading for the stairs. She and Rossini boarded the helo, and it lifted off and aimed for Naples, disappearing over the horizon in a matter of moments.

An hour and a half later, in the impressively decorated conference room of the National Archeological Museum in Naples, Dr. Sforza presented the finds at Villa Jovis to the six members of the Board of Antiquities who were in attendance, including their president, Benito Castolfo. She had edited the video clips and interspersed them with some of the best still shots. Dr. Rossini did an excellent presentation, describing the discovery of the chamber and the preliminary investigations with the wit and humor that had made him a favorite lecturer at several different universities. He had held forth for a half hour, and then Isabella stood and gave a more detailed description of the items removed. The photographs of the Tiberius manuscript elicited whistles of amazement and much murmuring among the board members, and the images of the leather coin purse and the horse effigy key also sparked lively discussion.

"In closing, gentlemen," Isabella said, "I don't think anyone can question the incredible significance of this find. The fact that we have an unopened wooden box or cabinet that is even now being cleaned of overburden, indicates that we may not have even uncovered the tip of the iceberg. However, the very public nature of the location and the small size of the chamber caused Dr. Guioccini and me to decide that the best way to preserve these items and curate them properly is to remove them from the chamber as quickly as possible and study them in a controlled, laboratory environment. I imagine that, by the end of the week, we will have all the artifacts cleared from the chamber. What I would ask of the board at this point is, are we ready to make any kind of public pronouncement yet? We have closed Capri's premiere historical tourist attraction to the public for three days now. According to the police chief at Capri village, several inquiries have already been made as to when Villa Jovis will be reopening. Would it be better to say nothing and press on with the work, or issue a non-specific statement about our excavations and the reason for the closing?"

Dr. Vincent Sinisi spoke up from the end of the table. He was in charge of the Bureau of Antiquities' Public Relations Department, so this was his bailiwick. Forty years old, handsome, and jolly, he was a favorite of the Italian media and a legendary ladies' man. "You raise a good question, Dr. Sforza. We certainly want to preserve the integrity of such a significant historical discovery, but at the same time, tourism is an enormous part of Italy's annual income. Handled properly, we can keep the site secured for the moment, and also guarantee a huge upturn in tourism when it is reopened. I think at this point, a carefully worded press release is in order. Let the people know something has been found, just don't tell them what. Let them know it is potentially very significant, and that we are very much on the job. Leave them wanting more. And then, when all the artifacts have been removed from the chamber, you, Dr. Sforza, will need to give a press conference with all the members of your team and announce the full scope of your discoveries."

Isabella frowned. She had never really dealt with the media before, and was not so sure that she wanted to. "Are you sure that is really necessary, sir?" she asked. "I would prefer to work in anonymity as long as I can."

Sinisi laughed. "Your days of anonymity ended when you uncovered the Tiberius manuscript," he said. "You are going to be the best-known archeologist since Howard Carter—Italy's own Lara Croft! If this chamber produces more historical treasures, dear girl, they may be selling Isabella Sforza action figures in the stores next year!"

Isabella blushed deeply—she knew about the gun-wielding, buxom video game icon he referred to, and resented the implication. But deep down, the idea of being the best-known archeologist since Howard Carter was awfully appealing. Her professional ambitions were at last being realized. "I doubt that, Dr. Sinisi," she said finally. "But if you think a press conference is necessary, I will do one."

RECENT EARTHQUAKE UNCOVERS ANCIENT "CHAMBER OF SECRETS"

(AP) The earthquake which struck the isle of Capri on Sunday, off the Italian coast, may have revealed an archeological treasure, according to the Italian Bureau of Antiquities. The damage that the trembler inflicted on an ancient Roman ruin known as the Villa Jovis tore open a small, hidden chamber which historians believe has been sealed since the time of the Emperor Tiberius, who ruled Rome from 14 to 37 AD. Excavations at the site are ongoing, and several significant artifacts have already been recovered which date the site to the first century. The Villa Jovis, a popular tourist attraction, will be closed to the public until further notice. Italian authorities have promised a full press conference next week, at which some of the discoveries from the ancient chamber will be revealed.

CHAPTER EIGHT

That evening, Isabella and Giuseppe enjoyed an exquisite Chinese meal at one of Naples' few oriental restaurants. In between the sizzling rice soup, pot stickers, and the main course, they discussed the dig—and their team members.

"Professor MacDonald likes to hide beneath that Scottish burr and his humble parish priest routine," said Isabella. "But he has impressed me with his technical skills. He certainly knows how to handle ancient documents."

"I've worked with Duncan on several digs," said Rossini. "He is a consummate professional when there is work to be done, but he is as fun-loving a soul as a priest can be. Understand, he takes his faith and his vows seriously, but he doesn't let them interfere with his enjoyment of life. If there is such a thing as 'the joy of the Lord' that Scripture talks about, he is full of it."

"Dr. Apriceno is a pleasant soul as well," Isabella continued. "A bit brusque at first, but she is a walking encyclopedia of paleobotany, and seems to enjoy her work a great deal. I had a chance to talk to her early this morning, and we hit it off right away. She reminds me of my mother's oldest sister—a bit gruff on first acquaintance, but as kind-hearted as you could want to meet."

"And what about the young American?" asked Rossini. "You and he seemed to be deep in conversation when Duncan and I walked into the trailer this morning."

Isabella blushed slightly. "He is a very intriguing young man," she said. "I've never met anyone quite like him. I don't know a lot about the Evangelical movement, but he is nothing like what I expected when I heard he was a Baptist from the American South. I expected someone much more—"

"Fanatical?" Rossini supplied a word.

"Exactly! They have been painted as being a bunch of primitive-thinking, incurious drones by everyone I've talked to. That's what he and I were talking about. He said that most of the people who create stereotypes about evangelical Christians have never actually gotten to know one. Of course, he may be the exception to the rule, and ninety percent of Evangelicals may fit the stereotype. But I am not going to believe everything I hear about them from now on, I can tell you that," Isabella finished.

"A wise position, to be sure," said Rossini. "But that still doesn't tell me how you feel about Dr. Parker personally. I have seen how you have been looking at him, my dear. Now, out with it."

She turned even deeper red. "You don't miss much, do you, Giuseppe?" she finally said. "If you must know, I find him very attractive. You know that ever since I lost Marc I have buried myself in work. He—it—I was hurt so badly that I thought I could never find another person that would make me feel the way he did. But when I look at Josh—or when I catch him looking at me, with those dark eyes that seem to drink in my every word and every movement— I find myself feeling things I haven't felt in a long time. But is it really romantic interest? Or am I just finally coming out of my shell enough to feel what most women feel when a handsome, kind man takes an interest in them? I am very conflicted right now, and I don't like it much."

Giuseppe looked at her with a warm smile. "Well, dear girl, you deserve to be happy. I think Parker is a young man of good character and warm heart, and if things happen to work out between you, no one will be happier than I."

She regarded him quietly for a moment. "That means more than you can know," she finally said. "But I've not even known the man for forty-eight hours yet. So let's not crack the champagne bottles too soon."

After dinner, she dropped Giuseppe off at the Ambassador Suites, just down the block from her own rather plain apartment. She wondered how easy it would be to go to sleep with all that was going on, but to her surprise, she nodded off almost as soon as her head hit the pillow. There was a faint smile playing around her lips as the light of the full moon shone through the window and illuminated her face, but she never knew it.

After Isabella and Giuseppe had left the Isle of Capri, Josh and Father MacDonald had spoken for a while to the three newly arrived security guards—Lucien Rigatorre, Cesare Giovanni, and Ibrahim al-Ghazi. Lucien and Cesare were native Italians, and Ibrahim was a third-generation Arab immigrant. MacDonald explained their duties and showed them where they could set up their tent. All three were very professional and courteous, but none seemed particularly interested in the ongoing work of the team. Their job was to protect the site from intruders and curious tourists, and that was something they took very seriously.

After getting them situated, the two archeologists returned to the chamber. Dr. Apriceno was still busy at work, but shut off the small, high-powered HEPA vacuum when she saw them enter. Both looked at the near end of the chamber in amazement. With the centuries of stone dust removed, they saw the polished marble floor and smoke-stained masonry clearly for the first time. There were a few additional bits of graffiti scattered here and there on the walls, but so far no other objects had been uncovered by the removal of the dust. All that seemed to remain coated with the thick, choking layer was the back wall and the cabinet that leaned against it.

Simone Apriceno looked like a cross between a giant dust bunny and an exceptionally busy chimney sweep. She was coated with the dust of centuries, except where her brown eyes glittered from behind the goggles she wore. She motioned to them, and they all stepped out into the sunlight for a moment. Off came the mask and goggles, but their outline remained visible in the dust and grime that coated the rest of her face. "It's getting very close," she said. "I'll need to go very, very slowly around the cabinet and back wall—I think there is something propped against the wall next to the cabinet, but the accumulation is so thick I can't tell for sure. It will be late this evening before I get the last of the dust removed, but by tomorrow morning, we should be able to finish studying the chamber itself and the objects in it."

"I think we are going to remove the oil lamp from its niche above the door," said Josh. "That's the only object left in the forward part of the chamber. It shouldn't take long to analyze and photograph, then tomorrow we will have a clean slate to begin studying the items in the back of the chamber."

"And then I am going to bury myself in pollen analysis," said Apriceno. "I don't think there is any chance at all that this chamber has been opened in two thousand years, but I want to be positive that there is no possibility of any tampering. If there are further documents or artifacts inside the reliquary, or whatever it is, they could be very, very important to our understanding of the first century AD. No one is going to question their historical integrity if I have anything to do with it."

With that, like a medieval knight lowering the visor of his helmet to do battle, she pulled her mask and goggles into place and marched to the rear of the chamber, picking up the nozzle of the HEPA vacuum and aiming it at the back corner of the chamber. The whirring of the motor resumed, and Josh looked over at the Vatican archeologist next to him. "Remind me never to get on her bad side," he said.

MacDonald laughed. "The lass does build a full head of steam pretty quickly, doesn't she?" he said. "Now be a good lad and fetch us each a pair of acid-free gloves, and a sanitary box to transport that lamp in."

Josh returned with the necessary equipment a few moments later, and they quickly lifted the ancient brass lamp from its centuries-old perch and lowered it into the box. They carried it to the mobile lab and set it on the photography table. The lamp was made of bronze, and not particularly remarkable except for the Roman eagle and familiar logo, SPQR, stamped onto one side. "*Senatus Populare Quirites Romana*," Josh said to himself.

"The Senate, People, and Citizens of Rome," Professor MacDonald translated automatically. "You know, although they have been much maligned and looked down on, the Romans were, I think, the greatest governors of men this world has ever known. Look at how long their government lasted. Over five hundred years as a Republic, and another five hundred as an Empire!"

"Not to mention the Eastern Empire that lasted another thousand years in Constantinople after the Empire in the West fell," said Josh. "When you think about it, almost two thousand years is the greatest run by any government in the history of the world."

"No wonder the founders of your Republic drew so many examples from Rome," Father MacDonald said. "They had a good template to draw from, all they had to do was make some tweaks to correct the most glaring flaws—separation of powers, checks and balances—things the Romans had but did not enforce."

"Do you think Caesar really meant to bring down the Republic when he crossed the Rubicon?" asked Josh as he focused the camera on the lamp, photographing it from every angle.

"That's a good question," MacDonald said. "I think he knew that a civil war would ensue, but I don't think he ever saw himself as the destroyer of the Republic. Frankly, I think Colleen McCullough's portrayal of him got that bit right—he believed that Cato and Bibulus and their ilk were the ones who were going to destroy Rome if not stopped. Pompey was nothing but a tool in their hands."

"I've never understood the adoration of Cato as a hero," said Josh. "He was dedicated to the Republic, to be sure, and scrupulously honest—but he was so stubborn and hidebound in his views that he would never tolerate changing anything at all. A government that ceases to innovate and evolve cannot endure. Change merely for the sake of change is not necessarily a good thing—I think our current President is living proof of that—but change to adapt to a radically evolving world is a necessity for survival."

They continued to discuss and debate the fall of the Republic and the responsibility for that calamity as they finished photographing, measuring, and cleaning the ancient lamp. It was a fairly pedestrian artifact, although the residual oil preserved in the bottom of it would have some interesting information to reveal about how the Romans illuminated their homes. That analysis would need to be done by a chemist, not an archeologist, however. They sealed the lamp in an acid-free bag and placed it in a storage cabinet next to the curule bench that had sat in front of the ancient writing desk. As they were putting it away, the door to the lab burst open and Dr. Apriceno came in, her face red with excitement.

"You're going to want to see this," she said. Josh and Duncan looked at one another. "Hurry!" she snapped. The two archeologists followed her across the ancient flagstones as she explained. "I am down to the actual cabinet itself," she said. "Or at least, I was about to be. I wanted to clean the ceiling, walls, and floor all around it first. I was working from top to bottom, going very carefully—I certainly don't want to move or endanger anything that is *not* dust and pollen. The area above the reliquary was clean and free of any other objects, just masonry and stone blocks. Then I cleaned on the left-hand side of the reliquary— a space of about six inches between it and the side wall. Again, nothing but ancient dust and cobwebs. But then when I started to do the other side—well, remember how I said it appeared there might be something leaning against the wall?"

By now they were inside the chamber, and she pulled a small flashlight out of her pocket and trained it on the right rear corner of the chamber, where the gap was about a foot wide between the wall and the side of the reliquary. The bottom of the gap was still thickly coated with several inches of ancient stone dust and dirt, which reached to a height of about two feet. From the sloped ceiling down, the dust had been carefully vacuumed away, going right down the side of the chamber until—

"Bloody hell!" gasped Father MacDonald, and then crossed himself as he realized he'd sworn.

"Holy ancient metal, Batman!" said Josh.

Leaning against the wall, its pommel and hilt ring revealed by the removal of the thick dust that had buried it, was a sword—a Roman *gladius* to be precise. The pommel was a polished, gleaming yellowish white that could only be antique ivory, and at the hilt was a golden crest that glittered in the harsh halogen light from Dr. Apriceno's pocket torch. It was still sheathed in a leather scabbard that had faded to black with age. "I'll get the camera," said Josh.

He ran back to the lab and grabbed the high-powered digital camera, which had already been used to document so much of the site. He switched to video mode and allowed Dr. Apriceno to explain how she had discovered the ancient weapon, then took a series of still shots close up. Most of the scabbard was still buried in the dust and rubble, so he focused on the pommel and hilt. After he finished, the team met outside.

"What do you think?" said Simone.

Josh nodded to Father MacDonald. "The Professor is the senior team member present," he said. "I'll let him make the call."

"I am going to recommend that you continue—*very* carefully—to remove the overburden of dust and rubble from the chamber and the objects in it," he finally said to Apriceno. "The discovery is documented, and anyone can see that the sword could not have been placed there any more recently than the objects around it; you have left the dust coating completely in place for the entire length of the blade. No wonder we could not see it earlier; there must have been some sort of dirt slide in that corner. You need to take core dust samples, of course, from the area all around it before removing any more of the grime, however. Tomorrow we can show it to Isabella and see what she thinks. It'll be a nice surprise for her when she comes back from the mainland."

The other two nodded their assent. "First, however," he said, looking at his cell phone to check the time, "we all need a break. Simone, you have been working with hardly a stop since seven o'clock this morning, and it is five in the afternoon now. We have some security in place to guard the site; I am going to suggest that we seal the chamber, go down to Giuseppe's house, and have that excellent supper that should be arriving there in about an hour."

Dr. Apriceno protested. "I am *so* close to being done," she said. "Another two hours and the reliquary and sword will be completely uncovered and ready for examination."

"Fatigue clouds judgment, dear lady," said the cleric. "I'd hate to see you make a mistake and damage a priceless artifact because you insisted on pushing yourself too hard. You can come back up after supper and finish the job—Josh or I will be happy to come and help, in fact. And if you are bound and determined to do so, you can even stay the night up here on the mountain—my old bones will not protest a night in an actual bed. But right now, you need to eat, drink, and breathe some air that's not full of two-thousand-year-old atomized concrete and limestone."

She threw up her hands in surrender, and Josh helped her zip up the plastic entrance over the chamber doorway while Dr. MacDonald went and explained to the security guards that the team was going to break for supper. Rigatorre, their leader, nodded his understanding and told the other two to take their posts on either side of the chamber entrance. The site secure, the weary archeologists began to trek down the Via Tiberio toward Rossini's home.

An hour later, they sat around the table digging into fresh-baked bread and buttery pasta with clam sauce, while Father MacDonald poured a glass of wine for himself and Apriceno. Josh sipped an ice cold Coke that he had purchased from the souvenir shop on the town plaza. Simone's hair was still wet from the forty-minute shower she had taken while they set the table and laid out the food. For the first time in three days, she had no dust or cobwebs in her hair or on her skin, and felt like a new woman.

"I always thought that we Southerners could outdo anyone in the world when it came to delicious, fattening foods," said Josh. "But I must say the Italians give us a real run for our money."

"Italian cuisine is not necessarily that fattening," said Apriceno. "True, we are fond of butter and bread and pasta, but we cook everything in olive oil, not the dreadful animal fats and hydrogenated vegetable oils you use in the States."

"It is mighty tasty," Josh agreed, taking another bite. "But nothing in the world can equal good old bacon grease when it comes to flavor.

After one of our Fifth Sunday 'dinner on the grounds,' you could lay back, close your eyes, and actually hear your arteries harden as your stomach groaned in gratitude."

"Did you really eat dinner off the ground?" the Italian botanist asked. "It sounds so unsanitary."

Josh laughed. "It's a regional colloquialism," he said. "It means that we would have a communal potluck dinner on the church grounds, after morning service, instead of going home to eat."

"Oh," she said. "Like a Holy Day festival. I loved those when I was a young girl. Well, listen to me, Dr. Parker. Whenever this dig allows me an evening off, I will cook you a traditional Tuscan dinner, and your American Southern cooking will never taste the same again."

"But can it possibly match the flavor of a fresh boiled haggis?" asked the Scottish priest, and then laughed as he was pelted with dinner rolls from either side of the table.

The food lasted longer than their appetites did, as hungry as they were, and Dr. Apriceno insisted they pack up the leftovers and take them to the security guards. "Are you sure that you don't want one of us to stay on the mountain tonight and let you get a decent night's sleep?" asked Josh as they made ready to head back up the old path.

"After tonight, my fieldwork is done," replied Apriceno. "From this point onward, I will be staring into a microscope in an air-conditioned lab while you fine gentlemen figure out how to get into that cabinet and what to do with its contents. I can sleep in a feather bed tomorrow night, but tonight I want to finish my job in that chamber and begin preparing all my slides for analysis."

"Suit yourself," said the priest. "But we will escort you up and do some lab work while you get back to the chamber."

They made the hike quickly, and Apriceno sighed and ran a hand through her clean, graying hair before donning the dirty mask and goggles again. The other two handed off the food to the grateful guards and entered the lab. Josh plugged the digital camera into the computer and turned on the huge LED monitor that allowed for maximum magnification of the pictures. They looked quickly at the photographs they had taken in the lab of the curule bench and the lamp, and then pulled up the most recent set of images.

"I wonder if this sword belonged to old Tiberius himself," said the priest. "He was a legendary general long before he became emperor."

96

"Whoever owned it, it saw a great deal of use," said Josh. "Look at the scratches on the pommel, and how dented and worn the grip is."

"Hold it," said the priest, looking at the picture Josh had taken of the butt end of the grip. There was a golden eagle embossed there, and it was surrounded by Latin letters, nearly obscured by wear and scratches. Josh scrolled the mouse and pulled the letters in closer and larger. The inscription finally became clear: *"Ferrum et honorem Iulii"* was what they read.

"The Blade and Honor of the Julii," Josh translated.

MacDonald let out a low whistle. "The sword of a Caesar!" he said.

"But which one?" Josh asked.

"Given that this chamber has been sealed since 37 AD," said MacDonald, "there are only three candidates. Tiberius, Augustus, or the great Triumphator himself, Gaius Julius Caesar."

Josh's mind reeled. This blade could have been carried in some of the greatest battles in history. "I think," he said, "that Isabella is going to be very surprised when she returns."

"Of that you may be sure," replied the priest. "I think I have had all the discovery I can take for one day," he continued. "I'm about ready to close this place up for the night."

Outside, the last light of the day was fading from the sky. From the chamber, the whirr of the HEPA vacuum said that Dr. Apriceno was busy at work once more. The two archeologists bid her goodnight and strolled companionably down the mountainside.

Caesar, I have stood in the presence of majesty on many occasions. I can remember your noble father, the Imperator Augustus, speaking before his armies when I was just a young military tribune, and you know that I fought as a legate under you in Germany as well, and saw the honor your legionaries rightly accorded you there. I have stood in the presence of many foreign potentates as well, from Herod to Mithridates. As you know, most Eastern monarchs are grasping, venal creatures whose only nobility lies in the trappings they cover themselves with. Trust me when I say that this bloodied and battered Galilean itinerant radiated as much honor and dignitas as any Roman patrician. But there was also something . . . alien about him. Otherworldly. His statement, as ridiculous as it no doubt sounds when I recount it, made perfect sense to me as I stood there looking into his eyes. But he was not done—he continued: "If my kingdom was of this world, my servants would be fighting to rescue me as we speak. As it is, my kingdom is not of this realm."

I asked the question more directly. "So you are a king, then?"

He nodded, and replied: "You say correctly that I am a king. For this purpose I have been born, and come into this world, that I might testify to the truth. Everyone who welcomes truth will hear my voice."

I pondered his statement a moment, and I said out loud the thought that leaped into my mind. "Quid est veritas?" But I had heard all I needed for the moment, and did not wait for his answer. This man was no threat to Rome, I was convinced of that. I stepped out onto the balcony and addressed the mob below.

"Absolvo!" I cried. "I find no guilt in this man!"

The crowd exploded with rage.

CHAPTER NINE

Simone Apriceno rolled out of her sleeping bag and stretched luxuriously. Between collecting the dust core samples from the scabbard of the ancient *gladius* and then clearing the remainder of the dust from the back of the chamber, it was nearly midnight when she put away her equipment and sealed the chamber for the night. But the job was done, finally—the accumulated centuries of dust were gone, and the artifacts in the chamber, without having been moved or shifted a millimeter, were exposed and revealed exactly as they had been left when the chamber was sealed. It was one of the most challenging tasks she'd ever been entrusted with, and she was proud of the way she had handled it. Every single surface in the room had a core sample of the dust and debris covering it collected from top layer to bottom, labeled and arranged with photographs of the surface before and after its collection. Unless something truly bizarre showed up in the pollen samples, no one would be able to question that the site had been undisturbed since the chamber was sealed. Now her colleagues could study and catalog the artifacts, removing them from the chamber if necessary, while she devoted herself to the microscope.

She pulled on her boots over a pair of clean socks and buttoned a khaki shirt up over the Grateful Dead T-shirt she had slept in, and then brushed her teeth with water from a bottle she'd left by her bed for that purpose. It was 6:15 AM according to her watch. She walked over to the trailer and found a stale pastry from the previous day and bit into it while she started the coffee brewing. It was dry but still sweet and wholesome tasting. After the coffee was done brewing, she walked outside and talked to the two security guards.

"Anything worth noting happen last night?" she asked.

"Just some beautiful stars and a meteor shower after the moon finally set," said al-Ghazi.

"That, and I learned the entire history of this Moor's family, going back to the fourteenth century," said Giovanni.

"I'm not a Moor, I'm an Arab-Italian," al-Ghazi replied archly.

"Notice he doesn't deny the three-hour lecture he inflicted on me," his friend shot back.

"It was only an hour or so, and you asked for it," the Arab replied.

Simone smiled at their banter and walked over toward the head of the trail. As if on cue, she heard the voices of the two male archeologists approaching. They were engaged in a heated theological debate, ambling up the trail together. Josh had a large box under his arm.

"I understand that traditions can be important," Josh was saying. "Every church has them. But to allow human traditions to trump the clear teaching of Scripture has always struck me as dangerous. I mean, Paul clearly said that the pastor of a church should be 'the husband of one wife and a good manager of his family.' You know that most of the Apostles, including Simon Peter and the Lord's brothers, were married. So why should the Church not allow men of God to also be family men?"

"We do ordain widowers," said Father MacDonald, "but the priesthood is a holy office, and those of us who undertake it must be willing to renounce the privilege of having a family for as long as we wear the cloth."

"But where does the Bible require that?" Josh asked.

"It doesn't," Father MacDonald acknowledged. "But tradition and Church doctrine does."

They looked up and saw her smiling down at them from the head of the trail. Father MacDonald tipped his hat at her, and Josh gave a wave. "My apologies, dear lady," said the priest. "This young rascal is determined to re-fight every battle of the Protestant Reformation with me!"

"Not at all," said Josh. "I am just trying to understand the Catholic position."

"Well," she said, "the work is done. All the stone dust and debris are gone, and the chamber is just as Tiberius left it for us."

"I hesitate to ask how long it took," said Josh.

"I was in bed by midnight," she said. "Or at least, in my bedroll. Tonight I claim one of those soft guest beds at Giuseppe's house."

"I would say you have definitely earned it," the priest said. "So, have we heard from our illustrious leader?"

"Not yet," said Simone. "Now, what is in that box?"

"We have fresh pastries, and some sort of meat and cheese wrapped inside a light fluffy bread roll," Josh said. "I don't know the name, but it smelled wonderful!"

"I had one of yesterday's pastries," said Apriceno, "but I wouldn't mind something with a bit more substance."

They were eating breakfast when Father MacDonald's phone rang. He picked it up and listened to the greeting from the other end. "Good morning, Dr. Sforza," he exclaimed. "I trust you had a pleasant and productive meeting with the board?"

"Productive enough," she said. "We released a short press statement this morning, to let the world know that we have made a discovery up here. However, we are not yet letting anyone know what we have discovered. It mainly lets the public know why the Villa Jovis is closed. Were there any developments at the site last night?"

"We did make a wee little discovery while you were away," the priest admitted. "I think you will be quite pleased when you see it."

"I'm en route right now," she said. "Send me a couple of pictures on my cell. Be there in about fifteen minutes."

The priest looked at the cell phone with a bit of distaste. "I haven't even learned to take pictures with this thing, much less send them. Dr. Parker, can you lend your technical expertise?"

"I took some shots with my iPhone as well as with the camera last night," he said. "Let me shoot them to her. Do you have the number?"

The priest read him the number, and Josh sent the digital files to Isabella's phone. Moments later, he got a text back. Reading it, he let out a chuckle.

"What does she say?" MacDonald asked.

"'I hate all three of you. Be there in ten minutes,'" he read.

They finished their breakfast and walked to the upper level to watch the helicopter land. There were handshakes and high-fives all around when Giuseppe and Isabella climbed out of the chopper and joined them.

The first order of business was to see the chamber now that it lay revealed. Dr. Apriceno unzipped the plastic doorway covering the entrance and all of them filed in together and stood with their backs to the front wall where the writing desk had stood. She waited till they were all in place, then plugged in the high-powered halogen lights she had rigged up the evening before. There was a collective gasp as the tableau before them was illuminated.

Because of the slope of the stairs above it, the back of the chamber had a much lower ceiling than the front end. Where the ancient desk had been, the roof of the chamber was a good four or five feet above them. But the back, where the reliquary rested, was only a bit above five feet in height. The reliquary stood about four feet high and rested in the low end snugly, with about a foot of room on one side and somewhat less on the other. Because of the poor lighting and the shape of the room, not to mention the endless shower of stone dust from the steps above, the back of the chamber had been hard to see at first. The reliquary had simply been a large square object standing in the corner, coated with massive amounts of dust and dirt. The *gladius* had been so completely covered that Rossini and Sforza had not even noticed it on their initial inventory of the chamber's contents.

Now the walls, floor, and artifacts were cleaned of the dust of the centuries, and stood there as they had been left twenty centuries before. The reliquary was a magnificently carved wooden box, about a foot deep and five feet wide. Carved into the dark wooden doors was a finely detailed Roman eagle, with the inevitable SPQR engraved beneath it. Latin letters above the eagle, along the top edge of each door, read *"Iuppiter Optimus Maximus, conservare dignitas de Iulii."*

"Jupiter Greatest and Highest, preserve the *dignitas* of the Julii," Josh translated. The cabinet was made of a very dark wood, and bore the nicks, scars, and polish of much use. It was obviously not a new piece of furniture at the time it was buried in this chamber.

"Amazing," Josh finally said. "To stand in the presence of so much history is —"

"Humbling?" said Rossini. "If this box is what I think it is, it once held the funeral masks of Julius Caesar, his father and uncles, and perhaps even Augustus himself. Alone, without anything in it, this is the greatest discovery of Roman archeology since Pompeii was unearthed!"

"And look at the sword!" said Isabella. "That weapon had seen much service before it was laid to rest here. One of the Caesars may well have carried it in Gaul, Brittania, Spain, or Egypt. Giuseppe, did you have any idea when you found this chamber what a discovery you were making?"

"Not at all," he said. "Do you think Howard Carter knew what he'd found when he uncovered those two limestone steps leading downward, buried in the accumulated backfill of a later tomb in the Valley of the

Kings? Do you think Heinrich Schliemann realized he had actually found Troy when he first sunk his shovel into the earth of Asia Minor? My friends, this is a discovery for the ages."

After a long look at the newly revealed artifacts, the five of them retreated out into the open air to confer. How to proceed from here?

"First things first," said Rossini. "Let's begin with the leather purse we found. It should be sufficiently rehydrated for us to remove the contents without damaging it. Then, we remove the sword to the lab for study and preservation. The scabbard is leather and will deteriorate if not stabilized. After we have analyzed both those items, we will need to figure out how to deal with the reliquary. The first determination we need to make will be whether to move it unopened, or open it up, see what is in it, and then decide if we need to remove the contents first, and then move the reliquary itself, or move it contents and all."

Isabella nodded. "That seems to be a logical course of action," she said. "Let's repair to the lab."

Once inside, Dr. Apriceno set about organizing the hundred or more vials of dust she had gathered from inside the chamber. She would conduct a preliminary examination on the samples collected from each surface in the chamber, and then fly the entire collection to the mainland for more rigorous analysis after her initial report was made. The other four headed over to the rehydration tank and watched as Professor MacDonald donned a pair of elbow-length, acid-free rubber gloves and selected two pairs of forceps from a drawer. He pulled out a section of the tank's bottom, laid the forceps on it, then reached through the rubber-lined opening on the side of the tank and picked them up.

With great precision, he grasped one edge of the drawstring bag's open end with the smaller pair of forceps, then took the other pair and gripped the opposite side of the bag's mouth. He tugged ever so gently, and the ancient drawstrings, having regained a measure of their suppleness, slid through the holes, allowing the bag to open up a bit. He then used the larger pair of forceps to hold the bag open while he reached into it with the smaller pair. He gingerly lifted out the ancient key first. The actual key itself was made of iron, which was blackened from age but remarkably free of rust. The horse head effigy appeared to be carved from some soft stone, or perhaps very deeply stained ivory, inlaid with gold and gems. He laid it on the tray he had placed the forceps on, and then reached back into the purse again. The second item he brought out was the pointed object that had baffled them in the X-rays. Once it saw the light of day, though, its nature was apparent.

"An arrowhead," laughed Josh. "I've picked up a few hundred of these back in the States, although all of mine were stone, not iron."

"Why would Tiberius save a common iron arrowhead?" wondered Isabella.

The priest was already back at work, probing the purse's interior with the small forceps. In short order he extracted four coins—two gold, one silver, and one bronze. Further probing discovered no more items inside the purse, but to be sure, he released the mouth of the drawstring bag with his forceps and picked it up by the bottom, shaking it gently to see if anything else fell out. Only the fragile, desiccated carcass of a spider tumbled out. He pulled the tray out and transferred the metal items onto the table for study, then slid the original tray back into the tank with a fine pair of tweezers and a clear plastic box. The spider carcass was dropped into the box for later study—if it could be dated, it would be a clue as to how open the chamber might have been in ages past.

After the spider mummy was placed in storage, the archeologists crowded around the items on the table. Dr. Sforza photographed both sides of each item from multiple angles, and each was measured with calipers and its dimensions recorded in field notebooks and on film.

"Looks like two gold sesterces, a silver denarius, and a bronze drachma," said Rossini. "All appear to date from the Augustan age, which is consistent with the time the chamber was sealed."

"Excellent preservation of detail, too," Josh said. "These may be the most well-preserved Roman coins I have ever seen." Everyone nodded in agreement.

"What about this arrowhead?" he asked. "I am very familiar with the stone projectile points we find back home, but not so much with these Iron Age points." The iron arrowhead was about two inches long, and nearly an inch wide at the barbs.

"It's not Roman," said Isabella. "It's way too big, plus the Romans poured theirs into molds in a mass production process. This one appears to be hand forged and hammered."

"Could it be Gallic?" said MacDonald. "Or German?"

"It does look like some Gallic points I have seen," commented Rossini. "Is that something scratched into the metal on one side?"

Sforza plugged the camera into the computer and quickly downloaded the image, then pulled it up on one of the jumbo monitors. Rough Latin characters had been scratched into one side of the arrowhead's wide blade. Although worn and faint, they appeared to read "*G I C Alesia.*"

"Gaius Julius Caesar—Alesia," said Rossini. "That was his most important victory, the one that broke the back of the Gallic resistance and made him the most famous military man of his day. Sixty thousand Roman legionaries, besieging fifty thousand Gauls in a walled city while simultaneously fighting off a relief army numbering in the hundreds of thousands. I loved reading that section of Caesar's *Gallic Wars* as a boy."

"I remember that." said Josh. "Although I'll admit I read about it in Colleen McCullough's novels first, and then Caesar's own account later. He built a wall around the city, and another wall facing outward to protect his men—what did they call it? Double circumvallation?"

"That's it," said Isabella. "But why would he keep a single arrowhead? And why would it be passed down to Tiberius?"

"Just guessing," said Josh. "But if he was wounded—or, more likely, if he suffered a near miss that should have wounded him or killed him and didn't—he might have kept it as a reminder of his legendary luck."

"Fortuna's favorite, that's what they called him," said MacDonald.

Finally, they looked at the key. The barrel was just over an inch long, and the drooping metal end was distinctively notched. "Typical Roman effigy key from the first century," noted Isabella. "I have seen a number of similar ones from Pompeii. We need to keep it handy, in case the reliquary is still locked."

Each item from the purse was catalogued, assigned a number, and placed in a padded tray, then placed in a cabinet where they could be stored until the entire mobile lab was returned to the mainland. There they would be taken to the brand new laboratory recently built to supplement the aging facilities at the National Archeological Museum in Naples. All the finds from the chamber would be rigorously tested to tease out every bit of information they contained, and to check for any evidence that the artifacts were not authentic.

Once the examination table was cleared, Dr. Sforza looked at the team. "Are we ready to remove the sword from the chamber, or should we take a break?" she asked them.

The four archeologists looked at one another, and MacDonald spoke. "It's not nearly noon yet," he said. "All of us had a decent breakfast, and I am a bit concerned about that leather scabbard now that it has been exposed to the air. I want to get it into a controlled environment as soon as possible."

"I guess that settles it, then," said Isabella. "We carry it to the lab and begin the preservation process before we break for lunch."

Dr. MacDonald began preparing a tray to transport the sword on. He chose one that was a full meter in length, more than long enough to lay the shortsword and scabbard across. Then he laid a layer of acid-free fabric across the tray, taping it down at the edges to keep the breeze from blowing it away, and prepared a cover that would come down over the whole thing and snap into place on the sides, thus eliminating any chance of exposing the delicate, ancient leather to the destructive UV rays of the sun. When he was done, the four scholars walked from the trailer to the chamber entrance.

"Josh," he said, "I am going to stand here with the tray ready. I want you to don these gloves and very carefully lift the blade and scabbard onto the tray, and then snap the cover in place. Then you and I shall lift it through the opening and carry it straight to the lab."

Isabella began filming and narrating as Josh pulled the gloves on and studied the sword carefully. The leather scabbard was rough and cracked with age, but did not look as if it were in imminent danger of crumbling apart. Nonetheless, he gripped the pommel of the sword itself with one hand and grabbed the metal sheathing at the point of the scabbard with the other, not touching the leather at all, as he gingerly lifted it and placed it onto the tray. Isabella handed him the lid, and he lowered it into place and locked the latches down on either side. Then he put his hands solidly under the tray and helped guide Father MacDonald as he backed through the chamber entrance and across the small courtyard to the mobile lab.

Within moments, the tray was placed on the examination table, and the archeologists gathered around. The scabbard was made of what was probably, at one time, some very expensive and durable leather—perhaps from Corinth? It was black with age, but the golden trim that the leather was decorated with was as bright as ever. There was some silver there, too, but it had tarnished and darkened over the centuries. The artifact was measured and photographed, and then Josh carefully flipped it over so the other side could be examined. This side looked identical with one exception—there was a flat silver plate, about two inches long and an inch wide, sewn into the leather. The silver was faintly engraved. Once more, Josh zoomed in with the camera, snapped away, and downloaded the pictures to the computer. In less than a minute, they were looking at a magnified image of the inscription on the oversize monitor.

"*Ad Romae mundissimo filius, gerunt cum honore—Aurelia Cotta Caesar,*" read Professor Rossini. "Roughly translated: 'To Rome's Finest Son, Wield It with Honor—Aurelia Cotta Caesar.' Aurelia was one of the greatest matrons of the Roman Republic, and the mother of its greatest general. My friends, this removes all doubt. We are looking at the sword of Gaius Julius Caesar."

"I don't understand," Josh said. "This chamber belonged to Tiberius. Why did he place his adopted grandfather's items here?"

MacDonald replied, "Julius and Augustus were gods by the time Tiberius was an old man," he said. "Not just in the sense of being deeply admired former rulers, either. They were genuinely worshipped by the people of Rome and by the many citizens of the larger empire. And Gaius Julius Caesar was in a league of his own. Many military men still regard him as the greatest general of all time. His sword, his lucky arrowhead, would have both been precious family heirlooms. Whatever his shortcomings as an emperor, Tiberius was a great general in his day. His conquest of Germany made him a hero to the people of Rome while his adoptive father Augustus was still alive. But at the time he wrote the letter we found, he was an old man, aware that his time was short. His only heir was a psychotic teenager who had never led men in battle—a spoiled brat, a 'serpent' as Tiberius called him. He probably thought that Gaius Caligula was unworthy to wield the sword of the *Divus Julius*, and so sealed it up in the chamber, along with the lucky arrowhead—and who knows what else?"

The Catholic scholar turned to the lab table and looked at the ancient weapon. "The rehydration tank will be an absolute necessity to preserve that scabbard," he said. "But, unfortunately, it would be terribly detrimental to the metal blade inside it. We are going to have to unsheathe the sword and stabilize it and the scabbard separately."

He turned to the tray and donned the protective gloves again. He carefully gripped the scabbard at its top, where the metal sheathing extended down over three inches. Then he took the pommel of the sword in his other hand, and firmly pulled the ancient weapon from its sheath. The blade had a few rust spots on it, but was remarkably well preserved, still gleaming for much of its length.

Rossini gasped. "That is the best-preserved example of a Roman *gladius* I have ever seen," he said. "Perhaps the best ever found."

"Think how many battlefields it saw, how much bloodshed, how much history!" said Josh. "I am in serious danger of losing my scientific objectivity and whooping like a crazy Cowboys fan, back when Cowboys fans still had something to go crazy over!"

Isabella laughed. Even those who knew nothing about American football still knew who the Cowboys were. "I think we all feel like that—maybe not the Cowboys part, but the excitement, yes! The sword of Julius Caesar! That is even better than finding Excalibur!"

MacDonald glared at them. "Could one of you quit mooning over this thing long enough to set another tray up here?" he asked.

Josh quickly put another tray on the table, and the *gladius* was placed upon it. Then the Catholic antiquarian opened another rehydration tank, set the controls, and slid the first tray with the scabbard still resting on it into the tank. "Now THAT was a good morning's work!" he said. "Let's take a break, eat a bite, and prepare to deal with the reliquary."

Noble Caesar, anyone who has lived in Rome for any time has seen a Roman mob in action at some point or other. Our city is famous for its fickle masses. But I have never seen such raw hatred for any human being expressed so loudly and strongly as this crowd of Jews screamed its hate at Jesus. Ironic, since a few days before half the city had been ready to crown him as their king. Once more, they took up that awful cry: "CRUCIFY! CRUCIFY!"

"Why?" I shouted. "What evil has he done?"

One of the priests stepped forward—although not so far as to step past the threshold of the Praetorium. Hounding an innocent man to his death was apparently fine according to his religious convictions, but setting foot in the home of a pagan like me would have made him unclean! "We have a law," he shouted. "And by that law he ought to die, for being a man, he made himself out to be a god!"

The situation was deteriorating, so I removed Jesus from their sight—as well as myself. They were determined to see blood, it seemed. Very well, I would give them blood. But not as much as they wanted. I turned to the Brutus Appius, the Centurion who led my household guard. "Take him and flog him," I said. "But don't kill him!"

The young Jew that had been brought in to interpret leaped to his feet in protest. I had forgotten he was there, but I looked at him now and saw his raw fear, barely held at bay in his concern for his master. "I am trying to save his life," I said, as gently as I could, and retreated to my quarters until the deed was done.

CHAPTER TEN

The four archeologists stepped across the ancient flagstones to the entrance of the chamber. MacDonald looked askance at the narrow, uneven opening the earthquake had created. "One thing is certain," he said. "We will have to widen that opening in order to remove the reliquary."

Isabella replied, "From the inside the original outline of the ancient door is clearly visible. It appears that Tiberius' steward actually added an entire layer of brick to the outside of this exterior wall from one end to the other to completely disguise the opening when he sealed up the chamber. We will restore the doorway to its original dimensions when we finish our excavations."

They stepped inside and turned on the lights. The ancient cabinet sat in the rear of the chamber, just as it must have rested there the last time Tiberius Caesar opened it. Slowly they approached. This was the last untouched artifact from the ancient chamber. It could hold a priceless treasure trove of history, or it might be completely empty. Another moment would tell the tale! None of them wanted to step forward at first, but finally Isabella closed in, and Josh followed. She had her camera recording as she narrated.

"We are inside the Tiberius writing chamber of Villa Jovis," she said. "It is 1300 hours local time. The cabinet, or reliquary, that you see before you has not been opened or moved since the initial discovery three days ago. It has two doors that appear to open outwards. The seam is snug but the two doors do not quite meet in the middle. Directly below the embossed Roman eagle there appears to be a small, conventional bronze latch or clasp. I am going to now ask my colleague, Dr. Parker, to very carefully see if the latch will still open."

Josh put on his gloves and gently reached out to raise the top part of the latch. It was funny, he thought to himself, how some tool forms were so functional that they had not changed in 2,000 years. This latch was slightly more ornate but not that different in shape from the screen door latches on his grandfather's old home in Oklahoma. The latch resisted very slightly, but then there was the tiniest pop as the corrosion that had started to fuse the hook and eye together gave way, and the hook rose up easily.

He looked at Isabella, who began speaking for the benefit of the camera once more. "Now we shall open the cabinet and begin our inventory of its contents," she said, giving him the nod. He grasped the door firmly by its top edge and pulled outwards. There was a tortured creak as the ancient hinges moved for the first time in twenty centuries, and the door swung open with a puff of dust. The shock of discovery was followed by a tremendous crush of disappointment.

"RATS!" Josh exclaimed. "*Quod sugit!!!*"

The three Latin scholars stared at him, and as they saw what he had seen first, each reacted. Isabella let out a small sob, Duncan swore in Gaelic, and Rossini just shook his head.

"That sucks indeed, my young friend!" he finally said.

The cabinet had been divided into numerous compartments and cubbies, and it looked as if all of them, at one time, had held scrolls and ancient documents. But the wooden partitions between them had been chewed through, and the priceless trove of information had been shredded to line the two large rat's nests that occupied each lower corner of the reliquary. Isabella stooped and scooped up the mummified carcass of one of the offending beasts. "*Stupid, roditore meno male!!!!*" she screamed, and flung it against the back wall of the chamber, where it broke into pieces and settled to the floor in a cloud of dust.

Father MacDonald finally spoke. "They are stupid, evil little rodents," he said. "But all is not lost. I have retrieved substantial content from documents in far worse shape than these," he said. "There is still a great deal of information here, but it will be the work of years to piece it together and decipher it. What a sad disappointment!"

Josh spoke up. "Well, I see where the key fits in," he said, pointing. All four of them looked to see the small compartment, lined on the sides with dull metal, which occupied about half of the space at the top right hand side of the reliquary. Its ornately carved, bronze-plated door was intact and firmly shut. There was a keyhole in the center of it.

"Thank God!" Isabella said. "It looks as if the rats did not get into it. Unless . . ." For a moment she forgot proper field techniques. She handed her camera to Josh, grabbed the ancient cabinet with both hands, and slid it out from the wall about a foot. She shone her light on the solid wood back. There were two holes gnawed into the paneling near the bottom, showing where the rodents had gained entrance—but neither was directly behind the locked compartment. She gave a huge sigh of relief. The others stared at her, speechless. Finally she laughed. "All right," she said, "that was one small breach of professional field procedure! Let's do it right from here on out! I am going to suggest that we carefully remove all the shredded documents first. We'll search for any metal or non-perishable artifacts that might have gotten buried in the rat's nests. After the cabinet is completely cleaned out except for the locked compartment, we will transfer the cabinet to the mobile lab and see if the key still works. Hopefully the key we have actually fits that lock and not some other long-lost treasure chest from elsewhere in the Villa Jovis!"

Over the next few hours, the three archeologists brought several acid-free cardboard boxes over from the lab and carefully lifted out the shredded ancient texts, separating papyrus and parchment fragments from wood chips, bits of straw, and the other odds and ends the rats had dragged into their nest. Their spirits lifted a bit when they saw that there were still a few decent-sized pieces of scroll amid the more finely shredded fragments. MacDonald paused as he studied a piece about three inches across. It was written in a clear, strong hand that was a marked contrast to the shaky, almost illegible Latin of the Tiberius manuscript.

"It appears to be part of a letter to Tiberius," he said. "Judging from context, it is from Augustus himself. It says: *Meum filium, meis est quod assistere Agrippa in vitali labore . . . Romani aquilae perdidit ad Parthos per Crassus, Saxa, et Antonius. Eorum damnum est ictu ad Romae dignitas quod . . . An bello aut agere, debent reversus!* One end of the fragment is rather chewed up, but a rough translation would be 'My son, my command is that you assist Agrippa in his vital effort' . . . there's a bit missing here . . . 'Roman eagles lost to the Parthians by Crassus, Saxa, and Antony. Their loss is a blow to Rome's dignitas that . . .' Rats ate a few words here too . . . 'whether by battle or negotiation, they must be returned!' One of Tiberius' earliest military assignments was the expedition into Armenia, where he was second in command to Marcus Agrippa, in an effort to recover the lost standards of the legions that had been defeated in Rome's earlier conflicts with the Parthians. These were his marching orders!"

"What a treasury of history those rats destroyed!" said Josh. "That is the one thing that none of us suspected!"

"Years ago, I did a restoration project for a monastery in Spain," said MacDonald. "They had a cabinet full of beautiful medieval books, laboriously copied in Carolingian minuscule during the ninth century, that had been destroyed by rats, just like these scrolls. Yet, amazingly, within ten years, eighty percent of the writing was recovered."

"I know that is true," said Isabella. "But the pristine nature of the other finds in the chamber let us get our hopes up so high! I envy you your optimism. I can't look at this shredded parchment without feeling sick to my stomach."

Josh studied a fragment he had recovered, slightly larger than the one MacDonald had read. It was in the same hand as the Tiberius letter, but clearer and less shaky. He read aloud: *"'Non curare quod senatus dicit, Seiani, Sit maiestatis iudiciis permanere! At Romae in putredinem et purgare intendo tantum de putredine possum antequam moriar, ut non pudeat coram Divus Iulius— Si ad illum senem triumphalem vere Dei esse!'* Hmm. This one is actually a complete paragraph from a letter Tiberius wrote. It reads something like 'I do not care what the Senate says, Sejanus, let the treason trials continue! Rome is rotten to the core, and I intend to purge as much of the rot as I can before I die, that I may not be ashamed to stand before the Divus Julius—if the old triumphator is truly the God we make him out to be!' It appears that Tiberius' reputation as a tyrant may not have been an exaggeration!"

Over the course of the afternoon, they filled three boxes with papyrus fragments and one with pieces of a parchment document. This last one was badly shredded, but the few words they were able to read appeared to be bits of erotic poetry in Greek. They also filled another box with various other scraps and pieces—some gnawed leather, two coins, and a fair amount of fabric that appeared to have been part of a woman's gown at one time. In the heart of one of the nests was a golden chain with a cameo portrait of a Roman woman in marble, on a background of black onyx or obsidian. It was housed in a golden mount that was inscribed on the reverse side with the name "Vipsania Agrippina."

Isabella looked at it sadly. "I remember reading in Suetonius' biography of Tiberius," she said. "He married Vipsania, the daughter of Augustus Caesar's most trusted advisor, Marcus Agrippa, and was deeply in love with her. But when Agrippa died, Caesar ordered young Tiberius to divorce his bride and marry Agrippa's widow Julia—the only daughter of Caesar Augustus, and the young stepmother of Tiberius' first wife! It was a miserable marriage, and according to Suetonius, Tiberius pined for Vipsania for the rest of his days and never forgave Augustus." She gave

Rossini a dark look. "That's what old men get for meddling in the romantic affairs of their juniors!" she said.

He laughed out loud, and Josh looked at both of them in puzzlement. They laughed at his bewilderment. "It is, how would you say in America, an inside joke!" Isabella told him.

By the end of the day, the ancient cabinet had been carefully cleaned out and all the fragments of history boxed up for reconstruction. As near as they could tell, there had once been at least five papyrus scrolls in the reliquary, plus the parchment one, at least two garments, a few coins, and the necklace. There were also some pieces of grain and seeds that the rats had brought in at some point. These were bagged separately and turned over to Dr. Apriceno.

When they were done, Isabella addressed the team back in the mobile lab. "I think we are done for the day," she said. "I suggest we repair to the village for supper and then retire for the night."

"Who spends the night on the mountain this time?" said Josh. "I certainly don't mind."

Rossini spoke up. "I slept in a five-star hotel last night," he said, "with the most amazing room service! I feel I need to sleep in a tent to atone for such luxury! But I will join all of you at Mrs. Bustamante's for dinner first."

Closing up the chamber and weighing down the tarp that covered the entrance, the four were joined by Simone Apriceno as they ambled down the trail together. She commiserated with them over the loss of the scrolls from the reliquary. But she waxed eloquent about her initial findings. "I found a very few modern spores on top of the dust deposits near the door," she said. "Those doubtless blew in there within twenty-four hours of the chamber being torn open. But all the core samples show nothing but stone dust, soil, and a perfectly stratified series of pollen deposits scattered throughout. All the deepest samples are pure first century flora—not a bit of contamination!"

"What about the rat's nest?" asked Josh.

"Those samples appear to be a bit more recent than the rest, but still pretty old," said Apriceno. "The seeds from the nest appear to be consistent with early medieval agricultural crops. But we will be able to carbon date the rat carcass itself, despite its being flung against a stone wall and broken into several pieces!"

"Hey!" said Dr. Sforza. "I was provoked!"

117

They made their way down the trail to Dr. Rossini's house and took turns showering in the two bathrooms. Josh turned on the American ESPN satellite feed on the living room television while the two ladies were still getting cleaned up, just to see what was happening in the world of sports. The Rangers were opening their season with a nice winning streak, thanks to improved pitching, but the Mavs were barely above .500 as they stumbled toward the playoff season with hopes dimming. As for the Cowboys—well, Josh had not had his hopes up since the mid-90s, and reports from the upcoming draft gave him no reason to change that assessment.

Rossini came in, his hair still damp, and glanced at the screen. "I don't know why I even get that channel," he said. "I don't even care for our European sports that much, and as for your American games—well!" He gave a hearty snort.

Josh laughed. "I'm a one-town fan," he said. "My dad's pastorates always seemed to orbit the North Texas area, so the Mavs, the Cowboys, and the Rangers are my teams. I have tried watching hockey, but I just can't seem to get into it at all. Mind if I catch some real home news?" He switched the TV over to the American CNN feed. The President, sincere and eloquent seeming as always, was pledging to reduce the deficit in a responsible manner, if only Congress would start acting in a more bipartisan manner and support his agenda. Funny, coming from a man who had borrowed five trillion dollars in his first four years, and seemed determine to pass that mark in his second administration! Josh turned the TV off. "Sorry," he said to Rossini. "It was spoiling my appetite!"

"Not a fan of your country's Democratic Party, are you?" asked Rossini.

"Not in its current incarnation," Josh said. "They've had some good ideas in the past, but here lately all they seem to know how to do is tax, spend, and borrow. And some Republicans aren't much better!"

"Count yourself fortunate," the Italian archeologist said. "My country has been through nearly seventy governments since World War II!"

Josh looked at him. "Maybe you can borrow our Constitution," he said. "We don't use it much anymore!"

They laughed together, and then rose to greet the two ladies as they emerged, freshly changed, from the guest room. Moments later, Father

MacDonald joined them from the main bedroom. Rossini beamed at the group. "It has been entirely too long since I have entertained this many guests!" he exclaimed. "Let us go dine together and be merry!" He offered Dr. Apriceno his arm and escorted her out the door. Josh looked at Isabella and did likewise. Father MacDonald shook his head in amusement and brought up the rear as they walked down the street to Mrs. Bustamante's restaurant.

The dinner was superb, both due to the excellent food and the fact that they had skipped lunch in their focus on the contents of the reliquary. The friendly Spanish restaurateur seemed to think that all of them were suffering from chronic malnutrition, and kept bringing out additional side dishes that they had not even ordered. When Dr. Rossini gently protested, she blushed and fled to the kitchen.

Isabella looked at her mentor and grinned. "Something you are not telling me, Giuseppe?" she asked.

"No!" he snapped. Then he arched his eyebrows ever so slightly. "Not yet, at least."

She threw her head back and laughed, and Josh joined in. She looked at him intently for a moment. What if both she and her old friend were finding a second chance at love at the same time? Josh suddenly glanced her way, and it was her turn to blush and avert her gaze. She was somewhat excited and angry with herself at the same time. How could she develop such strong feelings so quickly, about a man she barely even knew? She decided then and there that she wanted to find out more about this man before her heart ran away with her any further.

They sat at the table for two hours, excitedly discussing the chamber and their discoveries. So intent were they on their conversation that they did not notice the man in the white suit, two tables down, who intently listened to their every word. They only saw him when he gave them a friendly nod and smile as they left.

After supper, they walked back to Rossini's house. He bade them a cheerful good night and headed up the Via Tiberio a short time later. Josh had paused on the way back to the house to buy a Coke at the gift shop he'd discovered the night before, and he arrived at the villa just as Rossini was leaving. He watched the older man go with affection. Rossini was intelligent, articulate, funny, and also wise. Josh imagined that he would be a wonderful grandfather, and that made him think of his own grandfather, some ten years gone now. But thinking of

119

Granddad Parker made him think of the impulse purchase he had made with his sodas, and he walked into the villa as the others stood in the den talking.

"Ladies, and most reverent Father MacDonald," he said. "Our evening just got booked!"

Three pairs of eyes regarded him quizzically as he reached into the sack from the souvenir shop, bringing out a box of double six dominoes. "I am going to introduce you to the true sport of kings—Forty-Two!"

MacDonald raised an eyebrow. "Laddie," he said, "I am a student of monarchies past and present, and I can honestly say that I have never heard of any crowned heads playing dominoes!"

"Who said anything about crowned heads?" Josh asked. "Barney and Betty King were the couple who taught Dad and I how to play the game, so we have called it the 'Sport of Kings' ever since."

"I thought forty-two was the answer to the Ultimate Question about Life, the Universe, and Everything!" said Dr. Apriceno.

Josh laughed at the Douglas Adams reference. This lady was sharp. "It is indeed," he said. "But it's also a wicked fun domino game! Now, let's gravitate to the table and your education shall begin!"

They all knew how to play Spades, a card game with similar rules, so making the shift was pretty easy. Within an hour, they were bidding, setting, trumping, and plunging with wild abandon. Josh and Isabella managed to beat out MacDonald and Apriceno two games out of three, and before they knew it, it was a quarter till midnight. At this point the older two excused themselves, leaving the young couple in possession of the kitchen table.

At first they discussed the incredibly lucky series of hands that had let them come from behind to win the last game, but then Isabella looked at Josh curiously. "All right," she said. "I have been thinking for some time about our last conversation. I was going to tell you a little about myself when we were interrupted. As I said, I was born on a small farm in Tuscany . . ."

For the next hour and half they talked, and she told him more than she had related to anyone since her husband's death about her life, her hopes, her dreams. She wept all over again as she described the accident that robbed her of her husband Marc. Without even thinking about it, Josh put his arm around her and gave her a hug until the spasm of grief passed. Then, to take her mind off her newly remembered loss, he began relating a series of stories about his own rural Baptist childhood, most of them humorous. Before long she was weeping again, but this time with laughter. "Water snakes in the Baptistry!" she exclaimed. "My village priest would have exorcised you!"

Josh laughed. "That might have been preferable to the trip behind the woodshed I had with my father!" he said. He looked at the clock. It was one-thirty in the morning. "My Lord, Isabella, we need to go to sleep!"

She looked at the clock and was astonished at the time. "I had no idea it was this late," she said. "We have to be up at six thirty!"

"Well, I enjoyed getting to know you," he said.

"You made me laugh more tonight than I have in . . . . well, longer than I can remember," she said. "Thank you." And leaning up, she kissed him on the cheek before turning and heading to the guest room. Josh stood rooted to the spot for a very long time before he turned toward the sofa he had spread his bedding on.

The next morning they got up a solid half hour after the other two. Josh was exhausted, and his hair was doing funny circus tricks as he stumbled toward the bathroom sink, looking for his toothpaste and brush to banish the taste of the trolls who had apparently used his mouth as their latrine sometime during the night. Isabella was also looking a bit haggard when she came stumbling in and sucked down two straight cups of black coffee in less than five minutes.

Josh stumbled into the kitchen after brushing his teeth and opened the fridge to get the Coke he hadn't quite finished the night before. To his astonishment, he saw an ice cold 20 oz. Dr Pepper waiting for him! He held it up and pressed the cold surface to his cheek. "Is it just me, or is this bottle radiating a golden light and heavenly music?" he asked.

Isabella laughed. "I completely forgot that I bought that for you in Naples day before yesterday," she said. "I was looking for something in my purse last night before bed and found it, so I popped it in the fridge for you."

"You are an angel of heaven incarnate," he said as he took a long drink.

"I'll admit I had one myself when I bought yours," she said. "Not bad stuff, as soft drinks go. But I still prefer Madeira!"

"One of these days," said MacDonald, "you are going to have to tell me whatever stories or anecdotes you were telling her after we went to bed. I couldn't hear what you were saying, but her laughter carried through three walls!"

So, as they walked up the Via Tiberio, Josh began relating the old Grady Nutt story about the "Baptist Sunday Bulletin Balcony Bombardier Brigade." While some of the religious references were lost on the three Catholics, enough of the humor got through that all four of them were chuckling as they reached the top of the trail and approached the lab. Dr. Rossini was waiting, leaning on his cane, his face wreathed in smiles. "How pleasant it is for brethren to dwell together in unity!" he quoted the Scriptures as they walked up to him.

"You forget, *Signor Doctore*, forty percent of this group is sisters," said Dr. Apriceno.

"Trust me, dear lady," he said, "your feminine charms, and those of the fair Dr. Sforza, are such that I could NEVER forget your gender! I was using 'brethren' in a completely gender neutral context."

She jabbed him in the ribs with her elbow, and he grasped his side and moaned in mock dismay as she scowled at him. Isabella let them go on a moment, then said, "All right, team, it is time to face the greatest challenge yet. I think we need to move the reliquary before we attempt to open the locked compartment. How can we best accomplish this?"

Giuseppe spoke up. "I had anticipated that we would remove it at some point today," he said. "I think the best way to do it would be with a furniture dolly, after carefully wrapping it in soft cotton blankets. That way we can keep it upright, only leaning it slightly backward or forward, all the way from the chamber to the lab. We will need to enlarge the opening to do this, and I have already marked which bricks we will need to remove to get the width we need."

"Where are we going to get a furniture dolly?" asked Josh.

Rossini grinned. "Chief Rosario should be delivering it within the hour," he said. "So let's start removing some bricks!"

In short order the archeologists had removed some twenty-two bricks from the entrance of the chamber, leaving the door very close to its original dimensions. Rossini had already numbered each brick and photographed it original placement, so that the wall could be reconstructed at some point if need be. They had just finished neatly stacking the ancient masonry to one side when a hullo drew their attention. Chief Rosario was at the edge of the site, with two of the burly security men blocking his path.

"Giuseppe!" he shouted. "I do your bidding and you sic your goons on me? Is that any way to treat an old friend?"

"Let him through, men," said Isabella. "Chief, thank you so much for all your cooperation and assistance in this project since we began work. Is there any way we can repay you for your kindness?"

"Absolutely!" he said. "Just let me have a tiny peek at what you have found."

Isabella and Rossini looked at each other for a long moment. Josh, Duncan, and Simone looked on with curiosity. "You are the director of this dig, my dear," said Rossini. "But I will tell you that this man can keep anything you tell him in the strictest confidence."

"All right," she said. "Just the five-minute tour, though!" She turned to Rosario. "How would you like to see the sword of Julius Caesar himself?"

It was more like a half an hour, but when Chief Rosario walked down the hill he had a dazed expression on his face. A military history buff, he had actually trembled at the sight of their finds, and had sworn on his mother's grave to honor the confidence they had shown in him.

After he left, they took the packing blankets, bungee cords, and dolly into the chamber. The cabinet sat mute in the corner, its doors closed once more at the end of the previous day's labor. "How do we go about this?" Isabella said. "We always hired movers when we had to relocate!"

Josh laughed. "I worked at a furniture store in Hugo, Oklahoma, for two summers in high school, and one semester as a docent in a historic home while I was in college," he said. "If there is one thing I know how to do, it is how to move delicate antique furniture!"

The others watched as he draped the packing blankets over the cabinet and used bungee cords to bind them around it. Then he ever so gently eased the front side of the cabinet back, sliding the tongue of the dolly underneath it. He pulled the reliquary toward him, settling its weight on the dolly, and asked Isabella to hold it steady while he used more bungee cords to gently lash it to the dolly. Then he grasped the handles firmly and very slowly rolled it back to the entrance of the chamber.

"Now," he said, "I want us to grasp the dolly itself—not the cabinet, just hold it steady on the dolly!—and lift the whole thing through the entrance." They all held their breath, but in a moment the process was complete. Josh looked askance at the ancient flagstones between the entrance and the mobile lab. While they were worn smooth with age, they were still rough enough to guarantee a bumpy ride to his ancient cargo. Rossini looked at him thoughtfully, thinking the same thing.

"Lucien! Ibrahim!" he called. The two security guards came over quickly. "Can you help us VERY gently lift this cabinet into the trailer?" he asked. "Keep it upright at all costs!"

"Of course," said the burly Italian. With al-Ghazi and Josh helping to bear the weight and steady the load, the reliquary was safely deposited in the lab within moments. The two guards looked curiously at the objects in the various rehydration tanks and trays across the lab. Lucien Rigatorre gave a low whistle of amazement at the *gladius* lying on the sanitary tray. "Mama Maria!" he said. "Is that thing real?"

"It is indeed," said Dr. Sforza. "Two thousand years old and still sharp enough to cleave a skull!" They both stared for a moment as she briefly explained what it was and asked for their silence on the subject. Then she thanked the guards again for their help, and hustled them out the door as quickly as she politely could.

Dr. MacDonald retrieved the key from the drawer he had placed it in, and Josh carefully unwrapped the blankets and checked the cabinet for damage. Finding none, he gently raised the latch and opened the doors. All four archeologists watched intently as MacDonald gently placed the key inside the ancient lock and tried to turn it. Nothing moved. He gently twisted the key in the opposite direction. Nothing. He let out a long sigh. "I think the lock is frozen with rust," he said.

Josh thought for a moment. "I think I have just the thing," he said, walking over to the locker where he had stowed some of his professional gear. He returned with a blue and yellow spray can.

"What on earth is that?" said Rossini.

"WD-40," said Josh. "The greatest lubricant on earth. In the South we use it on everything from frozen lug nuts to arthritic elbows."

"Absolutely NOT!" said Isabella. "Who knows what damage it might do to whatever is inside if you spray it straight through the keyhole?"

"That's where this comes in," said Josh, pulling the tape off of the side of the can. What they had taken for a thin red stripe on the side of the can was actually a very narrow plastic tube that had been taped to it, looking for all the world like a drinking straw for someone whose jaw was wired shut. "I can attach this, insert it into the lock, and target the spray specifically at the tumblers, letting none of it go through to the inside of the compartment."

She looked at him skeptically. "Do you want to see inside this thing today, or not?" he finally asked.

"Very well, Dr. Parker," she said in a very stern voice. "But I will hold you personally responsible for any damage to whatever lies inside this compartment!"

Josh saw that she meant it, so he used the utmost care as he inserted the red tube into the lock. He angled it straight up and sprayed a very short burst of lubricant, then angled it straight down and did another. "Done!" he said when he finished. "Let's give it five minutes, and try the key again. That should give me just enough time to tell you about the three Baptist deacons and the circus clown!"

They listened, first in irritation, then with smiles, and finally with hearty laughter as he told the old joke, which actually involved three deacons, the clown, an ostrich, and a midget. By the time he hit the punch line—"What do you mean, I must be hatched again?" the five minutes had passed. The chuckles quickly faded as they watched MacDonald lift the horse head key to the hole. He slowly turned it to the left, and there was an audible click as the ancient tumblers moved. The door sprang open a few inches, and with his acid-free gloves he opened it all the way. Isabella was filming as Josh shone the light into the long-sealed cubbyhole.

Only a faint film of dust lay over the two scrolls that were inside. Each was sealed with faded red wax, bearing the now familiar signet of Tiberius Caesar. The scrolls appeared completely intact, though faded with age to a light brown color. His voice slightly trembling, MacDonald said "Josh, get me the padded forceps and two covered trays." Parker scrambled to get two trays and cover them with acid-free paper. He found his own hands trembling slightly as he held out the first tray. MacDonald carefully lifted the first scroll with the padded forceps and placed it on the tray. Josh carried it to the table, and they clustered around to look at it. The seal had obviously been made with the same

125

ring they had found on the writing table, but the remnants of an older, long-broken seal were visible beside it. The now familiar spidery handwriting of Tiberius had recorded a short description on the outside of the scroll. *"C. Iuli Caesaris Augusti testamento ultimum,"* read Josh. "'The last will and testament of Caesar Augustus.'" There were whoops of excitement from the rest of the team.

"Now the other one," said Father MacDonald. He carefully took the forceps and lifted the second sealed scroll from its two-thousand-year-old resting place and gently laid it on the tray that Josh held waiting. It was likewise sealed and inscribed, and Josh carried it to the table before trying to decipher the elderly Emperor's shaky Latin. He pulled the magnifying glass over the scroll once he got it situated, looked at the scroll, and then turned deathly pale. He staggered backwards two steps.

"Josh!" Isabella said with great concern. "What on earth?"

He could not speak. Somehow he was seated on the floor, although he had no memory of his legs giving out. He opened his mouth two or three times, and then gave up trying to get any words out. He simply pointed a trembling finger at the scroll lying on the tray. Father MacDonald looked through the magnifying glass and read the inscription. *"Testimonium Pontii Pilati Procuratoris Iudaeae,"* he read. "'The Testimony of Pontius Pilate, Governor of Judea.'"

Isabella paled. Rossini and Apriceno simply stared at each other in shock.

"Holy Christ!" said Father MacDonald. It was not an expletive but a prayer.

I was not pleased when my legionaries brought the Galilean back to me. As I had ordered, they had not killed him, but they had come very close. His back was scored to the bone in places, and they had placed an old purple robe over his shoulders and a crown of poisonous Galilean thorn branches upon his head. The soldiers hate the Jews, of course—this is not a choice posting for a hard-drinking, hard fighting Roman man—and given a chance to humiliate one of them, the men had taken full advantage of it, leaving the Nazarene a bloodied wreck. But, I thought, perhaps I could play Jesus' pitiful condition to my own advantage. I led him back out onto the porch of the Praetorium and shoved him in front of me, giving the mob a good view. "Ecce homo!" I shouted. Some of the crowd cried out in pity, but the priests once again took up that hateful cry: "Crucify! Crucify!"

I held up my hands for silence. For the life of me I did not know what to do. This man had an enormous following. If I put him to death, would the common people who loved him rise up in open revolt? But if I spared him, the ruling class, whose cooperation is so vital to our government here, would be turned against me, perhaps permanently. What to do?

I thought of something. Raising my hands for silence, I cried out, "People of Jerusalem, you know that it is my custom to release one prisoner to you during your Passover each year. This year, I give you a choice. Shall I release this Jesus of Nazareth, your king?" I laced my voice with sarcasm, trying to throw scorn on the very idea that this wretched figure could ever be considered royalty. "Or shall I release to you the murderer Bar-Abbas?"

Once more the crowd roared. "Bar-Abbas! Bar-Abbas!" they cried.

CHAPTER ELEVEN

A half hour had passed. Both scrolls had been deposited, seals intact, inside a rehydration tank, where the ancient papyrus could be rendered supple enough to unroll. Josh sat quietly at a table near the end of the trailer, staring into space. Few words had been spoken, as the magnitude of the find they had made was still soaking in. After setting the controls on each tank to the proper levels, Father MacDonald came and sat across from Josh. Within a few moments, the entire team had taken a seat around the table. Even Dr. Apriceno had left her microscopes behind for the time being.

"I don't understand," said Isabella to Josh when she joined the group. "Having a written document from the hand of Pontius Pilate is something of great significance, but why did you nearly pass out when you saw it?"

"Because I think I know what it is," said Josh. "Don't you, Professor MacDonald?"

The priest nodded. "It certainly would make sense for it to be there. I cannot imagine any other event from that time, in Judea, that would merit being placed in the Emperor's most confidential files."

"What are you talking about?" Isabella demanded. Then it dawned on her. "Do you mean that you think this is—Pilate's report about . . ."

"The crucifixion of Jesus of Nazareth," said Josh. He quoted a Latin passage: "'*Atque haec forte potes cognoscere Actuum Pontio Pilatus.*' Justin Martyr wrote that to the Emperor Antoninus Pius around 140 AD. The traditional translation is: 'And that these things did happen, you can ascertain from the Acts of Pontius Pilate.' Apparently it was known to the early church that Pilate made a report to Rome about the events surrounding the death of Jesus, and that his narrative supported their claims about those events."

"But how can you be so sure that this is that report?" she asked. "Couldn't it be something else entirely?"

"That is a possibility," said Father MacDonald. "However, I can't think of any other event that occurred during Pilate's ten years as governor that would merit the Emperor's interest to this degree."

Josh nodded. "There is also that curious reference by Tertullian," he said.

Isabella gave him a blank look. "I know who Tertullian was," she said, "but I don't remember any reference that would apply here."

Josh explained, "In one of his writings, dated to about 180 AD, Tertullian says that Tiberius proposed to the Senate that Jesus of Nazareth be recognized as a god, and that a statue of him be added to the Roman pantheon. Most scholars have dismissed the story due to lack of any earlier reference to such an event, but it could have its roots in Tiberius having read and been impressed by Pilate's report about Jesus."

She nodded. "This is a discovery of enormous significance," she said. "I need to call Dr. Guioccini and let him know about it. I imagine that the Antiquities Bureau is going to want to make the call on how we deal with this find."

"I think that I will need to report this to the Vatican as well," said MacDonald.

"What about our press release?" asked Josh. "Aren't we supposed to do some sort of press conference tomorrow?"

"I imagine that, from this point forward, those decisions may be made well above our pay grade," said Dr. Apriceno.

"I think that this should be a conference call," said Isabella. "I want all of you available to answer questions and give opinions." She patched her laptop into the lab's main computer and dialed in the number. A moment later Dr. Guioccini answered, and when she told him what she wanted, his face appeared on the jumbo monitor a few seconds later.

"All right, Isabella," he said. "I know you would not waste my time with something unimportant, so tell me—what have you found? I've already seen the pictures you sent of the sword, and received your email about the scrolls that were destroyed by rats. I'm guessing you have opened the locked compartment?"

"That is correct. Within the last hour or so. The compartment contained two undamaged scrolls, both still sealed with the signet of Tiberius Caesar," explained Isabella.

"Marvelous!" the lead archeologist beamed. "But there is more—the look on your face makes that very clear. So continue!"

Isabella swallowed. "Both scrolls have a written title that appears to match the handwriting on the Tiberius letter, scrawled on the outside of each roll just above the seal. One is called 'The Last Will and Testament of Caesar Augustus.'"

"Bravissimo, Isabella!" exclaimed Guioccini. "That is an incredible find! This is a great day for archeology, for Roman history, for all of Italy!" He paused, studying her face through the satellite uplink. "There is more still?" he finally asked.

"Yes, sir," she said. "The second scroll is also labeled. The title recorded on it reads 'The Testimony of Pontius Pilate, Governor of Judea.'"

The lead archeologist of Italy's Bureau of Antiquities paled. "You are quite certain of this?" he finally asked.

"Absolutely."

"Is there any possibility, in your professional opinion, that this chamber was tampered with between the time of Tiberius and today?" he asked.

"I don't see any way, sir!" she said. "We have followed proper procedure from start to finish, and everything in the chamber was buried under centuries of stone dust. The only thing that has breached that chamber since the first century were those cursed rats!"

He thought for a long time. Finally, he spoke. "Have all the artifacts been removed from the chamber?"

"Yes, sir. The reliquary was the last item to be removed," said Isabella.

"Very well. Secure all the artifacts in the mobile lab, inform the guards to keep an extra careful watch, and make sure that two of you stay on-site for the evening. I am going to call every member of the Bureau's governing board and we will be on Capri tomorrow morning to see the finds in person. Father MacDonald, I want you to inform the Vatican of this discovery and tell His Holiness that he may send an emissary of his choosing to attend the meeting as well. After we have viewed the site and the artifacts, we will need to have a sit-down meeting to discuss how to proceed, and how and when to release this information to the public. Dr. Rossini, can your house accommodate a meeting of about fifteen people?"

"Yes, sir," said Giuseppe, "although it will be somewhat cozy."

"Excellent! I am pleased to have such an excellent team working on this incredible discovery. I do not need to remind any of you just how important this find is. The other artifacts were amazing, but this has the potential to be earth-shaking! Absolute confidentiality is needed. I imagine one of our first orders of business will be to remove all the artifacts you have found from the island to our new research facility for further study. Until then, keep up the security, continue to catalog and analyze the damaged scrolls, and I will see all of you in the morning." He leaned forward to touch a button on his monitor, and the screen went blank on their end. The five archeologists looked at each other.

"Well," said Josh. "Who is good at jigsaw puzzles?"

They spent the balance of the afternoon laying out the hundreds of fragments they had brought out from the chamber the day before. It was tedious and frustrating work, with moments of exhilaration when they found two pieces that actually matched. But none of them could keep from stealing over to the rehydration tank every little while to look at the two sealed scrolls. What lay inside those ancient rolls of papyrus? What impact would it have? Being in the presence of so much historical suspense sucked much of the air out of the room; the jokes and jibes that had been a part of their banter up to this moment were banished. Finally, about six in the evening, Giuseppe had had enough.

"This is ridiculous!" he said. "I have tried to piece the same pair of scraps together six times! None of us are focused on our work, so I suggest we have supper and retire."

"Don't forget that more than one of us needs to stay up here tonight," said Isabella. "A little break for supper is fine, but I don't want the site unattended for more than a couple of hours, even with the security guards here."

Josh spoke up. "Would you like me to stay up here with you?" he asked.

She considered it a moment. She could see Giuseppe winking at her out of the corner of her eye, but dash it all! She enjoyed the young American's company, and also trusted him to be professional. "That is all right with me," she finally said. "But first some supper and a bit of time to clean up!"

They walked down the hill together as the shadows began to lengthen. Their conversation was less ebullient and humorous than the night before, but all of them were gripped with excitement at the thought of viewing a first-hand written account of the most pivotal event in history. Josh asked MacDonald how long before they could begin to unroll and read the scrolls.

"I imagine that if we break the seals within forty-eight hours of placing them in the tank, the scrolls will start to unroll a bit within the next day or so. It can be a long and tedious process. We usually are able to expose no more than about ten or fifteen centimeters of the scroll at a time. The Pilate scroll appears to be perhaps two meters in length. One thing I have learned about papyrus scrolls is that no two are alike. Some unroll fairly easily once rehydrated; others are very, very stubborn. I would say that it might be anywhere from two to ten days before we should be able to read the entire contents of each scroll from beginning to end."

"Can you imagine the reaction when we reveal this find to the world?" asked Giuseppe.

"I think the reaction will depend, to a great extent, on the contents," said Josh.

"What do you mean?" asked Isabella.

"Within intellectual circles throughout the West, there is a great hostility to Christianity in modern thought," replied the young American. "If this document is what we think it is, and the account confirms the New Testament narrative, there will be a large segment of the intelligentsia in Europe and the United States who will denounce it as a fraud and do their best to debunk it."

"Don't forget the Islamic world," said Father MacDonald. "It is an article of faith for them that the 'Prophet Isa,' as they call our Lord, was 'neither crucified nor killed, but it only had the appearance of it,' according to the Quran. If this narrative calls that into question, there will be opposition from them too."

"And, of course," said Giuseppe, "if this account disputes any of the claims of the New Testament, many Christians will clamor that it must be faked as well."

"You may be right," said Joshua.

They ate a quick supper at Rossini's house, ordering out from Mrs. Bustamante's excellent menu, and everyone took advantage of real toilet facilities to clean up, wash off, and shave. After a brief confab and an agreement that all of them would be on-site by seven AM, Joshua and Isabella walked up the Via Tiberio back to the ancient ruin where they had met and spend so much time together over the course of the week.

As they walked together, Isabella asked a question that she had been turning over in her mind ever since the earlier conversation between the team on the way down to supper.

"Josh," she said. "What will you do—if this is the account of Jesus' trial, and it contradicts the narrative your entire faith is based on?"

"I have been thinking about that ever since I read that inscription," he said. "I'll say this first—I really don't expect it to contradict the Gospel accounts. Why would Justin Martyr appeal to Pilate's report if it didn't back up what he was saying? It would be too risky to do so if the report contained information that was harmful to the Christian cause. But, if the *Testimonium* should contradict what is in the Scriptures, I would analyze its contents very carefully. I would see if Pilate was speaking from his convictions as a Roman or from first-hand testimony. If everything stood rock solid against my beliefs, I would, well—I'm not sure. I would take a long hard look at my beliefs, but I am not sure that I would abandon them altogether."

Isabella digested that a moment, and then spoke again. "Why is it so important whether or not Jesus actually rose from the dead? I mean, I was raised in the church like about every other Italian girl, and I have read the gospels and heard the homilies. Many of the teachings of Jesus recorded in the Scriptures are quite beautiful and express very high moral and ethical standards. But would they be any less so if it turned out that Jesus is still in his grave? Plato and Confucius died, but their teachings are still foundational to Western and Eastern intellectual thought."

Josh nodded. "There is an enormous difference, though, between the teachings of Jesus and those of every other philosopher in the history of the world," he said. "Plato, Aristotle, Buddha, Seneca, Thomas Aquinas, even Muhammad—all of them spoke as mere mortals. They never claimed to be anything but inspired teachers or enlightened individuals. Even Muhammad never claimed to be anything more than God's prophet. But Jesus of Nazareth was different. He actually claimed to be the Son of God—and more than that, he claimed that He and God were One. His teachings were entirely rooted in this concept of his own uniqueness, and if you take out His claim of divinity, then much of what He taught makes no sense at all."

"Did He really claim to be the Son of God," asked Isabella, "or was that claim retroactively applied to Him by those who came later? I have read the works of many modern scholars who say that Christ was deified long after His death, and that He Himself never made any claim to divinity."

Josh nodded. "Of course modern scholars want to say that, especially in America!" he said. "You must remember, my country still has more practicing Christians than any nation in the Western world. You don't win an audience in America by bad-mouthing Jesus! Or at least, you couldn't until very recently. And if you acknowledge that the Gospels accurately record the words of Jesus, then you have to either dismiss Him as an outright fraud or a delusional lunatic in order to reject His claim to divinity. So the easy way out, if you don't want to face the truth of who He was, is to say that the Gospels are a pastiche of myth and legend, built up around a historical figure, that transformed him from a revolutionary religious teacher to an actual deity."

"But doesn't that make more sense than God becoming a carpenter, of all things?" she asked. "After all, the Gospels weren't written down till over fifty years after the Crucifixion. A lot of stuff could be made up in that interval of time."

"If those are the correct dates, you might be right—although not necessarily, even then," said Josh. "However, modern scholarship has pushed the dates of the Gospels back considerably. For example, look at the books of Luke and Acts. Both by the same author, and written a short time apart—virtually every Bible scholar on earth agrees on that. But Acts ends with Paul under house arrest in Rome, awaiting trial before Caesar. It never tells us how the trial came out, if Paul was condemned or freed, and then we have Paul's pastoral letters which seem to indicate that he was released and made one last missionary journey before the Great Fire in 66 AD. That journey should be chronicled in Acts—but it isn't. I've always thought that the most logical explanation is that Luke wrote his Gospel, and the book of Acts, before Paul's first trial in Rome, as a defense brief of sorts. That would mean that both of those works were completed no later than 62 AD, less than thirty years after the crucifixion. And since the similarities in language lead most scholars to believe that Luke used both Matthew and Mark as sources for his account, then both those Gospels were in existence by then as well! That leaves only John as a later account, and even the early Church agreed that John wrote his Gospel from Ephesus when he was in his nineties, sixty years after the time of Christ and thirty years after the three Synoptic Gospels!"

"I'd never thought about it that way," said Isabella. "But still, thirty years is a considerable gap of time."

"It is, but do you think it is long enough to make up a claim as drastic as saying that a crucified rabbi, who died in disgrace, was actually the resurrected Son of God? And don't forget, Paul wrote Galatians around 48 AD or so, only fifteen years after the crucifixion, and it contains numerous references to Jesus as the Risen Lord of Life. Then there is the account in I Corinthians 15, where Paul recites a whole list of witnesses who actually saw Jesus after the Resurrection, and makes reference to having been taught that list right after he became a Christian—which was only five years or so after the event!"

She threw up her hands in mock surrender. "OK, OK!" she laughed. "So the Gospels accurately record that the early Church believed in the Resurrection. That doesn't mean it actually happened!"

"But if it didn't happen, then where did that belief come from?" asked Josh.

"Someone could have moved the body," answered Isabella.

"That wouldn't account for the resurrection appearances," Josh replied.

"Maybe Jesus wasn't dead when they placed Him in the tomb," she mused. "It could be that He revived and escaped and they mistook it for a resurrection from the dead!"

"That theory has been around for a while," said Josh. "But it has so many holes in it that it's hardly worth consideration!"

"Like what?" she asked.

"First of all, the physical trauma Jesus endured," Josh replied. "He was beaten, scourged, and nailed to a wooden cross, where He hung suspended by the weight of His arms for six hours, slowly pulling His shoulders out of socket and filling His lungs with fluid. And let's not forget John's account—he says that when the soldiers came to Jesus' cross, they didn't break His legs because He was already dead—but they did skewer Him with a spear! John felt that detail was important enough that he—or maybe the scribe who he was dictating to—immediately afterward added: *'And he who has seen has born witness, and we know that his witness is true; and he knows that he is telling the truth, that you also might believe.'* Now, suppose, despite all that, that somehow Jesus' heart was still beating when they took Him down from the cross. Somehow the fact that he was alive had to have escaped their notice, because they immediately took Him, wrapped Him in cloths soaked in aromatic spices, laid Him on a stone slab, and sealed Him in a tomb." Josh paused a moment. "So tell me, Dr. Sforza—" He raised his eyebrows as he gazed at her. "What happens to someone suffering from severe blood loss, shock, and trauma when you wrap him in damp, wet cloths and lay him on a cold stone slab?"

"I am guessing that he would develop severe hypothermia, slip further into shock and unconsciousness, and die?" she guessed.

"Bingo!" Josh said. "But let's suppose for a minute that, somehow, Jesus did survive, struggled out of his wrappings, pushed aside the stone, bypassed the guards posted over the tomb, and got away. He would be exhausted, near death, unable to use his hands or feet due to His injuries, and bleeding internally from the spear wound. Even if His disciples found him and somehow nursed Him back to health—well, I think it was C.S. Lewis who said something to the effect that: 'Could such a pathetic creature, weak, emaciated, and in desperate need of medical attention, be mistaken by anyone for the risen and triumphant Lord of Life?'"

Isabella was a bit overwhelmed by the force of his argument. Her scientific, rational side inherently struggled to reject any notion of a supernatural being breaking into human history. But at the same time, Josh made a compelling argument that such an event had actually happened some two thousand years before! She thought of another line of defense.

"But what if the disciples just made the whole thing up?" she said. "Suppose they really did write the Gospels, but the whole thing was just a fraud that got out of hand?"

"That's the last line of defense for the skeptic," Josh said. "And, there is a certain logic to it. But first of all, consider that the Apostles valued truth above all. They praised it and encouraged it among all their followers. They would have to be absolutely amoral to proclaim truthfulness so loudly while knowingly basing their whole new faith on a lie. And think about this—every account we have indicates that all of the early disciples except John were martyred for their faith—and even he was beaten on several occasions, and then exiled to Patmos for years. The apostles willingly went to their deaths proclaiming their faith in the risen Christ and believing He would raise them up again. If there is one thing that history demonstrates, Isabella, it is that men will die for a lie—

IF they believe it to be the truth. But who on earth would cheerfully die for a lie, KNOWING that it was a lie?"

"It does seem unlikely," she said.

"And one more thing," he said. "Even if the apostles lied, and made up the story of the Resurrection—what about good old Pilate, and the High Priest Caiaphas, and all the others who conspired to put Jesus to death? Don't you think they would have produced the body to scotch the story of the Resurrection as soon as it was proclaimed?"

"Well, you have made one thing very clear," said Isabella. "Two, actually."

"What would those things be?" asked Josh.

"You are certainly convinced by the evidence," she said. "And, you have done your homework on the subject. Your knowledge and eloquence are most impressive!"

"But you're not buying it?" he asked with a twinkle in his eye.

"Let's just say you have given me some things to think about," she answered. By now they were at the mountaintop.

Ibrahim al-Ghazi walked over from the tent where the security guards slept. "Dr. Sforza," he said, "do you mind if I walk into town during my off shift tomorrow?"

"Not at all," she said. "Is there something you need that one of the team could get for you, or is it something you need to tend to yourself?"

"Well, actually," the young Arab-Italian said, "I would like to go to mosque. I am not the most observant Muslim in the world, but my mother pesters me if I don't go at least once a month!"

Sforza laughed. "I think my mother has despaired of ever getting me to Mass again," she said. "But by all means, go ahead. Just remember, no loose talk about what is going on up here!"

"No worries," he replied. "I love archeology, and I think that your discoveries here are amazing!" He ambled back to his tent, and Josh and Isabella stepped into the lab and took a long look at the two ancient scrolls sitting in the rehydration tanks.

"We have barely talked about the will of Augustus," said Isabella.

"You're right," Josh said. "But honestly, that's hardly surprising. After all, we know most of what is in it. Several ancient histories have cited some of its terms. And, to be honest, even if we found that what

Suetonius wrote about the will was completely false, it would only be of interest to professional historians. The Pilate scroll, on the other hand, has the potential to affect the lives of billions of people worldwide!"

"Very true," she said. "But I am tired of talking about dusty old documents. I want to know more about you, Doctor Parker."

Josh looked at her, surprised. "What would you like to know?" he asked.

"I guess, mainly," she said with some hesitation—"Why isn't there a Mrs. Doctor Parker?"

Josh shrugged his shoulders. "I just never met the right person, I guess," he said. "I dated some in high school, but in college the whole social scene was such a turn-off, and I was so buried in my studies, and then in my work, that I just haven't really had time to go looking for someone. But, I suppose if someone ever comes knocking, they will find me at home," he added. That was as close as he would come to admitting he was fascinated with this beautiful Italian scientist.

She looked at him with amusement. "You are charming in the most awkward way!" she laughed. "I am going to commandeer this couch in the lab for my bed, so to avoid gossip; I suggest you take one of the tents for the night."

He looked at his watch. It was already well past 10 PM, and the ups and downs of the day had left him completely drained. "I am completely worn out," he said. "I think I will bunk down too."

She gave him an affectionate hug, and he stepped outside into the cool Mediterranean night. A million stars blazed overhead, and the moon was just cresting the eastern horizon. He walked over to the ancient chamber that had occupied their whole week. With all the artifacts removed, there was no need to cover it at night any more. In the dim light, it seemed somewhat forlorn, bereft of its secrets and desolate. He stepped inside and closed his eyes, trying to imagine the Emperor Tiberius huddled over the small table by the light of an oil lamp, writing letters that dictated the fate of a quarter of the world's population. Then he went to his tent and went to sleep.

By this time, your Excellency, I was rapidly running out of options. I pulled Jesus back into the Praetorium and looked at him in frustration. Those remarkable eyes stared into mine through the blood, bruises, and grime without a trace of fear, which began to anger me. "Where are you really from?" I demanded. He gave no answer. "Why will you not speak to me?" I shouted. "Don't you know that I have the authority to crucify you, or to set you free?"

He answered softly, "You would have no authority over me at all except for that which is given you from Heaven," he said. "You do not understand what you are doing; therefore the ones who delivered me up to you have the greater guilt."

Caesar, I am not a superstitious man, and I am certainly no coward. But I will tell you in confidence that his words shook me to the core. I felt as if I was the one on trial, and that this strange figure before me had somehow found me wanting. I led him back out before the mob. They were still screaming for the Galilean's blood.

"Behold, I bring him forth to tell you that I find no guilt in him!" I cried for the last time.

Then the old High Priest, Annas, lifted his voice to be heard. "If you release this man, you are no friend of Caesar! Everyone who proclaims Himself a King is Caesar's enemy!" The threat was very clear—he would report me to you unless I did his bidding.

CHAPTER TWELVE

Josh slept soundly, without dreams or interruptions, despite the hard ground beneath his sleeping bag. Isabella had a more difficult time getting comfortable on the narrow couch, but finally dozed off after midnight. They both woke up around 6 AM and brewed some coffee after changing clothes and brushing their teeth. The rest of the team arrived around 7 AM, and Isabella talked to them over breakfast.

"The entire Bureau of Antiquities will be arriving around eight thirty AM," she began. "They will want to tour the site and view the artifacts, and then Dr. Castolfo wants to hold a formal meeting of the board at Giuseppe's home. Speaking of which, Dr. Rossini, a couple of the board members are not the most ambulatory—Dr. Stefani is eighty-three, and gets around with difficulty, and Cardinal Raphael is the same age, although he is more spry. Do you think that Chief Rosario could have a couple of golf carts brought up to the head of the trail?"

"I will call him right now," said Giuseppe, stepping out of the trailer.

"Because of the spectacular nature of this find, we should be prepared to face sharp questions, both from the board and later, when we begin to release the news of the discovery to the public. Fortunately, we have recorded every part of the excavation on digital video, and have been meticulous in our documentation. It will be very hard for anyone to claim fraud, no matter what the scrolls actually contain. But I want our presentation to be clear, concise, and professional. Dr. MacDonald, I want you to lay out all the artifacts that can withstand open-air inspection, and have all the items that are still in rehydration tanks in clear view and ready for inspection through the glass. Be honest, professional, and humble—there will be about five hundred years of archeological and historical experience represented by these board members! Now, let us spend the last hour before their arrival getting the lab cleaned up and presentable," she finished.

In short order, the trash cans were emptied and several chairs were set up. The less fragile artifacts were laid out on trays with small labels describing them, and the items in the rehydration tanks were also labeled. The two scrolls from the locked cabinet were already changing slightly in color as the humidity was restored to them. Even the ancient seals were a richer hue of red than they had been, as the desiccated wax cells began to rehydrate.

They had barely finished cleaning up when the now-familiar sounds of a helicopter began to draw near. The entire team traipsed up the stairs to the large flagstone floor that had become a landing pad for the site. As the chopper settled to earth, ten people emerged one after the other. First on the site was Dr. Sinisi, looking tanned and fit, his legendary smile flashing in the morning sun. Next came the Head of the Antiquities Bureau, Dr. Benito Castolfo. A heavyset and serious individual, he was well connected in the Byzantine world of Italian politics, and was respected by academics both for his credentials as a classical historian and his bulldog-like determination to preserve funding for the preservation of Italy's rich past, no matter how dire the budget forecasts.

Next came Dr. Guioccini, who smiled at the team and gave Isabella a quick thumbs-up. He then turned to assist the elderly Dr. Marc Stefani, a renowned Biblical archeologist and the oldest member of the Bureau's governing board. After the old man had gotten his feet under him and taken his place beside the others, Dr. Antonio Neapolitano emerged. He was a prehistoric archeologist who had excavated numerous Stone Age sites in Italy. After him, Cardinal Caesar Raphael emerged. He was the Vatican's most respected archeologist and acted as a liaison between the worlds of science and faith, and was also Father MacDonald's supervisor and mentor. He made a deliberate show of helping the next member off the chopper with a courtly old-world flourish. Dr. Maria Tintoretto returned his gesture with a scowl. A respected historian of the first century, she was also a militant atheist and devoted much of her scholarship to questioning almost every aspect of the Church's early history—a stance that made her a frequent butt of jokes among Italy's overwhelmingly Catholic population. The fact that the Cardinal inevitably treated her with great courtesy and respect only increased her hostility, since she took it as a deliberate slight. After her came Dr. Luigi Castellani, a military historian and expert in Roman weapons and tactics. He was followed by Ricardo Gandolfo, who was not an academic but a special assistant to Italy's president in matters related to history and antiquities.

After they were all assembled on the ancient flagstones, Dr. Sforza introduced them to the team.

"Most of you know Dr. Rossini, the discoverer of the chamber," she said, "and you may be familiar with the work of Simone Apriceno, our paleobotanist. Father MacDonald is a renowned expert in ancient documents, and our American friend Josh Parker is an up and coming expert in first century classical archeology. His work at Ephesus was most impressive, and he comes to us with the strongest of recommendations."

The board members greeted the team cordially, although Dr. Tintoretto scowled at Father MacDonald. "I don't see why it is necessary to have a representative of a religious cult as a consultant on a scientific and historical excavation project," she snorted.

MacDonald gave her his best smile. "My clerical collar notwithstanding, dear lady, I will stack my professional credentials and qualifications up against any university archeologist you can find! Not to mention that, when the things we find have a strong bearing on the beliefs of one billion people, it only makes sense to have someone who understands those beliefs as witness to the discovery."

Cardinal Raphael nodded appreciatively, but Tintoretto simply glared and moved on. Isabella led them down to the level where the mobile lab was, and walked them over to the chamber first. "Every scrap of evidence we have found so far indicates that this chamber has been sealed up tight since 37 AD," she said. "The lack of moisture and heavy accumulation of stone dust covered and preserved all the artifacts inside remarkably well. Here next to the entrance we found a Roman era curule chair and a small writing table. On top of the table, covered by stone dust, we found an inkwell, a signet ring bearing the name and seal of Tiberius Caesar, an ancient quill pen, and most remarkably, a letter written by Tiberius himself to his steward, directing that the chamber and its contents be sealed up after he departed for Rome. In the niche above the door, we found an ancient bronze oil lamp, with a fair sample of congealed oil still preserved in its reservoir. The writing table also had a small drawer concealed beneath it. Inside we found some blank papyrus sheets and a leather coin purse which held an ivory horse head effigy key, a metal arrowhead, and some coins, all dating to the Tiberian era or earlier."

The board members were crowding into the ancient chamber, studying its walls and pointing at the ancient graffiti that still adorned them. Isabella let them continue for a moment, and then went on. "At the rear of the room was a reliquary about one point four meters tall and wide, and about point three meters deep. The exterior doors were unlocked. Leaning against the reliquary, still in its scabbard, was a perfectly preserved Roman *gladius* that, judging from the inscription on the scabbard, once belonged to Julius Caesar. Opening the reliquary, we were disappointed to find that rats had gotten into the cabinet in ancient times and destroyed most of the documents inside. However, having removed all the fragments, we believe it should be possible to reassemble most of the documents in time. We also found a beautiful cameo portrait—white marble on black obsidian—that apparently depicts Tiberius' first wife, Vipsania, as well as fragmentary remains of several garments."

"Interesting summary, Dr. Sforza," said Dr. Castolfo, "but now get to the reason we are all gathered here!"

She nodded. "There was a locked compartment inside the reliquary which we were able to open with the ancient key we found. Inside the compartment were two perfectly preserved scrolls. Each was still sealed with the signet of the Emperor Tiberius, but a short title had been inscribed on the outside of each scroll. One was labeled as the last will and testament of Caesar Augustus." There were some murmurs at that—apparently not all the board members were aware of what had been found inside the chamber. She paused until the board was focused on her again, and continued. "The last item was simply labeled as 'The Testimony of Pontius Pilate, Governor of Judea.'"

"Remarkable!" said Cardinal Raphael.

"An amazing discovery!" said Sinisi, beaming.

"Has either of the scrolls been opened?" asked Tintoretto.

"No," said Isabella. "They are both in rehydration tanks currently. Father MacDonald will supervise their unrolling when they are stable enough to be opened without damage."

"Are you sure you can trust his objectivity?" she asked.

"Doctor, this is outrageous!" snapped Cardinal Raphael. "Duncan MacDonald's professionalism is without reproach!"

"But will it remain so if something in that scroll contradicts the Christ myth that you people have used to hold back human progress for two thousand years?" she inquired venomously.

The president of the Antiquities Bureau cut in sharply. "Doctor, your hostility to the Church is well known, but your comments are unprofessional and frankly offensive. We are all scientists here!"

She looked at him and sighed. "I'm not accustomed to seeing true scientists wearing the trappings of an ancient fertility cult," she said. "But perhaps I overstepped. Doctor MacDonald, I apologize."

"Apology accepted, *Doctor*," said MacDonald, but the look in his eyes showed that he was still deeply offended.

"There is nothing more to see inside the chamber," said Isabella. "Let's go to the lab and you can view the artifacts for yourselves."

The group filed across the ancient courtyard, several of them admiring the ancient Roman architecture as they went. Dr. Stefani spoke to Rossini as they moved toward the lab. "Giuseppe, do you remember when I supervised your work at this site back in 1984?" he asked.

"Like it was yesterday," said Rossini.

"How many times did you and the other youngsters race up and down these steps at the end of the day?" the old man asked.

"Almost every day," said Rossini. "After sitting in a hole all day, scraping dirt back one layer at a time and bagging every masonry chip and corroded ancient coin we uncovered, it was a great way to stretch our legs and blow off some steam."

"And none of us thought that, the whole time, the greatest archeological discovery of the modern age was right beneath our feet!" said Stefani.

"Tiberius' steward did a good job of concealing the place," said Rossini. "Had it not been for the earthquake, who knows how long we would have waited for the chamber to be revealed."

"All things happen for a reason," said Cardinal Raphael. "God chose this moment to reveal whatever was concealed in that chamber."

"Or this was the first earthquake with enough magnitude to strike the area after time and erosion had weakened the wall sufficiently enough for it to collapse," snapped Tintoretto.

Josh had already decided that he did not like this woman, but kept his mouth shut for the time being. He was well aware that he was not only the junior member of this team, but also a foreigner. He cast a glance over at Isabella, who looked at him apologetically.

Moments later they were inside the trailer. The two benches from the small table inside had been scooted together to face the main workstation, and several folding chairs had been added. There was just room enough for the board members—with the exception of Isabella—to all be seated, while the team stood facing them. Isabella had prepared a montage of video clips and still shots of the chamber, beginning with the first ones of her and Rossini entering the chamber Monday morning. Rossini described his discovery of the chamber briefly, and then she showed the clip of them cleaning off the top of the ancient writing table, taking the time to show the artifacts they had uncovered. All but the ancient quill were on top of the large metal table arranged on covered trays in the order of their discovery. Sforza allowed the board members to pass the ancient signet ring around, since it was the most durable of the artifacts they had uncovered.

Then Father MacDonald and Josh described the process of cleaning and translating the initial letter from the Emperor Tiberius, and Simone Apriceno described the laborious process of cleaning the thick layer of stone dust that had enveloped every artifact and surface in the chamber. The photographs and video clearly showed the undisturbed nature of the sediments, and even the skeptical Tintoretto nodded in appreciation of the paleobotanist's impeccable field technique. When Apriceno arrived at the discovery of the *gladius* and its scabbard, everyone leaned forward.

Josh spoke for the first time, describing how he and MacDonald had carefully removed the ancient blade from the chamber and found the inscriptions on the pommel and scabbard. At this point Dr. Castellani spoke up. "Dr. Parker, I know that we need to move this proceeding along as quickly as possible, but may I please examine the blade for just a moment?"

Josh looked at Dr. Castolfo, who nodded, and handed the ancient weapon, hilt first, to the military historian. Castellani hefted the blade in his hand for a moment, then held it straight out and looked down the blade, seeing the original metal finish still gleaming in places despite the rust of twenty-one centuries. He closed his eyes and murmured softly: "Britannia, Spain, Alesium, Pharsalus, the Nile, Munda—this blade was used in the battles that shaped our world, by the greatest general who ever lived! Forgive me, ladies and gentlemen; I know you are more concerned with the scroll from Pontius Pilate, but for a military historian like me, holding this blade is a truly religious experience!" He sighed deeply and handed the blade back to Josh, who placed it on the table.

Isabella continued, describing the reliquary and showing its rich carvings and compartmentalized interior to the board, then showing them some of the scraps that they had recovered from the shredded hoard of ancient documents. Finally, she showed them the compartment up top, and the ancient key that had opened it. Then she sat down and allowed Josh and Father MacDonald to describe the final stages of the excavation, as they had removed the cabinet from the chamber and opened the small cubby that had held the two precious scrolls. Josh discussed how the scrolls had been removed and the inscriptions read the day before, and then led the board members to look at the two rehydration tanks where the ancient papyrus was slowly soaking up enough sterile moisture to allow it to be unrolled for the first time since 37 AD.

When the presentation was finished, Dr. Castolfo stood and spoke to the team and the board alike. "First of all," he said, "I want to congratulate the team on its amazing discoveries, and on the consummately professional field techniques you used to uncover and remove the artifacts, while working in a quick and efficient manner under unusual circumstances. Dr. Sforza, Dr. Guioccini, you could not have chosen a better team for this sensitive and significant excavation."

He paused a moment and applauded the team, joined by the members of the governing board. The five archeologists who had labored all week on the site bowed modestly, and then he continued. "Secondly, now that all artifacts have been cleared from the chamber, I think it is high time we removed everything to a more suitable laboratory for further examination. I have a team of technicians standing by; they will carefully transport all the artifacts back to the mainland, and then remove the mobile lab and all of the gear associated with it, so that Capri can have its tourist attraction back. Dr. Rossini, with your permission, I am going to appoint a temporary resident archeologist to cover your duties here on the island for now. You have certainly earned the right to take part in the analysis and curation of these artifacts!" Giuseppe nodded his assent, and the board's president continued. "I would ask all members of the team to remove your personal effects from the lab and the site before we head down to Dr. Rossini's home for our meeting. All the artifacts should be set up in our new research lab at the museum in Naples by tomorrow morning, and I would ask that all of you be there, ready to work, by ten o'clock in the morning. I know it will be Saturday, but I'd like you to get acquainted with our lab and make sure that none of the artifacts have been mishandled. You may catch regular transport to the mainland if you like, or return with us by helicopter this afternoon. Monday your work begins in earnest. I am looking forward to seeing the result of your continued labors on this remarkable discovery."

Josh and the team looked at one another. It would be a relief to be away from the island, but at the same time, he would miss this place where he had met and been accepted by four very impressive individuals. He was glad that he would be able to continue to work with them all for a good bit longer. Father MacDonald caught his gaze and gave him a wink, while Isabella glanced at him with a smile that made his knees go weak. Yes, it would be nice to get to work with her for a good long while yet!

Castolfo was wrapping up. "Now it is time for us to officially meet, as a board, with the five of you and discuss where we go from here. Dr. Rossini has graciously volunteered his home for this purpose, so at this point I will ask that we wrap up here and begin making our way down to Capri village. I believe that is all."

The board members rose and shook hands with the team, several of them offering words of congratulations and encouragement. Even Dr. Tintoretto seemed to be less confrontational. Cardinal Raphael stared for a long time at the Pontius Pilate scroll, while Castellani gazed lovingly at the ancient *gladius* that had once been carried by Julius Caesar. As the board members left one by one, Josh asked Isabella what she wanted to do about traveling to the mainland. Rossini, who was standing by her, said, "I think we should all spend the evening at my home and celebrate the successful conclusion of our dig!" The rest of the team nodded in agreement, and, with that settled, they quickly cleared their personal gear out of the trailer and tents before hiking down the hill toward the village.

* * *

As the archeologists were preparing for their trip down the mountain, Ibrahim al-Ghazi was cleansing himself before entering the small mosque that was a few miles down the road from Capri village. This ritual washing, called the *wudu* in Arabic, was obligatory before entering the mosque's prayer chamber. Once he was done, he stepped into the *musallah*, or prayer chamber, where the local imam was preparing himself to conduct the Friday noon service. The Muslim population of Capri was fairly small, and there were fewer than fifty people in the room when the service began a few moments later.

Ibrahim bowed and touched his forehead to the floor as he had done many times before. He was not a deeply religious man, but he did believe in Allah the Creator. Given the events of the last fifteen years, he thought, it was a shame that more Muslims could not adopt a tolerant attitude toward Western culture. It grieved him that so many of his co-religionists seemed to be stuck in a medieval mindset that saw ongoing jihad as the only way to advance their faith. He said his own prayer, incorporating the ancient words and phrases, but adding his own plea for greater understanding and peace between religions.

After the prayers were done, the imam stood and preached a short message, calling on the congregation to observe the Five Pillars, and reminding them that the best way to advance the cause of Islam in a nation of Catholic Christians was to live as exemplary citizens, to obey the laws, and respect the ways of their Italian neighbors. In short, it was a message of peace and moderation that Ibrahim was pleasantly surprised by. His parents' imam was much more confrontational, lacing his sermons with scathing denunciations of Israel, America, and Western culture in general, which was one reason he rarely attended their mosque anymore. He decided to thank the Imam after the service ended.

As the other worshippers departed, Ibrahim made a polite bow the imam, who had shed his traditional robes and was clad beneath in a well-tailored white suit. "That was an exceptionally good sermon," said Ibrahim. "I wish more imams preached your message of peace."

The imam smiled. "Ours is the religion of peace, is it not?" he asked. "How can I preach anything else?" Ibrahim nodded in agreement. The imam studied him curiously. "I am Imam Muhammad al Medina," he said. "You know, there are very few Muslims that live on this island, and I know all of them by sight, but I have never seen you before. Are you a tourist?"

Ibrahim shook his head. "No, I am working as a security guard on an archeological dig," he said. Surely that harmless admission would not hurt anyone.

The imam nodded brightly. "Oh, that would be Dr. Rossini's dig at the Villa Jovis! It sounds so fascinating. Have you gotten to see any of the artifacts yet? He told me that everything they found dates all the way back to the time of Tiberius Caesar himself!" That was partly true. Rossini had been talking to his fellow team members at Madame

Bustamante's restaurant, but Muhammad had been quietly listening in on every word.

Ibrahim smiled. Obviously this charming imam was a friend of Rossini's who was familiar with the dig, and could be trusted. "That is right!" he said. "But apparently they found something really big yesterday, because this morning a helicopter brought in ten people to view the site and meet with the team."

The imam nodded, his smile masking his keen interest. "I wonder what it could be?" he mused. "So many interesting things happened in ancient Rome."

The guard nodded, but decided he had said quite enough. "There is no telling," he said. "I'm just paid to keep the tourists out, and it looks like my job is nearly done. I think they have removed all the artifacts from the chamber, and are about to shut down the dig. At any rate, I have tarried too long. I am supposed to begin my watch in an hour. Thank you again for your sermon, and your prayers!"

"And thank you for your faith in the Religion of Truth," said the imam. "Go with Allah's blessing!" He watched as the young man walked away, and his smile faded quickly. Muhammad al Medina, the kind and tolerant imam of Capri's only mosque, was nothing but a mask; one of many that this man had worn in his fifty years. His true name he had nearly forgotten, but the name he claimed for himself was Ali bin-Hassan. That was the name under which he had fought the American crusaders, first in Afghanistan and then in Iraq, and the name by which the CIA was still searching for him. It was the name Sheik Osama had given him when he had joined al-Qaeda long before the devastating blow had been struck against the "Great Satan" on 9/11. He had fought in bin Laden's bodyguard at Tora Bora and protested mightily when the Sheik had sent him to Italy a few years later. "Bury yourself there," the terror leader had told him. "Forget jihad, tell the infidels what they want to hear. Make yourself a spokesman for the heresy known as tolerance until the time comes to strike another great blow for Allah!"

Ali knew what the Sheik had meant. One of bin Laden's dearest plans, known only to himself and a few trusted lieutenants (not, thank Allah, the treacherous dog Khalid Sheik Muhammad!), was to launch a mass attack on the Vatican itself, killing the infidel leader they called "the Pope" and dealing a body blow to Islam's oldest enemy, the Roman Catholic Church. But the fortunes of war had gone against al Qaeda, and the great Sheik was dead. Ali remained in touch with what was left of the organization's leadership, but the dream of burning the Vatican to the ground remained only that until Allah willed otherwise.

But now an unexpected development had occurred. Ali understood that the opportunity for Islam to become the world's fastest-growing religion had been created by two forces—the massive injection of Saudi oil money into missionary work, and the worldwide decline of the heresy known as Christianity. As long as those two trends continued, then the establishment of a worldwide Islamic caliphate was only a matter of time. But if something happened to cause a great revival of Christianity, the cause of jihad would suffer severely. Humanism could never defeat faith, he knew, but faith in a false god could hurt the Religion of Truth deeply. "Know your enemy," the ancient heretics had said. It was good advice. Ali knew the history of Christianity, and the great mistake that they had made in elevating the Prophet Isa (peace be upon him) to being the son of Allah, He who "neither begets, nor is begotten," according to the Prophet. Millions had believed the heresy promoted in the *injil*, the Muslim term for the Gospels of the New Testament. Now a chamber of secrets dating to the time of Isa had been found. Who knew if its contents would advance or hinder the propaganda of the Catholics? Nothing must be allowed to advance the cause of the cursed infidels any further! Not when Islam was winning the battle in the minds of so many. He resolved to find out exactly what they had discovered as soon as possible.

Ibrahim al-Ghazi was completely ignorant of the train of events he had set in motion as he hiked up the Via Tiberio to his job. He thought affectionately of the imam and his words, and thought that, if he saw Dr. Rossini, he would mention his encounter with a man who was obviously the archeologist's friend. But, as chance would have it, he did not see the doctor that afternoon. Or ever again, except on the evening news a week later.

* * *

Dr. Castolfo waited until everyone was seated to begin speaking. Rossini's dinner table had been extended to its maximum size and a couple of leaves added, but the entire board was still only barely able to fit around it. The team members had pulled in two small sofas from the TV room, and were able to sit together, facing the board. It was cozy, as

Rossini had said the day before, but it made it easy for everyone to see and hear what transpired.

"This unique discovery has the potential to reveal historical truths that will deeply affect the world's largest religion," he said. "All the more reason that we must proceed with the highest of scientific integrity and flawless procedure. The scrolls will be handled by a team of three highly trained lab technicians under armed guard until they are safe in the new research lab at the National Archeological Museum in Naples. Once they are safely there, access will be restricted to the members of this board and the five members of the excavating team. Should further examination by international experts be deemed necessary, the board will have to grant its approval. Whatever is in that scroll, even if it is only Pontius Pilate's grocery list, we do not want anyone to be able to question its authenticity!"

The other board members nodded their agreement, and Dr. Sinisi raised his hand for recognition. "Go ahead, Vincent," said the president.

Sinisi stood and addressed the room with his textbook charm. "What we have here is not only an archeological and historical discovery of the highest magnitude," he said, "but also one of the greatest opportunities for positive publicity in Italian history. When these findings are announced, the world is going to flock to Capri, to see the chamber, and then to Naples, to see the artifacts. We have promised the press an announcement on Monday, and I want us to tell as much as possible. Obviously, we cannot tell them what is in the two scrolls yet, but we can certainly reveal the other artifacts, and the fact that these two scrolls have been discovered and are being prepared for reading and translation. And then when we do announce their contents, the whole world will be listening with rapt attention. The spike in tourism could conceivably cure Italy's current budget woes and do much to restore our national prestige after the recent . . . well, after certain recent events."

Everyone in the room nodded. Even Josh had heard of the scandalous behavior of Italy's last president. Isabella stood, frowning, and asked to be recognized. When Castolfo gave her the nod, she spoke forcefully. "Dr. Sinisi, I do not want to compromise sound science in the name of promoting Italian tourism, patriotism, or any other ulterior motive. You have asked me to put on a dog and pony show for the media, and I will. The sword of Caesar and the other artifacts alone should be enough to create the buzz of interest you seek. The existence of the *Testimonium Pilatus* should NOT be revealed until we know what it contains."

Tintoretto spoke up. "I disagree, Dr. Sforza. You have been too influenced by these clerics masking themselves as scientists. If you keep the find secret, and its contents wind up debunking the foolish myth of the resurrected carpenter, the last thing any scientist should want is for the find to be smothered in secrecy, so the Church can bury it all over again! I vote for full disclosure!"

The Cardinal looked at her, barely concealing his distaste for her prejudice. "For that very reason," he said, "I am forced to agree with my colleague, Dr. Tintoretto. The Church has nothing to fear from history, and I am sure the Holy Father would agree with me on this. Let us announce what we have found, and let the die be cast!"

"But don't you fear creating a media circus that will make it impossible for us to do our work?" asked Rossini.

"The new lab has excellent security," said Castolfo. "We will hire additional guards and request additional funding so that there will be no danger of unauthorized visitors entering the laboratory. Now, on a matter this important, I do think that everyone's input should be recorded. First of all, the team itself. You are the ones who have made this fantastic discovery. How many of you favor full disclosure to the media Monday?"

Josh and Simone Apriceno raised their hands, while the other three team members looked on silently. Finally, Isabella spoke.

"This is the board's decision," she said, "and I am the youngest and least experienced member of the Board. But as a field archeologist employed on this dig, I must vote no. However, when we vote as a board, I will vote with the majority."

"So you are in opposition, as a member of the team?" asked Castolfo. "What about you, Giuseppe? And Father MacDonald?"

"I stand with Isabella," said her mentor. "We need to wait."

MacDonald hesitated before answering. "I shall cast my vote with my young American friend," he said. "Our doctrines must be able to bear investigation."

Castolfo turned to the assembled board of directors, and Isabella crossed the room to stand with them. "Well, colleagues," the president said. "How say you? Do we release the discovery of the scrolls or not? Let those in favor vote first."

Eight hands were raised in favor. Isabella's nay vote was joined by the elderly archeologist Marc Stefani, but she allowed him to voice the opposition. "I must ask that we wait," he said, his voice trembling with age. "I have been an archeologist for fifty years, and I have seen many careers ruined by a desire for too much publicity, too soon. This is a remarkable discovery—let us not endanger it by premature publicity!" Isabella nodded in agreement.

"Dr. Stefani, we all have the greatest respect for your opinion, but it appears you are outvoted this time," the president said gently.

"Although I agree with Dr. Stefani, as promised, I will retract my opposition and vote with the majority," Isabella finally said.

"Very well," Dr. Castolfo concluded. "The press conference will be held on Monday at the National Archeological Museum. I think an abbreviated version of the presentation you gave us would be a splendid way to announce your triumph to the world, Doctors. So tomorrow you can begin putting it together!" He turned to Dr. Rossini. "Thank you so much for your gracious hospitality," he said. "It is time for us to return to Naples, and for the artifacts to be removed to the permanent lab. I am asking all five of you to take the rest of the afternoon off—your excellent work has earned it!"

"But should we not help supervise the removal?" asked Isabella.

"Don't worry, Dr. Sforza," said Castolfo. "I have three professional curators directing the process as we speak. Everything will be in place, ready for you to begin work, tomorrow morning in Naples."

With that, the governing board of the Italian Bureau of Antiquities said their farewells and made their exit, leaving the members of the team staring at one another in silence.

SENSATIONAL ARCHEOLOGICAL DISCOVERY TO BE ANNOUNCED MONDAY BY ITALIAN GOVERNMENT

(AP) An anonymous source within the Italian Bureau of Antiquities has informed the press that a historical discovery of 'paramount importance' has been made on the isle of Capri, where an earthquake recently revealed a long-sealed chamber. While declining to describe exactly what the discovery might be, the source did say that it could have a "profound impact on both Roman history and the early history of Christianity." Speculation abounds as to what Monday's announcement will disclose, and journalists from around the world are congregating in Naples, in advance of Monday's press conference. The chamber has been confirmed as dating to the reign of Tiberius Caesar, who was Emperor of Rome during the earliest years of the Christian era, when Jesus of Nazareth himself is said to have been crucified.

I had done everything in my power, Caesar, to prevent the execution of an innocent man. But at this point our continued government of this troublesome province seemed to me to be hanging by a hair. Personally, I have never been more revolted by the hypocrisy of the Jewish leadership. I called for a basin of water, and sat down in the judgment seat overlooking the crowd. I dipped my hands in the water three times and carefully dried them, then spoke.

"I am innocent of this man's blood!" I cried. "I wash my hands of this whole affair!"

Old Annas spoke again. "Let his blood be on us and on our children!" he shouted back. Even his son-in-law Caiaphas scowled at this remark, and many in the crowd howled their opposition, but the old man glared at them and refused to retract his ridiculous statement. But then that hateful cry of "Crucify, Crucify!" drowned out their argument.

I had had enough. "Take him then, and crucify him!" I snapped to the legionaries. "But I find no guilt in him," I muttered as they left. There was one duty left to attend—listing the formal charge against Jesus, to be posted on the cross above his head. I took a broad-tipped quill and wrote in bold letters: "This is Jesus of Nazareth, King of the Jews!" and ordered my scribe to copy it in Greek and Hebrew. I would accord the strange man this much honor, at least. For in my heart, I think he may have been a king of some sort.

As I returned to my quarters, I found the young disciple of Jesus, whom I had quite forgotten, staring at me with tears streaming down his face. "Get him out of here!" I snapped, and retired to my chambers.

CHAPTER THIRTEEN

"Well, that was fun," said Josh a half hour later. He and Isabella Sforza stood side by side on Dr. Rossini's patio, watching the chopper carrying their discoveries lift off from the Villa Jovis on top of the mountain. Father MacDonald was stretched out on the couch taking a nap, and Dr. Rossini was hunched over a chessboard with Simone Apriceno, waging an epic battle that she was currently winning by a single pawn.

"I cannot believe that they want us to announce the discovery of those two scrolls before we even know what they contain!" she snapped. "I know that Sinisi is a shameless publicity hound, but this is foolish even for him!"

"It's all about PR and money, if Italy is anything like the States," said Josh. "Whenever the government spends too much, history always goes onto the chopping block—or the auction block! I guess they are thinking that the more public interest they can gin up about our discoveries, the more money they can milk out of the legislature in the next session."

"We Italians are proud of our heritage," said Isabella. "There is a great deal of public support already for historical and archeological preservation."

Josh snorted. "I wish that were the case in America!" he laughed. "You are familiar with the Battle of the Alamo, in Texas?"

"Of course," she said. "And I think Billy Bob Thornton was actually a much better David Crockett than John Wayne."

"Many Americans would shoot you for saying that!" laughed Josh. "But Thornton's portrayal was much more accurate, at least. My point in the question was this—the original Alamo compound covered nearly three acres. Most of the fighting actually took place along the perimeter walls or in the 'Long Barracks,' not in the famous chapel. But the city of San Antonio grew up around the site and was allowed to devour everything except the chapel and part of the Long Barracks. The actual place where Travis, the Alamo commander, died is now inside a shoe store. They even allowed a McDonald's to be built on part of the battlefield at Gettysburg, Pennsylvania. And as for archeology—well, understand, most of our sites are Stone Age Native American mounds and such, but still, they sit unexcavated, except by amateur hobbyists if they happen to be on private land, while museums often throw away entire artifact collections that have been bequeathed to them. American archeology is a sad remnant of what it once was, I can tell you that."

She regarded him with affection. He was such a bundle of contradictions, as religious as a preacher, but passionate about science, and with more common sense and decency than any man she had met since—she paused in her thoughts, stunned. It was the first time all day long she had thought of the name of her dead husband. Only a week before, she could not go a minute without recalling his face, his name, his touch. A part of her was angry at the betrayal of his memory, while a larger part was focused on the lanky American next to her. She was so lost in her thoughts that she did not even hear his question. When she saw him staring at her, she realized he was waiting for a response. "I'm sorry," she said. "I was a thousand miles away for a moment there."

"I was asking how you wanted to handle the press conference on Monday," he asked.

"Ah, of course!" she said. "Actually, I think that Dr. Castolfo had a good idea. We will prepare a shorter version of the presentation we did for the Antiquities Board, and bring out some of the more durable artifacts to show and tell for the reporters. They will love it."

"I think that all the other artifacts will be forgotten the moment we announce the Pontius Pilate scroll's discovery," said Josh.

Isabella looked at him sadly. "You know, that is probably true. And a shame it is, too. I understand the scroll's importance, especially if it is what we think it is—but the other discoveries are so amazing, they deserve their day in the sun."

"That is true," said Josh. "But you know, regardless of what is in the scroll, I am going to tell my grandchildren that I was the first person to draw Julius Caesar's sword from its scabbard in two thousand years!"

She smiled. "You know that, in order to have grandchildren, you are, at some point, going to have to have children first."

Josh blushed and changed the subject. "Boy, that one lady professor—Tintoretto, I think her name was? She has no use for the church, does she?" he asked.

"I am not sure what drives her to be so hostile to religion," said Isabella. "I am no true believer like you, but I actually got into an argument with her once because she openly expressed doubt that Jesus ever existed as an actual person!"

"Yet she was once the sweetest little Catholic girl you ever met," said Giuseppe Rossini, who had stepped up behind them without their noticing. They both started, and he laughed. "You two must have guilty consciences!" he said.

"Not particularly," said Josh. "We were just pretty intent on our conversation when you came up behind us. So what happened to the sweet little Catholic girl?"

"Well, it was several years ago," said the archeologist. "I was a young professor, and she was a beautiful twenty-two-year-old grad student. She had a torrid affair with a colleague of mine—a married man. Such things were and are common in universities all over the world, I guess. At any rate, she begged Giovanni, my friend, to leave his wife, and he refused. He was just enough of a faithful Catholic to fear excommunication if he abandoned his spouse, whose uncle was a Cardinal. Then Maria got pregnant, and when he still refused to leave his wife, she aborted the baby. Had to go to France to get it done, as I recall. When she returned, she confronted him with the consequences of his actions—I guess she was hoping to show how devoted she was to him. He called her a baby-killing monster and threw her out of his office. She put up a screaming fit that required security to physically remove her from the building. Giovanni's wife got wind of it and left him, and not long after that, he shot himself. Tintoretto blames the Church for his death and her failed chance at happiness. Ever since then she has dedicated her career to debunking every aspect of Christianity that she can. It has colored her attitude towards archeology to a degree that many in the field refuse to work with her—not because they are true sons of the Church, but because they feel her objectivity is completely compromised."

Josh gave a low whistle of astonishment. "Wow!" he said. "I knew from her face that she was someone who spent a whole lot of time angry—she just radiates hostility in waves. Now I see why." He paused, and then continued. "But we can expect a lot of that kind of hostility if the *Testimonium* indeed is what we suspect. Her kind of militant atheism is rare in the population at large, but in America it is very pervasive in the media, academia, and the entertainment world. There are a lot of people who get rich in my country ridiculing religion, especially Christianity."

Rossini nodded. "I used to think that American evangelicals were a whiny lot, with a persecution complex," he said. "But the more I watch American news and commentary shows, the more I see why they feel the way they do. Well, hopefully by this time next week we will have a good idea as to what the scroll says—at least the first part of it. Then we will see what kind of storm descends on us."

They passed a quiet afternoon at Giuseppe's, catching up on their rest and talking about trivial matters. Josh wondered how his folks were doing back home, and realized with a start he had not spoken to them since his arrival in Italy. He walked over to Isabella. "I was going to call my dad," he said. "Since we are making our big announcement on Monday, can I go ahead and tell him a little bit about what we have found?" he asked.

Isabella laughed. "Since the whole world will know Monday afternoon, I see no harm in letting family have a few hours advance notice. I imagine Sinisi is making a 'strategic leak' to the press as we speak! Just tell him to keep it quiet till Monday."

Josh stepped out onto the patio. Twilight was already gathering, and the songs of Mediterranean nightingales were already audible. He watched geckoes scramble under the porch light, ready to snag the small moths that would come flocking as the darkness grew. The phone rang several times before his father picked up.

"Hi, Dad!" he said as the familiar voice came on the line.

"Josh!" his father replied. "I saw a short mention of the Capri site in the paper yesterday! Is that the dig you are working on?"

"That's right," replied Josh. "We are working out of the Villa Jovis, which was once the home of the Emperor Tiberius. Listen, you and Mom are going to want to watch the news Monday, about five AM your time—it will be noon here. I imagine all the networks will be carrying it, if not live, then right after we finish our press conference in Naples. In fact, I imagine by Monday evening you and Mom may even be getting some calls from reporters."

"Goodness," the old pastor said. "What on earth have you found?"

"Not a word to anyone until Monday, Dad, OK? You have to promise before I can tell you," explained Josh.

"Of course," said his father. "I could not have been a minister for nearly fifty years if I was unable to keep a confidence!"

"I know," said Josh. "I just wanted it to be clear that this conversation is very much in confidence. For about seventy-two more hours, anyway."

"Well, now that we have established that," his father said, "out with it. You have got my curiosity going something fierce."

"All right," said Josh. "Here is a very quick summary of what has happened since I arrived Tuesday. The earthquake that hit here on Capri on Easter Sunday tore open a chamber that had been sealed since about 37 AD. Nothing inside had been disturbed since it was sealed, so everything was perfectly preserved. Before I even got here, they had already found a writing desk and stool, and a signed papyrus letter from the Emperor Tiberius himself, and his signet ring and inkwell! Then as we excavated the rear of the chamber, we discovered a treasure trove of first-century Imperial relics. We found the sword of Julius Caesar, and a reliquary cabinet that once held the funeral masks of the Julian family!"

"Amazing!" said his father. "I am proud you could be a part of such an exciting excavation."

"I haven't gotten to the exciting part yet, Dad!" said Josh with a grin. "Inside the reliquary, we found that most of the documents it contained had been shredded by rats. But there was one small compartment that was locked. Fortunately we had already found the key to the lock in a secret drawer of the writing desk. We opened the compartment and there were two perfectly preserved scrolls. One of them was the last will and testament of Caesar Augustus—well, at least that is what the writing on the outside of the scroll says. But the other—oh, Dad, I nearly fainted when I read it. The scroll is still sealed, but there is an inscription scribbled on the outside of it—it is in the same handwriting as the letter that Tiberius wrote. It says: 'The Testimony of Pontius Pilate, Governor of Judea'!"

There was a long silence on the other end. "You aren't pulling my leg, are you, son?" his father finally asked.

"No, Dad!" Josh assured him. "I'm not above a practical joke, but not about something this important. I think it must be Pilate's report on the Crucifixion. I mean, what else could it be?"

"We know that such a report was made," his father said. "You may well be right. And even if not, to have a written letter from the hand of the man who presided over Jesus' trial—son, this is wonderful!"

Josh thought about his next statement. "Dad, if this is the testimony that Justin Martyr referred to in his 'First Apology,' then this discovery could truly be the greatest archeological confirmation of Christianity ever found!"

His dad agreed. "You are right, son. Understand, of course, faith is exactly that. It cannot be proven, measured, or tested. But I have always believed, and taught you in turn, that faith need not be blind. Christianity rests on a firm foundation of real history. You may have well found a significant cornerstone of that foundation. Well done, my boy!"

"Thanks, Dad!" Josh said. His father had always been an encouragement to him, even when he disagreed with some of Josh's choices, but to hear such pride in the old man's voice warmed Josh's heart. So God did have a reason for leading Josh away from the pulpit and into an archeology degree! Josh then asked about his mother, and the church at home, and the Rangers' seasonal prospects, and so the conversation meandered along for another thirty minutes before Josh hung up. He never saw the figure lurking in the shadows, and it did not move away until he went back inside.

Ali bin-Hassan had heard enough. So the Christian infidels thought they had found proof of the Crucifixion of Isa, eh? As a devout Muslim, Hassan knew that virtually everything the Christians taught about Isa was wrong. The Prophet had revealed the truth in the Quran, that Isa "was crucified not, nor did he die, but it only had the appearance thereof." The *injil* of Barnabas, which the infidels rejected, told the true story: that Allah had caught the Prophet Isa (peace be upon him) up to Paradise, and caused the treacherous Judas to be transformed into his likeness, so that the Romans had crucified, not the Galilean, but the very one who had betrayed him! But of course, the media would never tell the truth. If the scroll were opened and read, it would be an inspiration and encouragement to Christians worldwide, and all the gains Islam had made might be threatened. Hassan made up his mind that the scroll, and its discoverers, must be destroyed. As he slipped quietly through Capri village, to the small house near the mosque where he lived, he thought about how to best accomplish that.

Back at the house, the five archeologists prepared for dinner. Rossini had ordered out from Mrs. Bustamante's place, since none of them felt like going out for dinner, and she had delivered the meals in person moments earlier. He knew that the restaurateur did not normally leave the kitchen during the supper hours, and thanked her profusely, paying almost twice what the food was worth.

"Giuseppe, you old fool, you gave me too much!" she protested.

166

"After the hospitality you have lavished on my guests, it is the least I could do," he said. "Not to mention the many kindnesses you have shown to me through the years!"

"Well, someone has to make sure the lonely old widowers on this island are properly fed!" she replied.

Giuseppe worked up his courage. "This lonely old widower would like to show his thanks," he said. "After I return from Naples next week, would you like to go the cinema, or perhaps an opera, with me?"

"I thought you would never ask!" the Spanish restaurateur replied. "I should be most delighted to be your date!"

Rossini was beaming from ear to ear as he served the dishes to his friends. Isabella watched him, then whispered to Josh, "I bet he finally did it!" He raised an eyebrow in curiosity. "He's been mooning over Antonia for a long time," she explained. "I think he must have finally asked her out!"

Josh looked at the lovely Italian next to him. Her olive skin was deeply tanned, and the tiny laugh lines around her eyes only enhanced her Mediterranean beauty. "Speaking of which," he said. She turned and eyed him expectantly. "I was thinking that, once we get to Naples, perhaps you and I could—you know, maybe one evening, go and—"

She smiled at his awkwardness. How could a man this handsome be so uncomfortable around women? "I would very much enjoy spending an evening on the town with you," she said. "But let's get this damnable press conference over with first!"

The dinner was magnificent—Mrs. Bustamante had outdone herself this time. Steaming plates of pasta with every sauce imaginable, savory chicken diced fine and marinated until it was falling apart, calzones stuffed full of every variety of meat, cheeses, and vegetables, with hot fresh Italian bread rolls. The archeologists fell to with a vengeance, but it was apparent after a half hour that there was no way they could begin to consume it all.

Josh was enjoying himself immensely. Father MacDonald, Scottish brogue in full swing, was needling him about petty religious differences, and Josh was swatting aside his comments with witty rejoinders that had everyone around the table keeping score. The young Baptist had even allowed himself a glass of wine, although he honestly did not like the stuff much. Finally, not even the sturdy Apriceno could finish another bite, and they began to wrap up the leftovers.

167

"Put them all in my freezer," said Rossini. "I will feed on them for the next month!"

Apriceno laughed. "No wonder you've gotten portly since you settled here, Giuseppe," she laughed. "The way that woman fattens you up, you'd think she had her eye on you."

"Maybe she does," Rossini shot back, setting of a new round of laughter.

As she helped Josh wrap up the last of the calzone, he noticed that Simone was sporting a large gold ring that housed an ancient Roman coin. "I haven't seen you wear that before," he said.

Apriceno replied, "It was a gift from my husband, when I returned from my first dig. The coin is from the Augustan era, and he picked it up for me at a gift shop here on Capri on our honeymoon. He said it was in celebration of my successful excavation. Ever since then, I wear it whenever my field work is done. Ricardo and I parted ways long ago, but this reminds me that once upon a time, we cared for each other, and he was proud of my work."

Josh nodded. "He was a foolish man to let you go, Doctor. You're a pretty remarkable lady!"

She laughed. "All men are foolish, especially young ones when they try to flirt with women old enough to be their mothers!" she responded.

Isabella slid between them, smiling. "Back off, Simone, I saw him first!" she snapped in mock anger. Josh fled the room in embarrassment.

Later that evening, with the food put away and the dishes washed, they sat around the table, playing dominoes and discussing interesting digs they had been on. Josh showed them his lucky necklace—a simple leather circlet with the first arrowhead he had ever found suspended from it. MacDonald discussed an ancient Roman military camp he had dug in Great Britain, just north of Hadrian's Wall.

"The camp was normal enough," he said. "Buckles, arrowheads, toga clasps, a crossbow trigger. There were three burials just outside its boundary—looked like Roman legionaries who had fallen victim to Pict raiders—probably some of me ancestors. One of the Romans still had a Celtic spearhead in his rib cage! But there was a slab of stone in the camp—polished limestone with crude Latin letters carved on it. It was a curse: 'May Hades take this land of cruel blue barbarians and walking dead men!' I have never understood what that last part meant."

Josh nodded. "That is bizarre," he said. "One of my early archeology instructors in America said he once excavated an Archaic site in Central Texas where he found five severed heads carefully buried under several massive limestone slabs, each one several hundred pounds, piled one on top of another."

Isabella listened with interest. "One of my Egyptology professors excavated a burial near Karnak, where he found an enormous mummified crocodile—with a mummified child interred inside it. The boy had not been eaten—his body was perfectly intact and not torn apart, like a croc kill. But he was carefully mummified, and then deliberately placed inside the crocodile's body, with all manner of wards and protective curses inscribed on the wrappings that encased them both."

"Superstition is a bizarre thing," said Simone Apriceno.

"Speaking of superstitions," said Rossini, "my mother always told me that if I stayed up too late after eating too much, I might turn into a giant vegetable! And I think it is time for me to heed her wisdom. Isabella, you and Simone have the twin beds in the far guest room, and Father MacDonald, you may use the near guest room."

"I'll bunk down on the couch like I did last time," said Josh.

"Better your young bones than my old ones, laddie," said the priest.

One by one the archeologists gravitated towards their rooms, until Josh and Isabella were left alone. She let out an enormous yawn, and stretched slowly.

"I am thinking that we probably do not need to spend half the night talking, like we did Wednesday!" he said.

"You are probably right," she said. "By the way, I have arranged for you to stay at the Ambassador Suites, along with the rest of the team, for your time in Naples. It is a nice place, and the Bureau has a longstanding arrangement with them, so your room will be fully covered. It's just four blocks from the museum, and not far from my flat."

"Good," he said. "It will be nice to have a room of my own, although Dr. Rossini's place is far more comfortable than those tents up on the mountain!"

"Josh," said Isabella. He looked at her. "I have enjoyed, very much, getting to know you this week," she said, and kissed him.

This was no friendly kiss on the cheek, but a full-blown lover's kiss, with a great deal of passion and emotion behind it. He was too stunned to respond at first, but then returned her kiss with enthusiasm. After a few seconds, they broke apart.

"A shame this house does not offer greater privacy!" she said, and left him standing there, his emotions in a confused jumble. Once more, it took him a long time to go to sleep.

The next morning the team packed their bags and assembled down by the docks to catch the ferry to the mainland. A van was waiting to take them to the Ambassador Suites, and after they had deposited their luggage in their rooms, they met at the museum. Josh had never seen the massive structure before, and was quite impressed with it. It was a massive structure, pink with rich dark brown gables and arches. He knew that it housed one of the largest collections of Egyptian relics outside Egypt, as well as many one of a kind Greek and Roman era artifacts, and looked forward to touring it later, as time allowed. When they got out of the van, he began to walk toward its front steps.

"Straight in and keep going, my young friend," said Rossini. "The new lab is actually behind the main museum, in a completely new, state of the art facility."

The team walked through the corridors of the museum, out a small back door, across a small parking lot, and approached a modern concrete structure, with narrow windows and a low roof, unobtrusively inserted between the many historic structures around it.

"A large part of the structure is underground," said Rossini, "and that is where many items are stored. But the labs we will be using are all on the ground floor, near the back of the building. You'll notice that the entrance faces onto the parking lot of the main museum, while the rear of the building presents only a blank face to the street behind it. That is by design. This is a place for scientists and archeologists to work, not for the public to come and gawk. I was on the committee that designed the place."

There was a small security desk just inside the door, where each of them was issued a special badge that gave them access to the entire museum complex. After they had received their badges, Rossini walked them back to the main laboratory, where Dr. Guioccini was waiting for them. "Greetings, my friends!" he said. "Welcome to your new workplace! This is where you will tease out all the secrets from the treasure trove of information you have discovered. Let me show you around."

He gestured to the large work area behind him, where stainless steel tables with magnifying viewers over them held many of the Capri artifacts. "This is where the solid pieces will be studied—the furniture, the sword and scabbard, the various coins and other items you recovered. You have banks of microscopes, numerous computer monitors and workstations, and full carbon-14 dating capability. Dr. Rossini and Dr. Sforza, you will be doing much of your work here." He walked down a short corridor and opened the door to a much smaller lab. Numerous rehydration tanks of various sizes lined the walls, along with smaller worktables and trays, with magnifying viewers and enough computer equipment to conduct a moon launch, or hack into the CIA's mainframe.

"This is our manuscript center," he said. "Drs. Parker and MacDonald, this is where you will unroll the ancient scrolls you have found and transcribe their message. The two undamaged scrolls are rehydrating in those two tanks"—he pointed at the back wall—"and the fragmentary manuscripts are undergoing stabilization in these banks of drawers." He indicated an area along the opposite wall. MacDonald and Josh looked at each other happily. This kind of work environment was something many historians and archeologists only dreamed of.

"Last of all," Guioccini said as he escorted Simone Apriceno to the end of the hallway, "here is our paleobotany lab. All of your pollen samples are housed in those drawers, arranged according to the labels you placed on them, Dr. Apriceno. We have a full range of microscopic instruments, and C-14 dating capacity. I want a full and complete battery of tests run on every pollen sample you collected from the chamber, double and triple checked for stratigraphic integrity. Let us know if there is anything found where it should not be."

After finishing the tour, he called all of them back to the main lab. "The press conference will be in the visitor's gallery of the main museum at noon on Monday," he said. "We want to show the world good, solid science—with a dash of theater thrown in. I want you to pick the artifacts you are going to show, and flag them so that we can move them to the facility. The more durable items should be no problem; however, the scrolls do not need to leave this laboratory until they have been opened and read. But I do want good, clear pictures and video of them to show to the press. I would like all of you to speak

Monday, and explain those things that relate to your area of expertise. You have the entire day, and tomorrow if necessary, to put together your remarks. I would like to have a run-through this afternoon, so I can have an idea as to what you plan to say. Any questions?"

They looked at one another and shrugged. Each of them had already been planning what they might say, and what finds they might share, since they found out about the press conference, and they had shared some ideas the evening before and on the way over this morning. It was just a matter now of stringing it all together. Dr. Guioccini smiled and nodded his farewell, and left them to it.

It was a difficult day after that—not physically, but emotionally. Josh had never been the center of media attention before, but he did not have a terribly high opinion of the American press. MacDonald had acted as a Vatican spokesman on archeological matters for years, and was a natural in front of the camera. Simone Apriceno disliked public appearances, but she had worked as a university lecturer and knew how to keep her comments simple and interesting. Rossini would also be a natural, and Isabella, although she disliked this type of dog and pony show, was forceful and attractive enough to hold the attention of any audience. Little by little, they worked out which artifact each one of them would present to the press, what remarks they would make, and how to present the discovery of the scrolls. Time flew, and by three o'clock, they were ready to present their run-through to Guioccini and Castolfo. The two board members were duly impressed, and the long day came to an end shortly after six in the evening.

Josh joined the team as they walked back to the front of the museum complex. Isabella's car had been in the museum employee parking lot for a week, and she bade them a fond good evening before heading for it. She knew her neighbor had been watering the plants and feeding her cat, but it was time for her to have a night at home. The museum's van conducted the rest of them back to the hotel, and Josh took the time to enjoy a long, comfortable shower in the privacy of his room. His thoughts were still in an uproar about Isabella. He had never been this strongly attracted to any woman, and yet he knew she did not share his faith. How could he bear to share his life with someone he might not get to share eternity with? And yet her beauty made him weak in the knees—he had not felt this adolescent, even when he was an adolescent!

He felt like some exercise would do him good, so he went down to the gift shop and purchased an overpriced pair of swim trunks, then returned to his room and ran through some of the karate exercises, or *kata,* that he had learned during his four years of martial arts study in college. The blocks, punches, and kicks, exercised in perfect sequence several times over, helped clear his head. After an hour of vigorous exercise, he went down to the pool and swam for another hour, then ordered some food delivered to his room. He ate a light supper, to atone for the feasting earlier in the week, and was sound asleep before ten o'clock.

As for Isabella Sforza, she lay awake long past midnight, looking at the photographs of her lost husband, and then thinking about the young man she had met just a few days before. She thought long and hard about the two of them, unable to decide what move to make next. Finally, she got out of bed and padded through her apartment barefoot, taking Marc's photos down and placing them in her dresser drawer. She would never forget him, never stop loving him, and never stop missing him—but it was time to move on.

Even after I had granted them their wish, Caesar, the Jewish priests were still not happy with my handling of the Galilean. I had just sat down to my noontide meal when I got word that one of Caiaphas' secretaries wanted to see me. Once more I had to leave the Praetorium, since their ridiculous religion would not allow them to cross the threshold of a Roman. "What is it now?" I snapped.

"The inscription," he said. "You wrote 'This is the King of the Jews.' It should read that he called himself the King of the Jews."

I had had just about enough from these fools at this point. "I have written what I have written!" I snapped. "I will hear no more of this!"

It was a strange day after that. Within the next hour, the sky grew black as night, even though there was not a cloud in view. The light of the sun simply faded—not blotted out gradually, as in an eclipse, but all at once, and did not return to normal for three hours. At the third hour past noon, a huge earthquake shook the city. My centurion told me that it happened at the exact moment that Jesus died, and he was much shaken, babbling that we had murdered a living god—although he was quite drunk when he said it.

Not long after that, a very different sort of Jew came to see me. His name was Joseph, and he ignored religious protocol and entered the Praetorium to speak with me. He explained that, while he was a Pharisee and a member of the Jewish Senate, he had not even been informed of the charges against Jesus, or been present at his trial. He asked me for Jesus' body, that he might give the Galilean a decent burial. I instructed my soldiers that he could take custody of the body, as soon as they had made sure that Jesus was truly dead. The least I could do for this harmless man I had failed to save was let those who loved him bury him according to their own religious rituals.

CHAPTER FOURTEEN

Josh would later remember that perfect April Sunday in Naples as one of the happiest days of his life. He rolled out of bed at seven that morning and pulled on his trunks, swimming a few laps at the pool, and then enjoyed a continental breakfast in the hotel's luxurious dining lounge. He gave his dad a call, knowing it would be evening back home. After a pleasant conversation, he decided to look for a church to attend. He figured that Italy would not be rich in Baptist churches, and he was right. So instead he decided that the old adage 'When in Rome. . . ' applied to Naples as well, and headed to the largest and most magnificent cathedral in the city, the Duomo de San Genarro. The soaring Gothic structure was one of the most beautiful buildings he had ever seen, and the Latin mass was colorful, moving, and gorgeous to behold. He had briefly visited the gorgeous Cathedral at Amiens in France years before, and had seen many ancient churches, both Catholic and Orthodox, in Ephesus and other cities where he had worked and dug, but rarely had an opportunity to attend services at any of them.

Joshua's feelings about Catholicism were mixed. He had a tremendous respect for the history and traditions that the Church had accumulated, and knew that both Christianity and Western Civilization owed the Church a tremendous debt for the preservation of both the Scriptures and the Greek and Latin classics through the turbulent early medieval era, which Josh still thought of as the Dark Ages. Josh had little respect for those fundamentalists in America who routinely portrayed the Catholic Church as the 'great whore of Babylon' and the Pope as an antichrist. On the other hand, though, the cavalier attitude the Church seemed to have toward the Bible was bewildering and frustrating to him. He understood the intellectual arguments used to justify the subordination of Scripture to tradition and Church Councils, but the idea that any cleric in the modern world, however learned, would place man-made traditions over the words of the Apostles themselves was incomprehensible to him. He also believed that whenever any church, Catholic or Protestant, abandoned the clear teachings of New Testament Scripture, they were riding for a fall. His arguments with Father MacDonald were partly good-natured fun, but also had a serious side—he respected the priest enough to hope that perhaps the man might at least come to understand his point of view. It wouldn't reverse five hundred years of negativity between Catholics and Protestants, but in Josh's book, anything that increased understanding between Christians was a good thing.

Once he left the Cathedral, he turned his cell phone on and saw that he had missed a call from Isabella. He called her back, and she sounded more relaxed than she had all week. A night at home, in her own bed, had apparently been exactly what she needed. She asked Josh to join her for lunch, and they met at a small bistro a few blocks from his hotel. The menu was mainly soup and salad, which was normally not Josh's favorite fare, but after a week of Mrs. Bustamante's rich cooking, he found it welcome change. Isabella looked positively radiant, her dark eyes flashing as she spoke.

"I thought this might be the last chance we have to dine out in anonymity," she said. "I'm not sure how the press conference tomorrow is going to go, but I imagine it will be widely viewed. So let's enjoy the day together!"

"You think we will be stalked by paparazzi after tomorrow?" Josh asked with a smile.

"I think paparazzi may be the least of our problems," she said.

"I guess you're right," he responded. "So what do you want to do?"

She laughed. "How about a museum tour for starters?"

The museum was officially closed on Sundays, but minimal staff remained on the grounds, and the team's credentials opened every door in the place. For the next three hours Josh was enthralled with Mesopotamian figurines, Egyptian mummies, Greek and Roman statuary, and ancient documents of all sorts. He had heard of the National Archeological Museum's incredible collections, but the reality of it all, even on a brief tour, eclipsed anything he had imagined. After going quickly through the main floors, Isabella took him through a locked door that was intriguingly labeled "The Secret Collection." Josh fled a few moments later, blushing a deep scarlet, when he realized that the Secret Collection was, in fact, the largest extant exhibit of Greek and Roman erotic art in the world! Isabella's laughter trailed after him as she locked the door behind them.

"You should be ashamed of yourself, trying to corrupt the morals of a preacher's son!" he gasped through his own laughter.

"Joshua, we are scientists!" she said, laughing. "We should not let outmoded moral codes from the past deter us in our quest for truth!"

"Truth?" Josh said. "The ancient Romans were perverts, and that's the truth!"

Isabella laughed some more. "I wish I could disagree, but unfortunately, you may have a good deal of scholarship on your side there! This place has awkward memories for me, too. When I was a grad student, the professors thought it was an absolute riot to send a pretty female lab assistant to go fetch some item from 'The Secret Collection.' It is available for public viewing on request, and some of the patrons that made the request were . . . well, interesting characters to say the least!"

"And so you avenge your past humiliations by inflicting them on me?" Josh asked.

"Something like that," she replied. "I guess in fairness, I should ask what you would like to do next."

"I'd love to see the art galleries at the Museo di Capodimonte," he said.

"I love Renaissance art!" she replied. "I haven't been there since before. . . " She paused. For the first time that day, she thought of her long-dead husband. *Forgive me, Marc,* she thought, and went on. "Since before I was married," she finished.

Josh saw the brief memory of pain flash across her face, and paused in the street. "Isabella," he said. "I know you must have loved him very much. It doesn't bother me when you mention him, or remember him. He must have been a remarkable man to attract a woman as wonderful as you."

"He was," she said sadly. But then she smiled again, and the memory of grief faded from her face like a morning mist chased away by a spring sunrise. "But I think you are pretty remarkable yourself!" she exclaimed, and leaned up to kiss him on the cheek.

"Well, well, what have we here?" a booming voice said from behind them. For the second time that day, Josh flushed red, as Giuseppe Rossini and Simone Apriceno approached.

"None of your business, *vecchia ficcanaso!*" laughed Isabella.

"Old busybody, is it?" said Rossini. "My child, you wound me! I just wanted to make sure this wicked American was not inflicting his charms on you against your will!"

"Hey!" Josh protested. "I am the victim here!"

"Giuseppe, you dirty old man, leave these young people alone!" said Simone Apriceno, elbowing her companion in the ribs.

"You see, Joshua, what happens when you let women into your life," the old professor said in a mock injured tone. Both women rounded on him for that, and the Italian banter flew back and forth for a moment faster than the bewildered young American could follow.

Finally he spoke in English to break up the mock squabble. "Isabella and I were going to the Capodimonte to look at the galleries," he said. "Why don't you two join us?"

"Actually, that is where we were headed," said Apriceno. "I haven't been there since I was a girl, and Giuseppe offered to give me the grand tour."

Rossini proved to be an excellent tour guide, knowing all the back stories and salacious yarns about the various artists and paintings housed at the famous gallery. Time flew, and before they knew it the security guards were ushering them toward the entrance. Their party had acquired a large group of followers who applauded Rossini on the steps of the museum for his entertaining commentary. He bowed with a courtly Old World flourish, and the tourists went their separate ways.

"Isabella, you let me choose the museum, but now it is your turn," Josh said. "What next?"

"Supper," she said. "And then dancing!"

Rossini protested. "I am afraid my dancing legs were ruined several years back," he said.

"Nonsense!" said Simone. "I have been watching you all week, and I have decided that you are exactly as crippled as you want to be!"

"Well, I might be able to manage a slow waltz," allowed Giuseppe, "if I had a very patient and considerate partner!"

So they found themselves eating a delicious supper at La Belle Gourmet, a popular French restaurant, and then crossing the street to the Don Giovanni Ballroom, a popular swing club for those who liked 1940s era Big Band dance tunes. For the next two hours they waltzed, tangoed, and fox-trotted with abandon. Rossini managed the slower dances quite well, and Simone Apriceno quickly figured out just how often he needed to sit and rest, and which moves were too much for his bad leg. Josh had never been much for dancing, but Isabella was a natural, and under her patient instruction he managed to master some of the simpler steps pretty quickly, although the faster tunes left Isabella with a bruised toe or two, and Josh with bruised ribs from where she elbowed him in retaliation. At one point he found himself sitting next to Rossini while the two ladies visited the powder room. The older man leaned toward Josh.

"Young man, I must thank you," he said.

"For what?" asked Josh.

"You have given Isabella her smile back!" he replied. "I haven't heard her laugh like that in years. Whatever the future may hold, you have done a good thing today."

Josh looked across the room as the two women emerged and walked toward their table. Isabella's eyes were flashing and her smile lit up the room. "You know," he said, "I don't think I have ever seen anyone more beautiful."

"My dear ladies," said Rossini, "as much fun as this has been, we have a very big day ahead of us tomorrow. Might I suggest we return to our respective quarters?"

"Spoilsport!" Josh said, but he was secretly relieved. Dancing with Isabella was enjoyable, but he was too keyed up to relax, and the day had worn him out. As they rode back toward the hotel together, chatting about various things, he asked Giuseppe, "Where is Father MacDonald today?"

"He and Cardinal Raphael were having some sort of meeting most of the day," said Rossini. "I spoke to him just before we met you, and he was getting ready to go to an evening mass."

"I would have enjoyed having him along," said Josh, "but I must say that it was a perfect afternoon and evening regardless!"

"Somehow, I don't see the good Father cutting a rug with us at the Don Giovanni!" said Isabella.

Moments later they pulled up at the hotel. Rossini got out with a groan, and Simone helped him toward the front door. Isabella asked the cab to wait and got out for a moment, taking Josh by the hand. "Josh," she said, "why don't you come and spend the night with me?"

Josh groaned inwardly. This was a moment he had anticipated and dreaded at the same time. With a quick prayer for strength, he responded. "Isabella, I have had a beautiful time with you tonight. But I don't think that is a good idea."

Disappointment, hurt, and anger chased each other across her features in quick succession. "I thought you were interested in me as much as I am in you," she said. "I see I was mistaken. Good night!" She turned back toward the cab.

"Wait!" he exclaimed desperately.

"Why?" she asked. "I do not make such offers lightly, and I do not like rejection. Why should I wait?"

Josh sighed. "I am interested in you!" he said. "I haven't been able to take my eyes off you from the moment we met. You are the most beautiful, intelligent, captivating woman I have ever known!"

She looked at him and saw the tortured sincerity in his eyes. "Then why make a fool of me?"

"That is NOT what I am trying to do!" he said. "You think I don't want your love? There is nothing I want more. I want your face to be the last thing I see when I shut my eyes at night, and the first thing I see when I open them in the morning—and not just tomorrow, but every day! But I refuse to accept your love in a way that dishonors you, and dishonors God."

She hesitated. Religion again, she thought. "I don't understand," she finally said.

Josh tried to explain. "I believe that sexuality is best reserved for marriage," he said. "Virginity is a gift you can only give away once. I have guarded mine for my entire adult life so that I can give it as a gift to my bride, on our wedding night. It is the Biblical, Christian approach to love. I've never met anyone I want to share that moment with, until now. But not until the time is right!"

Isabella finally smiled and rolled her eyes. "I have a hard time believing the Almighty Creator of the universe is going to be offended if you come spend the night in my apartment," she said.

"But he is a God of small things, as well as great," said Josh. "It just would not be right for me to do this. I do love you, and I want you to know that. I've never been in love before—I've never felt for anyone what I feel for you. But I want to do this right, because I only intend to do it once. If you can't share my beliefs yet, please, at least, respect them."

182

"I don't like this God of yours very much sometimes," she said. "In Italy, we believe that God winks at small things! But tell me—" She stepped closer. "Where does your God stand on goodnight kisses?"

Josh heaved a sigh of relief. "I think a goodnight kiss would be lovely," he said.

Isabella pulled him close and kissed him so hard that he was left gasping for breath. Several bystanders, watching the drama unfold between them, actually applauded. She turned to them and gave a quick curtsy and smile, leaving Josh red-faced on the sidewalk. He finally turned and headed into the hotel. Despite being very tired from the long day, he swam fifty laps before heading up to his room for the night.

* * *

The next morning the five team members met Dr. Castolfo at the lab. He walked them over to the main museum and showed them the area where the conference would be held. Over a hundred chairs were waiting for members of the media, and a few reporters were already touring the museum, looking for backdrops for teaser sound bites. Three long stainless steel tables were laid lengthwise across the front of the room, with five chairs behind them for the team members. Overhead, a large flat-screen digital monitor would play the video clips of the excavation they had prepared. After walking them through the room, Castolfo showed them the back door, which led to a narrow corridor and a rear exit to the museum. "This way you can bring in the artifacts you wish to display during the press conference unnoticed."

This done, the five archeologists went and retrieved the items they planned to show to the press. Rossini would discuss the initial excavation of the chamber, and then Simone Apriceno would show several vials of dust, numerous photographs and video clips of the original condition of the chamber, and several blown-up photographs of ancient pollen samples she had taken. In addition, she had the inkwell and signet ring from the top of the writing table as visual aids. Father MacDonald would show the Tiberius scroll itself, still immovably molded to the top of the ancient writing table. Josh would be discussing the translation of the Tiberius scroll, and then presenting the sword of Caesar. Isabella would begin by describing the discovery of the tomb, and conclude by showing the ancient key and cameo portrait they had discovered. Then, last of all, she would reveal the existence of the other two scrolls.

As they retrieved the artifacts they intended to display, Father MacDonald walked over to the rehydration tanks to look at the scrolls. "Josh, come here!" he exclaimed. "In fact, all of you look at this!"

It took a moment for them to realize what they were seeing, but then it registered. The seals on the ancient scrolls were loosening—in fact, on the Pilate scroll, there was a gap of two millimeters between the center of the wax seal and the papyrus it had clung to for so long. "I think they will both come right off now," said the priest. "Then it will not be long before the scrolls begin to unroll on their own. We should be able to read the first parts of each scroll tomorrow."

He then carefully reached through the access holes in the front panel of the tank, wearing the acid-free gloves used to handle ancient perishables. Using a fine scalpel, he very gently pried at the wax seals. Each one popped off without difficulty, and he used a pair of forceps to extract each seal from the tank. Since the wax was not nearly as fragile as the papyrus, the two seals were transferred to the viewing table for photography, then each was assigned a separate catalog number and transferred to a controlled climate storage cabinet. After this was done, they walked over to the tanks. Each scroll had visibly expanded once the seals were removed, and it was obvious that as the papyrus became more and more pliable, the scrolls would unroll on their own.

"How long do you think each one is?" asked Joshua.

"The last will of Augustus is definitely the shorter of the two," said Father MacDonald. "I imagine it will unroll to roughly one meter in length. The Pontius Pilate report is considerably longer—I imagine that it will be slightly over two meters! This is exciting, my friends. Tomorrow the mystery will begin to unfold!"

"And the eyes of the world will be on this lab," said Isabella. "How I wish that they had been willing to wait one more week before making the announcement."

"Too late for that now," said Rossini, shaking his head sadly. "It is time to begin making our way to the arena."

"Is that what they call the press room in Italy?" asked Josh.

"Why not?" shrugged Giuseppe. "It is a place where you can be eaten by the lions, is it not?"

At noon the press auditorium was packed with journalists from over twenty countries. Dr. Sinisi's "teaser" leak to the press over the weekend had worked well—combined with a slow springtime news cycle, it had created a huge audience for their announcement. The five archeologists sat behind the table, smiling for the cameras as Dr. Castolfo prepared to introduce them. At exactly noon, the president of the Board of Antiquities stood, and the cameras began to roll.

"Ladies and gentlemen of the press corps," he began in flawless English. "I would like to thank each of you for attending our conference this day. The discoveries made within the last week on the isle of Capri are of extreme significance, not just within our narrow world of history and archeology, but also in a much broader sense, as they may touch upon the beliefs of countless millions worldwide. I would like to introduce to you the five members of the team who have labored exhaustively this week to uncover, remove, and analyze the artifacts from the Villa Jovis ruins on Capri. First, our ancient documents specialist and Church historian, Father Duncan MacDonald. From America, our linguist and specialist in early Christian history, Dr. Joshua Parker. Specializing in the history of the late Roman Republic and early Roman Empire, Dr. Giuseppe Rossini. Then we have our Paleobotanist and expert on carbon-dating, Dr. Simone Apriceno. Finally, our lovely and remarkably talented team leader, an expert on Roman archeology, Dr. Isabella Sforza. She will take over the press conference from here. Dr. Sforza?"

Isabella stood, and flash bulbs popped throughout the room. Lara Croft jokes aside, the fact that this expedition had been led by a woman whose looks could have made her a fashion model was good copy, and every reporter in the room knew it. She smiled and began.

"For the last week it has been my privilege to work with this group of consummate professionals in one of the most remarkable discoveries in the history of modern archeology. I must ask you to bear with us as we present these finds in the order that they were made; I can promise you your patience will be rewarded by the end of our time together. To begin, I have asked Dr. Giuseppe Rossini, who made the initial discovery, to explain how that came about."

Rossini stood. Ibuprofen had calmed the throbbing in his leg from the night before, and his silver hair and charming manner captivated the room quickly. "I am the resident docent and curator of the ruin known as the Villa Jovis on the isle of Capri. For those of you whose history is a bit rusty, this was once the home of the Roman emperor Tiberius Caesar, who ruled Rome from 14 to 37 AD. Last Sunday we experienced an earthquake on Capri—not a huge catastrophe, but enough of a trembler to make me go check and see if the ruins of Tiberius' palace had been damaged. Fortunately, damage was minimal, but as I descended a staircase from one level of the ruin to another, I saw that part of its supporting wall had collapsed. This staircase had always been thought to rest on a solid stone pile foundation; however, the wall collapse revealed that a small chamber had been hidden underneath it all this time. When I shone my pocket torch into the room, I saw that the room and all of its contents were buried under such a thick coat of dust—mostly atomized stone from the stairs above—that they must have been undisturbed for many, many centuries. I could also see that the room was still furnished. Next to the opening created by the quake were a small table and a backless chair, such as was favored by the Romans in the days of the late Republic and early Empire. I immediately realized that these items might possibly date to the time of Tiberius himself, and called Dr. Sforza." He nodded at Isabella. "She arrived later that afternoon, and as you can see on the video above, we filmed the chamber as best we could before beginning to remove any of the dust. We collected samples from every surface before we uncovered anything, since the dust itself and the pollen it contains can help us date the chamber with some precision, and reveal if the contents had ever been disturbed. We did, that first afternoon, clean the top of the small table off—although we left one area of dust undisturbed so that the stratigraphy would be intact. We found several interesting items on top of the table, and I will let my colleague Simone Apriceno explain some of those."

Apriceno stood, her speech as quick and blunt as her personality. "I was brought onto the scene the next morning. It was obvious to me that this chamber was very, very ancient. The coating of dust was anywhere from two to four centimeters in depth on top of every object. The items on the table had been revealed for inspection, but the bottommost layer of dust was still clinging in places, and as Dr. Rossini had said, there was one completely undisturbed section left on top of the table. I collected this sample, and once the table and curule chair had been removed, I spent most of the dig in the chamber, collecting samples of the stone dust from every single surface, and then clearing the remainder of the dust so that the exploration of the chamber proper could begin. I also put several of the smaller objects found in the chamber under the microscope to see if any pollen was still clinging to them. Here you see a signet ring bearing the name and seal of the Emperor Tiberius. There is still a good deal of wax adhering to the ring, and I found two spores of pollen clinging to it which are consistent with flora from the first century AD. I also found similar spores clinging to this inkwell, which was used at the writing table we found, and a bonanza of pollen samples adhering to this ancient wax candle, which provided the wax for sealing the documents that were found. While pollen analysis is not as sexy or intriguing as many other fields of archeology, one thing that it can establish is the rough date at which the chamber was sealed, as well as whether or not the chamber was breached at any point between now and then. Thus far, every bit of evidence the microscope has revealed to me has confirmed that the chamber was, in fact, sealed up two thousand years ago, and has remained largely undisturbed ever since." Attention was wandering a bit, which frustrated her because these dolts could not understand just how critical her discipline was to confirming the site's authenticity. Still, it was time to pass the torch. "To discuss the more interesting artifacts that we uncovered in the chamber, I refer you to my colleague, the Reverend Doctor Duncan MacDonald."

MacDonald stood and smiled. "No doubt, ladies and gentlemen, you are wondering when we are going to get around to the remarkable finds you were promised. Well, that lot has fallen, in part, to me. I was called into the site because of my expertise in handling ancient papyrus and parchment documents. What Doctors Rossini and Sforza found on Capri was actually a private writing chamber used by the Emperor Tiberius Caesar. We know this because of the name and inscription on the signet ring that Dr. Apriceno just showed you—but we also know because of what else was found on top of the writing table." With a flourish, he pulled a white cloth off of the small table, which was lying on its side. "This is the writing bench which you saw in the video. As you can see, as they uncovered the dust on top of the table, my colleagues realized that there was a papyrus sheet lying flat on it. The weight of the stone dust on top of it had, over the centuries, pressed the document down onto the tabletop, where the papyrus bonded to the lacquer that had been used to wax the table while it was still in use. The result was that the letter was perfectly preserved, but bonded irremovably to the tabletop. The letter is written in the highly polished Latin vernacular that was common to the Roman upper classes during the First Century AD. And it is signed by the Roman Emperor Tiberius Caesar himself!"

With that, he rotated the table so that the top surface, with the letter still adhering to it, was facing the crowd of journalists. An excited buzz swept the room, and flashbulbs exploded in a mini-lightning storm. The priest waited patiently for the buzz to die down, and then continued. "While my Latin is quite proficient—that used to be a requirement in my line of work, you know"—a few chuckles from the Catholics in the crowd ensued—"in translating something as important as this, I felt it necessary to have some assistance. My young American colleague, Josh Parker, helped me translate the scroll. If I may give you a short history lesson, Tiberius was the second Emperor of Rome and the heir of Augustus Caesar. He despised the crowds and noise of Rome and retired to the island of Capri around 22 AD. He remained there, governing from afar, until he left the island to return to Rome in 37 AD—a journey he never completed, as he died en route to the capital. But this letter was written before he departed, and it reads as follows—"

He then proceeded to read the Tiberius letter in a straightforward voice, dropping his accent to a minimum. When he was done, he could see that the attention of the journalists was still with him, but he also sensed bewilderment. "Understand that to an archeologist, this find alone would be of incredible importance. But the chamber still had other secrets to reveal to us, which my companion, Dr. Parker, will now discuss."

Josh stood. "Good afternoon, ladies and gentlemen. One item in the chamber that we have not yet shown you is the large cabinet that was buried in the dust at the back wall. As we cleaned and translated the document, Dr. Apriceno was busy removing centuries of stone dust from the back of the chamber. As she cleaned, she realized that there was something besides an ancient reliquary back in the corner. What was leaning against the cabinet will no doubt go down as one of the most precious artifacts ever recovered by any archeologist, at any time or place. As you can see from the video above, there was a Roman shortsword, called a *gladius*, leaning against the cabinet. I can tell you that it is the most perfectly preserved Roman sword ever found. But that is not the only thing that makes it remarkable. On the pommel of the sword, in Latin characters, is inscribed the legend: 'The Blade and Honor of the Julii.' The Julii were an ancient family of Roman patricians, whose members included the first five Emperors of Rome. We knew the moment we uncovered it that this was the sword of a Caesar. The question was which one?"

Josh slipped on his gloves and lifted the *gladius*, now sheathed in its scabbard once more. "Fortunately the scabbard was also inscribed." He pointed to the small silver disk that was woven into the leather. "The Latin inscription reads, 'To Rome's Finest Son, Wield It with Honor— Aurelia Cotta.' Aurelia was a very famous Roman matron from the first century BC, once renowned as the most beautiful woman in Rome. But today she is better remembered as the mother of a famous son—in fact, she was the mother of the most famous Roman of them all. You see, this is the sword of Julius Caesar himself. It was carried in some of history's most famous battles, by a man that many historians, myself included, believe to be the greatest general of all time." With a flourish he drew the blade from its sheath, and the photographers had a field day. It took five minutes for the excited buzz to die down, and then he spoke again. "This artifact ranks right up there with the burial mask of Tutankhamen as one of the most remarkable finds of all time," he said. "But we had not yet opened the reliquary! Dr. Sforza, would you care to finish our presentation?"

Isabella flashed him a quick smile and stood once more. "Even as Doctors Parker and MacDonald were translating the Tiberius letter, I had noticed that there was a small, hidden drawer beneath the writing table. Once we figured out how to open it, we found some blank papyrus sheets and a small leather drawstring bag inside it. The bag contained several coins, an ancient arrowhead which we believe was a battle souvenir of the Emperor's family, and a beautiful, ornate key with a horse head effigy made of ivory." She held up the tiny key for all to see, and then lowered her hand so that the zoom lenses could focus in on it. "We figured that this key would open the reliquary at the end of the room. But when it came time to open the reliquary, we found that it was actually unlocked. Sadly, it was here that we encountered our first true disappointment of the dig. At some point since Tiberius had the chamber walled up, rats had tunneled into the back of the cabinet and destroyed nearly everything inside. By sifting through the debris of their nests, we have uncovered the fragmentary remains of one beautifully inscribed parchment scroll, and at least five different papyrus documents. Piecing together and translating these pieces will be the work of many months, but from the bits and pieces we have read so far, what we have found appear to be some special documents that the Emperor Tiberius saved and kept for himself. We also found pieces of several garments, and this beautiful cameo portrait of the Emperor's first wife." She held up the obsidian jewelry, and several reporters snapped pictures of it.

"But our luck had not run out completely. There was one compartment inside the cabinet that was locked up tight. That is where our mystery key came into play. It opened the locked compartment, and inside we found two scrolls, both perfectly preserved and still sealed with the Emperor Tiberius' signet ring. The scrolls are very dried out and fragile, and are currently undergoing rehydration, so that they can be unrolled without crumbling. However, Tiberius took the time to label each of the scrolls by writing along the outside of them after they were sealed. The first scroll, visible on the monitor above, reads 'The Last Will and Testament of Caesar Augustus.' The second scroll I think you will find to be of particular interest, and is the primary reason for this press conference today. It reads, 'The Testimony of Pontius Pilate, Governor of Judea.'"

The room exploded with an excited buzz, which only continued and got louder as she sat down. Journalists were excitedly jabbering at one another, and it took Dr. Castolfo several efforts before they quieted down enough for him to be heard. "Ladies and gentlemen," he finally said. "This concludes our formal presentation. The two scrolls will be read and translated as soon as it is possible to unroll them. At this time, our archeologists will be glad to answer a few questions."

An American on the front row leaped to his feet. Josh recognized him immediately as Eli Arnold, a talking head from one of America's most liberal news networks. Isabella nodded to him. "So you are telling us that this letter is from THE Pontius Pilate? The legendary Roman governor who supposedly ordered the crucifixion of Jesus of Nazareth?"

Isabella nodded at Josh, and he answered for the group—they had agreed that he would field the questions from the American media. "First of all, sir, there is nothing legendary about Pontius Pilate. He is recorded as Governor of Judea in many ancient sources, Christian, Jewish, and Roman alike. And yes, he would have been the governor of Judea throughout the last half of Tiberius' reign, when Jesus was crucified."

"So do you think this scroll may have something to do with the Crucifixion of Jesus?" Arnold asked.

"I think there is a very good chance that it does," replied Josh. "First of all, there is an ancient reference to a report by Pilate on that event, and secondly, another source mentions that Tiberius may have taken an interest in the stories of Jesus. It is not a far stretch to infer that he heard about them through the report Pilate filed to Rome. However, we do not yet know for certain what is in the scroll—only that Tiberius himself ascribed it to Pilate."

An Italian journalist, Antonio Ginovese, raised his hand next. "How long until the scrolls will be read and translated?"

Isabella answered: "We don't really know. Ancient papyrus is tricky stuff, and no two scrolls are alike. I can tell you that the scrolls are responding nicely to the rehydration treatment, and are beginning to expand and uncurl a bit. I am hopeful that in a couple of weeks or less, we will know exactly what they say. And that information will be released to the public as soon as possible thereafter."

Trevor Sharif rose next. He was a sharply dressed English journalist of Arabic descent. "What impact do you think that this find might have on Christianity worldwide?"

Father MacDonald fielded that question. "It has long been the position of the Church that faith has nothing to fear from history. The Christians of the world, both Catholic and Protestant, have a great interest in what the scroll contains, but our beliefs are rooted in eternal principles that will not change because of one archeological discovery."

"And if this scroll reveals the Biblical story of the Resurrection to be nothing but a clever hoax?" Sharif continued.

"If the Resurrection were a hoax, I imagine the truth of it would have come out long before now," MacDonald calmly stated.

Tyler Patterson rose next. He was the youngest, freshest face in American network news, an attempt by one of the cable networks to draw in young viewers. "So is Tiberius Caesar the Emperor who was portrayed in the HBO series *Rome?*" he asked.

Josh did his best not to do a face palm on international television. "No," he said. "The events portrayed in the TV series ran from about 50 BC to 37 BC—almost a century before Tiberius sealed these documents in his writing nook." At least, Josh thought, he had not asked about the movie *Gladiator.*

The military correspondent from FOX news stood next. "Dr. Parker," he said. "How sure are you that the sword in the sheath really belonged to Julius Caesar?"

"Well, with both the pommel of the sword and the scabbard engraved, I would say that we have established that beyond all doubt," he answered.

A French correspondent from the back of the room rose. "How positive are you that the chamber has never been disturbed?" he asked.

Dr. Apriceno responded; "My findings are still preliminary at the moment, but I see no evidence whatsoever that the chamber has ever been opened, or its contents tampered with. At this point I would be very surprised to discover otherwise."

An Italian newspaper reporter spoke next. "How is it that this chamber remained secret for so long?" she asked. "Hasn't the Villa Jovis been extensively excavated through the centuries?"

Rossini addressed that one. "It is indeed remarkable," he said. "But several factors worked together to keep the chamber secret. First of all, the ancient Roman steward Mencius Marcellus deserves a great deal of credit. When he carried out the orders from Tiberius to wall up the chamber, he did an excellent job of concealing its existence. Instead of just covering up the ancient door, he actually had the masons lay a completely new layer of stone from one end of the stair wall to another, so that there was no indication that a doorway had ever existed. Secondly, while the marble flagstones and decorations of the Villa Jovis were plundered repeatedly through the centuries for building materials, the staircase and concealing wall were of plain limestone, not considered very desirable. And the fact that such large staircases usually rest on a solid pile of stone and concrete meant that no one suspected there ever had been a chamber there. So circumstances conspired to preserve these remarkable artifacts through the centuries."

"These items seem awfully clean and well preserved to be so old," the reporter said. "How were they not rusted and decomposed after twenty centuries?"

"That is a perceptive question," said Rossini. "From what I have learned, the roof of the Villa Jovis remained intact until the fifth century and maybe even later. That would have kept any moisture from penetrating the chamber, and allowed a protective coat of dry, sterile stone dust to cover the artifacts. And even with the roof collapsed, the fact that the Villa sits on one of the highest points on the island meant there was no ground-level moisture to accumulate in the chamber. And even in ruins, much of the guttering and water channels of the ancient villa remained intact, so that moisture, the great corruptor of perishable artifacts, had little chance of invading the chamber. So the dust piled up, dried, and sealed these ancient relics until last Sunday."

Cynthia Brown, an American correspondent, asked the next question. "When can we see the chamber where these artifacts were recovered?" she asked.

"The Villa Jovis will reopen to the public this afternoon," said Castolfo. "If he is willing, I bet that Dr. Rossini would enjoy taking some of you on a walking tour of the site." Rossini nodded his assent.

Several more questions came from various sources, many of them variations on what had already been asked. It was nearly an hour before Dr. Castolfo rose and drew the conference to its conclusion. After the last journalist exited the room, Dr. Vincent Sinisi stood from where he had been quietly seated on the back row and applauded. "For a bunch of antiquarians, you guys are rock stars!" he said. "The conference could not have gone better! Come to the board's conference room upstairs— dinner is on me!"

The entire governing board of the Bureau of Antiquities was waiting for them, and burst into applause when they entered the room. There was a lavish buffet of seafood and pasta laid out, and soon the starving archeologists were allowed to sit and stuff themselves. All of them had been too keyed up and nervous for breakfast, and they addressed their food with gusto. As they wrapped up the meal, Dr. Guioccini came over and laid his hand on Rossini's shoulder.

"Giuseppe," he said, "There are twenty-five journalists waiting for your tour of the site. We have helicopters standing by. Are you about ready?"

Rossini heaved a long sigh. "I am ready for a long, delightful nap!" he said. "But, I suppose if duty calls, I must answer. But only on the condition that I can leave the site and return to my home for the evening when I am done!"

"Of course," laughed Bernardo. "You have earned it. Isabella, would you like to tag along?"

"No!" she said. "I have provided the cameras with enough fodder for one day. I would like to return to the lab and get some real work done."

"By all means," Guioccini said. "I cannot emphasize how happy the board is with today's proceedings. It is a proud moment, not just for

Italy, but for historians and archeologists all over the world! I imagine, when your work here is done, that each of you will be able to write your own ticket at any university on earth."

He and Rossini headed off together, and the four remaining members of the team looked at the cracked lobster tails and crab shells piled up on their empty plates. Josh gave a groan.

"Are you sure we have to go back to work?" he said.

"Come, lad, the Lord hates a whiner!" Father MacDonald replied.

And the team headed back to the research lab.

AMAZING DISCOVERY ON CAPRI!

EMPEROR'S CHAMBER OF SECRETS MAY BE TIED TO THE CRUCIFIXION OF JESUS

(AP) Italy's Bureau of Antiquities has revealed a remarkable trove of historical treasures uncovered by a recent earthquake at the Villa Jovis, an ancient Roman ruin on the Isle of Capri. The chamber where the artifacts were found was probably sealed in 37 AD, according to Dr. Isabella Sforza, the lead archaeologist on the site. Among the artifacts recovered are a personal letter from the Emperor Tiberius to his steward, a sword that is believed to have belonged to the famous Roman general and statesman Julius Caesar, and the last will and testament of Rome's first emperor, Caesar Augustus. But by far the most remarkable artifact to emerge from the site is a scroll, inscribed on the outside by the Emperor Tiberius and sealed with his signet ring, entitled "The Testimony of Pontius Pilate, Governor of Judea." Speculation abounds that the scroll, which has not yet been opened or read, may pertain to the crucifixion in 33 AD of Jesus of Nazareth, the founder of the Christian religion. Archeologists say that the scroll should be opened and read within the next two weeks.

(See photo layout on page A-2)

I am sorry to have troubled you for so long about this matter, Caesar, but I am afraid that the story does not yet end. The sun had not yet set on that endless Friday when emissaries from the High Priest came to see me yet again. As you can imagine, they found me in no good mood. Why could they not return to their sacrificial Passover lambs and leave me be?

"Noble proconsul," purred old Annas. "While he was alive, this troublemaker repeatedly said that if he was killed, he would return to life on the third day. Could we trouble you for some guards to watch over the tomb until after the first day of the week? We fear his disciples may try to steal his body and proclaim him alive again, and then the deception will only grow worse!"

"You have your Temple guards," I growled. "Guard the bloody tomb yourselves!"

They bowed and scurried out, anxious to return to their families before sunset, when their religious observance actually began. After they left, I called in my primus pilus centurion, Gaius Cassius Longinus, who had headed the crucifixion detail. He had sobered up some, but was obviously still troubled over his afternoon's work.

"The Jews think someone may attempt to disturb the Galilean's grave," I told him. "First of all, are you sure that he was dead when his family cut him down from the cross?" I asked.

"Absolutely," he said. "He had quit breathing a half hour before, but I still had one of my boys skewer his heart with a spear before I allowed them to cut him down. I have never seen anyone die so bravely, sir. Not a curse! In fact, he even prayed for us as he hung there. Asked his father to forgive us. I've never heard the like!"

"Never mind that," I said. "Just make sure a couple of your legionaries keep an eye on that tomb for the next few days."

CHAPTER FIFTEEN

They were still walking across the parking lot toward the lab when Josh's phone rang. He recognized the number instantly. "Dr. Martens!" he said when he picked up. "How are you, sir?"

"Well, they are letting me hobble around on crutches now," his mentor said. "I will graduate to a cane in the next day or two, and when I do, I am getting on a plane to Italy. What a discovery! Congratulations, Josh, I knew you would do me proud."

Josh smiled. He thought the world of Dr. Martens, and the praise of his old professor was sweet music to his ears. "Honestly sir," he said, "it was a team effort all the way. I have really enjoyed working with this fine group of archeologists. But I will say, when I saw the inscription on that scroll, my knees went out from under me—I'm just glad I didn't drop it. I can't wait till it begins to unroll and reveal its secrets. This is the biggest find in the history of Biblical archeology!"

"You're going to need an experienced paleographer to look at it when you get it open," said Martens. "I've studied ancient Greek and Latin script for years. I would love to get a look at that scroll and analyzing the handwriting."

"You and about every other classical archeologist in the world!" laughed Josh. "But, since you are friends with Dr. Guioccini, I bet you will actually be able to do so."

"I certainly hope so!" said Martens. "I just need to get this leg working properly again."

"How is Alicia doing?" asked Josh.

"Very well," said Martens. "She has been absolutely wonderful throughout this whole mess—still insists it was all her fault, but I was the one who strapped on the skis. She is a great help to me getting around, though, and I'm sure she'll be coming to Italy with me. By the way, that Dr. Sforza is a very lovely lady, and I have heard she is a talented archeologist to boot. How is she to work with?"

"She's pretty awesome," Josh said. "As a supervisor, I mean!" Isabella, who had been eavesdropping a bit, dug her elbow in his ribs. "Well, truth be told, she is pretty awesome all the way around. I've really enjoyed getting to know her."

The older man responded, "Sounds as if you've gotten to know her quite well. Don't tell me that heart of flint has finally begun to thaw a bit?"

"Maybe just a little, sir!" Josh said with a laugh, unwilling to admit that his heart had actually turned to Jell-O.

"Then she must be a remarkable girl indeed," said the professor. "You know Alicia only became interested in me after she utterly failed to get any response from you!"

Josh was stunned. He'd had no idea that Alicia had ever been interested in him. "Wow," he finally said. "Was I really that clueless?"

"Fortunately for me, you were!" said Martens. They chatted a minute more before Josh hung up.

Isabella looked at him. "Was that your father?" she asked, apparently having missed Josh's initial greeting.

"No," he said. "But he is a very dear friend, and my mentor in the world of archeology."

"Ah, Dr. Martens!" she said. "I have not met him, but his published works are an absolute necessity for anyone in our field."

"Well," said Josh, "you are going to get to meet him soon, I think. He is planning to come to Italy as soon as he is mobile."

"That's right," she said. "He was in a ski accident, wasn't he?"

"Yes, several weeks back," said Josh.

"So what were you clueless about?" she teased.

"That," Josh said with a raised eyebrow, "is none of your business, Doctor Sforza!"

"Must have been a girl!" she laughed, and he shot her a venomous glance.

By now they were back in the lab, and Dr. MacDonald was already hunched over staring at the rehydration tanks. They joined him, and saw that both scrolls had begun to unroll already. About six inches of the Pilate manuscript had been revealed, while the smaller Augustus manuscript had unrolled further, with about half the document now being revealed.

"Marvelous!" said MacDonald as they looked over his shoulder. "I believe we can actually read the Augustus scroll right now—being smaller, it has unrolled as far as the wall of the tank will allow. I think when I pull it out on the viewing table that it will unroll completely. Josh, would you assist me? And Isabella, would you be so kind as to fetch Simone from the other lab? I would like all of us to be here when we read this scroll."

"I think we should notify Castolfo and Guioccini as well," said Isabella, and MacDonald nodded.

"It's a shame Giuseppe is going back to Capri. I wonder if he has boarded the helicopter yet," Josh wondered.

"I don't know," said MacDonald. "And I am not sure if Guioccini was going with him or not. Hopefully Isabella will catch them before they depart."

As the others were summoned, Joshua carefully covered a lengthy section of the viewing table with acid-free paper, and set two padded steel clamps above it about a meter apart. Once the scroll was unrolled, they would serve to hold each end in place while MacDonald sprayed the scroll with a stabilizing solution that would preserve the ancient papyrus while also keeping it in a flat position. As soon as he was done prepping the table, MacDonald donned his gloves and lowered the front pane of the rehydration tank. He very gently lifted the scroll out of the tank and laid it on the table, where the curled end immediately unrolled almost completely. He pushed down gently on the end that was still slightly curled up until he was able to slide it under the clamp, and then slowly lowered the clamp onto the end of the papyrus until the entire scroll was flattened on top of the viewing table. He clamped the other end, which was already lying flat, in place, and then got out an aerosol can of his special stabilizing spray. Holding it about eight inches over the ancient papyrus, he deliberately sprayed from one end to the other, making several passes to be sure that every part of the ancient document was covered. The solution soaked in immediately, and the papyrus became a slight shade darker as the liquid bonded to its cells.

While MacDonald was still spraying, Simone Apriceno came in, and moments later Guioccini and Rossini entered, both flushed and out of breath. Dr. Castolfo followed on their heels. Isabella's call had caught the three of them on the helicopter pad, and they had asked the pilot to wait for a half hour so that they could witness the reading of the scroll. Castolfo was on his cell phone with the journalists on Capri, explaining that the guided tour would be postponed for a short time. Meanwhile, MacDonald continued his spraying until he had completely coated the papyrus with stabilizer, then moved the magnifying viewer directly over the ancient document and turned on the jumbo flat-screen monitor overhead so that they could all see the writing on the papyrus clearly.

"Well, ladies and gentlemen," he said. "The rehydration tanks have done their work very well. This scroll was the smaller of the two, and it was over halfway unrolled when we returned from the reception. It would have unrolled further, but the end of the scroll had come to a stop against the side of the tank. Once I removed it and laid it on the flat table, all but the last few centimeters unrolled very easily. Now the scroll is stabilized, and we can study it to our hearts' content."

Rossini admired the script on the large viewer. "What wonderful calligraphy!" he commented.

"Most ancient historians commented on the clear and forceful style of Caesar's writing," said Josh. "We can see from this that they were talking not only about his wordcraft but about his penmanship as well. This is about the easiest reading I have ever seen on any ancient document."

"Why don't you read it to us, Josh?" said the priest.

Parker complied in a loud, clear voice, reading in Latin:

"Teste Vestalis summo Iunius Porcia minor Kalendis Octobris, anno centesimo sexagesimo septimo post conditam Romam rite descripti in aede Vestae est testamento Caesaris Augusti. Imperatorem et principem Romanum imperium imperator legiones praetorianis scutum republica functus officio dictator consul Donec legatum Pontificis Maximi Senatoris et quaestore I Gaius Julius Caesar Augustus. . ." Joshua read the entire manuscript in Latin, glad that he had kept his proficiency in the ancient language.

"Not all of us are Latin scholars, Dr. Parker," said Simone Apriceno. "Can you give us a translation?"

Josh nodded, and began again. He went a bit slower, but the clear, strong hand was easy to read, and the Latin was clear and precise.

"'Witnessed by Chief Vestal Porcia Junius Minor, on the Kalends of October, in the seven hundred and sixty-fifth year since the founding of Rome, and duly registered in the Temple of Vesta, is the Last Will and Testament of Gaius Julius Caesar Octavian Augustus. As *Princeps* and *Imperator* of Rome, commander of the Imperial Legions and Praetorian Guard, protector of the Republic, having held the offices of Dictator, Consul, Senior Legate, Pontifex Maximus, Senator, and Quaestor; I, Gaius Julius Caesar Augustus, in the forty-third year of my authority over Rome and its Empire, do set down in this public will and testament my wishes for the disposal of my personal goods as well as my political offices.

'To my wife Lydia, I bequeath our three villas at Capri, Capua, and Sicily, one-third of all my personal fortune in an amount not to exceed a million sesterces, and my thanks for her steadfast partnership in all my ventures, public and private. To the Senate of Rome, I bequeath the statues I have erected in their honor, and the public buildings that I have erected at my own expense. Let it be known that I found Rome a city of wood, and left it a city of marble! If I have played my role well, then I would have all good Romans applaud at my exit.

'To my adopted son, Tiberius Caesar, I bequeath my offices as *Princeps, Imperator,* commander of the Legions, and all other titles and emoluments that I may possess at the time of my death, as well as all my wealth not otherwise disposed. I charge him to guard and protect Rome, to uphold the rights of her citizens, and respect the *mos maiorum* that has guided the government of Rome since time immemorial. I charge him to be a just and wise guardian of Rome's many provinces and client states, and to appoint none but good and wise men to govern them on Rome's behalf. I have groomed him for this task for many years, and I have no doubt that he will acquit himself well.

'To the people of Rome, I bequeath half of my personal fortune in an amount not to exceed two million sesterces, to be distributed evenly across all the Tribes, as well as the improvements I have made to the Circus Maximus, the many parks and gardens that I have built, and the stadiums I have endowed. Long may they endure as centers of rest and recreation for the hard-working citizens of Rome!

'Here ends the public will of Caesar Augustus.

'*Addendum:* To the Senate of Rome—I have, over the years, discussed with many of you the possibilities of restoring the Roman Republic, and allowing elected consuls to once more serve as the leaders of the Senate and People of Rome. After much deliberation and reflection, I have realized that the old Republic was designed for the governance of a city, not for the leadership of the civilized world. It was the fragile structure of the Old Republic that led to a century of civil war, and it was the cupidity and stubbornness of its last leaders that forced my father, the *divus Julius,* to cross the Rubicon and root out the rot at Rome's core. Rome is no longer a Republic, although it retains many of its Republican forms. Only one man can practically govern an Empire, until such time as the laws of the Republic can be so thoroughly rewritten that an elected body can effectively rule the world. Only the gods know when such an hour will come. I charge you solemnly to honor my wishes in this matter.

'*Second Addendum:* To Tiberius Caesar—I have left you the greatest inheritance ever bequeathed. Guard it jealously, yet handle it with care. It can make you into a god, but it can also destroy you, my son. Govern with justice, but with caution, and when the need for ruthlessness should arrive, do not hesitate to be as ruthless as the occasion demands. May the gods give you wisdom!'"

Josh paused. "There is a small, scribbled note at the bottom in the handwriting of Tiberius. It reads: '*Putat senex dedit benedictionem et maledictionem sicut ego? Imperio mundi nolo nisi ipse regeret.*' In English: 'The old man thinks he has granted me a blessing, but I will take it as a curse! I do not desire to rule the world, only to rule myself.'"

The roomful of antiquarians applauded, and he gave a little bow.

"This will have Roman scholars talking for years to come!" said Rossini.

"Indeed," said Guioccini. "But we are going to have some journalists talking very badly about us if we do not board that helicopter for Capri right away. Isabella, will you send pictures of the Augustan scroll and the video you just took of Josh translating it to my cell phone? I am sure the journalists would be quite interested in this development."

"Of course, sir," said Isabella.

"Actually," the president of the Bureau said, "let us hold off on telling them about this until tomorrow. We need to double check and transcribe the translation before we release it."

Castolfo lingered after the others had left. He walked over to the table to peer closely at the original scroll rather than look at the oversized monitor. He started to reach out, just to touch one corner of the ancient papyrus, and then withdrew his hand. He looked at the archeologists with a wistful smile.

"For many years I have stared at the statues of Caesar Augustus— both the flawless, deified Augustus of the later years and the more accurate, human Octavian of his youth. I have read Suetonius, Cassius

Dio, and Plutarch's stories of him, and the poems that Virgil wrote in his honor. But to behold this scroll, in his own writing—" The president of the Bureau of Antiquities' governing board gave a small shiver. "This is something I have never dreamed of. Thank you."

Without another word, he walked out. Josh walked over and looked down at the ancient scroll, the elegant Latin letters as clear and bold now as they had been when they were written. He thought about the fact that, when that will had been written and left in the Temple of Vesta, not a single book of the New Testament had been written, and Jesus of Nazareth had still been in his teens.

"It's humbling, isn't it?" said MacDonald, standing at his elbow. "To stand in the presence of such a magnificent piece of history?"

"I remember the first time that I looked at the Declaration of Independence," said Josh. "I was just so filled with awe, to be looking at the actual handwriting of Thomas Jefferson! But to think, when those men met at Philadelphia in 1776, this scroll had already been buried in that chamber for over seventeen centuries."

Isabella had joined them. "It is truly an amazing experience!" she said. "When Giuseppe called me eight days ago, I truly had no idea of what lay in store."

"What about the Pilate manuscript?" asked Josh, turning from the table and looking at the tank. The scroll had unrolled another inch or so, and he could plainly see the writing on it. "How long do you think?"

MacDonald looked at it carefully. "I want to be incredibly careful with this one," he said. "Its significance is so enormous, we can leave nothing to chance. But it is obvious the humidifying effect is kicking in already. This scroll appears to be twice as long as the other one, and it has already unrolled nearly to the side of the tank. Fortunately, these tanks were made to rehydrate ancient papyrus and parchment, with the expectation that they would unroll as part of the process, and so the side walls are modular and easily removed or extended." He reached out and grasped a small, vertical plastic grip that extended from the edge of the tank the Pilate document lay in, and carefully lifted and pulled. The entire side of the tank pulled out, doubling its length and giving the scroll more room. The priest reached on the shelf above the tanks and pulled down a roll of clear plastic adhesive tape and covered the slot that the side panel had left in the front plexiglass surface, to maintain the seal and keep the humid air inside.

"There!" he said. "Now the entire scroll should have room to unroll. I imagine that by tomorrow, or Wednesday at the latest, the *Testimonium Pilatus* will reveal its mysteries to us!"

"I wish we could start reading it now," Josh said, looking wistfully at the ancient script. The writing was almost impossible to read from the low angle he had.

"I do too, laddie," said MacDonald. "But at least, when we start it, we will be able to read it all at once!"

"There is that at least," said Josh. "What shall we do with the rest of the afternoon?"

"It's after three," Isabella said. "Let's review and edit our video and photographic records of the last days on-site, and then begin preparing our announcement to the press on the Augustan scroll."

"And then we can watch ourselves on the evening news!" MacDonald said.

"Why don't the two of you come on over to my place for supper?" said Isabella. "I'm no great cook, but we can order out and eat while we see how badly the press misquotes us."

And so it was that two hours later, the three of them sat together in Isabella's comfortable den, watching as the evening newscasts from all over Europe and the U.S. led with the story of their press conference. They started off with the American broadcast network, BNN, where the handsome and vapid countenance of Tyler Patterson smiled at the camera from just outside the ancient chamber on the island of Capri.

"Good evening, ladies and gentlemen, and welcome to BNN Around the Globe!" he said cheerfully. "I am standing on the island of Capri, just off the Italian coast near Naples. Behind me you can see the mysterious chamber of secrets left behind by the Roman Emperor Tiberius nearly two thousand years ago. Every year, thousands of tourists have tramped up and down the stone staircase above this tiny chamber, never suspecting its existence. Not until the earthquake that struck the island on Easter Sunday, eight days ago, did anyone suspect that this ruin held some of the most important discoveries in the history of archeology!"

Isabella leaned over toward Josh. "He may not be bright," she said, "but he does have a flair for the dramatic!"

"Who needs intelligence when you can be entertaining?" Josh asked.

Onscreen, Patterson continued. "In this chamber, before leaving Capri on his ill-fated return to Rome in 47 AD, Tiberius sealed up his personal correspondence and some family heirlooms, which were revealed in a press conference at the National Archeological Museum in Naples today."

The scene cut to the press conference, which had already been carried live all over the world. The most popular clip seemed to be Josh, drawing the sword of Caesar from its scabbard. Isabella nudged him. "You look ready to do battle with the Fourth Estate single-handedly!" she laughed.

Patterson's voice-over continued. "As remarkable and exciting as these ancient relics are, the most important discoveries were not physically present at the press conference. Two ancient scrolls were still being dehydrated so they could be opened and read." Father MacDonald choked at that gaffe. "One of these scrolls, according to the label written on the outside of it and visible in this video clip, is apparently the last will and testament of Julius Caesar Augustus, famous for creating the Roman Empire, and being Emperor at the time Jesus of Nazareth is thought to have been born."

Josh groaned at that one. "Can't they at least acknowledge that maybe the Gospels got Jesus' birth year right, within a forty-year window?" he asked.

The broadcast continued. "Last of all, the archeologists revealed the existence of this scroll, which has yet to be opened and read. But its label proclaims it to be the 'Testimony of Pontius Pilate, Governor of Judea.' Pilate is known to Christians worldwide as the Roman governor who reluctantly signed Jesus' death warrant in 33 AD. Speculation is rampant as to what this scroll might or might not contain. For our informed opinions, we have turned to our special religion correspondent, Pastor Joel Wombaker, leader of the Evangelical Lutheran Church in New York, and Dr. David Hubbard, leader of the American Atheism Foundation and well-known author of the book, *Life Without God: What the Church Doesn't Want You to Know*. Gentlemen, what does this discovery mean for modern Christianity?"

The screen split to show the two men seated in the network's New York studio. Wombaker spoke first. A stocky, powerfully built man with a shaved head and an irrepressible smile, his nationally televised sermon hour, *Blessed and Getting Better!* had edged out many of the older, more stolid TV preachers in recent years. "This is a great day for the Church!" he said. "Christians have long preached and taught that our faith is rooted in real, historical events, and having Pilate's report to Rome, if indeed that is what this document is, will show everyone that has jumped on the Bible-bashing bandwagon in recent years that we have been right all along."

"But what if Pilate's testimony says that Jesus did not rise from the dead?" pressed Patterson. "What if he says the disciples hid the body, or that the Romans themselves took it for some reason?"

"Well," said the preacher, "you have to consider that there is really no evidence that Pilate ever became a believer. So naturally he would try to find some natural explanation for such a strange event, especially in a report to his Emperor. Even St. Matthew tells us the priests bribed the guards to say that the disciples came and stole Jesus' body."

Dr. Hubbard had been impatiently rolling his eyes throughout the pastor's remarks, so Patterson addressed him next. "What are your thoughts on this discovery, Dr. Hubbard?"

"First of all, I find all this premature speculation distasteful and ridiculous. There is very little evidence that a person named Jesus of Nazareth even existed, much less that he was executed as described in the collection of fairy tales known as the Gospels! This may very well be a report to the Emperor about something else entirely."

"Isn't that a bit of a stretch, to say that Jesus never lived?" asked the reporter.

"Not at all!" snapped Hubbard. "There is not a single contemporary reference to him! Just a set of stories that were written down fifty to a hundred years later by a group of superstitious peasants. And if he ever did live, I imagine he was just a zealous rabbi who got into trouble for purely political reasons, not some primitive deity who decided for unfathomable reasons to incarnate himself into the body of a carpenter."

"You sure do seem to waste a lot of hate and anger on someone whom you claim never existed, Dr. Hubbard," said Wombaker. "But your claim that Jesus never lived is ridiculous in the extreme, almost as inaccurate as the dates you ascribe to the Gospels."

"What do you mean by that, Pastor Wombaker?" asked Patterson.

"The three synoptic Gospels, Matthew, Mark, and Luke, were written only thirty or forty years after the time Jesus lived, by eyewitnesses of his life in Matthew's case, and that of John's gospel, even though it was written a while later. Some of Paul's letters date a decade earlier, and Galatians dates within fifteen years of the Crucifixion. Roman historians and the Jewish writer Josephus all treat Jesus as a real flesh-and-blood person. And as far as Dr. Hubbard's editorial comments go, St. Paul said it best: 'The preaching of the cross is foolishness to those who are perishing.' Whatever is in this scroll, God's church is not the least bit afraid to face it."

The atheist's face darkened. "Probably because they planted it there in the first place!" he snapped.

Patterson raised an eyebrow. "What do you mean by that?"

"Get real," said Hubbard. "They discover this supposedly undisturbed chamber on Easter Sunday, and the first thing they do is call in a representative from the Vatican and the son of an Evangelical preacher from the American South? The whole thing stinks so badly I can smell it here in New York!"

Josh looked over at Isabella. "And so it begins," he said.

"Good thing we did our field work properly," she replied.

* * *

On another television set, on the isle of Capri, Ali bin-Hassan watched the coverage of the press conference as broadcast on the Arabic network, Al-Jizyah. The anchor stated: "Archeologists claim to have found several artifacts dating to the time of the early Roman Empire, including a scroll that may to contain the report Pontius Pilate filed to the Emperor Tiberius about the so-called crucifixion of the Prophet Isa, peace be upon him. Christian infidels believe that Isa was crucified and then rose again on the third day to prove that he was the Son of the Most High. The Religion of Truth teaches that he was neither crucified nor killed, but divinely sheltered from harm by Allah and then caught up to the heavens, while the disciple who betrayed him was killed in his place. Islamic scholars hope that Pilate's report will chronicle the true narrative, but many already fear that this is just another clever hoax to deceive the faithful."

Hassan snapped off the TV and stepped outside. All day long, nothing but reports and speculation about the mysterious scroll and its alleged contents—he must do something! He made his way down the trail behind his house that led to the beach. The half-moon was low in the sky, and he could see nothing but empty sand in every direction. The crash of the surf would foil any potential eavesdropping. He pulled a disposable cell phone from his pocket. The cell phone had been delivered earlier that year, and it was programmed with only one number. That number would ring in a vacant apartment in Cairo, where a remote router would relay it to a cell phone belonging to one of the most wanted men in the world—al Qaeda's current director of operations, Ibrahim Abbasside. The Ethiopian terrorist had masterminded a number of successful plots, and others that had been foiled by the infidels, but he had never been captured. In fact, the cursed American Crusaders had not even been able to come up with a photograph of him yet! Hassan had debated all day on whether or not to call the number, but now his mind was made up. He turned on the phone and brought up the contact list, and pressed "Call" on the only number it displayed.

The phone in Cairo rang twice, and he hung up. Two rings was the prearranged signal. Seconds later, his phone buzzed.

"Allah is merciful!" he answered.

"Indeed he is," came the reply. "Hassan, it is good to speak to you again. I know you must have called for a reason. What is it?"

"This so-called archeological discovery," he said. "It could pose a great victory for the infidel Christians."

"Fortunate that it was found in your own back yard, then," said the terror mastermind. "It is a shame that you were not able to act more quickly."

"By the time I became aware of it, the artifacts were already being moved to Naples," said Hassan. "But I am familiar with the area where they are being studied. A properly placed 'special delivery' would destroy the lab, the scrolls, and the infidels who found them."

"You know that 'The Prophet's Hammer' has been delayed by the improved security at Target Alpha," said Abbasside. That was the code name for a truck bomb intended to destroy St. Peter's Basilica. "The device is ready, sitting in a warehouse just south of Rome. I could have drivers deliver it to Naples. But it would require someone familiar with the area to place the package where it needs to be delivered."

"You mean—" said Hassan.

"Paradise will await you, my brother," replied the Ethiopian.

Hassan could barely contain his happiness. That he might finally earn Islam's highest honor, death by jihad! The thought of the joys of paradise overwhelmed him. "*Allahu Akbar!*" he exclaimed.

"He is great indeed," said Abbasside. "A new phone will be delivered in two days. It will ring sometime Thursday evening, giving you specific instructions as to where the package will be waiting. Delivering the package will be your responsibility—it must be done at a time when the so-called Pilate report is there beyond all doubt, and you must get close enough to the walls of the lab to ensure their utter destruction. Is that clear?"

"Yes, imam!" exclaimed Abbas. The line went dead immediately thereafter. The entire conversation had taken less than three minutes. As he walked up the trail to his home near the mosque, he could hardly contain his joy. No more mouthing platitudes that went against every fiber of his being! No more being the infidels' pet imam! Muhammad al Medina, the kindly, benevolent imam of the Capri mosque, had always been a fiction. In less than a week, the whole world would realize how great a work of fiction he had been.

That Saturday, Caesar, was one of the quietest days during my entire tenure here in Judea. The Jewish leaders, having gotten their way, were quiescent the whole time, absorbed in their Passover rituals. The Galilean's followers were in hiding, no doubt in shock and grief at his death. After that incredibly long and difficult Friday, I began to feel I could breathe again.

But Sunday morning, shortly before the noontide meal, Longinus came to see me. He saluted crisply, but his countenance was grim. Not just grim, either. It was as white as my toga. He was afraid.

"He's gone," he said.

"Who is gone?" I asked.

"That bloody Galilean! Jesus of Nazareth! His tomb is empty, his shroud an empty shell, and his body is missing!"

Rage filled me. "How could this happen?" I demanded.

"My three legionaries were camped some distance away," he said. "But there were twenty of those Jewish Temple guards watching the tomb, and the stone across the entrance would have taken a dozen men to move! They had even sealed it with a big wax seal, proclaiming death to any who violated the tomb."

"Then what happened?" I demanded.

"Just before dawn, they heard the ground shake, and the Jewish temple guards shrieking. My two boys started towards the tomb, and saw the Jews lying on the grass as if dead. The huge stone was moved several yards away from the entrance. Decius Carmella approached the opening, and then a blinding flash of light knocked both of them out cold. When they woke up, the Jews had fled, and there was a group of women at the tomb wondering what had happened. That is when they came and reported to me!"

CHAPTER SIXTEEN

Josh rose early the next morning, swam ten laps in the pool, then showered and got dressed. He was just finishing his continental breakfast when Isabella walked into the hotel's restaurant looking for him. He waved her over with a bit of trepidation. They had not really been alone together since he had declined her invitation Sunday night, and he was not sure how she felt about him at this point. But she was all smiles as she slid into the booth across from him.

"You are an early riser," she said. "That's commendable; it leaves much more time to get things done."

Josh smiled. "I never could stand to waste daylight," he said, "even as a teenager. So many of my friends would sleep till noon on Saturday, while I would be up as soon as it got light, fishing or catching snakes or hunting arrowheads! Of course, while they were partying till three in the morning, I was generally in bed by ten every night."

Isabella looked at him sadly. "You were something of a Boy Scout, weren't you?"

"Oh, I don't know that I would go that far," said Josh. "I loved a good prank as much as anyone, and did my share of juvenile adolescent stupidity . . . but I avoided things that I thought of as 'the big sins.' I didn't smoke, didn't drink, never was interested in drugs, and was frankly scared to death of girls."

"Somehow I don't find that hard to believe," she said with a look so frank it scared him.

"Listen, Isabella, about the other night—" he said.

"I was too forward," she said curtly. "I have been so alone for so long I just couldn't stand it anymore."

"If I could have my way, you would never be alone again!" he said.

"So what is keeping you from it?" she asked. "Having your way, I mean?"

"There are some obstacles," he said, blushing. "But none of them are insurmountable. Obviously, we come from different countries, have separate careers, and speak different native languages."

"Joshua!" she said. "You are ducking the subject. I like you a great deal. Despite my better instincts, I think I may be actually falling in love with you. The least you can do is be honest with me. What is it about the thought of sleeping with me that terrifies you so much?"

"I guess 'fear of the unknown' is too simple an answer, huh?" he asked ruefully. "I'll try to explain as best I can. I believe, with all my heart, that the Bible lays out a divine plan for human relationships as well as with our relationship with God. I don't want to live like so many of my friends, hopping from partner to partner, looking for satisfaction and never finding it, promising to love and cherish, and then five years later, cheating, lying, and running out. I want to have ONE sexual relationship—but I want it to last the rest of my life. To me, that means I pick the right person, and then WAIT until my ring is on her finger and my last name takes the place of hers before I take her home with me forever. I have been looking my whole life for that person—and for the first time ever, I really think that I may have found her. My heart tries to leap out of my chest every time I look at you! And it's not just physical attraction—although there is plenty of that, trust me. But there is more. I want to make you laugh. I want to hold you when you cry. I want to see you every moment of every day. And I want to keep you from being hurt ever again."

There was so much sincerity, so much longing, in his voice that Isabella was moved despite herself. She had resolved, after his refusal of her proposition, to back off and begin disentangling herself from this handsome but confusing man. That resolve had come with difficulty, after a lot of soul searching and a half a gallon of chocolate ice cream. She had even called her closest female cousin to commiserate with her for an hour that night. But now his deep brown eyes, his tanned handsome face, and above all, the simple love that radiated from him melted that resolve. She opened her mouth and spoke.

"Then why not?" she said. "There is something else—or I think you would have asked me already."

He gave a deep sigh. "As much as I love you, Isabella, I love my God more. And I am afraid to share my life with a person who does not share that love. I don't want to spend the rest of my life with a person that I cannot count on spending eternity with. I want you to love Jesus as much as I do, and then I can love you without reservation or fear. But if you are an unbeliever—a skeptic—I am afraid to give my heart to you. Because if you never come to share my faith, that would mean saying goodbye to you forever when I die. And I don't think I could stand that. And so I hold back—because I don't know what you believe. It is the one thing we have never had a chance to talk about, and I have been waiting—and dreading—the chance to do so!"

"What do I believe?" Isabella asked. She had not really thought about God in years. She had gone to mass often as a young girl, and had entertained a simple belief in a benevolent Creator through her teen years. She was not sure what she thought about Jesus of Nazareth. She knew he had been a real person, but the Son of God? For her, the twisted marble figure hanging on a cross above the altar was an abstraction, a symbol of a powerful philosophy. A historical figure that had been amplified into something far more than he ever meant to be. Now she was the chief investigator in an excavation which could, potentially, establish which version of Jesus was real—the radical rabbi who challenged the authority of Rome and the priests, the misunderstood mystic, or the dynamic Son of God portrayed in the Gospels? Her scientific training, her skeptical nature, and her deep-seated anger at God over the loss of her husband years before, all argued against the kind of Jesus that Josh seemed to accept without hesitation. And yet, deep down, there was a part of her that had never left the cathedral where she had knelt as a child. That part longed for something greater than herself, a God that could love her and be loved in return, a God she could cast her cares on without reservation. Yet she doubted the existence of such a being.

"I won't lie to you," she said. "I don't know what I believe. I want your God to be real—he certainly seems to give meaning to your life—but I haven't decided if he is or not."

Josh took her hand in his and pressed it to his lips. "When you decide," he said, looking straight at her, "I'll be waiting."

She averted her gaze so he wouldn't see the tears that started to form in her eyes. After a moment, she said, "You are a ridiculously good person! But while you are waiting for me, the lab is waiting for us. Let's get out of here."

They slid out of the booth and walked toward the front entrance of the hotel lobby, with Josh holding her hand as they stepped out into the street. It was a rainy morning, and the flashbulbs that exploded were extra bright against the dim sky. Half a dozen journalists had been huddled under the hotel's elaborate façade, waiting for them to emerge. Since releasing Josh's hand at this point would be too late anyway,

Isabella tightened her grip and smiled for the cameras. He followed suit, and the flashbulbs popped again, and then the questions began.

"Dr. Sforza!" An earnest young American stepped forward. "Andrew Eastwood, *Chicago Tribune*. Any new developments since yesterday's press conference? Has either of the scrolls been opened and read?"

Isabella had spent a good part of the afternoon preparing remarks about the Caesar scroll, and figured this would be a good time to tease the media a bit. "Well, we will be making an announcement to reporters a bit later this morning," she said. "One of the scrolls had rehydrated and opened enough to be read by yesterday afternoon, and we will be sharing the translation with you in a couple of hours."

"Can you tell us which one it was?" the young American asked.

She sighed. "The Pilate scroll is the longer of the two and will take a bit more time to rehydrate and unroll," she said. "But the Caesar's will opened up beautifully for us. However, if you want to know what it said, you will have to attend our press conference at ten AM. Now, Dr. Parker and I have a great deal of work to do this morning, so if you will excuse us—"

Another reporter spoke up. "Dr. Sforza," he said. "There has been a lot of speculation in the press as to the nature of your relationship with Dr. Parker. Would you care to clarify that for us?"

Isabella's dark eyes flashed with anger. "NO!" she snapped, and she and Josh pushed through the small crowd that had gathered and headed toward the museum. A few shouted questions followed, but she and Josh ignored them.

"You should have known that was coming eventually!" he said as they neared the museum's entrance.

She turned to face him, first glancing back to make sure that none of the reporters or paparazzi had followed them. "I will have to know what that relationship is before I can clarify it for anyone!" she said. "And right now, I think you will agree that we are at something of an impasse, wouldn't you?"

Josh nodded. "Unwillingly, but yes—for the moment. But I do believe we will surmount it!"

She smiled at his optimism, his sweetness, and most of all, at him. His simple goodness was impossible to remain angry with. "If believing in Jesus will make me more like you," she said, "I might have to consider it at some point." Then she kissed him quickly on the cheek and began striding briskly toward the museum entrance.

When they came in, MacDonald was waiting for them, beaming from ear to ear. "It's about time you two lovebirds showed up!" he said in his best Scottish accent. "Oh, this is absolutely marvelous!"

Josh raised an eyebrow. "What is?" he asked.

"The scroll! The *Testimonium!*" the priest exclaimed, nearly dancing with excitement. "It opened almost completely. Giuseppe is already prepping the table, and as soon as you can get some gloves on, we can remove it from the tank and begin translation!"

Josh swallowed hard. This was it. For all his brave talk, he was a little afraid to see what was written on the scroll. What if Pilate revealed that the entire resurrection story—the story that Josh, his father, and virtually every person Josh cared about had based their entire lives around—was really a two-thousand-year-old hoax? Or a dreadful case of mistaken identity? Every alternative theory he had ever heard regarding the Resurrection story crowded into his head at once. But then a simple prayer from the Gospel of Mark came to his mind, and he repeated it to himself. "I believe," he prayed. "Help my unbelief!"

Then he looked up and smiled at the Vatican archeologist. "What are we waiting for?" he said. "Let's go!"

The three of them almost sprinted through the museum toward the back entrance, where Dr. Guioccini was waiting for them. "I was about to send out a search party, Dr. Sforza!" he said with a smile.

"We were waylaid by the advance guard of the Fourth Estate," she explained.

"After a breakfast that probably did drag on a bit too long," Josh admitted. The priest and the Italian archeologist gave him a curious look, and he realized how it sounded. "In the hotel restaurant, where Dr. Sforza had to come looking for me," he added quickly, and the priest gave him a wink. Curse that man's mischievous nature! Josh thought. Isabella herself was a bit red in the face, but he was sure it was from their quick walk through the museum. Nothing seemed to faze her.

They stepped through the back doors and stepped across the blacktop to the new lab. Rossini waited for them at the door, and Dr. Apriceno was right behind him. "I must admit," she said, "this is a bit more exciting than my microscope at the moment!"

When they stepped into the lab, Josh walked straight over to the tank, where the Pilate scroll had unrolled almost to its full length. One end of it was resting against the side of the tank, despite the extension they had made to the tank's width the day before. It looked to be nearly six and a half feet long.

"How are we going to move it to the viewing table?" Josh asked.

"I've been working on that for an hour," the priest said. "Look at this." He had taken four of the trays that they used to transport smaller artifacts from tank to table, and used some sort of powerful glue to attach long aluminum bars across their bottom sides, making one long tray. He picked up the trays and shook them solidly to make sure the epoxy had taken hold, then flipped them right side up and began covering them with acid-free paper. The tabletop was already covered, and the securing clamps were positioned to hold the scroll in place while it was being photographed and studied. MacDonald worked quickly, folding the paper down over the outside edges of the trays and taping it in place beneath. Josh was already putting his gloves on.

Moments later, they lifted out the plexiglass sides of the two tanks. Isabella had also donned her gloves, and three pairs of hands slid underneath the ancient papyrus to gently lift it out of the tank and place it on the combined trays. Josh and MacDonald got on either end, with Isabella in the middle, and carefully lifted the ancient document on the trays and carried it to the table. Then they slid it off the trays and then Father MacDonald carefully teased each end as flat as he dared, positioning the clamps so as to keep them from rolling back up, but not to put any actual pressure on the papyrus until he could stabilize the material. Josh gave a quick glance at the flowing Latin script that covered the page. At a glance, he could see that the last two columns were written in a different hand than the rest. One name leaped off the page at him—"*IESUS NAZARENUS.*" Jesus of Nazareth.

The air went out of his lungs, and MacDonald looked up from his work. Unable to speak, Josh pointed.

"Holy Mother of God!" the priest said. "It means one thing to speculate, and think about it. But to see it before our eyes! Help me, lad, I canna stand it. Let's get this thing stabilized so we can begin the translation!"

The rest of the team, and Doctors Guioccini and Castolfo, who had slipped in as they worked, all watched with rapt attention as the Scottish antiquarian produced two spray bottles of his special solution and handed one to Josh. Working silently together, the two of them slowly and carefully sprayed the document from one end to the other, coating it with the stabilizer two times. The ancient papyrus darkened slightly as the fluid hit it and soaked in. Soon the entire mass of papyrus was an even, rich brown in color, and the two men stepped back.

Fully unrolled, the scroll was about sixteen inches in height, and almost seventy-six inches in length. There was a faint, ancient water stain at one end, but the writing was clear and legible throughout. Dr. MacDonald turned on the state-of-the-art digital camera, which was positioned directly over the table on a retractable arm, with its powerful light ready to shine down on the scroll as every character was recorded on film. Isabella was the first to step forward, and then Rossini came up behind her and laid a fatherly hand on her shoulder. Moments later, Apriceno, Castolfo, and Guioccini joined them. Seven pairs of eyes stared at the ancient scroll.

Finally Rossini spoke. "There are hardly words to express this moment," he said. "What we do in this lab today will echo around the world. The realms of faith, politics, science, and history may all be shaken. None of us, at this moment, know exactly what is about to happen. But I have the feeling that our lives will never be the same. So I want to say—here and now—that I have been honored to work with each of you. I could not have asked for a more diverse, interesting, and professional team of scientists. You humble me."

Josh clasped the elderly Italian by the hand, his eyes shining. "The feeling could not be more mutual, Giuseppe," he said. "You are a good man. Father MacDonald, I came halfway around the world looking for a mystery, and found a friend. Simone, you are an amazing woman. I wish you and my mother could meet. You remind me of her a great deal. And Isabella—" He found himself unable to go on.

"Enough of this silly mush!" said Father MacDonald. "That scroll is not going to translate itself!" He busied himself with the camera, and the team watched as he carefully photographed each column of ancient script and saved the images to the laboratory computer. In a few moments, he was done. Josh plugged his laptop into one of the USB ports and downloaded the images, while the Father pulled up the photos on one of the lab's computer workstations.

"Dual translation, like before, Joshua?" he asked.

"Ready when you are," Joshua replied.

"Gentlemen," said Dr. Castolfo. They both looked up. "Our press conference begins in thirty minutes. I do not want your absence to be noted, and I don't want to tear you away in mid-translation. So I must ask you to refrain from starting until after we have spoken to the reporters about the Augustus scroll. I will have armed security inside the lab and outside its doors until you return."

Josh started to open his mouth in protest, then shut it again. The doctor was right. It would not pay to start something and then have to get up, speak to the press, and come back. He gave a wistful glance at the laptop's screen, with the entire scroll pulled up in a series of thumbnail images, then sighed and shut it off. Isabella printed out her prepared remarks, and then copied the translation of the famous emperor's will. With a long sigh, he got up from the comfortable stool and walked over to stare at the original scroll one more time.

"Also," said Castolfo, "we need to keep our progress on the *Testimonium* between us for the moment. No need to inform the media until we have something to report."

"I don't know that Dr. Sinisi would agree," commented Isabella.

Castolfo smiled. "Sinisi calls the press when he goes to the restroom!" he said. "But I am going to overrule him on this one. In fact, I have given orders not to admit him to the lab until the translation is complete. We will decide when to share this scroll, and not have our hand forced by premature leaks to the press."

The five archeologists, and Castolfo, walked up to the press room. Guioccini agreed to stay in the lab and keep an eye on things. The museum's security guards underwent rigorous security screening, but he wanted to be there anyway, just to be sure that nothing was disturbed. Even with twenty-four-hour security cameras, the potential significance of the ancient document was such that he felt he had to be there if none of the team members were.

The press conference went smoothly and quickly. As soon as the reporters realized the Pilate scroll was not the subject of the announcement, the intensity of their interest sagged. They took the translation and photographs of the Augustan scroll and glanced at them, but only a few had questions. Those inquiries were fairly routine—although the young reporter from Chicago who had accosted them outside the hotel actually seemed to be both interested in and informed about the subject.

"Dr. Sforza," Eastwood asked, "can you tell me how this document changes our understanding of the origins of the Roman Empire, and of its First Emperor?"

Isabella brightened at this opportunity to educate the public. "We have known for centuries that Augustus proclaimed Tiberius as his heir even before his death," she said, "but the fact that he specifically bequeathed all of his elected and appointed political offices to his adopted son shows that for him, the Empire was, as you Americans might say, a done deal. The short postscript to the Senate makes it plain that, even if he had once toyed with the idea of restoring the Republic, he had abandoned that notion as impractical. What is really interesting, though, is the appended note by Tiberius himself. It has always been known that he hated the city of Rome and did not seem to care for the Imperial throne, but this personal note, inscribed on Augustus' will, makes it evident that he apparently never wanted to be Emperor at all. Biographers will speculate for years on what he meant when he said his only desire was 'to rule himself.' We still have high hopes that the fragmentary manuscripts we retrieved will help further our understanding of the troubled relationship between Tiberius and his adopted father, Augustus."

The young reporter nodded. "So do you think Tiberius was the monster that the early histories portrayed him as?"

Isabella thought for a moment. This young man had obviously done his homework, and the question deserved an honest reply. "There are many histories that are very critical of Tiberius and his reign," she said. "It is worth noting that the further removed from his lifetime the sources are, the more wild and bizarre the stories they record about him. The earliest sources, which are also the sketchiest, paint a picture of an emperor who was stern and unhappy, but not a monster. I will say that the text of the letter we recovered seems to lean more towards that point of view. Certainly, it seems to refute the tales repeated by Suetonius portraying the old emperor as a twisted and cruel pedophile. But, at the moment, there is not enough information to make a solid statement one way or the other."

Eastwood nodded, seemingly satisfied with the answer. Isabella looked around the room and saw that no one else seemed eager to question her.

"Well, then, gentlemen, if that is all—" she began.

"One last thing," said Cynthia Brown. "When do you think the Pilate scroll will be ready to read and translate?"

Isabella paused. "Sooner rather than later," she said. Then the team exited before anyone could ask them what that might mean.

Caesar, I write these last pages with my own hand, because I am not sure that I trust even my faithful scribe with the words that follow. As soon as Longinus made his report, I ordered him to arrest some of the Temple guards who had been at the tomb and bring them to me immediately. It took a couple of hours, as they were closeted with the priests in some secret meeting. My legionaries discreetly nabbed two of them as soon as they left, and dragged them to the Praetorium.

At first they tried to pass off the story that the disciples of Jesus had stolen the body as they slept near the tomb. This tale was obviously a concoction—a guard detachment of twenty all asleep at the same time? The band of frightened peasants that had been too afraid to rescue their beloved rabbi, suddenly risking life and limb to retrieve his ravaged corpse? Ridiculous! I ordered them scourged, and their story soon changed.

What they told us was that before dawn Sunday morning, about half the detachment was asleep as the other half stood in front of the tomb, bored, and talking among themselves. Suddenly there was a blinding flash of light and a great earthquake that knocked them all to their knees, and the stone in front of the tomb was flung about ten yards away, nearly crushing one of them. As they stared at the entrance of the tomb, two glowing balls of light descended from the sky and assumed human form at the entrance. These two beings turned and looked at the guards, and every one of them fell down as if dead. When they came to, the tomb was empty, and two Roman soldiers were there unconscious as well. They fled to the Temple to report what they had seen to the High Priest, leaving my men stretched out on the grass.

The story sounds unbelievable, but even after another dose of the cat-o-nine-tails, they refused to change it. I ordered them both put to death and buried outside the city walls, so that no one would know what they had told me. Then I summoned the High Priest and met him outside the Temple District.

"What has happened?" I demanded.

"Exactly what I warned you of!" he snapped. "The Galileans came at night and stole the body of the Nazarene!"

"You mean all of your Temple guards let themselves be overpowered by a dozen frightened fishermen?" I sneered.

"There were nearly a hundred of them!" he said, obviously shaken that I refused to believe him.

"So how many did your guards kill?" I asked.

"None!" he said. "The blackguards overwhelmed them as they slept!"

His lies were so preposterous I did not want to listen any more. I turned on my heel and called over my shoulder: "It sounds like your guards were derelict in their duty. Let me know if you want them crucified, too!"

By evening the city was abuzz with rumors that the crucified Galilean had been seen again, by several of his disciples and by a group of women as well. There were also stories that the earthquake had torn the veil of the Temple, that several long-dead holy men had been seen wandering the streets preaching about the Messiah, and that the disciple who betrayed Jesus had hung himself. The Jewish priests were strangely silent, and I did not know what to believe myself.

The next morning, I walked down to the tomb where the crucified Jesus had been interred four days before. The heavy stone that had been rolled across the entrance was indeed several yards away, and one side of it was strangely scorched. The seal that had been placed on it was now a half molten blob of wax. I looked into the tomb, but there was only the lingering scent of myrrh and some empty linen wrappings lying where the body of the Nazarene prophet had been placed. I sat down on the stone outside, lost in thought.

"Why do you seek the living One among the dead?" a voice asked me.

I looked up to see the young disciple of Jesus whom I had recruited to act as my interpreter at the trial. He was alone and unarmed, and I motioned my legionaries to let him approach. He looked to be just out of his teens, and his expression was one of confidence and . . . for lack of a better word, joy.

"What happened here?" I demanded.

"Here the man you killed returned to life," he said simply.

"That is impossible!" I snapped.

"All things are possible with God," he calmly replied. "Our prophets have long predicted that the Lord's Messiah would be betrayed, tormented, and killed, and then rise again from the dead. I watched it happen. I saw Him tried, I saw Him nailed to the cross, and I saw your soldiers drive a spear through His heart. I wrapped His body in the shroud, and I stepped into the tomb yesterday morning to see the same empty cloths you just did."

"An empty tomb and an abandoned shroud don't mean a corpse came back to life!" I snapped. "They mean a grave was robbed, and I intend to find out who did it!"

His eyes softened. "Noble governor," he said. "I saw that you did your best to spare Him, and I am grateful. As long as I live to tell the story, I will tell that you did your best to save His life. But there is more to the story than the empty tomb. I know that He lives because I have seen Him myself! Alive, healthy, eating supper, the wounds of his ordeal healed! I have touched the nail scars in his hands! If you had seen what I have seen since yesterday morning, you too would believe in Him!"

The audacity of this peasant stunned me! That he would dare to forgive me for simply carrying out my duties as governor! I raised my hand to strike him, and then lowered it again, unnerved by his unwavering stare. Whatever he had seen, I realized that it had left him utterly without fear. As quickly as my dignitas would allow, I turned on my heel and left that accursed place.

And that is the end of my tale, Caesar. I have tried to conduct myself as a Roman prefect and proconsul should. I still do not know what it is I have done. Have I been the victim of an incredibly elaborate fraud? Have I lost my mind? Or was I the unwitting accomplice in the murder of a god? I do not know. So I leave judgment of this matter in your hands. Mine are too stained with blood to deal with it any further. I beg you, Caesar, recall me from this benighted place and let me return to Rome! I remain, respectfully yours, Lucius Pontius Pilate, Governor of Judea.

CHAPTER SEVENTEEN

As soon as they were out of sight of the journalists, Josh and Father MacDonald began walking faster and faster, both of them hitting a jogging pace by the time they got to the door of the research lab. Guioccini was still waiting inside, but there were two armed security guards outside the door who looked carefully at their ID badges before allowing them in. It was already apparent that the Bureau of Antiquities was taking this find very seriously.

The scroll was exactly as they had left it, spread out fully on the table. Its color had lightened a bit as the stabilizing compound bonded with the papyrus and slowly dried. Both men stared at the ancient document for a few moments as the rest of the team assembled behind them.

"Did you take a peek for yourself, Dr. Guioccini?" asked MacDonald.

"Not really," replied the lead archeologist. "I translated the first line, then made myself back off. You and Dr. Parker will have this privilege to yourselves."

The priest nodded and turned to Josh. "I think that my photographs have clearly captured every line of the original script," he said, "and you will be able to magnify them as needed on your laptop. I am going to suggest that we separately translate the entire manuscript, then swap notebooks and compare results."

"Agreed," Josh replied. "Keyboard or longhand?"

"I'm old school," the priest said. "I just like using a yellow legal tablet."

"Not a problem," Josh said. "Writing longhand does seem to flow more naturally when translating a handwritten document."

"All right then," said the priest. "I suggest we begin."

For the next four long and tedious hours Josh pulled up the photographs one after the other, carefully translating the ancient epistle one word at a time, occasionally pulling out his battered Latin-English dictionary when he ran across a particularly obscure term. He was focused on the individual words and phrases and did his best not to think about the actual narrative at first, but as he got further and further into the story he found himself looking back at his earlier writing, looking at the ancient text, and shaking his head in amazement. The letter was quite long and wound up taking about half the yellow tablet up when he was done. Despite the cool temperatures and low humidity of the lab, the perspiration was pouring down his brow when he finally set down his pen. He looked up to see the entire team, and Castolfo and Guioccini, staring at him. He looked over at MacDonald and saw that he was still writing. Deliberately, Josh covered his yellow pad up with a binder and went over to the fridge to pull out one of the Dr Peppers he had stored there as soon as he arrived on the mainland. He drank half the can in one long sip, then let out a long sigh.

Isabella sidled up next to him. "Well?" she whispered, not wanting to disturb MacDonald.

Josh grimaced. "Not yet!" he said. "I want to double and triple check our translations against each other before we start reading it. This is way too important to screw up!"

Isabella nodded, frowning. "My scientific half wants to congratulate you on your professional ethics, but my nosy woman half wants to tie you down and torture you until you tell all!"

"Talking bondage are we, my dear?" asked Rossini. "I didn't think you two were that far along yet!"

Josh flushed beet red, but Isabella simply glared and elbowed her old mentor. "You know my grandfather was in Mussolini's secret police!" she snapped. "I know how to deal with compulsive eavesdroppers!"

The grey-haired professor laughed and put one hand on each of their shoulders. "After everything we have been through since I found that chamber," he said, "I think this wait is the most nerve-wracking!"

"Can you believe it's only been ten days?" asked Josh.

"The quickest—and slowest—ten days of my life," replied Giuseppe.

"Well, laddie, shall we compare results?" asked MacDonald. He had gotten up and walked over unnoticed as they conversed.

"I'm ready when you are," he said. "But let us make one concession to the twenty-first century, shall we?" He walked over toward the lab's one copier, a Konica Minolta, and entered his security code. He frowned when the machine beeped and a red light came on.

"Sorry, professor," said Dr. Castolfo, rushing over. "Due to the extraordinary need for security, all copying now requires my code as well as the user's."

"Smart move," said the priest, and then copied his yellow tablet one page at a time after Castolfo entered the code.

Josh fetched his own tablet and did likewise. Now each of them would have their own original translation notes as well as a precise copy of the other's work, so they could compare word by word, line by line, at the same time. Once the copies were made, each of them retreated to his original position and began the comparison.

This part of the work was easier. The clear, strong Latin hand was easy to read, and for the most part, their work matched exactly. A few times they had translated synonyms instead of the same word, but the meanings were not altered. It took an hour to read through the whole thing silently, comparing and correcting as they went along. When they were finished, they moved their legal tablets to a large table where they could go over their work together. The handful of discrepancies was quickly ironed out, and about an hour after making the copies, they looked at each other and nodded, then turned to the group. Apriceno had wandered back to her lab, so Giuseppe quickly ran to get her. Isabella had stepped down the hall also, but she returned before the other two.

"Our work is done," said the priest. "We each translated the rather lengthy epistle individually, compared our notes, and reconciled the few slight differences between our versions of the manuscript. What you are about to hear is, as we suspected from the moment of its discovery, the report filed by Lucius Pontius Pilate, Prefect of Rome and Proconsul of Judea, to the Roman Emperor Tiberius Caesar about the crucifixion of Jesus of Nazareth. Joshua, would you like to do the honors?"

Josh shook his head. "No, Father," he said. "In this case, I will defer to your seniority and experience. You have earned this right in my book!"

The priest beamed at him. "Ya know, laddie, for a Protestant heretic, you are a true gentleman," he said.

Isabella, Rossini, and Apriceno all said at the same time, rather loudly, "GET ON WITH IT!"—unconsciously echoing one of Josh's favorite scenes from *Monty Python and the Holy Grail*. Castolfo and

Guioccini chuckled, and Josh suppressed his smile as the Scottish cleric began to read.

"Lucius Pontius Pilate, Senior Legate, Prefect, and Proconsul of Judea, to Tiberius Julius Caesar Augustus, Princeps and Imperator of Rome, Greetings.

"Your Excellency, you know that it is the duty of every governor to keep you informed of events in the provinces that may in some way affect the well-being of the Empire. While I am loath to disturb your important daily work with a matter that may seem trivial at first, upon further reflection, and especially in light of subsequent developments, I find myself convinced that recent events in Judea merit your attention. And I would be telling an untruth if I were not to say that I am concerned that other accounts of these happenings may reach your ears which are not just unfavorable but frankly slanderous of my actions and motives. The situation was one of unusual difficulty and complexity, and hard decisions were called for. As always, I tried to make the decisions that I felt would most lend themselves to a peaceful and harmonious outcome for the citizens of the Republic and the people of Judea . . ."

The room was already quiet, but as the Scottish cleric read on, the silence became tangible. When he reached the dramatic narrative about Jesus' trial, Josh could not restrain the smile that began to form. All these years of defending the Gospels as accurate accounts of the life and death of Jesus of Nazareth were not wasted! Throughout his labors, he had carried that tiny seed of doubt in the back of his head that his faith could minimize but never entirely eradicate. The sense of vindication he felt upon hearing the words out loud for the first time was overwhelming, but he tried to caution himself against overconfidence.

The others reacted in their own way. Giuseppe seemed to lapse into deep thought as the narrative reached its dramatic climax, nodding occasionally, but his eyes turning inward as he reflected on the impact of this discovery on history and faith around the world. Isabella's eyes widened as the account of the trial was read, and as MacDonald neared the end of the story, she looked long and hard at Josh, then sunk her gaze to the ground. Simone Apriceno remained as unflappable as ever, nodding occasionally, but her face betraying no emotion. Dr. Castolfo was fascinated, engrossed in the narrative from the beginning. Guioccini shook his head in disbelief several times as the narrative unfolded. MacDonald's clear baritone voice filled the lab, all trace of his accent gone, and his words as clear and crisp as those of a seasoned stage actor reading a long-practiced and well-loved part. His voice rose slightly, and then softened, as he read the account of the empty tomb.

." . . that is the end of my tale, Caesar. I have tried to conduct myself as a Roman proconsul should. I still do not know what it is I have done. Have I been the victim of an incredibly elaborate fraud? Have I lost my mind? Or was I the unwitting accomplice in the murder of a god? I do not know. So I leave judgment of this matter in your hands. Mine are too stained with blood to deal with it any further. I beg you, Caesar, recall me from this benighted place and let me return to Rome! I remain, respectfully yours, Lucius Pontius Pilate, Governor of Judea."

He looked over at Josh and gave a small nod. Josh spoke to the group then. "There is one tiny addendum at the end of the manuscript," he said. "It is not the handwriting used throughout the first section, which was probably penned by Pilate's scribe, nor is it in the same hand as the last two pages, written by Pilate himself. But it does bear a very strong resemblance to the handwriting on the Tiberius letter, and the postscript Tiberius added to Caesar's will. It simply reads as follows:

"'Sergius—this is the most remarkable tale I have read in a while. I would say that Pilate made the whole thing up for my entertainment, were it not for the angry letter I have from Caiaphas the High Priest—and the fact that dear old Pilate is the least imaginative soul in Rome! Send someone you can trust to Judea and see if you can verify any of this remarkable story. And return this original to Capri when you have had it copied—I think I shall keep it with my personal records.—Tiberius Caesar Augustus'

"And that is the entire manuscript, folks. What think you?"

Castolfo spoke first. "I think that there is going to be a political, theological, and historical firestorm that will make the hubbub over the Judas Gospel look like a college debate contest!"

Guioccini nodded. "It certainly will put the historical revisionists on the defensive," he said. "And I imagine the more radical elements of the Muslim world will not be too happy either."

Isabella nodded. "The American intelligentsia is going to have a field day with this one," she said. "Some of the more radical ones, like Hubbard, are going to accuse us of every kind of fraud conceivable."

Simone Apriceno smiled. "I always believed the Church got it right," she said. "Maybe not all the doctrinal derivatives, but the central claim of a Resurrection always made more sense to me than any of the so-called explanations did."

Josh was somewhat surprised. Nothing in her earlier conversations had led him to think she was a person of faith.

Giuseppe Rossini was also beaming. "I agree with Simone. I have not always been a strong Christian, but in my heart, I always believed that Jesus was the Christ of God. Losing my wife made me question that, but I was coming back to my beliefs long before I uncovered that chamber."

"Let's not be too hasty," Isabella said. "After all, Pilate makes no claim to have seen the risen Jesus. Only that the disciples had already made that claim, and that something bizarre did happen at the tomb."

"Do you have any alternative explanation, Dr. Sforza?" Josh asked.

She thought for a moment. "Not really," she said. "But what do you think, Joshua? We have talked about your religious beliefs and your scientific convictions over the last ten days. How do you feel now that you have read Pilate's entire statement?"

Josh thought for a long time before he answered. "I'd be lying if I said there wasn't a sense of vindication," he said. "I've been reading and studying the historical records and accounts of Christianity's origins all my life. I have read all the major apologetic works from Justin Martyr to Lee Strobel, and I have read many of the criticisms as well, from Thomas Jefferson to Bishop Spong to Bart Ehrman. All along I have been convinced that the Gospels were the best, earliest, and most accurate account of Jesus' life, and therefore I believed that His life was indeed a supernatural one. But in the end, no historical proof can justify faith. I believe in Christ because of what He has done in my life and the lives of so many through the centuries—not because Pontius Pilate confirmed that the Gospels got the details of Jesus' trial down correctly."

Father MacDonald nodded. "The boy speaks true," he said. "Faith, in the end, is still 'the substance of things hoped for, the evidence of things not seen.' I have always believed that the Holy Church and Her Scriptures rested on a foundation of pure, accurate history. It's nice to see that belief confirmed to some degree. But I was not going to let the writings of a long-dead governor shake me from my belief in Jesus as the Son of God, regardless."

"That's a lot easier to say now than it was when that scroll was sitting there unopened, though, isn't it, Duncan?" asked Rossini.

The priest threw back his head and laughed. "You can say that again, old friend!" he replied.

"I must ask all of you not to breathe a word of this to anyone yet," said Castolfo. "I will summon an emergency meeting of the Board of Antiquities tomorrow morning at nine AM. I want all of you in attendance, and I want a clean copy of the translation ready to be handed out to the members. I would also like some recommendations as to what other scholars we can invite to come and examine the scroll and verify the excellent work done by Professor MacDonald and Dr. Parker. The more eyes we have on this document now, the better. As soon as the board gives approval, we will begin planning a press conference to release the findings to the public."

Guioccini spoke up. "I would like to have my old friend Dr. Luke Martens brought over as soon as possible," he said. "He was my first choice to be on the excavation team, but was recuperating from a broken leg and not up for the manual labor on Capri. He was the one who recommended Joshua to us, and I think we all agree that was an excellent choice. Now that we are working in the lab, and he is a bit more mobile, I can think of no scholarly opinion I would like to have any more than his."

Josh nodded. "I'll second that," he said. "Dr. Martens is dying to get over here anyway."

MacDonald spoke up. "I would like to invite Cardinal Heinrich Klein to come as well," he replied. "He is too old to do fieldwork, but he is the Vatican's leading historian and specialist in ancient Latin manuscripts."

The group soon began speaking all at once, talking about the various scholars and specialists each wanted to invite to examine the manuscript, and discussing the remarkable contents of the ancient report among themselves. They split off into pairs and trios and moved apart, the better to hear each other over the buzz of conversation. Josh soon found himself standing face to face with Isabella.

"Congratulations, Josh," she said. "It looks as if your faith was not ill placed. So were there any surprises in what you read?"

He nodded. "One big one," he said. "For years, even conservative scholars have wondered exactly how the Apostle John knew what transpired between Jesus and Pilate. Most skeptics think the entire dialogue he described between Jesus and Pilate was completely made up. But it seems that John was right there in the room during Jesus' interrogation, and never forgot what he heard. It seems he never forgot his promise to Pilate, either—he said more than any of the other Evangelists about Pilate's reluctance to send Jesus to the cross."

She nodded, somewhat somberly.

"You don't seem very happy," he said.

"This is difficult for me," she replied. "I am a scientist through and through, and the idea of a supernatural God coming into the world as a carpenter—healing people, raising the dead, then dying to atone for the sins of the world! It's all well and good for a Sunday morning homily at the Cathedral, but to think of it as historical fact—well, that's going to take some getting used to."

Josh looked quickly around the lab, and then planted a quick kiss on her cheek. "Isabella," he said. "Don't be afraid of faith! It won't change who you are. It will only make you better!"

She looked at him fondly, touching her cheek where his lips had brushed it. "I wish I could believe that," she said.

Moments later Dr. Castolfo's voice rose above the others. "This has been an incredible day's work!" he said. "Tonight, supper is on me!"

Josh realized that it was well after six in the evening, and that he was ravenously hungry. It seemed everyone else in the room was, too, as the conversations began to shift from matters of theology, history, and politics to which restaurant would provide them with the most privacy and the best food. However, since the Bureau's president had made the offer, the pick was his. An hour after he had declared that he was picking up the tab, they found themselves seated in a private ballroom at A Finestella, a fine old restaurant overlooking the bay. Pasta and seafood was the specialty, and huge steaming platters of shrimp, clams, calamari, scallops, and prawns followed one another from the kitchen to the table, preceded by succulent aromas that set every mouth to watering. The archeologists had all skipped lunch, it turned out, and before long they were digging into the delicious cuisine with gusto.

Josh carefully chewed a mouthful of the tenderest calamari he had ever eaten, seasoned with butter, garlic, and a hint of basil and oregano. "You know," he said to Father MacDonald, "if there is no seafood in heaven, I am not entirely sure I want to go there!"

"You may be out of luck then," said the priest, "for the Apocalypse of John says that 'there will be no more sea.' Will you forfeit your soul for a prawn?"

"Don't be silly," Josh said. "All that means is that the shrimp and scallops in heaven live on dry land!"

Isabella, who had consumed about three glasses of wine that evening, found this comment hilarious for some reason, and giggled for several minutes over it. Across the table from them, Simone Apriceno and Giuseppe Rossini were bantering like teenagers as they discussed his best possible strategies for his upcoming date with Signora Bustamante. Castolfo and Guioccini looked fondly at the team as they quietly discussed the plans for the next morning's meetings.

The dinner party finally broke up after 8 PM, and the team quickly decided that they would return to the lab early and type up the translation for the board, rather than go back to work so late. Josh gave Isabella a quick kiss goodnight outside his hotel, and she waved fondly as he got into the elevator. He was glad that she had decided to respect his convictions about their relationship. If only she knew how very difficult it had been for him to refuse her offer that Sunday night! He was too drained by the day's events to do any swimming for the evening, and settled instead for a long, warm shower before crawling between the sheets.

In his dreams, a lean, hawk-nosed figure in a toga stood before him, leaning over a table where a long scroll lay, nearly finished. He knew instinctively that it was Pontius Pilate. The man looked troubled, even tormented, as he sealed the scroll he had just finished writing. Then he turned and saw Josh, and opened his mouth as if to speak. Suddenly, a huge gout of flame came shooting from the sky and consumed him, the scroll, and all the furnishings in the room. Josh heard the sound of mocking laugher in his ears before he jerked awake. It was a long time before he went back to sleep.

The next morning's work went very quickly; Josh was a rapid-fire artist on the keyboard, and he typed up a complete transcript of the Pilate letter in less than an hour and handed it to Father MacDonald for proofreading. After checking the text over for errors and typos and comparing it to their notes from the day before, they copied the transcript and placed each copy in a black plastic binder marked "*Segrete e Riservate*" on the outside. Then the team met privately for about a half hour. They decided to let Isabella read the finished translation to the board members, and then the members of the team could speak to answer specific questions.

The time passed very quickly, and by 9 AM they were ushered into the conference room where they had met before. Nine faces were seated on the far side of the table. Dr. Castolfo was the picture of dignity and decorum in the large center seat, and next to him Dr. Guioccini looked tanned and elegant. Cardinal Raphael regarded them serenely, without a hint of concern across his pale, wrinkled visage. Dr. Sinisi was wearing a beautiful Armani suit and a pale yellow tie that set off his deeply tanned skin nicely. His customary smile was so bright it hurt to look at, causing Josh to wonder how much the man spent on tooth whiteners. Professor Neapolitano, however, wore a suit that looked as if it came from a second-hand shop, and what was, perhaps, the world's ugliest lime green bow tie to set it off. Next to him Dr. Tintoretto scowled across the table at Father MacDonald, who returned her glare with a sweet smile and a slightly arched eyebrow. Marc Stefani eyed the team with an undisguised curiosity that belied his years, trying to figure out from their expressions what this meeting was all about. Signore Gandolfo was all smiles, ever the perfect politician, trying to make every person there feel as if he had their best interests at heart. And Professor Castellani, at the end of the table, looked frankly bored—or maybe just drowsy. As the clock next to the antique fireplace struck nine times, Dr. Castolfo rose up and spoke.

"Well, my friends," he began, "our team has moved with great speed and professionalism in opening and translating the two ancient scrolls from the site at Villa Jovis. I am sure all of you are aware of the text of the Augustus scroll, which was presented to the public yesterday. I am excited to say that the second scroll, the so-called *"Testimonium Pilatus,"* was opened, read, and translated yesterday afternoon. Dr. Guioccini and I were there for the historic moment, and I have summoned all of you so that you may be the first outside the seven of us to actually hear the contents of this amazing epistle. I have asked Dr. Sforza to speak for the team in presenting to us the contents of this incredible discovery."

Isabella stood, looking professional but lovely in a black skirt and light green blouse, with a single jewel suspended at her throat from a gold chain. It caught the light as she began speaking.

"I cannot explain what I am about to read. All I can tell you is that these are, without a doubt, the words of Lucius Pontius Pilate, written nearly two thousand years ago. Since there is very little I can say to clarify or change what is here, I am simply going to share the contents."

In a clear low voice, speaking with great deliberation, she read for the next twenty minutes. As the narrative unfolded, some of the board members sat in silence, while others raised eyebrows, shook or nodded their heads, and in other ways betrayed their emotional reaction to what they were hearing. When she finished with the short postscript that Tiberius had tacked on at the end of Pilate's tale, she looked at the board members curiously.

"That concludes the manuscript," she said. "It is time to discuss what we do for our next step."

"More scholarly examination of the original papyrus should be the first order of the day," said Castolfo. "Dr. Guioccini and I have already begun putting together a list of noted archeologists and antiquarians we should like to examine the scroll."

"We MUST tell the public!" said Sinisi. "This is the most earth-shattering discovery in the history of archeology! Think of the controversy! Think of the publicity! Think of the tourism! People will pay a hundred Euros apiece to stare at the scroll and count it cheap! This could be the greatest boon to the Italian economy since the War!"

"I AM APPALLED!" shouted Doctor Tintoretto. "Do any of you take this seriously? Can you be so easily duped? This is a travesty! The document is obviously forged! Tell me, Father MacDonald"—the priestly title dripped with vitriol coming from her mouth—"when did you substitute this abomination for the real scroll? Or was there ever a real scroll to begin with? Did the Church plant this fraud on the island a century ago, and wait for it to be discovered? I wouldn't put anything past your two-thousand-year-old social club of pederasts and misogynists!"

"Now see here, lass—" began MacDonald, but she had already turned to Dr. Castolfo.

"Professor, I demand that this document be removed from the hands of this team immediately and subjected to rigorous carbon datings. I warned you what would come of letting these *cultists* be involved with a serious archeological dig!" she snapped.

"ENOUGH!" roared Joshua. The whole room fell silent, and every eye fixed on the lanky young American. His face was flushed, but his dander was up and he would not back down. "I have kept my silence before this board up till now, since I am both a foreigner and the youngest person here. But I will NOT sit here and listen to my integrity and that of my colleagues be any further impugned! Doctor Tintoretto, you have let your hatred for the Church rob you of all   scientific objectivity. You have closed your ears to every version of reality that does not conform to your irrational prejudice."

Tintoretto's eyes bulged with fury, and she hissed, "Listen here, you jumped-up American cowboy—"

"NO!" Josh interrupted. "I have sat and listened to your bile since before we left Capri, and kept my mouth shut. It is my turn to speak out now, and I will have my say! Surely you know that the four Biblical Gospels were all composed in the first century AD. That puts them, at a bare minimum, within seventy years of the events they report. If you are up on the latest research, you also know that the first three Gospels are almost universally dated thirty to forty years earlier, in the decade of the sixties. That means that they were written barely thirty years after the trial of Jesus. And all of them agree that something remarkable happened, that the tomb of Jesus was empty on the third day. Any historian worth his salt will tell you that the earlier the source, the more reliable it is—and that if several early sources all agree on a central narrative, it is probably because that narrative is true. Well, lo and behold, all the Gospels do agree! And now we find a document that predates them by thirty years, and guess what? It confirms them! Remember the old adage from Arthur Conan Doyle? 'When you have eliminated the impossible, whatever remains, no matter how improbable, must be the truth.' It may not confirm to your beliefs—your prejudices, to be perfectly honest—but you need to reconcile yourself to the fact that it appears the Gospels were right and you were wrong!"

"I will not be spoken to like this by an *evangelical cultist!*" snapped Tintoretto, leaping to her feet and fleeing the room. Josh sank back down into his seat, his face still red, as every eye at the table followed her exit, then turned to him. Dr. Castolfo waited until the clicking of Tintoretto's heels faded into the distance, then stood and began softly applauding. One by one, the other board members joined him, and Josh flushed an even deeper red.

"I have been waiting for years for someone to put that rather unpleasant woman in her place," the board president said. "And it turns out the only one with the courage to do so was our plucky young American friend!"

"Good grief," said Josh. "I figured you would be asking me to leave the country after that!"

"Tintorreto is a sad and angry person," said Cardinal Raphael. "I feel a great deal of compassion for her, but I would be lying if I said she makes the Biblical injunction to love one's enemies easy. Now, however, I feel we should return to the matter at hand."

"Indeed," said Castolfo. "I am going to suggest that we ask Cardinal Klein to come from Rome immediately, and Joshua, I will ask you to call Dr. Martens and issue our invitation. His wife will be welcome to accompany him, since he still needs help moving about. The museum will, of course, cover all expenses. Bernardo, perhaps you can call Dr. Henderson at the Smithsonian also?"

Sinisi spoke up at this point. "We need to let the public know!" he said. "I think we should call a press conference before the week is out and share the translation with the press!"

Castolfo sighed, and looked at Isabella. "Dr. Sforza, what do you think?"

Isabella thought a moment. "It goes against my grain to agree with the board's resident publicity hound," she finally said. "But I think Vincent is right. The whole world is waiting, and the longer we wait the more the skeptics will say that we doctored the evidence. Put it out there now, let the world see the scroll, and let the examinations begin!"

Castolfo looked up and down the table. "Shall we take a vote?" he asked the members. They nodded, one by one, and he called for a show of hands. The vote was eight to one, with Dr. Castellani objecting and Tintoretto marked as abstaining.

"Very well then," he said. "We will hold a press conference Friday morning. I will ask the team to begin preparing their remarks, and now I must go after Maria and see if I can calm her down a bit. Again, I would like to thank the members of the Capri team for some truly exemplary work. Well done! Meeting adjourned."

ITALIAN AUTHORITIES TO ANNOUNCE TRANSLATION OF PONTIUS PILATE SCROLL FRIDAY

(UP) The Italian Bureau of Antiquities has announced that the scroll by found on the island of Capri, allegedly written by Roman governor Pontius Pilate some two thousand years ago, has been translated by a team of Latin scholars. Other experts are being flown in to Naples to verify the translation, and the contents of the ancient letter will be shared with the public in a press conference this Friday at 11 AM.

The Publicity Director of the Antiquities Bureau, Dr. Vincent Sinisi, has confirmed that the scroll does, in fact, deal with the trial and execution of Jesus of Nazareth. "I don't want to give anything away," he commented, "but this is going to give historians, theologians, and reporters enough material to debate for a long, long time!"

The scroll was discovered in a chamber that was revealed on Easter Sunday, when an earthquake struck the Italian coastline and damaged the wall that had concealed the chamber since the time of the Roman Emperor Tiberius Caesar. A team of archeologists was convened on site and removed the artifacts from the chamber to the National Museum in Naples, where they have been analyzing the relics ever since. Experts have all agreed that the other documents from the chamber are authentic and date from the first century AD.

In what may be a related note, Dr. Maria Tintoretto has announced her resignation from the Antiquities Bureau effective today. She has called a press conference Friday afternoon at three to explain the reasons for her abrupt departure. Sources close to the museum say that the noted skeptic is upset with the release of the scroll's contents to the public in such a hasty manner.

CHAPTER EIGHTEEN

Ali bin-Hassan read the article a second time, sipping his morning coffee as he did so. The drink was as black and bitter as the hatred that he nourished in his heart, the hatred that sustained him in his ongoing jihad against the cursed infidel. So they had opened and translated the scroll so soon? That meant he was running out of time. It was Wednesday, and the press conference was scheduled in two days' time. The "package" would be delivered to Naples tomorrow, and he resolved that the infidel scientists would never have a chance to read the ancient scroll to the press. He had toyed with the idea of waiting to see what the scroll said before destroying it and the infidels who had discovered it. After all, if it debunked the false claims of the Christian *injil*, it could be a useful propaganda tool for the cause of Allah's champions. But, after further reflection, he had decided it was not worth the risk. If the document confirmed the heresies of the Christians, the damage would be impossible to undo, even if the scroll and the archeologists were obliterated by his attack. It would have to be Friday morning, early in the day, before they removed the scroll to the press briefing room.

That meant that he would need to prepare his statement as well. Once he decided that an explosive attack was the best way to deal with this problem, he realized that he would need to explain his actions to the world. He had a sophisticated laptop and a nice digital video camera, and he was almost done preparing his remarks. Once they were completed to his satisfaction, he would film himself delivering them, and upload the video to his laptop. A remote command from his cell phone would email the video to all the major wire services whenever he chose; all he had to do was text the command to his PC. It would be the last thing he did before detonating the package and sending himself to Paradise. As he got up from the table and tidied away his breakfast dishes, he practiced his introduction out loud.

"In the name of Allah, the Just, the Merciful, and in the name of His holy prophet . . ."

* * *

"All expenses paid?" Dr. Martens said. "That is wonderful! I have been meaning to take Alicia abroad since we married, but this blasted injury has kept me from it—and Naples is gorgeous this time of year! I am on crutches now and getting stronger every day. The flight will be a bit of an ordeal, but nothing I can't handle. I appreciate your arranging this for me!"

Josh laughed. "I had nothing to do with it," he said. "Yours was the first name Dr. Guioccini suggested to the board when we began discussing bringing in outside experts."

"So are you going to tell me what the scroll says?" asked Martens.

"Not over the phone," said Josh. "We are really throwing down a veil of secrecy over this until the press conference. And I certainly would not want to prejudice your own translation efforts!"

"That is no way to treat your old friend and mentor, Joshua!" said Martens. "But it is good professional ethics. I look forward to seeing you soon."

"Your flight is at nine AM your time," said Josh. "Can you get to the airport that early?"

"I was released from the hospital yesterday," Martens said. "Alicia and I can pack up and drive to the airport Hilton here in a couple of hours, and just spend the night. Then we'll be in the boarding line bright and early."

"Great," said Josh. "I can't wait to see you again!"

* * *

Late Wednesday evening, near the remains of the ancient seaport of Ostia, a hired driver named Luigi Figaro approached the large rental truck he had been asked to deliver to Naples. According to the manifest, it was loaded with eight crates of potting soil for use at a botanical garden. However, he was to deliver it to a storage facility in the north part of town, where a garage slot had been reserved. Apparently the gardeners were not going to be ready for it till next week. Luigi shook his head. It struck him as an odd way to do business, but what did he know about growing flowers? He was getting paid, with an extra bonus if he got the thing delivered before 6 AM Thursday. It was easy money, as traffic was light after 8 PM and the drive was only a few hours.

He peeked in the back and saw the crates stacked on top of one another. He wrinkled his nose at the rich, fecund smell of fertilizer and dirt, and then he shut the cargo door, climbed in, and started the engine. He tuned the radio to his favorite station and pulled into the evening traffic.

* * *

Josh and the archeological team were meanwhile wrangling over how to present the scroll to the media. Dr. Sinisi had joined them, since publicity was his bailiwick, but Dr. Castolfo was also there to rein in his enthusiastic colleague.

"I tell you, you MUST have the actual scroll in the media room! Photographs and video footage will not do this time!" Sinisi was saying.

"I dinna like that idea," growled MacDonald. "My solution does stabilize the ancient papyrus, but that much flash photography is not good for the two-thousand-year-old ink."

"We do have some special glass cases that neutralize the worst effects of bright lighting," said Castolfo. "Why don't we rig up one of those for it? That way, the reporters can see the actual document, but it will still be temperature and humidity controlled, and protected from bright lights."

The Vatican archeologist nodded in reluctant assent. "Very well," he finally said. "I still don't like it, but I see the point in having the actual manuscript there. Now, if you will excuse me, ladies and gentlemen, my colleague Dr. Klein will be arriving shortly. I am going to the airfield to meet him."

"Very well," said Castolfo. "It has been a long day, folks, and tomorrow will be a very busy time of preparation. I suggest we call it a night."

Josh lingered for a moment as the others headed to the door. "Dr. Castolfo," he said.

The Bureau's president looked at him and said "Yes, Dr. Parker?"

"I heard that Dr. Tintoretto has resigned from the board," the young American replied. "I can't help but feel partly responsible. I regret the intensity of my outburst."

The older man sighed. "I have known Maria many years," he said. "She is a very angry person, and over the years her anti-Christian mania—and there is not another word for it—has grown stronger and stronger. I am not a religious man, but at the same time I am also enough of a historian to recognize the truth of what you said. The tomb of Jesus was indeed empty, whatever the reason. Pontius Pilate's testimony proves that beyond a doubt. Her obsession with debunking Christianity is so strong that when the scroll confirmed what the Gospels said, cognitive dissonance set in. It did not agree with her version of reality, so to her it must be a fraud. Otherwise her entire worldview has been proven wrong, and her fragile personality could not handle such a paradigm shift."

"I wonder what she has planned for her press conference," Josh said.

"I am sure she will announce that the scroll is faked, that the discovery was staged, and the translation biased," said Castolfo. "However, she has zero proof of any of those assertions other than her own opinion. I will make sure a couple of the reporters in the crowd know what to ask in order to expose just how completely subjective her claims are. Your work, and that of your colleagues, is very valuable, and your field technique beyond reproach. Dr. Apriceno's findings should prove beyond a shadow of a doubt that the reliquary was completely undisturbed, and that the scroll was placed there two thousand years ago. That should neutralize any allegations of fraud that she cares to make."

Josh nodded. "I've known some pretty militant atheists over the years," he said, "but I have never seen anyone so bristling with hostility. Still, it is saddening that she has allowed her prejudices to destroy her objectivity."

He walked to the door where Isabella waited for him. She slipped her hand into his as they walked toward the front doors of the museum. "So what are you doing this evening?" she asked.

"I was thinking of setting up my webcam and having a chat with my parents," he said. "I would like to introduce you to them, if you would care to join me."

"It's a virtual world these days, isn't it?" she said. "Not that long ago, I would have had to either wait to meet them in person or else join in on a conference call with bad audio. Now it's the two-way video links that used to exist only in *Star Trek* episodes."

"You like *Star Trek*?" Josh asked.

"Well, of course," said Isabella.

"Original series, *Next Generation*, or *Voyager*?" he queried.

"No *Deep Space Nine*?" she replied.

"Nobody really likes that one," he said.

"That's rather harsh," she said. "I thought Commander Sisko was one of the most intriguing characters in Roddenberry's universe!"

They were happily engaged in sci-fi nerd talk as they walked out the door, and for the second time that week the explosion of flashbulbs caught them by surprise. Once more they had been caught holding hands in public, Josh thought. Somehow, the idea didn't bother him one bit, though.

"Doctor Sforza! Any comment on the Pilate scroll?" shouted one reporter.

"Why yes," she said. "I have a great deal to say about it!" A hush spread over the crowd as every journalist trained his microphone on her. "Sadly, I can't share those comments till Friday," she said sweetly, setting off a chorus of groans.

"Can you at least tell us how you were able to get the scroll opened and read so quickly?" asked the *Tribune* reporter Drew Eastwood.

"That is a fair question and does not violate the confidentiality I have agreed to," said Isabella. "So I will give you an answer. Ancient papyrus that has been rolled up for centuries dries out and remains in the rolled-up position. When we find such a scroll, we place it in a rehydration tank that restores the moisture gradually. As the papyrus soaks up the moisture, it becomes pliable again and unrolls on its own. The more moisture it soaks up, the faster the unrolling process. These two scrolls were both so well preserved that they unrolled in close to record time. When we shared the Augustus scroll with you gentlemen on Tuesday, the Pilate scroll had already begun to unroll. Once it flattened out, we treated it with a special solution developed by our own Dr. MacDonald that stabilized the papyrus so that it could be handled without fear of damaging it. As soon as the solution dried, we began the process of translating it that afternoon."

"Were there any difficulties with the translation? Was the text complete and legible?" Eastwood persisted.

Isabella looked at him with a new respect. This young man was persistent and determined, but he also was well-informed, courteous, and asked no stupid questions. She decided to answer him honestly.

"You are very close to overstepping the bounds of what I am allowed to share at this point," she said. "But you are not quite there yet. So I will tell you this much: the Latin script was very clear and the document undamaged. We are quite certain that we have recovered the words completely and accurately. The text was translated independently by two of my colleagues, who then compared their results very carefully.

There were no major discrepancies. Now as to what the text actually said—you'll have to wait till Friday!"

The young blond journalist nodded respectfully, and Isabella decided then and there that when the time came to give an exclusive interview, he would be her choice recipient. But now the rest of the pack was shouting questions.

"Can you at least tell us if the account agrees with the New Testament versions of Jesus' trial?" shouted a British journalist.

"No, sorry!" she replied.

"Do you know why Dr. Tintoretto resigned from the Board of Antiquities?" asked the Italian TV reporter Antonio Ginovese.

"I have an idea, but since she has called a press conference, I think it would be better to let her answer that question," said Isabella.

"Does it have anything to do with her hostility to Christianity and the Church?" shouted Tyler Patterson.

"No comment!" she replied.

"Are you and Dr. Parker romantically involved?" asked Valeria Witherspoon, a correspondent for a popular British tabloid.

Isabella sighed. At some point, this would have to be dealt with, but she hated having her personal life under the media's microscope. "You folks have caught us holding hands twice," she finally said. "You may draw your own conclusions!"

"Dr. Parker." Witherspoon aimed her next question at Josh. "How does your pastor father feel about your having a Catholic girlfriend?"

"You'll have to ask him about that!" said Josh. "Now no further questions!"

With that they hailed a cab, even though Josh's hotel was only a few hundred yards away, and got in quickly and slammed the doors. "The Ambassador Suites," she said to the driver. He pulled away from the curb, down the block, around the corner, and under the awning.

"Buy you supper?" Josh offered.

"That sounds splendid," said Isabella, "but something light, please, after that huge feast last night! I am fond of Simone Apriceno, but I have no desire to wind up looking like her!"

"There is a little salad and sushi bar up on the penthouse level," said Josh. "It's great for a quiet dinner together. And afterward, there is an excellent business center where we can link up to the Internet and talk to my family!"

"Why not go to your room?" she asked. "Don't you trust me?"

Josh leaned over and kissed her. "Maybe it's myself I don't trust," he said softly in her ear. "Besides, do you want the press reporting that you spent the evening alone with me in my room?"

She sighed. "Why on earth are they so interested in whether or not you and I are romantically involved?"

He laughed. "That, my dear lady, is the price of celebrity! And of course, the fact that you are absolutely gorgeous only adds to the interest."

She slapped his arm lightly. "You Americans and your flattery!" she laughed.

The sushi bar was good, and since it was on the penthouse level, they didn't have to worry about gawkers from the street wandering in. Josh enjoyed the smoked eel, shrimp, and octopus, while Isabella favored the crab, scallop, and tuna rolls. After a light meal, they made their way to the business center, where there were individual carrels with laptop hookups. Josh quickly plugged in, and then placed a call to his folks on his cell phone. It was mid-morning in Oklahoma when his mother picked up on the other end.

"Hello, Joshua!" she said.

"Hi, Mom!" he replied. "Can you and Dad get on the computer? I want to chat with you both."

"Certainly, dear," she answered. He heard her voice call out, "Ben! Josh wants to talk to us on the computer. How do I connect to that movie talking channel again?"

He repressed a smile. His dad had taken to the digital age like a fish to water, hosting video conferences for area pastors and teaching online courses. His mother, on the other hand, regarded the laptop solely as a device for playing solitaire. He heard over the cell as his dad came to the computer, and moments later their familiar faces were looking at him from the screen of his laptop.

"Hi, Dad! Good to see you guys again!" Josh greeted them.

"Hello there, son! You seem to have become quite the celebrity," his dad said. "We've had all kinds of calls to the church office from reporters and TV folks, wanting to know all about you."

251

"Yeah, our little dig has become big news," Josh answered. "I hope the publicity is not too much trouble."

"It's increased interest in our church, that's for sure!" his dad said. "I told everyone that has called that I will give an interview only if they attend Sunday services first. We should have a dozen or so by this weekend!"

Josh grinned. "It may be a lot more than that, after Friday," he said.

"What do you mean, son?" his dad asked.

"We translated the Pilate scroll," said Josh. "Our press conference is Friday at eleven AM local time. That will be about one AM in Oklahoma. You're going to want to stay up, Dad, that's all I can say!"

His father beamed. "I'm so proud of you, son! Is it what we thought it might be?" he asked.

"Er, I can't really say, Dad," Josh replied. "All I can tell you is that you will definitely want to be watching when we read the translation!"

"Not even a clue for your old man, eh?" the silver-haired pastor asked.

"Sorry, Dad, not with my boss standing right here!" Josh replied. "But I do want you to meet her. Mom, Dad, this is Dr. Isabella Sforza, the supervisor of the dig I've been working on. Isabella, these are my parents—Dr. Ben Parker and his wife Louise."

Isabella sat down next to Josh and leaned toward him, where they could see her clearly. "Hello," she said. "I have been looking forward to meeting you both. This isn't as nice as being there, but it is better than a phone call!"

"So you're the Italian beauty who can't seem to let go my son's hand, eh?" asked Brother Ben. "You have no idea how long we have been waiting for him to get interested in girls!"

"Dad!" said Josh.

Isabella laughed. "Your son is a delightful young man, and a perfect gentleman. I have been enjoying my time with him greatly."

Josh's mother smiled sweetly at Isabella. "May I ask you something, dear girl?" she queried.

"Why of course, Mrs. Parker!" Isabella replied.

"Do you love him?" she asked.

Isabella was taken aback by the forthrightness of the question, but she answered as best she could. "You know," she replied, "I believe I do!"

"Then please marry him!" Louise Parker said. "I would like to have grandchildren before I am ninety!"

Josh thought he would sink through the floor in embarrassment, but his dad came to his rescue. "Now Louise," he said, "let's not scare her off! So Josh, how do you like Naples?"

"It is a beautiful city," he said. "I haven't had much time to take in many of the sights, but the museum that I am working in is simply amazing! Isabella gave me the grand tour last weekend. Hopefully, before I am done here, I can fly you and Mom out for a visit. I'd like to show you Capri as well!"

They talked for another fifteen minutes or so, and then Josh said his farewells and severed the connection. He looked at Isabella, who was grinning at him. "Sorry about Mom," he said. "She can be a bit—well, a bit direct sometimes!"

Isabella laughed out loud. "You have never met my mother!" she said. "She would already be asking what we want to name the first child!"

"I think I would like to meet your parents sometime soon," he said.

Her expression softened. "I am afraid you won't be able to meet my papa," she said. "He died two years after Marc did. But soon I will take you to meet my mother, and then we can compare notes on which of us has the most 'direct' mama!"

"I guess I had better head to my room soon," he said. "Morning comes early, and tomorrow is a very busy day."

Isabella looked at him fondly. She was tempted to ask if she could tuck him in for the night, but she had decided that embarrassing him wasn't as much fun as it had seemed at first. Still, she wished that her apartment wasn't so empty. Josh's presence seemed to fill the room all around her, and she didn't want to leave him yet.

"Shall we take a walk on the observation deck first?" she asked him.

"That sounds fun," he replied. There was an elevator from the penthouse level that opened on a small rooftop garden overlooking the Mediterranean. As they stood at the rail, they could see the dark silhouette of the isle of Capri in the distance. The waning half-moon was hanging in the sky like a silver spotlight, and the quicksilver reflections sparkled on the water's surface.

"It is beautiful, isn't it?" she said.

"Not as beautiful as you," he replied, slipping his arm around her shoulders. She leaned her head against him and they stood like that for a long time.

* * *

The next morning, as the archeologists assembled and began planning how to present their findings to the press, a ferry boat left the island of Capri for the mainland. Among the smiling tourists and businesslike locals, the mild-mannered Imam Muhammad al-Medina blended in perfectly. He chatted for a while with a Catholic fisherman, Antonio Ginovese, who lived a few doors down from him, about the weather and the general state of the Italian economy.

"Imam Muhammad," the man said as they neared the mainland, "I would like to thank you."

"Whatever for?" the Muslim cleric replied.

"I had such a terrible view of Muslims before you came to our island," he replied. "All I ever saw on the news was the violence and carnage that seem to follow Islam everywhere. I thought everyone who prayed to Allah was a potential Osama bin Laden. But you have shown me that a Muslim cleric can be a kind-hearted, god-fearing, neighborly friend. I am glad you helped me overcome my prejudices against your people."

Muhammad al-Medina—the mild mannered, moderate Muslim cleric who lived in peace with his Catholic neighbors—regarded him with a curious expression. Ali bin-Hassan, the relentless jihadist who was on his way to pick up a car bomb, smirked behind the false identity he had so carefully crafted. The infidels were so trusting, so easy to deceive! "Antonio," he said, "I just hope you remember, that when you see me, you are looking at the true face of Islam!"

Hassan turned and walked away, and the Italian fisherman shuddered. He genuinely liked the moderate cleric, but that look in his eyes as the Imam delivered that parting shot had sure seemed hateful. Oh well, he thought. It was just his old prejudices trying to re-assert themselves. By the time he crossed the gangplank to shore, he had completely forgotten about the conversation. He would remember it vividly, however, after the next day's newscasts.

* * *

That morning, the outside experts had begun to arrive at the museum. Cardinal Heinrich Klein, renowned antiquarian and longtime friend of Benedict XVI, had come in early and asked to study the scroll. He had gone over the entire document with a powerful, illuminated loupe, occasionally switching to black light to see how the ancient ink looked under UV illumination. After about an hour's examination, he sat at the workstation and began carefully translating the manuscript for himself, referencing the blown-up photographs MacDonald had taken, and never once looking at any of the translations that the team had already completed.

When he was completely finished, he called for the original, handwritten versions prepared by Josh and Father MacDonald. He read each of them carefully, and then read the reconciled version that they had come up with and prepared to hand to the press the next day. Only then did he speak to them.

"Excellent work, gentlemen!" he told them in his strong German accent. "You were careful and deliberate, and I can find no errors in anything that you did. As for the contents—*mein Gott!*—this is a truly amazing discovery! The enemies of the Cross will truly be put to shame!"

Josh smiled. This man was a legend in Biblical textual studies, and coming from him, such remarks were high praise indeed. "Thank you, Your Eminence," he said. "Father MacDonald made it a very easy task! He is a consummate professional and a great archeologist."

"The lad is too modest," the Scots priest replied. "He knows twice as much as I did at his age, and in another decade or two he'll be giving me a run for my money!"

They stood and excitedly discussed the ramifications of Pilate's testimony. Worldwide, the twenty-first century had not been kind to the Church, with one expert after another emerging every few months with a discovery—usually dubious but always well-publicized—that called another aspect of New Testament history into question. Traditional scholars were always quick to reply, but they seemed to be constantly on the defensive. There was no doubt the Pilate scroll would give the Church some ammunition to go on the intellectual offensive, and all of them looked forward to the consternation among the anti-Christian intelligentsia with some relish.

Later that afternoon, Josh was sent to the Naples airport to meet his mentor Dr. Martens. The flight was to arrive at 3 PM local time, and it appeared as if it might even be a little ahead of schedule. Josh had the limo driver wait outside and walked over to the reception area, holding up a cardboard sign he had made at the lab. He had written in Latin: "*Doctoris Luke Martens, aestimetur professore antiquitatum,*" as a joke. That was the title that Dr. Martens had demanded all first-year grad students call him.

Since he was on crutches, Martens was one of the first passengers to disembark, with Alicia by his side. Blonde, leggy, and as beautiful as ever, her face lit up when she saw Josh, as did her husband's. Josh made his way to the rope line and embraced his old mentor, and accepted an enthusiastic kiss on the cheek from Martens' young bride.

"All right, Dr. Parker," she said. "I want to meet this Italian hottie who has succeeded where all the girls at college failed!"

Josh laughed. "I had no idea they were trying so hard!" he said.

"That is because you were too afraid to talk to any of them, my boy," said Martens. "You were the shyest young man I have ever taught! But it is good to see you again and good to be on terra firma! You have no idea how glad I am to be out of that infernal aircraft! Even in first class, the seats are NOT made to accommodate a full-length leg cast! Now, how far is it to the museum from here?" he asked.

"About twenty minutes across town," Josh replied. "We have a limo waiting for you."

"You have to hand it to the Italians," the older archeologist said. "They do know how to roll out the red carpet!"

Josh grabbed their luggage and carried it for them to where the car waited. Alicia, who had never traveled outside the States except for mission trips to the Dominican Republic and Mexico, was agog at the beautiful Renaissance architecture, and the occasional Roman-era structure that peeked out from the twenty-first-century clutter. "I cannot imagine what it would be like to live surrounded by so much history," she breathed.

"And here I thought all you cared about was fish and extreme sports!" her husband said.

"I can't be married to you and not appreciate days gone by," she said. "And I just adore beautiful architecture—and Italy seems to be the global headquarters of the insanely talented builders' society! Look at that cathedral! Those spires must be two hundred feet tall!"

The two antiquarians sat together and quietly enjoyed her fascination with the historic surroundings. In a matter of minutes they arrived at the museum's front doors. Isabella was waiting for them, and Luke and Alicia helped the American professor get out of the limo and levered up onto his crutches. He accepted their help with good grace, but both knew how much it grated on him to be limited in his mobility when there was such exciting work ahead.

"Welcome back to Italy, Dr. Martens," said Isabella.

"Dr. Sforza!" he replied. "It is so nice to finally meet you in person. I loved your paper on that Roman temple of Minerva you excavated. You managed to pull an impressive amount of data from a very limited number of remaining artifacts!"

"Limited! More like nonexistent!" she laughed. "But the architecture of the place was interesting, to say the least. Is this your lovely wife?"

"Alicia Martens," said the American, holding out her hand. "I hear you and Josh here have become something of an item!"

Isabella rolled her eyes. "You can't keep anything out of the papers these days," she laughed. "But I must say I have become rather fond of your friend here."

Alicia nodded. "If the feeling is mutual, then you have succeeded where half the girls in Texas and Oklahoma failed," she said.

"Oh please!" said Josh. "She makes me sound like some sort of OSU Romeo. I was just trying to pass her husband's insanely demanding grad courses when I allegedly attracted all this female attention. Personally, I don't remember any of it."

"Really?" said Alicia. "What about the time that Larissa Sorrells asked you to come up to her dorm room for an all-night study session?"

"She was taking advanced calculus, and I was studying Latin grammar and Roman government," said Josh. "I figured it was some sort of practical joke, and stayed away."

Alicia rolled her eyes. "See?" she said to Isabella. "He is impossible!"

Sforza laughed in turn, and then looked over at Josh. "I think I like your friend here," she said. "Now, Alicia, until after the press conference tomorrow, no one but the team members and our visiting experts are allowed back into the lab. I am going to ask Josh to take your husband on back to the lab, and I will show you to your hotel rooms, if that is OK."

"Sounds fine to me," Alicia replied. "Any place around here a girl can go for a swim?"

"Josh assures me the hotel pool is excellent, and it's not a long cab ride to some of our public beaches—however, they are starting to get rather crowded as the weather warms up," said Isabella. "What is it with you Americans and your obsession with water?"

* * *

Josh helped Dr. Martens navigate the corridors to the back of the museum, and then across the courtyard to the research lab. Bernardo Guioccini was waiting for them, and his face broke into a smile at the sight of his old friend.

"Luke! What a delight to see you again!" he boomed. "My word, man, what has this child bride of yours done to you?"

"I did it to myself, you old misanthrope!" Martens replied. "Tried to dodge a little snow brat on an easy slope and hit a tree! Now I want to see the discovery my young friend here has made."

"But of course," said Guioccini. "Come on back to the lab. Cardinal Klein just translated it earlier today and has been comparing his version to that of your young protégé, and his student Father MacDonald. Happily, they both passed muster. But I am sure you want to see the original and make your own notations before seeing theirs."

"I have been thinking of nothing else for the last week," said Martens. They had entered the lab by this time, and he made a point of circling the room and looking at every artifact that they had retrieved from the chamber before turning to the opened scroll that was still spread out on the viewing table. He stared for a long time at the sword of Julius Caesar, and then read the will of Augustus, studying the strong, clear Latin handwriting for several minutes. Finally he went to the viewing table and carefully leaned over on his crutches, studying the ancient papyrus for a long time before he spoke.

"*Quid est veritas?*" he breathed softly. "Pilate spoke more than he knew, didn't he, Joshua?"

Josh nodded, looking over his shoulder. It was still hard to believe that he was staring at the writing of the man who had sent Jesus of Nazareth to the cross! Martens carefully studied the scroll for about a half hour, and then turned to Josh. "I have to get off this leg," he said. "And I will need a laptop and a yellow pad."

* * *

Valeria Witherspoon wanted a scoop so bad she could taste it. She had dreamed of being a journalist ever since she was a teenager, but after graduating with a degree in photography and print journalism, the only job she could find was with the *UK Tattler*, a lowbrow tabloid that specialized in scandalous pictures of celebrities and royals, along with articles about space aliens and the Illuminati. She hated it with a passion, but it paid the bills, and every week she sent out résumés to respectable newspapers and magazines, hoping in vain for a return call. So far there had been none.

But the story of the Pontius Pilate scroll had captured the imagination of the sleaze industry just the same as it had everyone else's. Jesus was still great copy in the UK, even if only fifteen percent of the population actually attended church. In the two years she had worked for the *Tattler*, they had run stories that Jesus was married, Jesus was gay, Jesus never existed, and that Jesus was a reincarnation of Buddha. Now they wanted to run a story on the Pilate scroll, and had sent one of their writers to Naples along with Valeria. Her job was to get the pictures that would go with the article.

That assignment had modified slightly after the press got wind of the burgeoning romance between the American archeologist and his Italian counterpart. Her job now was not just to get pictures of the ancient scroll, but also to try and get some personal shots of the two antiquarian lovebirds—preferably skinny dipping, making out, or otherwise cavorting in a manner that would draw the attention of the scandal-loving British public.

The problem was that the lab where the main work was being done was completely off limits to the press. The modern building sat behind the ancient Renaissance palace that housed the museum, across a small, highly restricted employee parking lot that was surrounded by a ten-foot-tall concrete panel wall. Part of that wall actually connected to the back of the lab building, but there were no windows or doors leading out onto the Via Aventine, the business district street that ran directly behind the lab. However, in doing some reconnaissance, she had discovered that one of the adjacent buildings actually had a second-floor window that opened onto the street about a meter above and half a meter to the left of the wall. She was convinced that if she could crawl out that window and step onto the top of the wall, she could run down its length to the roof of the lab and quietly perch there, getting numerous shots of the scientists and historians coming and going. Maybe even get a shot of some relics being transported to and from the main museum building! This could be the scoop that finally got her out of the tabloids and into the mainstream media, she thought. Tomorrow morning she would find out.

* * *

That evening Josh and Isabella treated Dr. Martens and Alicia to dinner. The two women had hit it off right away, and Isabella found out a great deal about Josh from Alicia– and found she liked him even more after hearing it all. To her surprise, she found that both Martens and his young bride were also as rock solid in their Christian faith as Josh was. Hearing the three of them go back and forth between the realms of science and faith took some getting used to. Isabella was still torn on the issue of personal faith. She had fallen in love with a man who loved his God more than he loved her, and somehow expected her to be all right with that. She wasn't sure she could ever be so accepting of a love that transcended their affection for each other. But as she saw the clear adoration with which Alicia regarded her older husband, she began to think that these people had something that she was missing. Not only that, but something she wanted very badly.

* * *

Ali bin-Hassan—he would never be called by that other name again, he had decided when he left Capri—drove out to the storage facility that evening and looked over the truck. He paid the fee and told the attendant that he would take it out in the morning, but explained that he wanted to check out the cargo first. A few folded Euros and the bored employee disappeared back to his booth, and Hassan climbed inside the truck and began to work.

Each crate contained a thin layer of topsoil covering a 200-pound bale of ammonium nitrate, with a detonator at the bottom of each bale. All were connected with black wires that were virtually invisible against the black plastic sheets the crates rested on. The receiver set that would trigger the detonators was packed in a plastic bag and set on top of one of the bales, then covered with the same thin layer of soil. The remote that would activate the receiver was next to it, also sealed in a plastic bag. All Hassan had to do was turn on the receiver, drive to his target, and press the red button on the remote. Then the truck and all its cargo would explode with the force of several tons of TNT.

After he was done inspecting the deadly package, he climbed in his rented car and drove a short distance to a seedy motel, where he was to spend the night. There he carefully bathed himself and shaved his body, in the age old purification ritual of the jihad warrior. He bowed deeply toward Mecca and said the *shahada* with a passion and intensity he had not felt for years. He felt the mask he had worn for half a decade dropping away like a physical weight as he prepared for virtuous slumber. Tomorrow he would enter Paradise! He hoped that Sheik Osama would be proud.

* * *

Josh rose the next morning refreshed and ready for the day. He had discovered that he rather enjoyed the attention of the media, and most of all, he was looking forward to telling the whole world that the faith he had cherished his whole life was indeed based on real, solid history, not mythology and fairy tales! As he dressed, he reflected on what a wonderful, wild ride his life had become in the last two weeks. He had gone from being an unknown scholar in an obscure field to being one of the best-known archeologists in the world. And, to top it off, he had met the girl of his dreams in the process.

As he got dressed, he thanked God again for sending Isabella his way. He prayed, too, that she would find her way to the same saving faith that burned in him. He had always hoped to find his other half and get married someday, but now for the first time in his life he attached a name and a face to his prayers. Oh dear Lord, he thought. Let her be the one! Let her find You and love You as I do, so that we can be one with you together and forever!

His morning devotions complete, he grabbed a quick continental breakfast and made his way to the lab. He was one of the first ones there, with only Simone Apriceno and Giuseppe Rossini ahead of him. He greeted them with enthusiasm, and moments later Dr. Sinisi and Father MacDonald showed up also. MacDonald was carrying a two meter long, half meter wide plexiglass box with a sterilized aluminum base.

"That ugly thing?" Sinisi asked. "How can we present this priceless, ancient artifact to the world public for the first time ever resting on what looks like an old lasagna pan?"

"Sorry, laddie, but this is the bottom of the carrying case!" snapped the priest.

"Well, could we use it to carry the scroll into the briefing room, and then set the scroll on a piece of clear plexiglass and place the cover over it again?" asked Sinisi. "That way it will appear to be resting on the mahogany tabletop that will bring out its colors and textures so much better!"

MacDonald sighed. Sinisi's obsession with style over substance would try the patience of His Holiness himself, thought the priest. But the man did have his uses, and MacDonald also wanted the ancient manuscript to look impressive when the media finally got a look at it. He thought for a moment.

"Tell ye what," he said. "There is a good sterile sheet of clear plexiglass over there. I will load it in the bottom of the cart, and we can put the scroll on top, and then use the service tunnel to take it over to the press briefing room and see how it looks. Good enough?"

"Excellent!" said Sinisi. "I know it's early, but let's run it over there and take a look. We'll use the service tunnel to avoid taking the manuscript into the sunlight."

The tunnel ran under the parking lot, and was narrow and dimly lit, but it was perfect for transporting light-sensitive objects between the buildings. Virtually all personnel, however, preferred to walk across the restricted parking lot in the bright daylight. MacDonald carefully placed the scroll inside its portable display case and used a bungee cord to lash it to the top of the cart, since the tray stuck out a good bit on either end of the apparatus. Sinisi tucked the clear sheet of plexiglass under his arm and walked beside the priest as they rolled the cart toward the service elevator.

* * *

Hassan picked up the rental truck at 7:30 AM and made the drive across town as quickly as he could while scrupulously observing all traffic laws. It certainly would not do to be pulled over with 1,600 pounds of explosives in the back of the truck and a remote-controlled detonator in his front pocket! The route he had chosen, the Via Piscus, made a T-intersection onto the Via Aventine directly behind the museum. He could power across the intersection as soon as the light turned green, and then plow into the back wall of the lab as he punched the button on the detonator. The infidels would never know what hit them.

There was one detail left to attend to as he approached the intersection. The light was red and only one vehicle was in front of him, with its turn signal on. As soon as the light turned green and the vehicle was out of his path, he would floor the accelerator and begin his journey to Paradise. Knowing that it was too late for anyone to stop him, he took out his cell phone and dialed his computer back on Capri. The email program he had set up selected the message with his video manifesto attached and sent it to five major news organizations at once. There would be no speculation as to who carried out this attack.

The light was now green, and the Volvo in front of him turned out of his path. He picked up the detonator and jammed on the accelerator.

"*Allahu Akbar!*" he shouted as he the truck shot forward and he pressed the button.

* * *

Valeria Witherspoon was thrilled. She had paid the shopkeeper fifty Euros to gain access to the storage room whose window was right next to the wall separating the lab from the street. The concrete top of the wall was less than half a meter wide, but flat and smooth. She kicked her shoes off, climbed out the window, and held onto a sturdy drainpipe as her feet found the wall. Her camera was slung at her side instead of around her neck, so it would be less likely to pull her off balance. Quickly putting one foot in front of the other and looking at the laboratory roof instead of at the ground below, she traversed the distance in a matter of seconds without being seen. Once on the roof of the lab, she walked toward the side that faced the museum. She was in luck! The American archeologist Parker and his love interest, Dr. Sforza, were just leaving the lab. Witherspoon dropped to one knee and focused her camera on them. They paused just outside the back door of the main museum building to converse. She couldn't hear what they were saying, but her camera was out and snapping away as they talked. Then the tall American leaned down to plant a quick kiss on Sforza's cheek, and

Witherspoon caught the moment perfectly. She was already envisioning the caption that would go with the picture on the *Tattler*'s cover when she heard behind her the sound of an engine accelerating rapidly. She was turning to look over her shoulder when the world dissolved into a sheet of flame and smoke. She was vaguely aware of being tumbled upwards, end over end, her hair on fire and her camera flying away from her. Then she slammed into the back wall of the museum and slid down to the asphalt in a lifeless heap.

EXPLOSION AT ITALIAN MUSEUM

(UPI) BREAKING NEWS . . . A large explosion has destroyed the laboratory where the 'Pontius Pilate scroll' was being prepared for presentation to the public later this morning. Details are still emerging, but eyewitnesses have reported an enormous blast that leveled all but one wall of the research laboratory where the artifacts from the widely publicized dig on the island of Capri were being curated. At least one eyewitness says that the attack was the result of a truck bomb being driven into the rear of the lab at a high rate of speed.

Ambulances are on the scene and early reports indicate that there are numerous fatalities. The press conference about the Pilate scroll, scheduled for 11 AM this morning, has been postponed. Dr. Vincent Sinisi, publicity director for Italy's Bureau of Antiquities, could not be reached yet for comment.

At the same moment the blast occurred, numerous media outlets received a video from a Muslim cleric calling himself Ali bin-Hassan, claiming responsibility for the blast in the name of Al-Qaeda. The person in the video claims to be Hassan, and also states that he recently lived on the isle of Capri under the name Muhammad al Medina. The video has been sent to Italy's police and Interpol in an effort to determine the truth of these claims. Further coverage will follow as the details emerge.

CHAPTER NINETEEN

For the rest of his life Josh would struggle to recall exactly what he and Isabella had been talking about at the moment the lab exploded, but he was never able to. They had been walking over to the main museum, leaving Simone, Cardinal Klein, and Dr. Rossini in the lab, to see for themselves the setting in which the Pilate scroll would be presented later that day. The last thing Josh remembered was leaning over to give Isabella a quick kiss in the relative privacy of the parking lot when the blast grabbed them both and hurled them ten feet forward, into the back wall of the museum.

For a second or two, he was unable to hear, move, or see. Then he lifted his head and watched as burning rubble and bricks came falling from the sky like a grotesque hailstorm from hell. He crawled to Isabella as the rain of ruin continued, covering her body with his. Somewhere in the midst of the chaos he heard a sickening splatter and watched a mangled human body strike the side of the museum about twenty feet above his head, then flop to the ground a few feet away from them. Seconds later a burning camera, trailing its carrying strap, struck the pavement next to him and burst into shards of flaming plastic.

Isabella was weeping softly beneath him, blood streaming from a cut on her forehead. As the hail of debris ended, he pulled her to her feet.

"Are you hurt?" he asked anxiously.

She shook her head. "Shaken up a bit, but everything seems to be working," she said. He could barely hear her over the roaring in his ears; both of them had ruptured eardrums, as it turned out.

He turned back to the ruined lab just in time to see the last of the ceiling collapse. The nearest wall to them was the only one still standing—the entire back half of the building was simply gone, replaced by a large smoking crater.

"My God!" he said. "Giuseppe! Simone!" They both began to run toward the destroyed lab, hoping against hope. Halfway there, Josh stopped cold, staring at the object on the ground before him. It was a human hand, with neatly polished nails. On one finger gleamed a ring made from an ancient Roman coin. Isabella burst into hysterical tears at the sight.

Josh swallowed hard and made his way to the lab's front door, which hung crookedly on one hinge. The acrid smoke pouring from the hallway choked him, and he saw that the wide, carpeted hallway that had once led all the way to the rear lab barely went back ten feet now, blocked by the collapsed ceiling and walls around it. Then he saw two arms protruding from beneath the rubble, a beam from the ceiling covering them. One of the hands was still moving!

"Isabella! Help!" he shouted, grabbing boards and ceiling tiles and throwing them aside. Flames were spreading rapidly through the destroyed structure, and he needed to get this person out quickly. In a matter of seconds they had each grabbed one end of the beam and levered it upward. Josh found a large chunk of concrete to prop it with, then he and Isabella each grabbed a hand and pulled hard. A bloodied figure, covered with white plaster and streaked with blood, emerged from beneath the wreckage. Both legs were smashed and mangled from the knees down, and blood poured from several wounds on his torso, but he was still alive. It was Dr. Rossini. Together they carried him out to the parking lot. He groaned in pain and opened his eyes, but could not speak. Josh pulled off his belt and used it as a tourniquet on one of his legs as the sound of sirens began to grow in the distance. Then he and Isabella put their backs to a parked car, ignoring the shattered window glass all around them, cradling their friend in their arms and waiting for help.

* * *

"All in all, you are a fortunate young man," said the white-haired Italian doctor in passable English. His name tag identified him as Dr. Manuel Castrillon. "A mild concussion, two ruptured eardrums, and some bruises and cuts . . . considering your proximity to the blast, you could have come off much worse."

Josh shook his head. He had not felt this groggy since he took a line drive to the forehead in Little League when he was twelve. "What about Isabella?" he asked.

The doctor smiled. "She's in the next exam room," he said. "She insisted I see you first, and I agreed because she appears to be fine except for that cut on her forehead, which has already been tended. I'll go see her now."

"I'm coming too," said Josh, hopping off the bed. It was a bad idea—vertigo overwhelmed him and he had to grip the sides hard to make sure he did not fall over. But in a moment his balance returned, and he willed himself to follow the doctor to the next room. Isabella sat there, an expression of utter devastation on her face. Josh took her hand and kissed it, then stepped back so the doctor could do his work.

The physician looked in both her ears and eyes, testing her pupils to see if they dilated properly. Then he asked Josh to step out while he did a quick physical exam. Josh moved into the corridor and leaned against the wall, breathing heavily, his head in his hands. Suddenly he heard the familiar chirp of his cell phone from the exam room where he had been moments earlier. He stepped in and found his jacket in a tray next to the bed with his other personal effects. He picked up the phone and saw his dad's picture on the photo ID.

"Hello?" he said after picking up.

"Thank God, son!" his father's distraught voice came over the line. "Your mother and I saw the explosion on the late news and feared the worst. Are you hurt?"

"Not really," he said. "Bumps and bruises, but nothing that won't heal. Listen, Dad, I will talk to you later, but I need to check on Isabella. I'm OK; just ask the Church to pray for all those who aren't."

"All right, son," his dad said. "Call soon! I hope Isabella is all right."

Josh ducked back into the other exam room after a quick knock. Isabella was buttoning up her blouse. "She got off even lighter than you," said the doctor. "One ruptured eardrum and some bruises and contusions, plus that little gash on the forehead. I put a couple of butterfly stitches in it and placed a bandage over it, which she needs to leave in place for now. If possible, I would like to keep both of you for observation overnight—"

"First things first," said Josh. "How is Dr. Rossini?"

The Italian doctor frowned. "Not good," he said. "They took him to the Critical Care ward and were prepping him for surgery last I heard. But that was an hour ago."

"Is there a place where we could sit while we wait for him to come out of surgery?" Isabella asked.

"Let me see," said Castrillon. He punched a few commands into the computer in the exam room and looked at a lengthy list of names. "It appears he has been assigned a room on the third-floor Intensive Care when he comes out. Why don't you just wait there, and they will bring him in as soon as they finish operating."

So it was they found themselves seated in a quiet room with a hospital bed between them. There were two chairs, one a recliner, which Josh insisted Isabella take. A television was mounted on the wall, and he turned until he found an English language cable news broadcast. The attack on the lab was headline news, and he turned up the volume to catch the details.

"This is Meagan Hauser with GNN news," the perky anchor said. "Details are still emerging from the horrific attack at the National Museum of Antiquities in Naples, Italy, three hours ago. The confirmed death toll stands at seven so far, with several victims still being treated. Among those victims whose names have been released are Dr. Simone Apriceno, a well-known paleobotanist; Cardinal Heinrich Klaus, a respected Vatican archeologist and church leader; British journalist Valeria Witherspoon; and two American tourists, Tristan Wooten of Campbell, Texas, and his fiancée Brooke Blue of Commerce, Texas, who were hit by debris from the truck bomb while shopping in a nearby market. Also killed was the self-confessed bomber, Islamic radical Ali bin-Hassan. Hassan emailed his videotaped confession and manifesto to our station and several other news outlets moments before the blast. This is a short clip of what he said."

The screen went black, and then a grim, bearded face appeared. Josh was shocked to recognize the man—he had seen him at least twice during his five days on Capri, hanging around Mrs. Bustamante's restaurant. The imam was speaking in English during this part of his statement, so no subtitles were necessary.

"The infidels have defiled the lands of Allah with their unbelief, and done their best to shake the will of the faithful around the world," the cleric intoned. "Now they produce this forged scroll to prove that the Prophet Isa—peace be upon him—was in fact the son of Allah, who neither begets nor is begotten. This forgery is a clear attack upon the religion of truth, designed to shake the faith of the simple. Such an assault on the truth of Islam cannot be tolerated! Those who defile the name of Allah and his prophets cannot be suffered to live. Those who question the truth of the Holy Quran must die. That is why this lying scroll and those who would foist it upon the world must be destroyed. *Allahu Akbar!*"

Isabella clicked the remote and the cleric's face disappeared. She stifled a sob.

"To think that the best and kindest man I have ever known could be crippled for life by such a medievalist thug!" she said. "It is more than I can bear. Oh, Josh, Giuseppe has been like a father to me." He took her in his arms and held her tight as she wept again.

About a half hour later, the doctors wheeled Giuseppe into recovery. Both his legs were gone at the knee, and there was an oxygen mask over his mouth, but his eyes were open and clear. Isabella took him by the hand, and he squeezed gently. The faintest suggestion of a smile crossed his lips.

"I can only let you stay a moment," the doctor said. "He is very weak, and the prognosis is still uncertain. His children will be arriving soon."

Rossini's mouth was moving, and Josh and Isabella leaned in close to hear what he was saying.

"I am glad . . . the two of you are all right," he said in a weak whisper. "Isabella, you make me so proud. Don't let this attack quench your fire for truth! Joshua . . ."

"Yes, Giuseppe?" said Josh.

"Take care of her for me," he said. "You are a fine young man. Make her happy. And . . . tell Antonia . . . that I may not be able to make our date." He smiled faintly and closed his eyes. Then they fluttered open one more time. "I want you to know, Josh . . . I am not afraid. If He rose from the dead . . . I know death can't hold me either." His eyes closed again. His breath became slower and more regular.

Josh stood with tears in his eyes. He looked at Isabella, who was sobbing as if her heart would break. "Let's get out of here," he said.

They paused long enough to sign the papers agreeing not to hold the hospital liable if they both keeled over and died as soon as they left the building, and then Josh led her out into the waiting room. To his surprise, Dr. Martens, Alicia, and Dr. Guioccini were waiting for them.

"I cannot tell you how glad I am to see the two of you in one piece!" said the Antiquities Bureau archeologist.

"These Okies are tough, Bernardo," said Martens. Alicia simply took Isabella by the hand and then caught her up in a gentle hug. Josh looked over at Guioccini.

"The scroll?" he finally said.

"Safe and sound!" said the Italian. "Sinisi and MacDonald had taken it out of the lab only a few seconds before the blast. For once Vincent's insatiable obsession with appearances proved to be a very good thing."

Josh let out a long sigh of relief. "Where is Father MacDonald?" he asked.

"He just went up to be with Rossini. I think he wants to be there . . . in case," said Guioccini.

Josh nodded. He didn't think Rossini would survive the day, but he did not say so. "So what next?" he asked.

"We are going to take Isabella home. It is important that I speak with both of you for a few minutes, and then I am going to let you both rest. You have been through enough for one day," Bernardo added.

The four of them climbed into a waiting limo. Martens was managing his crutches better, Josh saw. He commented on his mentor's quick recovery.

The older man laughed. "Actually, it still throbs like crazy. But after this morning's carnage, my ski injury just doesn't seem nearly as important. How are you feeling, Josh?"

Josh thought about it for a long time. "Numb," he finally said. "I just don't think I can absorb one more blow today. I knew the scroll would attract opposition, and I was ready to go to bat for it—but the idea that someone would kill just to keep its message from being heard! It's still hard for me to believe."

"Islam has been at war with the rest of the world since its inception," said Guioccini. "Not all Muslims are, of course—most of them are simple, peaceful people who simply want to worship their god and raise their children in peace. But Islam is the only one of the world's great religions whose holy scriptures call for an ongoing war against all nonbelievers. Most Muslims want to put the 'sword passages' behind them as a violent stage their faith went through in its infancy—but others do not. Those who believe that jihad is essential to Islam regard Christianity as the greatest threat to their cause. This scroll—which seems to prove that the most important claim of the New Testament is based on actual facts, not myth and legend—is the worst threat to their faith in a generation."

Josh clinched his jaw, and his eyes took on a steely hue. "I will NOT let those bastards win!" he snapped.

Guioccini nodded. "Nor will I, my young friend."

Moments later, they pulled up outside Isabella's apartment and helped her out of the limo. Now that the initial shock and adrenaline had faded, both she and Josh were beginning to feel sore all over. Fortunately, they both had been prescribed some Percocet to help them deal with the pain. After the elevator deposited them on her floor, Isabella let them into the apartment. They all sat down around her small dinner table. Guioccini spoke quickly.

"The two of you have been through a horrible ordeal," he said, "and I do not intend to impose on you long. But I want to propose something to you. This attack was made for the purpose of suppressing your discovery. The best way to honor the sacrifice of those who died this morning is to go right ahead with our plan to release it to the public. I would like to reschedule our press conference for tomorrow afternoon at three PM. If you are physically able, I want you two to be the ones to share our findings with the media. Are you willing to do that?"

Josh looked at Isabella, and she met his glance with a determined nod. He looked at Guioccini and nodded himself.

"There is no way I am going to let them silence us," he said. "We will be there!"

"Then I shall not keep you longer," said Guioccini. "Please, both of you get some rest. I will—" He was interrupted by the ringing of his cell phone. He glanced at the incoming number and wrinkled his brow. "Yes, Dr. Castolfo?" he said.

The voice at the other end was clearly agitated, and as he listened, Guioccini became equally agitated. "She can't be!" he snapped. "Yes, Benito, I will turn it on immediately!"

Josh looked at him with a raised eyebrow as Guioccini grabbed the TV remote. The Italian archeologist looked at him with anger radiating from his eyes. "Tintoretto has gone ahead with her press conference," he said, turning on the television.

The news channel showed the familiar façade of the National Museum of Antiquities in the background. Smoke was still visible rising from behind the building. Maria Tintoretto stood on the steps, her expression grim. She was about to begin speaking, and Guioccini turned up the volume.

"I would like to thank the members of the press for agreeing to meet me this afternoon," she said, "especially in light of the horrific events of this morning. Let me begin by offering my sincere condolences to the families of those who were killed or injured in this terrible attack and my personal best wishes for those recovering from their injuries."

"No prayers?" asked a reporter.

"Talking to an empty sky does nothing to heal wounds or cure diseases," she snapped. "But you have touched upon part of the reason why I am here, so let me explain. As most of you know, two days ago the so-called 'Pontius Pilate scroll' was translated and read to the members of the Bureau of Antiquities. It was immediately apparent to me that this so-called artifact was nothing but a clumsy forgery, a piece of pro-Christian propaganda most likely planted by the Church some time ago in hopes that it would be found and used to bolster their belief in an archaic and obsolete god-myth. However, as the board discussed it further, it also became apparent to me that our members were entirely taken in by this fraud, and were ready to present it to the world as a genuine chronicle from the time of the legendary Jesus of Nazareth. When I raised my voice in objection, the president of the board allowed me to be shouted down and verbally abused by the American member of the dig team, who is the son of a fundamentalist preacher and a religious primitive of the worst sort. What I wanted to do was demand that the surrounding artifacts from the chamber be subjected to the most rigorous of testing, and the scroll itself be carbon-dated, before it was presented to the public. When I was not even given a chance to finish my proposal, I walked out and resigned from the board."

There was a buzz of comments among the press representatives, and several reporters began shouting questions. Tintoretto raised her hand and the media grew quieter. "I will take questions, but let me finish my statement. Obviously, I had no idea what would happen this morning—no one did—but I do want to draw your attention to the circumstances. This '*Testimonium Pilatus*' was to be read and presented to you this morning as an authentic historical document. Supposedly, all the other artifacts from the chamber on Capri would prove its antiquity and authenticity once they were tested. But now, behold! The lab is destroyed, and all the associated artifacts are gone forever. This completely removes them from all scientific scrutiny! So we are handed the scroll as a fait accompli, with absolutely nothing to back up the claim that it is nearly two thousand years old. Awfully convenient, don't you think, ladies and gentlemen? I tell you, this has the cold, oppressive hand of the Holy See written all over it! I submit to you that the discovery, the announcement, and this morning's terrorist attack were all engineered by the Church in order to make this fraud appear credible!"

The reporters roared back in amazement, anger, and disbelief. Antonio Ginovese spoke loudest and first. "Doctor Tintoretto!" he shouted, and she nodded. His cameraman stuck the mike closer to her as Ginovese repeated his question. "I know you are aware one of the victims of this attack is a respected and powerful Cardinal of the Church. Surely you cannot be proposing that the Vatican ordered the murder of one of its own princes?"

"Why not?" she sneered. "The Church has always been eager to pave its path to power with the blood of its own believers. Martyrdom, they call it, don't they?"

Guioccini was livid with rage. "That BITCH!" he roared. "I am going down there right now! This cannot be allowed to stand unanswered! I will send a car for you later, Luke!" He literally ran from the apartment.

The rest of them continued to watch the press conference in disbelief and outrage. The American, Andrew Eastwood, was asking another question. "Dr. Tintoretto," he said. "Can you tell me how you know for certain that the '*Testimonium*' is a fake when the rest of the Antiquities Board seems to accept it as an authentic and ancient manuscript?"

"Because it describes events that did not and could not have possibly happened!" she snapped.

"What events are those?" asked the American reporter.

"The same ones chronicled in that fourfold fairy tale known as the Gospels," she replied. "That this obscure carpenter was in fact a deity who rose from the dead!"

"So your problem with the scroll is not with its condition or the circumstances of its recovery, but with the fact that it confirms the Gospel narrative?" he pressed. Josh mentally blessed the dogged young reporter for his persistence.

"I have many problems with the circumstances of its recovery!" she shot back. "For example, why did the team include both a representative from the Vatican AND an American evangelical? Why were the two of them left alone on Capri while Dr. Sforza returned to the mainland to meet with the board? There was ample opportunity for a substitution to have been made inside the chamber!"

Josh groaned and rolled his eyes, and then felt his cell phone vibrating in his pocket. He glanced at the Caller ID and saw that it was Father MacDonald, then answered.

"Father!" he said. "I am glad to hear from you."

"You won't be, laddie," said the voice of the priest. He sounded a hundred years old. "I have bad news. Rossini . . ." For a moment MacDonald could not go on, and Josh heard him stifle a sob. "Giuseppe is with the saints now, lad."

Josh didn't even remember hanging up. He looked at Isabella, and she started crying anew at the expression on his face. He slowly nodded, and then went to her and held her as she sobbed bitterly.

Luke Martens got up and placed his hand on Josh's shoulder for a moment in silent prayer, and then he and Alicia made their exit. Josh waited till they were gone, scooped Isabella up in his arms, and carried her to her bed. She never quit clinging to him and weeping. He laid her down gently and pulled the blankets over her, then sat on the edge of the bed. Finally she spoke.

"First Marc," she said. "Then my papa . . . and now Giuseppe. Every man I have ever loved has been taken from me, Josh!"

He pressed his lips gently to her bandaged forehead. "I'm not going anywhere," he said gently.

Her gaze fixed on him. So much love shone from his eyes that she finally managed a tiny smile. "You know," she said, "this is not the way that I hoped to finally get you here!"

He laughed. "It wasn't something any of us expected," he said. "But I will stay here tonight and keep an eye on you. I don't want to be alone, either. Let me get you one of those painkillers, and I will stay with you till you can go to sleep."

"You won't leave then?" she asked plaintively.

"Only as far as the couch," he promised.

He walked back into the den and turned to the television, which was still on. Dr. Guioccini had gotten to the front of the museum in a matter of minutes, and was now addressing the reporters as Tintoretto tried to interrupt. "This press conference is the most gross and disrespectful breach of professional ethics and personal integrity I have ever seen!" he thundered. "The forensics teams are still picking up pieces of Simone Apriceno from the ruins of her lab, and this vile woman calls a press conference to denounce our beloved colleague as a fraud? For shame, Doctor Tintoretto! Even your anti-religious mania should allow for more decorum than this!"

Tintoretto snarled back, "I cannot stand by and see the Board of Antiquities squander its scientific credibility to support this obvious forgery!"

He glared at her. "If it is such an obvious fraud, then why are you the only person to condemn it as such?" he asked. Before she could answer, he turned to the reporters. "Ladies and gentlemen of the press," he said. "I regret that this woman could not put her prejudices on hold for a single day to let us mourn our dead. But we will not let hatred from rigid atheists or religious fanatics silence the truth of our findings. The Pilate scroll was, in fact, spared from the blast because it was being transferred to the main museum at the moment the suicide bomber struck. We are still determined to share both the scroll and its contents with you tomorrow, to show that the enemies of scientific truth and professional integrity will NOT be allowed to win! I invite you all to be here at three PM tomorrow to see the *'Testimonium Pilatus'* for yourself. At that time we will reply to all the objections made by Dr. Tintoretto in detail. And as for you—" He rounded on the former board member in fury. "You, madam, are trespassing on museum property. You will vacate the premises immediately or I will have you physically removed!"

She paled. "You would not DARE!" she snapped. "I am an employee of this museum!"

"Not anymore," he said. "I spoke to the board on the way over and they have just unanimously agreed to terminate your contract. Now, I would politely ask you to depart!"

Tintoretto stormed off the steps and disappeared into the crowd of journalists as the reporters' cameras clicked furiously. Guioccini watched her depart and then walked into the museum, ignoring their shouted questions. Josh turned the TV off, picked up the bottle of pills, and went back to Isabella.

Her tears had stopped, but her eyes were still red with grief. He gave her a Percocet and sat on the edge of the bed. She took his hand in hers and pressed it to her cheek, closing her eyes for a moment or two. Then she looked at him directly.

"I don't get it, Josh," she said.

"What don't you get?" he asked.

"You say that God loves us so much that He sacrificed Himself for us in the person of his only Son. You say that He hears and answers prayer. You say He deserves our absolute love and devotion," she said.

"I believe all those things to be true," he said calmly.

"Then why is there so much shit in the world?" she asked bitterly. "Why do children starve, and good people die of cancer, and innocent girls get raped and evil clerics blow up innocent people in the name of Allah? Why is Giuseppe dead?" Unable to contain her emotions, she broke into fresh sobs.

Josh looked at her long and hard. "If you expect that my faith somehow gives me all the answers to the unfairness of life, you are going to be disappointed," he said. "I don't know all the answers. I have asked the same questions of God that you just asked me. But I do know a few truths that might just help you understand a little," he said.

"Right now I need all the help I can get," she said.

"OK," he said. "Here goes. There are two things that keep this world from being the perfect place God made it to be. The first of these is what has cursed man from the beginning—the fact that God made us with free will. Since the garden, every man and woman has been free to choose their own path. There are people in the world who voluntarily choose to do evil. God usually does not stop them—not because He is complicit in their evil, but because He will not force someone to behave as He wishes them to. Secondly, and hand in hand with that, there is the presence of sin. Sin is the cancer that eats up everything that is good in people and replaces it with bile and hatred. Sin is what twisted Dr. Tintoretto's life and filled her with anger and misery. Sin is what drives fanatics to murder in the name of a supposedly compassionate god. Sin ties us in knots and keeps us from reaching for the good and perfect life that God has waiting for us."

She nodded, understanding but not convinced. "And there is something else," Josh added. "That is the fact that God is omniscient and we are not. When something like today happens, all we see is the short-term pain and anguish and not the eternal consequences. Sometimes great evil can be turned into an even greater good. And sometimes pain is the way that God draws us nearer to Himself. Did I ever tell you about my cat, Lovecraft?"

Isabella actually laughed a bit. "You named your cat after a writer of Gothic horror stories?" she asked.

Josh sighed. "I told you I was a total nerd," he said. "Lovecraft was a pretty Siamese, friendly and approachable. Far and away the best-natured cat I have ever owned! Of course, she had to be, given that I was a very typical mischievous teenager. But one evening, we went off to Wednesday church services, and Lovecraft the cat found her way into our garage. Dad had been bass fishing that Saturday, and left a rod and reel leaning in the corner with a lure still on it. The lure was something called a 'Devil's Horse'—about three inches long, shiny, and with three treble hooks attached to it. I guess the lure was hanging free and the cat batted at it with her paw. The treble hook bit in and got hold of her. The more she yanked and pulled, the deeper it went. So, being a cat, she tried kicking at the lure with her back claws to make it let go—and she got a hook in her back leg as well. By now the rod was broken and the garage has got fishing wire everywhere. When panic and flight did not work, Lovecraft tried aggression again. She BIT the lure to make it let go—and got a third treble hook through the cheek!"

Isabella looked at him, laughing and crying at the same time. "I think I know that feeling!" she said. "Everything you do makes the situation worse!"

"Exactly!" Josh said. "So we get home from church and Dad's fishing rod is smashed, there is fishing line all over the garage, stuff is strewn everywhere, and in one corner, tangled in a huge ball of fishing line and miscellaneous things that had gotten caught up with her, was my poor cat, yowling, hissing, and ready to claw the eyes out of anyone who got close!"

Isabella was giggling now, as the Percocet took hold. "So what did you do?" she asked.

"I wasn't able to do anything," Josh said. "I was only ten years old. But my Dad got a beach towel and threw it over the cat, wrapping her up tight. Then he uncovered one pierced cat member at a time, pushed the hook through the wound until the barbs came out the other side, used wire cutters to cut the barb off the hook, and then pulled it back out. You should have heard the cat howl! It sounded like she was being disemboweled! And despite the towel and two pairs of hands helping, she still managed to claw my dad up pretty good. After he got the last hook out and cut her free of all the fishing line, she bit him for good measure, went streaking out of the garage and under the house, and did not come out for two days!"

"Poor kitty!" Isabella said.

"The thing is," Josh continued, "to her limited understanding, Dad was just torturing her. There was no rhyme or reason to his actions that she could understand. All she felt was the pain. But the whole time, he was actively working to free her from the mess she had gotten herself into. And she clawed and bit him for his troubles!"

Isabella was quiet now, her rich brown eyes staring up at Josh.

"That's us," he said. "That's our whole world. We are so caught up in our own sin, our own misery, and their consequences that we can't even begin to see a way out. And when God tries to help us, we fight back because we can't see the situation from his perspective. All we see is more pain, so we lash out at Him. But the whole time He is just patiently trying to extricate us from the mess we landed ourselves in by our own stubbornness and pride."

Isabella was quiet for a very long time, and he thought that perhaps she had gone to sleep. But when she spoke, her voice was soft but very clear. "Thank you, Joshua," she said. "It doesn't make everything better—but it helps me understand. A little. I still wish Simone and Giuseppe did not have to die."

Josh's own tears started up again, surprising him. "Me too," he said softly.

"I love you," she said as she faded off to sleep.

"I love you, too," he breathed softly. He held her hand for a long time, and then limped in to the couch to call his parents.

* * *

Hundreds of miles away, Ibrahim Abbasside watched the evening news with disgust. The fool Hassan had blown himself up and let the very thing he was seeking to destroy get away! The scroll would be read to the press tomorrow and there was nothing anyone could do to prevent it.

Abbasside stepped outside and paced under the light of the moon for a while. The sobs of his fourth wife could still be heard from their bedroom. She was only fifteen, and pleasingly proportioned, but had made the mistake of talking to him during the news broadcast. The bruises would heal soon enough, he thought, and perhaps she would have a better understanding of a junior wife's place when they did.

So the scroll was going to be read and publicized, he thought. The infidel Italian woman, Tintoretto, had already created a narrative of fraud and disbelief around it—may Allah grant her mercy! he thought. Of course, the authorities would then announce that the scroll itself must be tested to verify its age. That meant that, at some point, it would have to be moved, he mused. That could present an opportunity—to do what?

If the scroll were destroyed before it could be tested, then its claims would lose much validity. In time, it would be forgotten, and the religion of truth could continue to grow and thrive, while the heresy of Christianity would continue its slow decline. That was it, he nodded. He would have to get close enough to the museum to be ready to strike the moment the scroll left the grounds there, which would mean abandoning his long-time sanctuary. But, he decided as he strolled back into the small cinderblock building he called home, this time there would be no intermediary to carry out the job. Sometimes, he thought as he walked past his cowering child bride, if you want a job done, you just had to do it yourself.

NEW DETAILS EMERGE IN MUSEUM BOMBING
AL QAEDA LINK CONFIRMED

(UPN) Authorities continue to investigate the deadly terror attack in Naples, Italy yesterday, when eight people were killed at a research lab that is part of the National Museum of Antiquities complex. The attack killed archeologist Giuseppe Rossini, paleobotanist Simone Apriceno, Cardinal Heinrich Klein, a renowned archeologist with the Vatican Museum, British journalist Valeria Witherspoon, Museum security guard Lucien Luccatori, and an American couple, Tristan Wooten and Brooke Blue, who were vacationing in Naples and were struck by wreckage from the blast.

The suicide bomb was made up of approximately 1500 pounds of ammonium nitrate fertilizer rigged with an electronic detonator. The bomber, Ali bin-Hassan, has been confirmed to be a high-ranking Al Qaeda leader who trained in Afghanistan with Osama bin Laden. He sent a video statement to several media outlets proclaiming that he was acting in order to prevent the 'Testimonium Pilatus,' a recently discovered first century manuscript that reportedly describes the trial of Jesus of Nazareth, from being read to the press at a conference scheduled for Friday.

Ironically, the blast did not destroy the ancient papyrus scroll, which was in another building at the moment the explosives were detonated. The Museum has announced that the postponed press conference will be held Saturday, despite the fact that one disgruntled board member has denounced the discovery as a fraud. Security around the Museum has been beefed up in anticipation of the press conference.

CHAPTER TWENTY

Josh woke up the next morning with a groan of agony. Every muscle in his body ached with a pain that was only surpassed by the throbbing of his head. He slowly levered himself upright, trying to remember where he was and why he hurt so much. He saw that he was in an unfamiliar apartment, and then the memories came crashing in. The lab destroyed, his friends dead, priceless artifacts gone forever . . . the memories hurt almost as much as his injuries. He picked up the bottle of painkillers and staggered to the sink, pouring himself a glass of water, and took two of them. Then he looked at the clock and saw it was nearly nine in the morning. His muscles were beginning to loosen up a bit, and he limped down the hall to Isabella's room a bit more steadily than he had stumbled to the kitchen.

She was still sound asleep, her face finally relaxed and calm. Her blouse had ridden up a bit, exposing her perfectly toned belly. A single scabbed-over scratch, courtesy of broken glass from the lab, marred its feminine perfection. He lovingly pulled the blanket over her and sat down. She stirred and gave a deep groan, then opened one eye.

"Josh?" she said. "What are you—" Then her face resumed its grieved expression as she remembered the awful events of that dreadful Friday. Finally she let out a long sigh. "I was so hoping it was all a dream," she said. "But I know it wasn't."

"I woke up thinking the same thing," Josh said.

She sat up with a deep groan. "I am not sure what hurts worse," she said. "My body or my soul!"

"Well, I can pray for one and provide narcotics for the other," Josh said. She gave him a faint smile and took the Percocet gratefully. She swallowed the pills with several gulps of water and rubbed her eyes.

"What time is it?" she asked.

"A little after nine in the morning," he said.

"I guess we had better get to the museum before noon," she said. "Why don't you let me take a shower and get dressed—unless you would like to go first?" she added.

"All my clean clothes are at the hotel," he said with a rueful smile. "You go ahead and get ready and then you can walk me there. Or better yet, catch a cab. It's only a few blocks, but I am not terribly steady on my feet just yet."

"All right," she said, sitting up. The effort caused a wince of pain. "I keep thinking I will find some part of me that does not hurt," she said.

"I'm still looking," he replied. "So far, my left ear and my right pinkie finger are about it."

She got up slowly and grabbed a few things, then trudged down the hall to the bathroom. Josh limped into the kitchen and looked in the fridge. He saw some eggs and a few slices of smoked ham, and decided to make some breakfast. In a few minutes he had a frying pan heated up, and was grilling the ham with a dash of butter. After it was lightly browned on both sides, he pulled it up with some tongs and cracked about a half dozen eggs into the bowl. He stirred them with a whisk, adding salt and pepper, then diced the ham and stirred it in.

"That smells delicious!" Isabella said as she walked in a few minutes later, toweling her hair dry. She had opted for a simple pair of khaki pants and a beige blouse, with a small golden pin in the shape of a dove on the left side.

"I realized neither of us has eaten a bite since breakfast yesterday," he said. "And, no matter how bad the heartbreak, the body still needs fuel. Grab us a pair of plates, please."

The eggs and ham disappeared very quickly, and each of them drank a cold glass of water to wash it down. Josh quickly washed and rinsed the dishes, and Isabella put them away. Both of them were feeling the pain fade from their bodies as they stretched, walked, and used their sore and bruised muscles. The Percocet helped, too.

By the time they were done, Josh decided that maybe the walk to the hotel would do him good. It was about six blocks, and they covered the distance quite rapidly, considering all they had been through. About 100 feet from the front door, however, Isabella grabbed his arms and pulled him into the front door of a curio shop.

"What is it?" he asked.

"Look around the hotel entrance!" she said.

Sure enough, about two dozen reporters, most of them with cameras around their necks, were milling around, waiting for Josh to come out. He let out a long sigh, looking down at his clothes, which were still filthy with ash, dirt stains, and blood. What would the papers make of him showing up with a freshly cleaned and showered Isabella, while still wearing the clothes he had survived the explosion in?

"Go into this shop for a moment, and wait for them to leave," Isabella said.

Josh looked around the corner doubtfully. "I don't see any tents," he said, "but that looks like a pretty permanent base camp to me. We'll still be here at suppertime if we wait for them to disperse on their own!"

She gave him her first real smile since the explosion. "Dr. Parker," she said, "just watch me work!" She brushed past him and took off toward the hotel at a brisk pace that belied the pain he knew she must be feeling from yesterday's trauma. She got within about twenty feet of the press corps before one of the photographers recognized her, and within moments they were thronging around her, asking for comments. Josh could hear her strong clear voice over the traffic.

"Gentlemen, Dr. Parker will not be down for at least an hour—he is still very sore from the blast and just woke up a few moments ago when I called him. I would like to make a statement, but if it is all right with you, let's walk over to the museum steps before I speak. It's a much better backdrop for the cameras, don't you think?" she asked. Josh watched in amazement as she headed down the street with the press following meekly behind her, looking like a flock of sheep following a shepherdess to their watering hole. He waited a few minutes, purchased a newspaper at the shop, buried his face in it, and walked over to the hotel.

Forty-five minutes and one very long, hot shower later, he emerged from the elevator into the lobby to find Isabella, Dr. Martens, and Alicia waiting for him. He greeted them warmly and gave Isabella an affectionate kiss. "You really saved me just then," he said. "There was no way I could have faced that pack in my condition!"

She looked at him fondly. "It was the least I could do," she said, "after the way you took care of me yesterday. Father MacDonald is waiting for you at the museum. He wants to talk about the press conference this afternoon, but also about Giuseppe's funeral arrangements. They are talking about holding his service Monday afternoon, and Simone's the next day."

Josh nodded. "Of course I want to attend," he said, "but why would Duncan need to talk to me about the arrangements?"

"Apparently Giuseppe's son wants you and I both to speak," she said.

Josh was stunned. "I am deeply honored," he said, "but I only knew the man for a couple of weeks! Why on earth does the family want to hear from me?"

Isabella gave a gentle shrug. "Apparently you made a profound impression," she said. "At least, that is what Giovanni, his son, told Father MacDonald."

Josh shook his head in wonder, and the four of them headed over to the museum together. "So what did you tell the press?" Josh asked Sforza as they walked toward the entrance.

"I talked about Giuseppe and Simone," she said. "I paid tribute to both of them, and said nothing that I regret."

He put his arm around her. "That couldn't have been easy," he whispered.

"It wasn't," she said. "I was in tears by the time I was done. But I did it for them as much as I did it for you. The press has focused so much on us that both of them have not gotten the attention and credit they deserved. Giuseppe made the discovery, and Simone's lab work, although cruelly interrupted, still established the authenticity of our finds to a great degree. I want them remembered as the true heroes of our story."

By now they were inside the Museum, and Josh started striding toward the back of the building to the door that led to the lab—and then caught himself. "I just realized I have no idea where to go," he said softly.

"This way, laddie!" said a familiar voice behind him. He turned to see Father MacDonald, smiling but looking older and sadder than Josh had ever seen him. He took the priest's hand in his own and they embraced warmly.

"I am glad that you are all right, Father," Josh said.

"Likewise, lad! I felt the blast deep in the service tunnel, and all I could think was that you and Isabella had been in there with the rest of the team when Sinisi and I walked out. I feared the worst," confessed the Scotsman.

"We were just walking over to the main building when the lab blew up behind us," said Josh. "Both of us were picked up by the blast and hurled into the side of the building. We were lucky to escape with a few cuts and bruises, and rattled heads."

The priest nodded. "Giuseppe and the others were not so fortunate. I was able to speak with him before the end, and he—well, he was a good man. He died trusting God and doing what he loved. I will miss the old bugger a great deal, though. True friends are few and far between, and he and I have known each other for so many years. The others . . . well, they all died instantly. I have spent the night praying for their dear souls."

The group fell silent for a moment, and then Isabella took charge. "I take it we are now operating from the old lab?" she asked.

"Indeed," said MacDonald. "Lead the way, dear."

She took them down two or three side corridors in quick succession to a service elevator bank marked "Restricted Access." An armed security guard checked their names against a list he held, and then nodded them through. The elevator buzzed down three levels, and they found themselves in a large but cluttered laboratory. Several tables had recently been cleared, and on one of them the Pilate scroll was resting in its plexiglass case. Dr. Guioccini and Dr. Castolfo were waiting for them, along with a very subdued Dr. Sinisi.

"Joshua, Isabella," Castolfo said. "I hope the two of you are somewhat better this morning?"

"Functional," said Josh, "but that's about it. I feel like I lost a round with Rocky Balboa."

Isabella smiled. "Joshua protected me from the brunt of the blast," she said. "I am sore but I will be ready to talk to the press this afternoon. I want the world to know that our friends did not die in vain."

Josh nodded. Then he looked over at the next table and gasped. Scabbard slightly blackened but still intact, there lay the sword of Julius Caesar! He walked over and stared. "How on earth did it survive?" he asked.

Castolfo laughed. "After the blast, we were all focused on clearing the rubble and searching for survivors at first—then for bodies. Finally, about eight PM last night, I walked over to where my car was parked. The sword and scabbard had been hurled aloft by the blast and punched through my windshield when they came down—left sticking straight up like Excalibur!"

Josh looked more closely and saw that there were indeed fragments of fresh glass imbedded in the ancient leather. "Remarkable," he said. "After the Pilate scroll, I think that this was quite possibly the most wonderful find from the site. I am glad to see it survived."

He turned to the scroll itself next, studying the clear, flowing Latin script once more. "So what is the plan today?" he asked.

"I think we start with a quick recap of the scroll's discovery, a strong rebuttal of Dr. Tintoretto's baseless accusations, and a tribute to our fallen friends," said Isabella. "Then we hand out the copies of the scroll in Latin and in English, and read the translation to the press. Then we take their questions."

Castolfo nodded. "I think that is the best course of action to follow," he said. "Before the events of yesterday, something more theatrical might have been in order. But given the death and destruction, your straightforward approach is much more appropriate."

Sinisi spoke up for the first time. "My friends," he said. "I cannot express in words how sorry I am for this terrible loss. I know that my natural enthusiasm can be grating at times to you field scientists, but I will say I am profoundly thankful that I talked Professor MacDonald into taking the scroll over to the press room yesterday. Otherwise, four more of us would be dead, and this priceless treasure destroyed forever. Understand, I am not trying to take any kind of credit. Truth be told, I begin to think the Almighty is protecting this document! I just want you both to know how very glad I am that you are alive and unharmed. I'm even glad the Father here was with me and not in the lab."

MacDonald growled. "You are a pompous ass, Sinisi—but I owe my life to your 'enthusiasm,' as you call it, so I guess I will have to think better of you in the future. I canna tell you how much that annoys me!"

Castolfo smiled at this. Despite the tragedy, there was still a bond between the team and the board members that could not be shaken. "I have asked the cafeteria to send down some sandwiches," he said. "I personally don't feel like eating, and I doubt that any of you do either, but the body must go on even when the spirit is crushed. After we are done, we will take the scroll up to the press room and begin setting the stage. Reporters will be allowed in at two thirty, and the briefing will begin promptly at three o'clock. Does anyone NOT want to speak?"

The three surviving members of the team looked at one another. Not a one of them said a word. Castolfo and Guioccini looked at the three scientists for a moment, and then the board president nodded. "I cannot tell you how much I have come to respect and admire each of you," he finally said. "You are a credit to your respective disciplines, and to your faith."

"What lies ahead after this afternoon?" Josh asked.

"That is a good question," said Guioccini. "Dr. Castolfo and I have been discussing it for some time now. Dr. Henderson, from the Smithsonian, will be arriving in Rome on Tuesday. We have decided to do the carbon-14 testing on the scroll itself at the new lab in the Palazzo Massimo in Rome. They have the newest spectrographic equipment, and it will only be necessary to remove a tiny fragment of the scroll to get an accurate date. Later next week we will transfer the scroll by automobile to the Palazzo and conduct the testing next Friday. The results should silence Tintoretto once and for all. As for the scroll's permanent residence, since it was found so close by, agreement has been reached that it will be permanently exhibited here in Naples."

"I would like to see it formally designated in all subsequent scholarly works as the Rossini Papyrus," said Isabella.

"That is a wonderful gesture, Isabella," said Guioccini. "Dr. Castolfo and I have already discussed it, and agree—with one slight amendment. We propose to call it the Rossini-Sforza Papyrus."

She sighed. "I don't really care," she said. "Not about my name being on it, at least. As long as our friend is remembered, I am content."

"We have a large crew sifting through the rubble of the lab alongside law enforcement," said Sinisi. "It is possible that some of the more durable relics from the chamber may have survived the blast, and if they did, we will make sure that they are displayed with the scroll here at the museum."

"Do you really expect to find anything?" asked Josh.

"The flames were put out pretty quickly," said Sinisi. "I doubt any papyrus survived, but there is a chance some of the other pieces did. Fortunately all the photographs taken at Capri, and in the lab, were downloaded to the museum's hard drive and saved. We know what every last scrap of material from the chamber looks like!"

About this time, a museum cafeteria worker arrived with a tray of sandwiches and sliced fruit, and the six scholars enjoyed a brief and mostly silent meal. Josh looked down the table at Father MacDonald, missing the familiar banter between him and Rossini. A thought occurred to him about his last conversation with Giuseppe.

"Did anyone call Mrs. Bustamante?" he asked.

The three team members looked at one another in dismay, while the board members looked puzzled. Finally Isabella spoke.

"Let me go ahead and do it," she said. "He asked us to speak to her, and we were just too stunned and exhausted last night to even think about it."

Josh stood, groaning as his sore muscles complained. "Would you like me to go with you?" he asked.

She nodded. "I wasn't going to ask, but I will not say no either," she replied.

They took the elevator up to her office, and she dialed out on the land line—the museum's massive stone structure made cellular communication difficult. The phone rang twice on the other end before the familiar voice of the restaurant owner answered.

"Bustamante's Fine Dining," she said. "We are closed for the day, due to the death of our friend Dr. Rossini."

"Antonia, this is Isabella Sforza. I was a good friend of Giuseppe's," she began.

"I remember you, dear girl!" said the Spanish widow. "Giuseppe's face always lit up when he talked about you. He was a dear, dear man."

"He thought very highly of you, too, Antonia," said Isabella. "In fact, the last time I saw him, in the hospital after the blast, he asked me if I would speak to you."

"He thought of me? At the end?" she asked.

"He told me to tell you—" Isabella began, then swallowed hard, choking back the tears. "He wanted you to know that he was very sorry he could not keep his date with you."

There was a muffled sob from the other end, and a long pause. "The old fool!" snapped Bustamante through her tears. "I had eyes for him these last five years, and he waits this long to ask! We could have had some good years together if he had not been so shy!"

Isabella was crying now, the tears running down her face as she listened. "He loved his wife so much," she said. "I don't think he really thought he could ever be that happy again. Only here in the last two weeks did it seem to me he finally began to move on. I am sorry the two of you did not have a chance to find each other sooner, but I do know this much—they would have been very good years for both of you."

Bustamante nodded. "I cannot be angry with him, really," she said. "Loyalty is so hard to find, how can I fault him for being faithful to her memory? But oh! dear girl, I will miss him so much. He was my favorite customer and a dear friend."

"I hope to see you at the memorial service on Monday," Isabella said.

"I will be there," the Spanish restaurateur replied. "He loved you like a daughter, you know."

"I know," said Isabella. "And I loved him as a second father. I am afraid I must go now, Mrs. Bustamante. I will see you on Monday."

"Goodbye, my dear, and thanks for calling," said Bustamante.

Isabella hung up and sat at her desk for a long time, staring at her hands. Josh put his own hands on her shoulders and kissed the top of her head.

"That was a sweet thing to do," he told her.

"It was his request," said Isabella. "How could I do otherwise?"

"I guess it is time to go down to the lab," he said. They left Isabella's office and headed toward the elevators. When they got there, they found the scroll and its case already set on the rolling cart that had carried it from the other lab moments before the explosion on Friday. Sinisi smiled when he saw them.

"I am glad you got here before we left," he said. "Come along and I will show you the set-up."

The press conference was being held in the museum's old ballroom to accommodate the huge crowd of journalists already gathering outside. There were chairs for over 300, and an elevated stage at the front, with a large black curtain drawn. Very carefully, the cart was wheeled from the elevator near the front of the room to a small ramp that led up to the stage. The beautiful mahogany table was set near the front of the stage, with six chairs arranged behind it. In the center of the table was a large sheet of clear plexiglass. MacDonald lifted the carrying tray off the cart with Sinisi's assistance, and then the two of them donned acid-free gloves to raise the plexiglass top off the tray and then gingerly move the scroll onto the plexiglass stand prepared for it. The new base was very slightly angled to tilt the ancient scroll toward the audience. Once the scroll was centered on the new base, the clear plexiglass shield was placed back over it. The material was so transparent and non-reflective that the cover was barely visible.

From beyond the curtain, they heard a mass of voices entering the room from all three doors at once. The press had been allowed in, and so the six of them quickly began preparing to face the cameras. There was a small lavatory backstage for last-minute grooming and calls of nature, and within a few minutes everyone had checked their hair and clothes in the mirror and situated themselves behind the table. The team sat in the middle seats, with Josh and Isabella at the center and Father MacDonald at his right. Sinisi sat at the end next to MacDonald, while Castolfo and Guioccini sat on the other side of Isabella. Josh glanced over at her, and saw how tired and pale she was. He was sure he looked no better, but he gave her hand a squeeze and smiled for her anyway.

At three o'clock the curtains drew back, and a storm of flashbulbs exploded at the sight of the ancient scroll. Josh flinched reflexively, recalling the blast from the day before. Isabella shot him a quick smile, and then Sinisi rose up to speak.

"Ladies and gentlemen of the press, after the tragic events of yesterday, all of us felt that the best way to honor the sacrifice of those we lost was to show that the cowardly terrorist who murdered our friends failed in his goal of destroying what they discovered. As you can see, the *Testimonium Pilatus* is intact and undamaged. I have asked the surviving members of the team to present it to you today." Sinisi finished his remarks and looked over to Isabella, who stood and looked at the assembled press corps.

She looked pale but determined, and the bandage across her forehead was painfully obvious in the strong light. When she spoke, her voice was soft but very firm. "The scroll you see before you was found inside a locked cabinet which had been sealed inside the 'Tiberius chamber' of the Villa Jovis since 37 AD. My colleague and friend Dr. Apriceno had to excavate about six centimeters of dust to even reveal the cabinet itself. We carefully chronicled every step of our excavation from start to finish, to show that there was no chance whatsoever that the chamber or the artifacts within it had been tampered with, despite the reckless comments by a disgruntled former board member."

294

She walked around to the front of the table, facing the press members directly, and lowered her voice to a quiet and conversational tone. "The 'Tiberius chamber' was discovered by my dear friend and mentor, Professor Giuseppe Rossini. I was the first person he called when he found the chamber revealed by an earthquake on Easter Sunday morning; I was, with him, the first person to enter it—he refrained from stepping inside from the time he found it until I could join him almost six hours later. Dr. Rossini was a friend and mentor to an entire generation of classical archeologists; he was a man of honor and decency, with a sense of professionalism that was tempered only by his warm and compassionate heart."

The assembled reporters were completely silent. Her raw grief, and the warmth in her voice as she spoke of her old friend, had turned a room full of eager, panting newshounds into a sympathetic audience that felt her pain and grieved with her. She looked around the room and saw their reaction, then continued.

"As soon as it became evident that we had discovered a trove of untouched relics from the first century, I called my superior, Dr. Guioccini, who helped me assemble a team of brilliant archeologists to assist with their excavation and removal. The one whose work would be the most important in establishing the antiquity of the chamber and its contents was Dr. Simone Apriceno. She spent the better part of five days collecting samples of dust and pollen from every single surface in the chamber. Once we got back to the mainland, her work in analyzing the pollens and other botanical residue inside the chamber was almost nonstop. She spent more time in the lab than any of us, and although her work was cut cruelly short by the cowardly terror attack on this facility, the results that she was able to complete all show that the chamber was undisturbed and intact—other than some visiting rodents about five hundred years ago!"

The reporters nodded to each other. It was apparent that Dr. Tintoretto's accusations had not found a sympathetic audience with most of them. Isabella managed a tiny smile, and then went on.

"Simone was someone I had not worked with before, but we quickly became close friends. She was a big-hearted, generous soul who loved to laugh and dance. I only regret that we did not meet sooner.

"It took us less than a week to completely catalog everything in the chamber. The reliquary cabinet containing the two scrolls was the last item to be removed. The two scrolls were not discovered until the entire cabinet was safe inside the mobile lab on Capri. Once the importance of the find was realized, the Antiquities Bureau elected to move all the artifacts from the chamber to the mainland. This was accomplished one week ago today. After the papyrus manuscripts reached the new research lab here in Naples, Dr. MacDonald took over the curation process, as an expert in ancient document preservation and restoration." At this point she nodded at Duncan, who stood and surveyed the reporters calmly, then began to speak.

"Dealing with ancient papyrus is a tricky business. I had no idea how long it would take for the two ancient scrolls to unroll, nor how intact they were. Fortunately, these scrolls had been preserved so well inside the locked compartment where we found them that they unrolled as quickly as any papyrus I have ever handled. As you know, the shorter scroll, the last will and testament of Caesar Augustus, unrolled in a matter of two days, and many of you were present when we shared its contents at the beginning of this week. By the time we held that press conference Tuesday, the Pilate scroll had already begun to open. As soon as it was safe to do so, we unrolled it and began the work of translation. It was my privilege to work with a brilliant young scholar in ancient Latin, Dr. Joshua Parker of Oklahoma. We both translated the scroll separately, using high-resolution photographs of each page, and then going to the original any time there was a question about a single character. Only when both of us had completed our efforts did we compare notes. The scroll was completely undamaged and written in a strong, clear hand, making it so easy to read that there were no discrepancies at all between our translations. To be doubly sure, we invited two more noted scholars, my own instructor in ancient Latin, Cardinal Heinrich Klein, and Doctor Luke Martens from Texas. Both of them conducted their own separate translations of the scroll and found our work to be without error. I would like to take this moment to offer my condolences to the many friends and students of Cardinal Klein, who was a brilliant antiquarian and a teacher to so many historians and archeologists over the course of his fifty-year career. His loss is a cruel blow, not just to the Church he served so faithfully, but also to the discipline of history and Latin studies to which he brought a consummately professional and scholarly approach."

The Scottish cleric looked out at the audience, sensing that they were beginning to get restless. "After all four translations were diligently compared; we began preparing to present the scroll and its contents to you, the world media. It may seem hasty, but given the fact that one member of the Antiquities Bureau's governing board was already preparing to denounce the finds as fraudulent—without a shred of proof, I might add—we decided that a direct and swift presentation of the facts was the best way to deal with her accusations. We were transporting the scroll to this building from the research lab yesterday morning in preparation for the press conference when the terrorist attack leveled the building and killed our friends. I was spared because I was personally transporting the scroll when the attack occurred; my comrades Joshua and Isabella were walking over to this building from the lab to discuss our preparations at the moment of the blast and likewise survived. Cardinal Klein, Dr. Apriceno, Dr. Rossini, and our security guard Lucien Luccatori were all slain in the attack, as were the young British photographer Miss Witherspoon and two American tourists, Tristan Wooten and Brooke Blue. Once we had recovered from our initial shock, we decided, with the Board's approval, to go ahead with our plans to share the scroll with the public—so that the evil fanatics who carried out this attack will realize the extent of their failure!" His Scottish accent grew stronger, and his voice crackled across the room like thunder as he finished his remarks. Then his expression softened and he continued. "At this time, the written translations of the scroll will be passed out, and I have asked my colleague, Dr. Joshua Parker, to share the contents with you aloud."

Josh swallowed nervously and stood. His body was still stiff and aching from the blast and his head was beginning to throb again. But as began to speak, his aches and pains faded away. He began simply.

"I cannot begin to add to or improve upon the comments already made. I came across the ocean to work with a group of people I had never met, and found some of the best friends imaginable. And yes, one who is now more than a friend." He flashed a quick smile at Isabella. "But all of that is not the reason we are here. What we have found at the Villa Jovis is the most remarkable discovery in the history of Biblical archeology—a document thought to be lost for nineteen hundred years. Scholars have long known that Pontius Pilate forwarded some sort of report to Rome regarding the trial and execution of Jesus of Nazareth, in 33 AD. Justin Martyr, writing to the Emperor Antoninus Pius in the mid-second century, challenged him to find the truth of the story of the crucifixion by reading Pilate's account. But by the time Constantine

297

legalized Christianity in 316 AD, the report that was filed in Rome was long lost."

The reporters were listening closely now, even as some of them were perusing the copies of the document Josh was holding that were now being passed out. He continued: "But we know now there was another copy—Tiberius' personal copy, which he filed along with several other documents in his hidden writing nook on the isle of Capri at the Villa Jovis. This is the copy which we have found, and here is what it says: *Lucius Pontius Pilate, Senior Legate, Prefect, and Proconsul of Judea, to Tiberius Julius Caesar Augustus, Princeps and Imperator of Rome, Greetings.*

Your Excellency, you know that it is the duty of every governor to keep you informed of events in the provinces. . .'"

The room fell silent as, for the first time, the world heard the long-concealed testimony of the Roman governor who crucified Jesus. Josh read carefully, making sure to go slowly enough that he did not stumble over his words or skip any part of the document. Flashbulbs were going off all over the room, and as he reached the story of Jesus' trial and crucifixion, the buzz in the room steadily grew. His voice rose louder over the hubbub as he reached the final paragraphs of Pilate's story:

"'The next morning, I walked down to the tomb where the crucified Jesus had been interred four days before. The heavy stone that had been rolled across the entrance was indeed several yards away, and one side of it was strangely scorched. The seal that had been placed on it was a half molten blob of wax. I looked into the tomb, but there was only the lingering scent of myrrh and some empty linen wrappings lying where the body of the Nazarene prophet had been placed . . ."

By now a profound silence had fallen over the room as the import of these words sunk in. Josh read on to the end of the narrative: *"'And that is the end of my tale, Caesar. I have tried to conduct myself as a Roman prefect and procurator should. I still do not know what it is I have done. Have I been the victim of an incredibly elaborate fraud? Have I lost my mind? Or was I the unwitting accomplice in the murder of a god? I do not know. So I leave judgment of this matter in your hands. Mine are too stained with blood to deal with it any further. I beg you, Caesar, recall me from this benighted place and let me return to Rome! I remain, respectfully yours, Lucius Pontius Pilate, Governor of Judea.'"*

Josh paused a moment, looking out on a sea of astounded faces. He spoke again before the shouted questions could begin. "That is all of the original text, but there is a short note appended to the end in the same handwriting that we found in the short letter from Tiberius Caesar to his steward. The emperor, as you can read, ordered an investigation into the truth of Pilate's story. This, incidentally, confirms a late second-century account which says that Tiberius Caesar was aware of the story of Jesus' resurrection and may have even recommended that Jesus be included in the Roman pantheon of gods. I realize that this was a long document, and I appreciate your patience in listening to it all. At this time we will take any questions you might have."

Cynthia Brown spoke up. "Dr. Parker," she said, "don't you find it a bit odd that this manuscript parallels the New Testament accounts so exactly?"

"Not at all," said Josh, "and neither should anyone else. For the last century or so, there has been a concerted effort on the part of academics worldwide to call every point and detail of the four Gospels into question, while elevating the so-called 'Gnostic Gospels' as being perhaps more accurate or authentic. However, in all fairness, this effort was never based on sound historical scholarship, but rather on ideological hostility to the principal claims of Christianity."

"That seems a bit of a reach, don't you think?" she persisted.

"No," he said. "The four Biblical gospels are the only biographies of Christ that were composed in the first century, while the eyewitnesses of Jesus' life were still alive. Two of them, Matthew and John, were written by eyewitnesses; Mark and Luke were companions of the original Apostles and compiled their gospels from the accounts of those who were, as Luke put it, 'from the beginning eyewitnesses and servants of the word.' All the other documents that have been put forward—the Gnostic Gospels, the New Testament Apocrypha, all the sensationalist books of the last fifty years proclaiming this alternate theory or that to contradict the New Testament narrative—all those things were written centuries later by men who were in no position to know the truth. So now we find the account written by the man who presided over Jesus' trial, and guess what? It agrees with the earliest eyewitness accounts we have. Why should anyone be surprised?"

Drew Eastwood spoke up. "If the evidence for authenticity was so convincing, why did Dr. Tintoretto denounce the document as a fake?"

Josh looked over at Castolfo, who nodded for him to answer. "There are others here who can testify with more credibility than me, but all her written work—at least, all I have read—drips with hostility toward Christianity in general and the Catholic Church in particular. Her antagonism toward Christianity was so strong that she was unwilling to admit the possibility that the *Testimonium* might be genuine. To her mind, if it supported the Biblical narrative, then it had to be a forgery—no other alternative would be considered."

The young reporter nodded. "What are you going to do to address her concerns?"

"Such serious charges have to be answered, obviously. We want the work of our team—especially that of our fallen comrades—to be above any question of fraud. The work that Simone Apriceno completed clearly shows that the chamber has not been disturbed since Roman times, but since all of her samples were destroyed in the blast, we have agreed to allow the *Testimonium* itself to be carbon dated at the Palazzo Massimo in Rome. That should put any doubts about its authenticity to rest once and for all," Josh concluded.

Tyler Patterson spoke up, his perfectly groomed hair gleaming with slight silver highlights at the temples. "So would you say that this find vindicates the claims of Christianity once and for all?"

Josh paused a moment. "Speaking as a Christian rather than as a scientist for just a moment," he finally said, "Christianity does not need vindication. In the end, faith is not something that can be logically proved or disproved. It is a decision of the heart. I will guarantee you that those who do not want to believe will find some excuse to reject what is written here—not on any valid historical grounds, but because they do not want accept the accountability that goes with acknowledging Jesus as the Son of God. They will call Him a magician, an illusionist, a space alien, or whatever it takes to avoid changing the way they live. For those of us who believed in Him already, it's nice to see history confirm what our Scriptures teach us—but it doesn't change the fact that we already knew who He was, long before this chamber was ever uncovered."

Eli Arnold spoke up. "So what you are saying is that faith and fact are unrelated?"

Josh shook his head. "No," he said. "History, archeology, and ancient documents can take you a long way down the road to faith—but in the end, faith itself is still a journey of the heart. Your head can only take you so far."

Antonio Ginovese spoke up. "Back to the scroll that you discovered," he said in accented English. "What will happen after it has been carbon dated?"

"It will be permanently housed here at the National Museum of Antiquities," Josh said, "along with any other associated artifacts that we can recover from the wreckage of our lab. We have decided that the document shall henceforth be referred to as the Rossini-Sforza Papyrus."

Several other questions were shouted aloud, but Dr. Castolfo spoke up. "Gentlemen, there will be time for questions and interviews later on," he said. "Do not forget the physical and emotional trauma these young people have endured over the last twenty-four hours. We need to let them get some rest, and we have our friends to mourn. Thank you for your attendance today. This press conference is now ended."

The reporters groaned and protested, but then began a hasty exodus as they rushed to meet TV and newspaper deadlines. As the auditorium cleared, Josh slumped back to his chair in exhaustion. The curtain in front of the table slowly slid shut, and he took Isabella by the hand. Now the world knew.

DID THE GOSPELS GET IT RIGHT ALL ALONG?

"TESTIMONIUM PILATUS" CONFIRMS NEW TESTAMENT ACCOUNT

(from the New York Times International Edition)

Two weeks after its discovery on the isle of Capri, the ancient document known as the "Testimonium Pilatus" has been translated, and was released to the media in a spectacular press conference this afternoon. The document, which covers a six-foot-long papyrus scroll, is apparently the original report that Roman governor Pontius Pilate sent to Rome concerning the trial and execution of Jesus of Nazareth, whom the world's two billion Christians claim to be the Son of God. Pilate, who apparently was concerned that his role in the trial might be reported back to Rome in negative terms, gave an account that parallels the four Biblical gospels to a remarkable degree. He describes Jesus' growing reputation among the people, and his own concern that the Nazarene's arrival in Jerusalem might spark some unrest among the people of Judea.

Pilate also confirms the Biblical claim that it was the Jewish religious leaders who instigated Jesus' arrest and trial, making it clear that he believed the Galilean to be innocent of all charges and tried repeatedly to have him released. His account of the conversations he had with the accused Jesus are very close to those recorded in the Biblical Gospel of John, which may be explained by the fact that Pilate asked one of the disciples of Jesus—most likely John himself—to act as interpreter when he interrogated Jesus.

The scroll contains three different handwriting styles—one apparently belonging to Pilate's scribe, and the shorter, final portion written in Pilate's own hand, according to the scroll itself. Finally, there is a short postscript in a hand that matches the writing on several other documents discovered at Capri, attributed to the Emperor Tiberius. The Roman Emperor apparently took a great interest in the case, and asked for one of his officers to investigate the story on his behalf.

By far the most controversial claim in the ancient scroll is its description of the Resurrection of Christ. While Pilate himself did not witness the event, he interrogated the guards who were posted at the tomb, and their accounts match the Biblical claim that the stone was rolled away and the body of Jesus gone on Sunday morning, following the Friday crucifixion. . .

(Continued on page A2) (Complete Text of the "Testimony of Pontius Pilate" on page A3)

CHAPTER TWENTY-ONE

After the press conference ended, the team members waited quietly behind the curtains while the auditorium slowly cleared. The adrenaline and determination that had driven Josh and Isabella to get up and face the day had faded, and both of them were aching and exhausted. While MacDonald and Sinisi carefully returned the scroll to the mobile platform and then took it back to the museum's lab, Dr. Castolfo picked up a phone and spoke some sharp orders in Italian. After he was done, he turned to Josh and Isabella.

"You two have done more than I would have dared ask," he said. "I know that it was a physical strain for both of you to be up and around so soon after your ordeal, and as your employer, I am ordering you both to go home and get some rest. I have summoned a limo to one of the museum's side entrances, and it will whisk you both away in short order. Joshua, your friend Dr. Martens and his wife will be waiting for you at the hotel to get you up to your room. Isabella, I will be glad to escort you to your apartment. I do not want to see either of you until Monday, is that clear?"

Josh nodded. "I feel like I could sleep till Monday!" he said.

Isabella agreed. "I feel like all the air has gone out of me," she said. "I used to have an inflatable toy dolphin when I was a little girl that I carried to the beach, and it always made me sad when Papa let the air out of it at the end of the day. But right now I feel like it looked just before he rolled it up and tossed it in the trunk!"

Josh smiled. The analogy fit his feelings as well. Of course, his boyhood beach toy had been an inflatable dinosaur rather than a dolphin, but the comparison still rang true. He stood slowly, every bruise and abrasion making itself felt, then helped Isabella to her feet. She leaned on his arm as they made their way after Dr. Castolfo down a restricted corridor to one of the museum's side entrances.

"Your tribute to our friends was beautiful," he said.

"Thanks," she replied. "I had been turning over what to say in my head for a while. It's funny how close you can grow to someone in such a short time. I barely knew Simone Apriceno for two weeks, yet I miss her cruelly already."

"It is odd how quickly we grow attached to total strangers, isn't it?" he answered, giving her arm a gentle squeeze.

She looked up into his eyes and smiled. "You are right! So much awfulness has happened since we met," she said. "But meeting you at least makes it seem a little bit worthwhile. Josh—" She paused.

"What is it, Isabella?" he asked.

"I don't think I could survive if I lost you, too," she said.

"Isabella, nothing is going to happen to me," he said. "But the beauty of faith is that our loved ones are never truly lost; just separated from us for a little while."

She looked at him, and the sadness crept back into her eyes. "You make faith sound so appealing," she said. "I just don't know that I am ready to take that step yet. It is too soon."

By this time they were at the side door of the enormous museum complex, where a large black limo was waiting for them. The windows were tinted, but as they passed the front of the museum Josh saw a few correspondents on the steps, cameras rolling as they pontificated on the story of the scroll and its implications. He was curious to see how it would all play out in the press, but too tired and sore to care much at the moment. A few moments later, the limo pulled up at the front of his hotel, and he saw Dr. Martens and Alicia standing at the door waiting for him. He gave Isabella a quick kiss and got out, walking as quickly as his injuries would allow him, to meet them. Several reporters who had been waiting nearby immediately converged on him.

"Dr. Parker!" shouted one American. "Would you like to make any comment about the events of the last two days?"

Martens spoke up loudly. "Gentlemen, this young man has been through a great deal in the last forty-eight hours. If you had seen him last night at the ER, you would realize what a heroic effort it was for him to even be at the museum today. Please let him through so he can get some rest."

"It's all right, Doc," Josh said, as he reached the door and turned around, seeing a small forest of microphones and cameras aimed at him. He privately swore never to make fun of celebrities' paparazzi problems again. "Let me make a very short statement," he said, "and then just please do me the favor of leaving me alone for a day or two."

The reporters grew silent. Josh thought for just a moment about everything that he had experienced since he got the phone call from Dr. Martens out on Lake Hugo just two weeks before. What could he possibly have to say that had not already been said? Finally he spoke.

"The discovery of the *Testimonium* is no doubt the single most important find in the history of Biblical archeology, but in one important aspect, it is not unlike the others that have been made in the last one hundred and fifty years: it confirms the historical truth of the Biblical narrative. Christianity is the only faith in the world whose central claim rests upon a single historical event: the Resurrection of Jesus of Nazareth. Most of you know that my father is a Protestant minister. For my entire life I have heard him thunder from the pulpit that if Jesus was not physically raised from the dead on the third day, then the entire foundation of our faith is a falsehood. My dad believes—and I share that faith—that if Jesus remained in His tomb on the third day, then most of what He said and taught becomes meaningless. As profound as the sayings of Christ are, they are all rooted in His claim, and His belief, that He was the Son of God." Josh paused a moment, his head throbbing, but went on in a determined manner. "If that claim was false—whether Jesus of Nazareth knowingly claimed to be something He was not, or He mistakenly believed Himself to be the Son of God when in fact he was merely a deluded mortal—then two thousand years of Church history are based on a lie. I have been through an extensive education—eight years of college from my Bachelor's to my PhD. I have been instructed by some men who were devout Christians, some who were curious agnostics, and a couple who were militant atheists. I kept my faith through all my years in college because none of them were able to answer this fundamental question: if Jesus was not the Christ, then who moved the stone from the tomb?"

He drew himself up and looked directly at the cameras. "The testimony of Pontius Pilate proves that the authors of the Gospel did not make up their story. Does Pilate's account conclusively prove that Jesus was the Son of God? No! As I said earlier, those determined not to believe will find any number of reasons to reject, question, or explain away what Pilate recorded. But what the *Testimonium* does is prove what I have said my whole life: the Gospel writers did NOT make up the story of the Resurrection. Like everything else they wrote, it was based on historical fact. All those who have spent the last couple of decades trying to undermine the Gospel stories are going to have to carefully reexamine their scholarship—and their motives! That is all, gentlemen. I am exhausted, I am hurting in places I did not know I had, and my head is about to spontaneously combust if I don't lie down. If I don't wake up in three days, send a nurse up with a caffeine IV!"

The reporters gave a good-natured laugh, and Josh slowly turned and entered the hotel. Alicia held the door open for him, and Dr. Martens waited within, leaning on his crutches. They made their way to the elevator bank and climbed into a waiting car.

"Well said out there, Josh!" exclaimed Dr. Martens. "Atheists all over the world are gnashing their teeth right now! You are a fine scholar and a man of faith—I am proud to have been one of your teachers!"

Alicia leaned over and gave him a friendly kiss on the cheek. "You did us all proud today, cowboy!" she said with a laugh.

Josh smiled, and then winced. He had not been kidding about his head. It felt like someone was cutting a hole in the top of his skull with a jackhammer. "I kept thinking about the question that I was asked back at the museum," he said. "I know that faith can never be completely vindicated or proven by any scientific discovery, but at the same time, I know that what can be proven is that our faith rests on a sure foundation of history. That was what I wanted to clarify. I wonder what my dad would think of my comments? I pulled up several lines from his standard Easter sermon."

Martens nodded. He and Josh's dad had been friends for a number of years. "I think Ben is probably a very proud papa right now," he said.

They got out of the elevator on Josh's floor and headed down the hallway to his room. "I think," Josh said as he swiped his key card in the door, "that I will forego my usual swim this afternoon."

Alicia laughed. "Now I know you are hurting," she said. "We used to joke that an Oklahoma ice storm couldn't keep you out of the pool!"

"Well, the college pool was heated, so no, they didn't!" Josh said. "Speaking of hot water, I think I am going to go and take a very long, very hot bath, take my Percocet, and sleep for a day or two. Thanks to both of you for being such a support to me—not just these last few days, but ever since I have known you. I am lucky to have such awesome friends!"

"Good night, Josh!" the professor and his young wife said together, and Josh closed the door and headed into his suite.

* * *

Dr. Castolfo had walked Isabella up the steps to her apartment, refusing to speak to the group of reporters who had finally figured out where she lived and were staked out in front of her building. He promised them a short statement after he accompanied Isabella to her rooms, and the journalists made no attempt to follow them into the building—although the presence of the burly doorman and two uniformed policemen may have had more to do with their courtesy than his promise.

In the elevator, he finally spoke to her. "So, Isabella, without meaning to pry, do you think your affection for this young American is going to be taking you away from our facility?"

She shrugged. "At this point I have no idea," she said. "I've only had one romantic relationship in my entire life before this one, and it led to a happy marriage that was cut short far too soon. Josh makes me happier than I have been since Marc died, but whether that happiness will turn into something more permanent, what will happen then? Well, I suppose right now that is in God's hands."

Castolfo raised an eyebrow. "I did not know that you were a religious person," he said.

"I wasn't," she replied. "But after the last two weeks—well, I guess I can honestly say I no longer have any idea exactly what I believe."

The Board of Antiquities president gave her a fatherly smile. "I believe, dear girl, that you need some pain medication and a couple of days' worth of uninterrupted rest!"

Isabella nodded. "You will get no argument from me," she said.

Once inside her apartment, she pulled on a warm pair of sweat pants and a T-shirt that had been washed so many times it was softer than the finest wool. She took a Percocet and washed it down with a swallow of bottled water—the stuff that came out of her apartment's pipes was invariably coppery tasting and awful—then went to her room and lay down.

She saw the phone by her bed and, on impulse, dialed Josh's cell number. He picked up on the third ring.

"Is everything all right?" he asked her.

"Yes, I just wanted to hear your voice before I went to sleep," she replied drowsily. "Are you OK? You were hurt more than I was."

"I'm actually a bit better now," he said. "I'm soaking in a tub so hot I half expect someone to start peeling carrots and potatoes into it at any moment! In a few moments I'm going to pour myself into some old gym clothes and sleep until I wake up—however many days that turns out to be."

"I wish you were here," she said. "Not so I could take advantage of you, just so I could look into your eyes until I fall asleep."

Josh replied after a short pause. "Soon," he said. "Very soon I hope that we will be able to spend not just one night, but every night together."

"Joshua, are you proposing to me?" she asked.

"You know I want nothing more," he said. "But first, I want you to fall as much in love with God as you have with me. Better yet, I want you to love Him even more! Then I'll know we can truly be together forever."

She sighed. "Your God makes things awfully complicated sometimes, my love! Good night!" She hung up before another long theological discussion could begin, but as she went to sleep, she found herself thinking. How on earth could a mortal person fall in love with an infinite God?

* * *

Ibrahim Abbasside watched the news conference, and then the comments by the young American archeologist, on a television set in Benghazi, Libya. The newsfeed provided a flowing Arabic translation below the video images, but he did not really need it—his English was quite passable, his Italian even better. He had picked up a flawless set of travel papers from a local cell leader, identifying him as Abdullah Ali, a wealthy Ethiopian antique dealer. It would be a good cover for him to find out some more information about the museum and its environs, and to spy out when the scroll was going to be transported to Rome for study.

His ambush would have to be during the transport process, he thought. The museum would be heavily guarded after the previous attack, and the security in Rome had proven itself impenetrable by his organization. But a traveling convoy—there were many choke points between Rome and Naples where an ambush could be carried off quickly and with a high probability of success. However, he would need help. This operation was beyond the capability of one man. Fortunately, the sleeper cells that had been waiting for the last five years to strike at the Pope were still available, although he was certain that most of the members would not survive. Of course, martyrdom was the highest goal of every jihadist; it was the only activity that carried with it a guaranteed admittance to Paradise. Although Abbasside was convinced he was more valuable to the struggle alive than dead for the moment, he knew that when the time came, he would not hesitate to sacrifice himself for the glory of Allah.

But how much damage had already been done by the release of the scroll? All other stories were forgotten in the rush of news from Italy; around the world infidel Christians rejoiced, while the skeptics and doubters who had done so much to undermine faith in Islam's greatest rival were still trying to figure out how to assimilate this discovery. Abbasside's own faith in Islam remained unshaken—the *Injil* of Barnabas clearly stated that Allah had caused the disciple who betrayed the Prophet Isa (peace be upon him) to be transformed into Isa's very likeness so that the turncoat would die in the Prophet's place. Apparently the transformation had been so complete that even the Roman governor had been fooled. But Pilate was not the only one. Already, one prominent skeptic and atheist had announced that this discovery had convinced him of the truth of Christianity, and a well-known former Christian pastor, who had become a virulent critic of the faith he had rejected, now stated that he was ready to be reconciled to the Church. What impact would this discovery have across the Muslim world?

Abbasside knew that years of exposure to decadent Western music and films had weakened the grip of Islam on the minds of many young Arabs. The invention of the Internet, while a great boon to planning and executing attacks on the West, had also given thousands of young Muslims who might never see a New Testament access to the infidel Scriptures. He had heard imams talk of young, faithful Muslims suddenly stricken by doubt about the Prophet Muhammad (peace be upon Him) and wondering if perhaps Isa had been what the church claimed him to have been all along! It was unconscionable! The veteran terrorist was determined that this scroll could not be allowed to undermine the faith of one more follower of the Prophet!

* * *

Alessandro Zadora, the Police Chief of Naples, was still trying to piece together the clues from the horrific blast that had destroyed the new research lab at the National Museum of Antiquities. The self-confessed bomber turned out to have been a long-term Al Qaeda sleeper who had been dormant for the better part of a decade. However, al-Medina had not left Capri for more than a year before the blast. So who had bought the explosives and loaded them onto the truck? That investigation was baffling him, so he had called in the State Security Police Force's leading anti-terrorism expert, Antonio Lucoccini, to help him in the investigation.

The two men had worked together before, and had a healthy respect for each other's professional abilities. Zadora was surveying the wreckage of the lab, counting the yellow flags that indicated where pieces of the bomb and the truck that delivered it had been found. Al-Medina's body had been completely shredded in the blast, pieces of it being recovered in more than twenty locations, too badly damaged to help investigators much. So far, only a few clues had been located as to the device that had caused so much devastation: a small fragment of the detonator, a badly damaged remote control, and a few pieces of the crates that had contained the explosives themselves. It appeared to be a standard ammonium nitrate bomb—the fertilizer was easily obtained in small quantities, and occasionally larger amounts of it were reported stolen.

"This place is a mess! Looks like a bomb went off or something!" a familiar voice said behind him.

"Always the wise guy," said Zadora, turning to face Lucoccini. "If I wanted a comedian, I could have hired one from a local nightclub and left you in Rome taking bribes!"

"Now that hurts, coming from an old friend! Any leads on who supplied the bomb?" asked Lucoccini.

"We've barely recovered any pieces of the device at all," said Zadora. "The fertilizer was most likely stolen—there have been several thefts of ammonium nitrate the last few years. Some have been recovered, some not. Our best shot is going to be with the detonator, but we need to find more pieces of it before we can begin to figure out who might have put it together."

They walked together through the wreckage of the lab. Two police technicians were lifting a shattered Formica tabletop with the help of a small forklift. Underneath they found some half-melted plexiglass, a crushed stool, and some sort of very black wooden desk or small table, its legs broken and laid flat. Zadora reached down and turned it over to find an ancient piece of parchment, streaked with soot, somehow glued to the surface of the wood. It was covered with writing. "Someone call the archies in," he said. "We found some more of their junk."

"Junk?" said Lucoccini. "That's the Tiberius letter, you uncultured rube! Haven't you watched any of the news about what they were working on?"

"I've been tracking a serial rapist, two kidnapping cases, and a child murderer for the last month," snapped Zadora. "All I've had time to watch is my blood pressure going up!"

"And then came this," said Lucoccini thoughtfully.

"Exactly!" his friend snapped. "And then came this!" They watched as one of the museum staff made his way down the ruined hallway between them and the main building. "Hard to believe a two-thousand-year-old scrap of paper was worth this much trouble, isn't it?"

* * *

At ten thirty Sunday morning Josh heard a steady pounding sound insert itself into his dreams. He groaned and rolled over; trying to return to the creek bed he was walking down in northeast Texas, ten years old again, with a pocket full of arrowheads and not a care in the world. But the persistent pounding sound kept forcing itself into his mind until he finally sat up with a lurch and realized that someone was knocking on his door. Grumbling, he pulled on a T-shirt and stumbled through the suite, realizing as he did so that the soreness in his limbs and the pounding in his head were much more subdued than they had been the day before. Still, he was not very happy—he had left the "Do Not Disturb" sign out, and really felt as if he could have slept for another eight or ten hours.

"Who is it?" he shouted, not even looking through the keyhole.

"Are you going to lie in bed all day while the fish are biting?" a familiar voice answered.

"DAD!!" He threw open the door and embraced his father, who stood there grinning, with his mother right beside him. "How on earth did you get here? How long have you been here?"

His father released him, and Josh's mom stepped up and hugged him too.

"It's good to see you, son!" he said. "After we saw the news of the explosion, your mother and I were sick with worry, even after you

313

called. Then Brother Bowers called and asked if we would like two tickets to Naples, leaving later that night. Who could turn down such an offer?"

Josh nodded. That would be just like Brady Bowers, a deacon in his father's church who had made a bundle in the dotcom boom of the nineties and gotten out before it went south. He had dedicated his life to Christian charities and church planting, and was one of his dad's closest friends. Josh looked at the familiar faces of his parents and found his eyes welling up with tears. Thank you, Brother Brady! he thought.

"You have no idea how glad I am to see you two," he said. "It's been a very tough few days."

His dad nodded sympathetically. "I've been watching every bit of news coverage I could," he said. "We saw the big press conference from the airport, and then caught your remarks to the press right before we boarded the plane." The old pastor grinned. "Those were some downright eloquent statements—a couple of them seemed a bit familiar!"

Josh grinned. His dad always had a way of making him feel better just by being there. "I suppose I must have picked something up after being dragged into church three times a week for my first eighteen years!" he said.

His mother looked at the room. "Those museum folks must like you," she said. "This is a lot nicer than our room!"

Josh laughed. "They have been very gracious hosts," he said.

About that time his phone rang. It was Luke Martens. "Did your folks find you all right, Josh?" he asked.

"Woke me from a sound sleep," he said.

"Your mother wanted to bring you breakfast at seven thirty," he said, "but I talked her into giving you another three hours. Why don't you all come down to mine and Alicia's suite? We've ordered a big brunch."

"That sounds good," said Josh, suddenly realizing he had not eaten in nearly twenty-four hours.

"Isabella is coming too," said Martens. "She called a little while ago and had just woken up. She wants to meet your folks."

"Great!" said Josh. "Is Duncan coming too?"

"No, but we can watch him on television," said Martens. "He was on one of the Sunday morning shows in the States—they taped it late last night, but we recorded it on our DVR so we could watch it with you guys."

"Awesome!" said Josh. "I'll be down shortly."

He turned to his folks. "Feel free to have a seat on the couch," he said. "I'm gonna jump in the shower and wake myself up for a minute, and try to make myself presentable. Then we can go down and eat with the Martens."

He disappeared into the bathroom, and his mother leaned over toward his father and whispered: "I bet that Italian girl is going to be there! Josh never cares if he is presentable or not!"

Ben Parker looked down at her with a small grin. "You're an impossible woman!" he said.

A half hour later, they walked into the suite where Dr. Martens and Alicia were staying, to find Isabella had beaten them there. Josh introduced her to his parents and then firmly placed himself between Isabella and his mother, determined to shield her from the third-degree inquisition he knew would be forthcoming for as long as possible. Isabella looked much more relaxed and comfortable, having exchanged the large bandage on her head for a smaller, simpler Band-Aid. The lines of stress and grief had eased somewhat, although she was still more somber and grim than the vibrant young archeologist Josh had met on Capri two weeks before.

The group of six arranged themselves on the sofa and easy chairs and Luke Martens turned on the TV and DVR. The program had aired several hours ago in the States. It was the popular morning show hosted by none other than the impeccably groomed Tyler Patterson.

"Good morning, world!" he boomed his familiar greeting. "And welcome to the *Sunday Morning Report!* The whole world is abuzz with debate about the *Testimonium Pilatus*, the two-thousand-year-old Roman scroll that was discovered in the island of Capri two weeks ago today. Is it authentic? Does it truly prove that Jesus of Nazareth rose from the dead? Or is it part of a *da Vinci Code*–style plot on the part of the Church? Here in our studio to discuss the matter is Pastor Joel Wombaker, host of *Blessed and Getting Better*, America's number one Sunday Christian broadcast, and Dr. David Hubbard, renowned atheist spokesman. Joining us from Italy are Dr. Duncan MacDonald, Catholic priest and a member of the original excavation team, and former Antiquities Board member Maria Tintoretto. Welcome to you all! Now, Father MacDonald, you were one of the original team members. Why don't you tell us why, in your opinion, the *Testimonium* is absolutely genuine."

The screen split and Duncan appeared, wearing a khaki shirt with his clerical collar. "Good morning to ye, Tyler!" he said in a sprightly fashion. He enjoyed using his Scottish accent to lull verbal opponents into thinking he would be an easy mark before closing in with a devastating response to their argument. "Now bear in mind, laddie, that the actual chamber was discovered by Giuseppe Rossini and Isabella Sforza. I was not called into the site until the next day. However, the minute I got in there and looked around, it was very obvious that everything in that chamber had been left in place for many, many centuries. The stone dust that had filtered down from the steps overhead had created a two-inch-deep layer over everything, and the only part of it that was disturbed was where Dr. Sforza and Giuseppe had entered the tomb and cleaned the dust from Tiberius' writing desk—which, I am proud to add, was recovered earlier today from the site of the blast, damaged but with the Tiberius letter still attached and intact!"

Josh smiled at that. So the Tiberius letter had survived! He supposed it was a good thing they had not even tried to detach it from the top of the desk. He refocused his attention on the screen.

"The reliquary where the Tiberius scroll was found was in the very back of the chamber and was the last item removed," the priest was saying. "Being leaned against the back wall, it was covered with a very thick layer of dust, and had been partly buried in a dirt slide, so that we could not even tell what it was at first. Once we got inside it, we did discover that rats had chewed up most of the contents of the reliquary, which proved to be a bitter disappointment. However, there was a small locked compartment up by the top shelf that looked intact. We actually moved the entire cabinet into the mobile lab before we tried to open it."

"So how was it the rats were not able to get into this compartment as easily as they had the rest of the cabinet?" asked Patterson.

"Well, I did say it was locked, didn't I?" said MacDonald. "Fortunately, we had discovered the key, an exquisitely worked item, in Tiberius' writing desk earlier that week. With a little lubrication we were able to insert the key and get the tumblers to move, and the door sprang open. The compartment had solid wooden walls which extended to the very back of the cabinet. The only way the rats could have gotten in would have been to chew a hole directly behind the compartment, and they had already opened a large hole near the bottom which was all they needed to go in and out. Rats don't eat papyrus; they just use it to line their nests. Apparently there were enough other documents in the rest of the reliquary to give them all they needed!"

"Pastor Wombaker, what thoughts would you like to add?" Tyler interrupted the priest.

"I think the *Testimonium* is a wonderful discovery, which proves to the world what the Church has been saying all along—that Christianity rests on a firm foundation of reliable history," said the TV preacher, flashing his famous grin. "All the fellas who have been trying to put Jesus back in His tomb for the last twenty years or so have all got egg on their faces this morning!"

"Indeed?" said Patterson. "Dr. Hubbard, do you have any egg on your face today?"

"No sir," said the atheist. "I am on a low-cholesterol diet. But seriously, Tyler, this whole thing stinks to the high heavens. I mean, first, as soon as the discovery is made, they fly in a Vatican representative and the son of a rural Evangelical preacher to do the excavation? What kind of science is that?"

"Just as solid as hiring an evolutionist to excavate dinosaur bones!" snapped MacDonald. "Listen here, laddie, I am one of the most experienced handlers of ancient papyrus in the whole world, and young Dr. Parker is almost as good as I am! We were called in for our scientific credentials, not because of our religious beliefs!"

"If anyone believes that, I have some ocean front property in Kentucky I'd like to sell them!" snapped Hubbard. "Now, sir, I don't doubt that you know your ancient documents and inks pretty well. That would make it pretty easy for you to fake them, now wouldn't it?"

"You can't fake C-14 dates, laddie," replied MacDonald. "Nor can you fake twenty centuries' worth of atomized stone dust! Every single test we ran on the dust from that chamber showed it was two thousand years old!"

"Dr. Tintoretto, you were a member of the Board of Antiquities that oversaw the excavation. You are also an outspoken critic of this

317

discovery. Can you tell us—were there any irregularities in their field techniques that would have created a window for a hoax of this magnitude?"

"Certainly there were! The excavation director left the site overnight, leaving these two Christian cultists in charge of the excavation during that time. Who knows what they could have gotten up to while she was gone?" the Italian scholar sneered.

"Now see here!" snapped MacDonald. "It is perfectly normal for the lead archeologist to report in to her supervisors. During the time Isabella was gone, Dr. Apriceno was busy removing centuries of dust deposits from the chamber, after taking samples from every surface to make sure that there was no question of disturbance."

"It's rather convenient, for the Church's purpose, that those samples are all destroyed now, isn't it?" she asked in a mocking tone.

MacDonald's voice was quiet, dead calm, and seething with rage. "Considering that eight people are dead, three of them dear friends of mine, and that every bit of testing would have confirmed the authenticity of our finds, I would say it is decidedly *inconvenient!*" he snapped.

"Well, let me pose this question to our two doubting Thomases," said Patterson. "If the carbon dating next week shows the scroll to be two thousand years old, will that satisfy you that it is genuine?"

"Not really," said Hubbard. "It only proves that the papyrus is that old. It proves nothing about the writing on it!"

MacDonald was opening his mouth to respond when Tyler cut him off. "Well, folks, time for a commercial break! When we come back, more on the investigation into the bombing at the Naples Museum. Thank you, Father MacDonald, Dr. Hubbard, Dr. Tintoretto, and Pastor Wombaker!"

The four scholars were all trying to talk to each other at once when the program cut to commercial. Martens cut the TV off. Josh shook his head.

"Desperate people are pretty sad, aren't they, son?" his dad asked.

"You can say that again," Josh replied.

"Well, you have made at least one convert," said Isabella, handing Josh a newspaper. It was the *Chicago Tribune's* international edition, and she had it opened to the op-ed page. "It seems our friend Mr. Eastwood has been pretty impressed with your discovery and commentary."

Josh looked at the column, entitled, "Confessions of a Former Atheist."

"Well, I'll be," he said as he began to read.

CONFESSIONS OF A FORMER ATHEIST

BY ANDREW EASTWOOD, FOREIGN CORRESPONDENT

One does not have to be a Christian to understand the power of Jesus' words; simple in vocabulary, cosmic in scale, stately in their rhythms and deep in their impact, they changed the world. But most of the world's Christians will immediately tell you that their faith does not rest upon Jesus' eloquence as a speaker, or his skill as a philosopher, or even his reputation for working miracles. From the time of the Apostle Paul, the central claim of Jesus' followers has been that this Galilean rabbi who lived two thousand years ago was in fact the virgin-born Son of God, sent to reconcile a lost humanity with a loving Father by sacrificing Himself, and then conquering death after it had claimed Him. Such an extraordinary claim demands extraordinary proof, and the proof that the Church has pointed to for twenty centuries is the story of the empty tomb and the Risen Christ, seen by his followers for forty days, then ascended into heaven to await the End Times.

I was raised in the Church, but like most young people, when I went off to college I shed my religion like an old pair of socks. Eager to chase women and anxious to be thought of as an intellectual heavyweight, I drank deeply from the wisdom of my professors, who told me that Christianity was nothing but another fertility cult, similar in its claims to dozens of other mystery religions of the time, and that if there was a historical Jesus, he bore no resemblance to the Suffering Savior of the Gospels. That secular perspective liberated me from the oppressive morality my parents tried to force on me, freeing me to make love to whoever I wanted, drink as much as I wanted, and to convince myself that I was the captain of my fate, the master of my soul.

But over the years, I found that lifestyle increasingly empty. Some of the confident claims of my college professors did not bear up under scrutiny—the so-called resemblances between Christianity and other fertility cults, for example, I found to be either manufactured or greatly exaggerated. And, I will admit, the faith and confidence of those who had remained in the Church intimidated me. They seemed to be happy and fulfilled in a way that I was not.

Still, I remained confident that the Gospels were largely fairy tales. If believing in such nonsense made my friends happy, more power to them. I was too smart to fall for the story of a magical carpenter who healed the sick, rose from the dead, and then disappeared into the sky. Even in my spiritual loneliness, I felt confident in my intellectual superiority to those who bought into such simple myths.

But when I was sent to Naples to report on the discoveries at Capri, I was forced to reexamine my beliefs and my skepticism. What if the Gospel stories really were true? I did not want to accept it. I found myself hoping that Pilate's tale would show that Jesus' body really had been stolen, or burned, or removed on government order, so that I would know once and for all that my skepticism had been well-placed. Well, we all saw how that worked out. The Testimonium, which in this reporter's opinion passes the bar of authenticity with flying colors, shows that the early Church did not base its claims of a Resurrection on wishful thinking and mistaken identity. Something miraculous really did happen in Jerusalem in 33 AD, the Sunday morning after Passover.

And something miraculous happened in my life as well. As I heard the words read by Dr. Parker Saturday afternoon, fifteen years of carefully cultivated skepticism and secularism collapsed within me like a house of cards. I found myself leaving the press conference, filing my obligatory story, and then seeking out the nearest church. There, for the first time since I was eighteen, I knelt at the altar and spoke to the Almighty. "Hello, God. It's me, Andrew. Remember me?"

It turns out He did.

<<<TRANSCRIPT OF A PHONE CONVERSATION FROM THE CIA'S COUNTERTERRORISM OFFICE, APRIL 22, 20** BETWEEN COL. LINCOLN BERTRAND AND FIELD AGENT DOMINGO GARCIA>>>

GARCIA: Got an interesting bit of intel from the North African data stream, Colonel.

BERTRAND: What's shaking in the world of bad guys, Dingo?

GARCIA: Looks like "the Ethiopian" may be on the move, sir.

BERTRAND: Abbasside? No one has heard a peep about him in five years. Are you sure?

GARCIA: No, sir, not a hundred percent, but chatter is indicating that a high-ranking operative has moved from Somalia northward to Libya in the last twenty-four hours, seeking ID papers and a passport to the European Union. The info is fragmentary and garbled, and we weren't able to intercept a photograph, but the physical description we intercepted matches what we know of Abbasside, and the deference the everyday jihadist drones are showing to him indicates that he is pretty high up the food chain. I've collated the information and will be forwarding it to you momentarily via secure email. There's only two or three of the highest ranked AQ leaders still at large, and he is the only one we suspect of holing up in that corner of the globe.

BERTRAND: Good work, son. Any idea of his destination?

GARCIA: Could be London—scuttlebutt says that there is some sort of op supposed to go down there this summer. MI6 is scrambling to penetrate the local affiliates and see if they can figure it out. My gut tells me Italy. The attack there last week failed to take out its target, and the chatter among monitored AQ cells indicates a high degree of concern that this scroll will be damaging to Islam.

BERTRAND: I think London is more likely, personally, but by all means monitor all the chatter from known Italian cells as well. And keep data mining and see if any other possible targets might be in the works. We do NOT need another successful terror attack, given all the unrest in the region. Excellent work, and thanks for keeping me in the loop. Keep a status report coming every twelve hours, or more often as events warrant.

GARCIA: Aye, sir! Signing off!

CHAPTER TWENTY-TWO

After watching the talking heads bicker for a while, Josh heard a knock at the hotel room door, and when Alicia answered it, two waiters entered the room pushing silver service carts piled high with dishes of food. The Martens' suite had a good-sized dining table, although with the six of them it was a bit cozy. As they took their places, Josh noticed with some trepidation that his mother took the place directly across from Isabella.

The food was delicious, and all of them were hungry. Josh could feel the soreness leaving his body as the hot, nourishing Italian foods, rich in cheese, butter, and garlic, filled him with warmth both literal and metaphorical. After the wrenching events of Friday and the draining press conference on Saturday, he felt as if he were slowly returning to normal. After some routine chitchat about the weather and the beauty of the city of Naples, Josh's dad turned to Isabella.

"My dear girl," he said, "I must admit that I was quite shocked to see you and my son holding hands on the evening news back in the States, when he had barely mentioned you up to that point. That being said, I am delighted that you two have such an interest in each other."

Isabella smiled warmly. Josh's dad reminded her of an old cowboy from an American Western, with a faint drawl, a tanned, leathery face, and a kind smile. She said, "Well, sir, I must confess that I found him pretty irresistible from the start."

Josh laughed. "Not nearly as irresistible as I found her!" he said.

His mother beamed. "I am just so proud my baby boy has finally gotten interested in girls!"

Josh rolled his eyes. "Mom, I have been interested in girls since I was ten years old!" he said. "I just had a hard time . . . expressing that interest."

He was blushing to the roots of his hair, and Isabella was enjoying herself enormously. "Well," she said, "I can see where Josh gets his good looks."

Reverend Parker smiled. "And I can see why he found you so charming!" he said.

Mrs. Parker looked over her glasses at Isabella. "You two aren't . . . you know—"

Isabella leaned forward with a conspiratorial air. "Sadly, your son has resisted my every effort to plunder his virtue!"

"MOM!" Josh shouted, flushing scarlet, while Dr. Martens and Alicia leaned against one another hooting with laughter.

Reverend Parker did his best to look stern. "A good thing, there!" he said. "I am not familiar with Italian customs, but in Oklahoma we have these things called 'shotgun weddings'!"

Isabella looked at him with an air of studied innocence. "Now why would anyone want to marry a firearm?" she asked.

About that time another knock came at the door, and Josh rushed to answer it, eager to be away from his parents for a moment. Father MacDonald stood at the door, looking a little more rested and relaxed than he had on television.

"I heard that there was a party going on," he said with a touch of his old mischievous humor.

"What the heck!" Josh said. "Come on in. Mom and Isabella are taking turns to see who can embarrass me the most!"

"Well, I certainly would not want to miss that!" the Scottish priest said.

Josh walked him in and introduced MacDonald to his parents. "Mom and Dad, this is Father Duncan MacDonald, one of my colleagues and a renowned Vatican archeologist. Duncan, this is my father, Reverend Ben Parker, and my mom, Louise Parker."

"A pleasure to meet you, Father!" said Parker, holding out his hand. He had always gotten on well with Catholic priests in the communities where he pastored, regarding them as a different department, but working under the same management he did.

"Good day to you, Father MacDonald!" said Josh's mom. "I must confess to you that I was raised by two old hard-shell Pentecostals who taught me that Catholics were all the devil's minions—but I never could see my Jesus rejecting some sweet people just because they were too fond of his mother!"

Josh groaned. His folks were in rare form today. MacDonald, on the other hand, threw back his head and roared with laughter. He took Louise's hand and placed a gallant kiss on it.

"Well, dear lady," he said, "I can see where Josh gets his gift of charm from! I have never been so sweetly insulted in my whole life!"

"Oh, I meant no offense, Father!" Mrs. Parker said. "I truly love our Catholic brothers and sisters."

MacDonald chuckled. "No offense taken, my dear. Josh and I have been re-fighting the Protestant Reformation since we met, but we've become good friends in the process. He's got a keen mind and a good heart."

Reverend Parker patted his wife's arm. "She is an impossible woman," he said. "I only married her to spare some other man such an awful fate!"

She turned to her husband. "And here I thought you said it was because I had an excellent set of 'breeder's hips'!"

Now it was Reverend Parker's turn to blush. "That's quite enough, dear!" he said. Then he turned back to Father MacDonald. "I must admit, sir," he said, "I just don't feel right not going to church on Sunday. Is there an afternoon mass my wife and I might attend somewhere?"

MacDonald raised an eyebrow. Not many Protestant ministers from America volunteered to attend an Italian Catholic service. "I would be glad to take you and your wife to the three o'clock mass," he said. "But I am afraid I do need to take Josh and Isabella from you for an hour or so first."

"What's going on?" Josh asked, but as the words left his lips he remembered. "Is it about Giuseppe's service?" he asked.

The priest nodded, and the room grew quickly still. The humor drained from the air in an instant. "His son and daughter will be waiting for us at twelve thirty," he said. "I told them we could meet over at the museum boardroom and go over the service together."

"I'm still not sure why they want me to speak," Josh said. "I loved Giuseppe dearly, but I only knew him for a couple of weeks."

"Why don't you come with me," said the Scottish priest. "I'll let his son explain it to you."

Josh and Isabella excused themselves and stepped out of the room after MacDonald. As they made their way toward the elevator, Josh realized that being with his parents had already begun to heal him, both spiritually and physically. He still grieved for his friends, but his father's steady presence and his mother's deliberate silliness had reduced that grief to a manageable ache instead of a devouring gloom. In his heart, he said a prayer of thanks that they had come.

"Dr. Parker!" the hotel's maître d'hotel said as they passed the front desk.

"Yes?" Josh said.

"I hate to bother you, sir, but could you pick up your messages? They are really starting to stack up!" the man said.

"I picked them up Friday, didn't I?" Josh asked.

"Well, actually, it was Thursday evening," the manager said.

Josh nodded. "Of course," he said. "The last few days have got me a bit rattled. Let me have them and I will read them as we walk to the museum."

"That might be a difficult proposition," said the rather prissy Englishman.

"How so?" asked Josh. "How many are there?"

"Three laundry bins full, and counting!" said the maître d'hotel.

Josh slumped, stunned. "All right, then," he said. "Send them to my room and I will go through them later."

MacDonald looked at him, amused. "Seems as if you are officially now a celebrity, lad!" he exclaimed.

Josh rolled his eyes. "That is the last thing I need!" he replied.

After running through the usual gauntlet of reporters outside the hotel, they briskly hiked down the block to the museum. Josh was stunned when he saw a large crowd gathered outside, many of them holding signs. The largest group was holding up crucifixes and other Christian emblems. A few of their signs were in English, and Josh read them across the square. SEE, WE TOLD YOU SO! The first one read. Another read CHRIST IS RISEN INDEED! Yet another carried that hoary old warning uttered by every prophet of doom from Jeremiah onward: REPENT!

A second group seemed composed primarily of Muslims. More of their signs were in English, not Italian, and some were in Arabic. One read in bold letters: VIOLENCE IS NOT THE WAY OF THE PROPHET. A shame all Muslims didn't share that philosophy, Josh thought as he remembered his slain friends. Another sign said JESUS: A PROPHET, NOT A GOD! And another contained the Shahada, the age-old confession of the Islamic faith: THERE IS ONE GOD AND MUHAMMAD IS HIS PROPHET. One angry-looking cleric carried a more militant sign: DEATH TO THOSE WHO PRACTICE *SHIRK!* Josh knew that in the Quran, the sin of *shirk* was to associate the glory of God with another. Muhammad and the caliphs who followed him all taught that, by honoring Jesus as the Son of God instead of just another prophet, all Christians were guilty of *shirk*.

The third group was the smallest, and seemed to be composed primarily of well-dressed, academic-looking men. One of them held up a sign that was simply a cross with a red slash through it. Another waved aloft a quote from Voltaire: MAN WILL NEVER TRULY BE FREE UNTIL THE LAST PRIEST IS STRANGLED WITH THE BOWELS OF THE LAST KING. Another simply read: HAVEN'T WE KILLED ENOUGH PEOPLE OVER GODS THAT DON'T EXIST?

Josh shook his head. Here was freedom of speech in its rawest, purest form. The three groups shouted slogans back and forth, and some of their leaders argued vociferously near the center. He and his two companions skirted along the edge toward the doors of the museum, and almost made it in without being recognized. By the time the demonstrators saw them and stampeded toward the door, they were close enough to slip in without being detained. The security guard firmly locked the doors in the faces of the howling crowd, and Josh and Isabella looked at one another with relief.

"Sorry, lad," said MacDonald. "There was only a handful gathered when I headed over to the hotel, but their numbers are growing by the minute."

"I've called the police and asked for extra security around the museum from this point forward," said Dr. Castolfo, who had been waiting for them. "Of course, that is over and above the extra security we have had in place since the attack Friday. I am not exactly on Police Chief Zadora's 'Friends' list anymore!"

Josh sighed. "I wonder how long this will go on?" he asked. "And how will we be able to get any work done at all?"

"One thing is clear," said Castolfo. "When we transport the scroll, we will have to have some heavy security along for the ride!" He paused, and then looked at Josh and Isabella sympathetically. "But that should be the least of your concerns. Giuseppe's children are waiting for you in the boardroom. Take all the time you need and I will drive you back to the hotel when you are ready to return. Follow me." He turned and led them to the second floor, where the ornately appointed meeting room of Italy's Board of Antiquities was located. Josh paused at the door, remembering his trepidation when he had shared the contents of the scroll with the board only a few days before. Then he stepped in and gasped in shock.

Giuseppe Rossini stood before him—about twenty years younger, but the smile, the crinkles around the eyes (albeit less pronounced), and the wavy dark hair were identical. He gulped and realized he was staring, then said, "I am sorry, Mr. Rossini. You look so much like your father that it is a bit unnerving!"

Guillermo Rossini smiled. "You are not the first to say that, Dr. Parker," he replied in heavily accented English. "I've actually had a couple of my father's old girlfriends hit on me before."

His sister rose and joined him. Very pretty and feminine, she still carried the strong stamp of Giuseppe's heritage on her features as well—piercing blue eyes, aquiline nose, and a smile that was just as infectious and ingratiating. "It is good to meet you, sir," she said in impeccable English. Josh remembered that she had gone to college at Yale, according to her proud father. "I am Andrea Rossini-Pellata."

Isabella stepped through the door and embraced them both. She had met them on several occasions when she was Giuseppe's student, although the last time they had met was at their mother's funeral. They chatted together in Italian for a moment, and then turned back to Josh.

"I am sorry, Dr. Parker, Father MacDonald," said Andrea. "We forgot our manners for a moment."

Duncan smiled. "I haven't worked at the Vatican this many years and not learned some of your local lingo, my dear!" he said.

"I am just an ignorant foreigner, but, please, call me Josh," Parker added.

"Well, Joshua," said Guillermo, "come and sit at the table with us. My sister and I have been dying to meet you for the last two weeks."

They moved to the large conference table together, and sat down, clustered at one end. Guillermo took the head of the table and gestured for Josh and Duncan to sit at his right, while the two ladies sat across from him. Once they were settled, Giuseppe's son looked fondly at the American.

332

"You are probably wondering why we have requested that you speak at our father's funeral," he said.

"The thought has crossed my mind since your request was relayed to me by Father MacDonald here. I loved your father as a good friend, but my acquaintance with him was very brief. Surely there are others who would be better able to remember him publicly," Josh said.

Brother and sister looked at one another and smiled. "You have no idea of the impact you had on our father's life," said Andrea. "That is the reason we chose you. He thought very highly of you during your brief acquaintance."

Josh looked puzzled. "I don't understand," he finally replied.

"I thought you might not," said Guillermo. "So I printed these out for you." He handed Josh a sheaf of papers. "I ran them through an Internet translator, but Andrea assures me it got the gist of his words correctly."

"What are they?" asked Josh.

"His nightly emails to us," replied Giuseppe's son. "Dad wrote faithfully, every evening that he could, to tell us about his day and stay in touch. I copied and pasted all the paragraphs where he talked about you, and the discovery you shared. I want you to read them as soon as you can. Then I think you will have a better idea what to say tomorrow afternoon at the service."

"I must admit I am now very curious," Josh said. "If I may—"

"By all means," said Andrea. "We need to do some catching up with Isabella, and go over the order of service with Duncan as well."

"Two o'clock tomorrow, right?" asked Josh as he moved down to the other end of the table.

"That is correct, Josh," said the priest. "And Simone's service is at one o'clock the next day."

Josh nodded and sat down, the conversation at the other end of the room quickly fading to a low buzz. He looked down at the first email and began reading, and it seemed as if immediately he could hear Rossini's booming voice echo through the room.

"My dear children," read the first one. "You must forgive your old man his failure to communicate the last couple of days. I have made a remarkable discovery up at the Villa Jovis, uncovered by the earthquake that rattled the island on Easter Sunday. I cannot, as yet, tell you exactly what it is, but I can tell you that Bernardo and Isabella have assembled an international team to conduct the excavation here at the site! A remarkable team they are, too. You have heard me talk about my old friend Duncan MacDonald, the Scottish priest and expert on papyrus. He is here, along with Simone Apriceno, the paleobotanist who helped me out on that dig at Crete back before I hurt my leg. Isabella and I are the team leaders, and there is one other fellow in the group as well—a remarkable young American named Joshua Parker. He seems a very pleasant fellow, even though he is one of those Evangelical Christians you read about in the American press. I must admit, I was expecting him to be more of a knuckle-dragger! But he comes to us with first-rate academic credentials and seems to be very solid in his field techniques. He knows a lot about first-century Rome as well. I think I will enjoy working with him, even if he does seem to have eyes for Isabella. Of course, every man who sees her tends to suffer from that malady!"

Josh smiled, remembering how sternly Giuseppe had warned him against tampering with Isabella's emotions when they first met. He turned the page and read the second email.

"Dear Children, the work at the Villa Jovis goes on, and the discoveries are remarkable! While much work remains to be done, I can tell you we did find a signed letter, perfectly preserved, bearing the actual signature of Tiberius Caesar, the second Emperor of Rome. We are continuing to excavate, and more discoveries are coming forth every day. It is far and away the most exciting discovery I have ever been party to!" Josh smiled, remembering how enthusiastic Giuseppe had been about their discoveries in the chamber.

The missive went on: "I am becoming better acquainted with Dr. Parker, and the better I know him the more I like him. He is a first rate scientist and a man of faith, something that is very rare these days. He not only believes that all the New Testament tales about Jesus of Nazareth are literally true, he can argue point by point why history proves them to be so! In fact, he has forced me to re-examine some of my own beliefs in the process. He is quite a good-looking young fellow as well, and unless I miss my guess, he has caught Isabella's eye. She looks at him in a way I haven't seen her look at anyone since Marc died—and he returns her gaze with equal ardor. It does my old heart good to see her happy again, and I don't think Joshua is the sort to take advantage of her affections."

Josh flipped through several more of the emails. In each of them, Giuseppe informed his children about the excavation as much as his professional confidentiality would allow, and also talked about his growing friendship with the other members of the team. But again and again he returned to the subject of Josh. "Our latest discovery, without saying too much, has the potential to either compromise or confirm some very important parts of the New Testament narrative about Jesus," he wrote after they had found the Pilate scroll. "Joshua is as unflappable as ever. He is so firmly convinced of the historical truth of the Biblical claims about Jesus that I don't think he even considers the possibility that our discovery might reveal a very different story. I must admit, I envy him his certainty. I will write you more on the topic as soon as I can, but for the moment I am under a vow of confidentiality."

Josh kept reading. After the contents of the chamber were transferred to the mainland and the archeologists enjoyed their night on the town, Giuseppe had written faithfully, commenting again and again how delighted he was to see Isabella and Josh falling in love with one another, and hinting that he might be developing a romantic interest of his own, although he never mentioned Mrs. Bustamante by name. After reading several more, Josh came to the last email in the stack.

"My dear children," Giuseppe began. "The Pontius Pilate scroll is translated at last, and tomorrow we will share its contents with the world. I will not share the particulars with you yet, but I will say this much—the Church got it right! Maybe not in all the terrible things done in the name of Jesus since He walked the earth, but in the narrative the Gospels tell us, the Church preserved the correct story. You know that your mother and I were both raised in the Catholic Church, and you also know that my faith took a long sabbatical since her untimely death. No more! Tonight I went to church and celebrated Mass with a heart full of love for God, and I have a Bible on my end table as I write this. I know that our church does not place as much emphasis on the Scriptures as Protestants like Joshua do, but I am aflame with curiosity to reread the accounts of the Passion in light of what I now know. I owe young Joshua a great deal—his rocklike faith that our discovery would confirm the Gospel accounts has inspired me. My heart overflows with love of God, and his Christ, and you, my children. The next time we see each other, perhaps we can all attend church together. It would certainly make your old father's heart proud. I am blessed in my family, in my friends, and I have been blessed to be a part of this greatest discovery in

335

the history of Biblical archeology! I shall write you again, after the press conference tomorrow, and share with you in full what I can only hint at now. Your loving father, Giuseppe Rossini."

Josh put the text down, his cheeks wet with tears. He deeply missed the jolly Italian archeologist, and reading Rossini's account of their time together had made him feel as if the old man were in the chair across from him again. But at the same time, he rejoiced that Giuseppe had rediscovered his faith before leaving this earth, and he thanked God that he had been allowed to have some small part in that process. He folded the papers and rejoined the others.

"So now you understand why I asked you to speak tomorrow?" Guillermo said.

"Indeed," said Josh. "I am still not sure what you would like me to say, though."

"We thought perhaps that you would simply like to talk about the work you and our father did together," said Andrea. "And, we would like you to read this."

She handed him a Bible—he recognized it as the basic Gideon Bible that was placed in every hotel room in the world—or at least, in countries where Bibles were allowed. "You can see where he underlined a passage just before he put it down for the night," she said.

The Bible was open to *Il Vangelo de Giovanni,* and Josh read the underlined passage: *Io sono la risurrezione e la vita, chi crede in me, anche se muoia, vivrà. Credi tu questo?* Josh mentally translated: "I am the Resurrection and the Life; he that believes in Me, though he were dead, yet shall he live. Do you believe this?" In the margin next to it, Giuseppe had written and underlined two words: *"Che Faccio!"*—"I do!"

Josh looked up at the two Italians and smiled. "Thank you for the honor you have done me in allowing me to speak," he said. "I enjoyed your father's company a great deal, and I am glad if I was, in some small way, able to help him reconnect with his faith. But please don't assume it was anything about me that helped him find God again. I think that God placed us together for a reason, and He is the one you should thank."

The siblings looked at one another. "Both of us are believers," said Andrea. "We understand that God made sure our father was reconciled with Him before the end of his life. But we also believe that God used you to accomplish that, and we will always be grateful." She rose and embraced Joshua. "Now we just need you to bring Isabella into the fold, and then take her to the altar!"

Joshua blushed a little bit—somehow he seemed to do that whenever the topic of Isabella and marriage came up—but he looked her in the eye and said in a loud whisper: "Don't give away my battle plan!"

Isabella looked at him across the table and sighed. "I guess I can't get you where I want you without your God tagging along, can I?" she asked.

Josh smiled at her. She was so beautiful, he thought. "Actually, dear, He won't be 'tagging along,' He will be in the driver's seat," he said.

MacDonald shook his head. "You two!" he said. "Some days you make me regret my priestly vows, other days you make me profoundly thankful for them!"

They left the boardroom and found Dr. Castolfo waiting for them. He took them to one of the museum's side entrances and ushered them into a waiting car with tinted windows. After they were comfortably seated, he turned to them and asked how things had gone.

"As well as they could, under the circumstances," she said. "I will deliver a formal tribute to Giuseppe as a colleague and friend, and then Josh will talk about how our time together had such a big impact on Giuseppe's life and faith. Father MacDonald will be delivering the eulogy and celebrating the Funeral Mass."

"I am sure it will be a very fine and appropriate service," said Castolfo. "The entire Board will be present, of course. It is sad to mark the passing of such a fine man."

"I wanted to ask you something, while we have a moment," said Josh.

"By all means, Doctor. What can I do for you?" replied the board president.

"I think I would like to give an exclusive interview to one of the reporters that has been covering this story," Josh said. "And I think Isabella would like to join me."

"I have come to a great respect for your professionalism, Joshua," said Castolfo. "You may do so with my blessing, and that of the board. Who do you plan to favor with the exclusive?"

"Andrew Eastwood of the *Chicago Tribune*," said Joshua. "He is far and away the most intelligent of all the reporters I have talked to. He has a knack for asking the right questions, and has an impressive background in Roman history."

"An excellent choice," said Castolfo. "Don't you agree, Isabella?"

"Absolutely!" she said. "I was thinking that I would enjoy giving him an interview at some point."

"Excellent!" Castolfo responded. "I will get his contact information and text it to you later today, so you can reach him directly."

"Thanks," said Josh. "I was wondering how I could get ahold of him without simply calling him out from a pack of reporters."

After skirting around the ever-growing mob of protesters in front of the museum, their car had pulled up at the hotel, and Josh and Isabella got out together. She had agreed to go to Mass with Josh and his parents. They were waiting for them, together with Dr. Martens and Alicia. Father MacDonald had remained at the museum with the Rossini siblings. They called a cab and piled in, running the gauntlet of reporters yet again. Josh sighed as they headed to a nearby cathedral. He hoped, at some point, to get his private life back again.

The service was beautiful, although Josh's mom, like many Baptists, was a bit confused about exactly when she was supposed to stand and kneel. The priest's homily was in a rapid-fire Italian that Josh had a hard time following, but he did catch several references to the Resurrection, and at least one direct quote from the *Testimonium*. The Church was wasting no time in trumpeting Pilate's confirmation of the Passion narrative, and that made Josh very proud. Maybe this would provide a spark for the revival of Christianity in Europe, which had been needed for so long.

After Mass, Josh had the cabbie drop Isabella off at her apartment to freshen up, then escorted his parents back to their hotel room. Although he had not put in a heavy day, he was nonetheless exhausted—the injuries from the blast, although now healing, still ached and drained some of his native vitality from him. After seeing his folks to their room, he went up to his suite and collapsed on the bed. He dug his cell phone out of his pocket and saw that he had received a text from Dr. Castolfo.

Opening it, he saw the name "Eastwood" and a phone number. Better now than later, he thought, and dialed it.

"Andrew Eastwood, award-winning journalist!" a cheerful voice chirped from the other end of the line.

"Well, it can't be too hard to excel in your field, considering how many imbeciles there are adorning it!" Josh replied.

"You, sir, have touched the perimeter of wisdom!" Eastwood shot back. "Is this, by chance, Dr. Parker speaking?"

"Indeed it is," Josh said. "Your remarkable acuity shows itself once more!"

"Well, to what do I owe the pleasure of this call?" said the reporter. "And do you mind if I record it for posterity?"

Josh laughed. "No need," he said. "I want to give you a chance to record me at length. Isabella and I have decided that you will be the recipient of our first exclusive press interview."

"Hot dog!" exclaimed the young reporter. "That is a much sought after honor! Why me?"

"Well, the short answer is that you are the only one out there who asks the questions that I would ask, if I were a reporter," said Josh. "We both also really enjoyed your editorial in this morning's paper. Tomorrow is kind of a tough day, but are you free later this evening? Say around eight thirty?"

"I was going to have dinner with the Pope," said Eastwood. "But I can blow him off! Where shall we meet?"

"Come to the hotel this evening, and I will tell the doorman to let you in," said Josh. "Isabella and I will take you up to the sushi bar on the penthouse level, and we can talk at some length in relative privacy."

"Cool beans!" said Eastwood. "See you then!"

Josh hung up with an amused smile. The reporter looked and sounded like an excited high school student, but according to his biography at the paper's website, he was actually thirty-five—older than Josh or Isabella. The main thing Josh liked about him was that Eastwood brought a high level of accuracy and intelligence to every story he touched, and that he had not only recognized the remarkable impact of the *Testimonium,* but had responded to it with an open profession of faith in the pages of one of the world's most read newspapers. The young reporter had *chutzpah,* Josh thought, and such a rare quality deserved a reward.

It was three o'clock in the afternoon, and he looked at the huge stack of mail that had been dumped just inside his door, and then at his bed. Fatigue won out, and he lay down for a nap, leaving instructions to be woken at six. He then called Isabella and told her the time and place, then closed his eyes and surrendered to oblivion.

* * *

Ibrahim Abbasside watched the three crowds of clashing demonstrators outside the museum with amusement. He had blended in with them perfectly, hoisting a sign in English that read JESUS: A PROPHET, NOT A GOD! in bold red letters. He knew that the Western intelligence agencies had never managed to get a good picture of him, and so he reveled in being able to hide in plain sight among the crowds outside the museum. He had even caught a brief glimpse of the two infidel scientists and the priest as they scurried into the building that afternoon. His hands had twitched at the sight, longing for the familiar grip of an AK-47. How he would have loved to set their bodies dancing as the bullets riddled them! He had killed four nuns in Somalia in exactly that manner, sending their infidel souls to hell for daring to offer medical treatment to sick children in the name of their false god, Christ—never to be confused with the Prophet Isa, whom he revered.

But Italy had pretty strict gun control laws, and the Beretta in his pocket would have to do when the time came. But when to catch them unawares? He knew that killing Parker and Sforza would not be enough. He had to destroy the ancient scroll, and remove forever the possiblity that science might confirm it as genuine. Already the infidel priests and pastors were trumpeting from their pulpits that history had proven their faith to be true, and he must put a stop to it! If he could reduce the scroll to ash, it would limit the damage and forever leave the question of the *Testimonium*'s authenticity hanging.

When to do it? He figured that the infidel archeologists would wait until after the funerals of the victims from Ali bin-Hassan's failed attack to move the scroll to Rome for testing. He had already, through a series of covert messages, put two sleeper cells on alert for immediate activation. When the scroll moved, they would strke. But when would that be? And what route would they take? He needed the answers to these questions, and soon.

<<<TRANSCRIPT OF A PHONE CONVERSATION FROM THE CIA'S ANTITERRORISM OFFICE, APRIL 23, 20** BETWEEN COL. LINCOLN BERTRAND AND FIELD AGENT DOMINGO GARCIA>>>

GARCIA: Colonel, I have some fresh news for you.

BERTRAND: What is it, Dingo?

GARCIA: Looks like the Ethiopian is in Italy now.

BERTRAND: Do you have his location fixed?

GARCIA: No, sir, but if I were a betting man, I would guess that he is in or near Naples. We picked up some intercepted conversations, and two sleeper cells have been activated—one near Rome, the other closer to Naples. I am guessing that they are planning to try and destroy that scroll again.

BERTRAND: (sighs audibly) I suppose that will mean bringing the Italians in on it, won't it? Crap, I hate that. Their police leak like an Arkansas mobile home roof!"

GARCIA: I'd recommend getting ahold of Antonio Lucoccini, Colonel. He is probably the straightest arrow in that quiver, and he's been hankering to nail the Ethiopian ever since those four Italian nuns got perforated in Somalia.

BERTRAND: No one holds a grudge like a Sicilian, eh? Good call. I'll begin collating the data. Forward me all the specifics you can, I'll launder them for security, and then bring him into the loop. With any luck we will nip this thing before it goes down. Good work, Dingo. Keep me informed!

GARCIA: Aye, sir. I'll be in touch soon.

CHAPTER TWENTY-THREE

Alexander Vizzini was a Sicilian by birth and a career criminal by choice. His life of crime had made him rich beyond the dreams of avarice, enabling him to wear the most expensive suits and squire young models around town whenever he felt like it. And yet, the worst of his criminal activities would only have netted him a dozen or so years in prison if prosecuted to the fullest extent of the law. Vizzini had never physically harmed another person, and in fact, he made a point of never carrying a weapon, although his bodyguards were well armed. Of course, his potential jail sentences were theoretical: Vizzini had never been arrested or even named as an accessory to a crime. He was a dealer in information, with a specialization in electronic intelligence.

Vizzini had taken to the information age like a fish to water—he had a natural gift for electronics, and had learned the ways of the Internet back in the good old days of dial-up modems and 27KB connections. The faster information traveled, the quicker he followed, and with the world becoming increasingly interconnected, he haunted the phone lines and email servers, dipping into communications effortlessly and leaving not a trace behind. As he became aware just how easy it was to tap into government computer and phone networks, he had begun selling the information he gathered to a select group of customers. The Sicilian mobsters were among his best-paying clientele; he enabled them to stay a step ahead of the police by tapping into radio networks, emails, document files, and telephone conversations. He also dealt out information to a variety of foreign governments—not the Western powers, with their silly ideas of the rule of law and limited government, of course—but he had done work for a number of rogue states, all for a high fee. The only thing he insisted on was never being told how the information would be used. As a rule, he avoided watching news broadcasts and reading the papers for that very reason. He was mildly repulsed by bloodshed.

He was enjoying a gourmet meal at his favorite restaurant when his special cell phone rang. This number was available only to those who had done business with him before. They were allowed to pass it to others who had need of his services, and his business grew strictly by referrals. The number had not been changed in ten years, but he did not worry about it being traced. The program he had built to host it randomly directed the calls through locations around the world, and then relayed them to his cell without a trace. If the CIA or Interpol had been monitoring this caller, their computers would have told them that the number being dialed was that of a hardware store in Cincinnati, Ohio. Tomorrow it would go to a veterinarian's office in Greenville, Texas.

"This is the Spider," he said. He had chosen the name for himself years before, and rather liked it. He imagined himself as an impeccably dressed arachnid, poised in the center of a web, sensing every vibration from its far-flung strands.

"I have need of your services," said a voice on the other end. The Italian was passable, but carried a North African accent. "You come highly recommended from mutual friends."

"What services do you require?" he asked.

"I need to monitor all phone calls coming in and out of the National Museum of Antiquities in Naples for the next week," the client replied. "Including any lines that are encrypted, and any cellular calls made by members of the Board of Antiquities."

"Simple enough," Vizzini replied. "To where do you want the information directed?" The client rattled off an email address. "Very well. Do you want transcripts, or the actual audio files?"

"Both, if possible," the African said.

"I shall require one hundred thousand Euros deposited to this account within the next two hours," said Vizzini. "The intercepts will begin tomorrow morning, and continue through next Sunday. At that point, if you wish to continue surveillance, it will cost you an additional fifty thousand Euros a day."

"I imagine a single week will be sufficient," said the client. "But if it is not, shall I contact you at this number?"

"Precisely so," said Vizzini. "And feel free to recommend me to your friends."

"I have no friends," said the voice on the other end, and hung up.

Vizzini shrugged and pocketed his phone. Such strange people required information sometimes.

* * *

Josh had tried to sleep for some time, but found that he could not rest. With nothing better to do, he began to read through the mail that had been delivered to him. The first letter was postmarked from Dayton, Tennessee—home of the Scopes Monkey Trial of the 1920s, he recalled with a wry smile.

"Dear Dr. Parker," it read. "I think that your discovery may be very significant. As you translate Pilate's statement, be sure to look at the document under UV for the watermark of the Freemasons. They have been involved in every assassination in history, as I am sure you know—"

He balled that one up and tossed it in the wastebasket, then opened another.

"God bless you for your work, good sir!" it began cheerfully. "I have been telling my students for years that those who believe the Bible have nothing to fear from good, solid science or honest history, and you are proving my argument for me! As a longtime Christian schoolteacher, it is refreshing to see reports in the news that verify the truth of Scripture instead of tearing it down! I will be watching your press conference Friday with my entire World History class."

Josh set that one aside to answer. The next one was postmarked Friday evening, and had an address in Naples. He opened it to find a flowing script on rich, manila-colored paper. It was in English, although awkwardly phrased.

"Dr. Parker," it began, "I was deeply saddened to see the coverage this morning of the attack on the museum's lab and the deaths of your colleagues. I am even more saddened by the knowledge that it is one who claims to share my own faith that has done this thing. As an imam, I have devoted my life to reforming Islam to better relate to the modern world, and I have urged those who pray at my mosque to renounce violence and live in peace with those of all other faiths. Some listen, and some do not. But I want you to know that not every follower of the Prophet is a monster like the man who slew your friends today. I wish you luck with your continued investigations into history. I, too, believe that religion has nothing to fear from true science. May you recover quickly, and may some of your discoveries have survived this cowardly deed. Sincerely, Muhammad Ali-Hussein."

Josh added that one to the pile to be answered as well. He knew that there were many peaceful Muslims out there, and he wanted to give them as much encouragement as possible. Over the next two hours, he read through nearly a hundred letters. Many were from sincere

Christians, supporting him in his work and offering their prayers and, in one envelope, a neatly folded hundred-dollar bill "to help with expenses." There were two or three angry letters from atheists and skeptics denouncing him and the team's discoveries as obvious frauds, and even one death threat. There were also about a dozen letters from young ladies expressing an interest in altering his single status. "Don't trust that Italian tart," read one. "She will string you along and break your heart! You need a good old Baptist girl from Alabama who knows how to make a pecan pie!" That one made him smile, but the next one he opened with feminine handwriting on the address had about four photographs enclosed that made him blush furiously before he stuffed them into the trash can, making sure that some of the other discards covered them up. He could imagine the snide remarks if Isabella, or worse yet, his mother, saw them!

He had lost track of time when his telephone rang. It was Isabella, waiting for him in the lobby. He looked at the clock and realized that Andrew Eastwood should be waiting for him as well! He pulled on a light jacket and headed for the elevator.

He found Isabella and Eastwood chatting together in the foyer of the hotel. They greeted him with a wave, and Isabella came over and gave him a gentle hug—both of them were still sore from Friday's trauma. Then the reporter came over and shook his hand.

"Dr. Parker, it is a distinct pleasure to meet you," said Eastwood.

"Likewise, sir, and feel free to call me Josh," said the archeologist.

"And my friends call me Drew," replied the reporter.

They made small talk on the ride up the elevator, and then had a seat in the sushi bar. After they ordered their food, Eastwood got down to business.

"I like to take things in chronological order when I am building a story, so I am going to begin with you." He indicated Isabella. "Dr. Sforza, what did it feel like the first time you set foot in that chamber on Capri?"

"When I looked in and saw that it was still furnished, and that everything in there was coated with centuries of dust, I felt like a little girl at her birthday party!" Isabella said. "I could not wait to see what lay beneath the gift wrapping of the ages."

"How long after Dr. Rossini found the chamber did you arrive on Capri?" he asked.

"He made the discovery that morning, and I was on-site by early afternoon," she said. "Giuseppe was one of my early mentors as an archeologist, and one of my dearest friends. As soon as he saw that the chamber was undisturbed, he backed out of it and called me—he didn't even set foot inside it till I got there," she said. "We entered the room together, and began uncovering the items on the table first of all."

"Tell me what that was like," asked Eastwood.

"Understand we had no idea what the chamber was for, or what was in it," she said. "I knew that the furniture looked Roman in design, especially the curule magistrate's chair, but it wasn't until we began dusting the items on top of the writing table that it really began to sink in that we were looking at something that had not changed since the time of Tiberius Caesar!"

"What did you uncover first?" he asked.

"An inkwell," she said. "And it still had ink residue all over it. Some of the ink had dripped on top of the desk itself, and that's when we realized that the table had been used right there in the chamber. Then we found the signet ring with Tiberius' name on it, and we were so excited! The candleholder and the wax candle, and then the quill—but for me, the moment I will never forget was when I watched Giuseppe dusting off that ancient quill and realized it was lying on top of an intact papyrus document! Then, after we cleared the dust from that first document and saw the signature of Tiberius Caesar—it was the kind of moment every archeologist dreams of!"

"I had dreams of being an archeologist when I was a kid," said the journalist. "You make me wish I had stayed with it. Now, Dr. Parker, when did you enter the story?"

"I was fishing with my dad on Lake Hugo in Oklahoma when I got a call from Bernardo Guioccini," said Josh. "He actually wanted my friend Dr. Martens to come and work the dig, but Doc was recovering from a broken leg and was not yet mobile two weeks ago. So I caught a flight and got to Naples late the next afternoon."

Over the next hour and a half, they told him all about how the dig had progressed, and how the friendships among the team had grown at the same time. They spoke fondly of the departed and of Dr. MacDonald, and explained their growing excitement as the nature of their discovery became apparent. Eastwood was an attentive listener who rarely interrupted, his comments simply serving to guide their narrative along the way. Occasionally he snapped a picture as they spoke, but didn't interrupt the flow of the story otherwise. Finally, after they recounted the horrific aftermath of the explosion, he asked them the one question they had not been too forthcoming about.

"So what is the story with the two of you?" he asked. "It is obvious to all that there is some kind of relationship developing, but the whole world is curious to know what it is!"

Josh and Isabella looked at one another at the same time, and then looked back at him.

"It's complicated!" they said at the same time, and then burst out laughing as they looked at one another.

Eastwood smiled. "Is that your only comment?" he asked.

Josh said, "Well, it's not only complicated, it's pretty personal. How about if we just leave it by saying we have become very fond of each other?"

Isabella nodded. "He speaks true," she said. "We don't really know what the future holds for us at this point, so I suggest we don't share anything else with your readers on that front."

Eastwood made a wry face, and then smiled. "You guys have given me so much that I guess I can't complain," he said. "The fellas in the press pool are going to want to kill me already!"

Isabella smiled. "Tell them not being a moron has its rewards," she said.

"And let them in on the secret of my success?" Eastwood scowled. "No thanks!" He paused for a moment. "You don't have to comment on this one if you don't want to," he said. "But I'm going to put it out here for you anyway. According to a local news source, as he was leaving Capri to pick up the car bomb, Ali bin-Hassan told one of his neighbors—who thought he was a peace-loving local imam at the time—that he hoped the man would remember that Hassan represented the true face of Islam. Do you think he was right?"

Josh sighed. No matter how he answered this question, he was bound to offend someone. At the same time, he trusted the young reporter not to misquote him or distort his answer, so he decided to answer anyway.

"Of course not!" he said. "There are over a billion Muslims in a world of over six billion people. If all Muslims believed in jihad, there would be none of us 'infidels' left. The vast majority of the world's Muslims are peaceful people who want to be left alone to practice their religion in peace. However, there is a minority in the Muslim world who are committed to jihad. I think the roots of this belief lie in the Quran itself, and the man who spoke it into being. Muhammad was a man of war, which even the most devout Muslim will freely admit. He spent a good part of his life leading his followers in battle and preaching against his enemies. Those who follow the path of jihad today simply believe that Muhammad's declaration of war against unbelievers is a literal mandate for the ages, while those who reject jihad recognize it for what it is—a part of the history of their faith, not a plan for its future."

Eastwood nodded at Josh's explanation, and then stood. "Listen, I cannot thank the two of you enough, and I have intruded on your evening already. I'll take the elevator down and give you guys some time to yourselves. Have a great evening!"

He ambled toward the elevator, and Josh and Isabella watched him go. "You know, when the press first started stalking us, I couldn't stand any of them," said Josh. "But that gentleman almost gives me hope for the American media."

"Let's see what kind of story he produces from our conversation first," Isabella replied. "I have seen some very well-conducted interviews hacked to pieces and wind up an unreadable mess!"

Josh looked at her lovely face, drinking in its features. "So is our relationship really that complicated?" he asked.

She sighed. "It shouldn't be, but it is," she said. "I have come to the conclusion that I love you very much. I am just not sure that I can love your God as much as I love you!"

"Even though He loves you so much more than I ever could?" Joshua asked.

"You keep saying that," she replied, "and I want to believe you. You make Jesus sound as if He is the answer to every problem. But I cannot see Him that way yet. If it is any consolation, I want to see Him that way. I look at your certainty and I am envious of it! I just can't share it quite yet."

Josh kissed her on the cheek. "You are getting closer every day, Isabella. Faith doesn't often come in great blind leaps. Sometimes it just dawns on us little by little. Would you do one thing for me, though?"

She looked at his eyes, fascinated by the intensity of his gaze. There were so many emotions there. "What do you want me to do, Joshua, *mi amor?*" she asked him.

"Would you read John's Gospel tonight?" he asked. "Or at least, over the next few days? Not as a historian, or as a scientist—read it as if you had never seen or heard of it before. Read it with your heart as well as your eyes. See if, perhaps, it helps you find your way toward faith."

She sighed. Joshua's God got on her nerves sometimes, but she could not turn down this strange young man who had captured her heart, "Very well," she said, "but I make no promises about how I will react!"

He smiled and kissed her again. "I don't ask for promises," he said. "Just an open mind. I have never felt anything like this before—the way you make my heart sing when you walk into the room, and the way I forget to breathe when you look at me. I don't want to live another day that you are not a part of my life."

A part of her wanted to shout, 'Then why bring your God into it?' But she knew Josh well enough by now to know that his God went where he did, and that if she was going to make room in her heart for Josh to stay, she would have to find a place for his God too. So instead of shouting, she sighed and said, "You make things complicated, you know!"

They sat together after that for a little while, sipping green tea and watching as the guests slowly left, then Josh paid the bill and they took the elevator together. They got off on his parents' floor and stopped in to see how the elder Parkers were doing.

Ben Parker came to the door in an atrocious pair of Bermuda shorts and an obviously new T-shirt showing the skyline of Capri on it. "Hello, son!" he said with a big smile. "And you too, Isabella! Have you youngsters had a nice evening?"

"We were talking to a reporter, Dad," said Josh. "He seems like a decent sort, and we decided to give him our first exclusive interview."

"Ah," said Reverend Parker. "Was it that young Eastwood fellow who wrote the editorial you showed me yesterday?"

"None other," said Josh. "He has written the best coverage of our discoveries from day one, so we thought we would share our first exclusive with him."

"Probably a good pick, then," said his dad.

"Reverend Parker," said Isabella, "why is your television unplugged and turned to the wall?"

The old minister laughed. "Well, my wife made the mistake of turning it on after nine PM, and she found some of your local programs a bit too—um, revealing for her taste!"

Isabella laughed. The rather explicit and raunchy nature of Italian TV had been part of her cultural background since she was a teen, but her visits to the States had taught her that American TV only hinted at things Italian TV showed.

"I guess it would take a little getting used to," she said.

The pastor nodded. "I don't think she has any intention of getting used to it," he said. "However, she has had great fun telling all fourteen members of her senior ladies' Sunday School Class about it! I think she is still on the phone!"

He paused, and sure enough, Joshua heard his mother's voice coming from the bedroom of their suite, saying: "I am totally serious, Evelyn! Naked as a jaybird—in a cereal commercial, no less!"

Josh rolled his eyes, and said "Well, I guess I had better leave you two for the night. Rest well, Dad!"

"I will, son. Would you like for your mother and I to come to the funeral service tomorrow?" he asked.

Josh nodded. "I've never spoken at a funeral before," he said. "I could use the moral support."

He walked back toward the elevator. It came to him suddenly that he was absolutely exhausted. He looked at Isabella. "Are you going to be all right?" he asked her.

"Physically, I need a good night's sleep, and maybe one more of those Percocets," she said. "Emotionally, I just don't know how well I can deal with burying poor Giuseppe tomorrow. I am still so angry! One of the best and kindest men I have ever known murdered so senselessly."

"Evil is a hard thing to come to terms with," said Josh. "It is bad enough to lose someone, but when they are taken from you maliciously—well; it makes it hard to believe that there is justice in the world."

She nodded. "I think that is one reason I have such a hard time embracing your God," she said. "I still think He should be able to fix everything, so that what happened to our friends never happens again!"

"He will, in His own time," said Josh. "I really believe that." The elevator stopped at his floor, and he leaned in for one last kiss. "Goodnight, love. Rest well."

She watched the closing doors hide his face, and then turned away, watching the lobby come rushing up toward her through the glass side of the elevator. She let out a long sigh. In so many ways, Joshua was the perfect man—in some ways, even more so than Marc had been. She could imagine the two of them sharing an exciting life together, working on digs, collaborating on papers, and yes, raising several children. But could she come to share his unshakeable faith in a loving God—a God who came to earth as a carpenter two thousand years before? She had been asking herself this question for a week now, and still had not come up with a satisfactory answer.

Remembering her promise, she stopped at a bookstore on the way back to her apartment and bought a Bible. She knew she had one buried in the boxes at her office, but had not kept one in her home since she was a little girl. She had never read any of the Gospels straight through for her own pleasure, although she had been required to read them for a Biblical archeology course she had taken in college. Even growing up in the Catholic Church as a girl, reading entire books of the Bible had not been encouraged—although short passages were included in the missal nearly every Sunday.

She went home and showered, then pulled on an old, comfortable T-shirt and some terrycloth shorts to sleep in. She took a long drink of cold water and a single Percocet to ease the throbbing from her sore muscles. Turning on her bedside lamp, she found the Gospel of John and began to read: "In the beginning was the Word, and the Word was with God, and the Word was God. The Word was with God in the beginning, and through Him all things were made . . ."

* * *

Joshua was exhausted, but still too keyed up to sleep. He flipped through the channels, avoiding the racy programs that had scandalized his mother, and finally found an English language news station. He caught up on events back home—the baseball scores showed him that the Rangers had opened their season with a nice winning streak, but it appeared the Mavericks were not going to make the playoffs yet again. He sighed. It was sad when a storied franchise entered a rebuilding phase.

He flipped over to one of the late-night talk shows. Will Mayor was on every Sunday night back in the states, and his show was just starting on one of the international movie channels. He was a foul-mouthed, sarcastic atheist who loved nothing better than bashing religion and right-wing politicians at every opportunity; he was one of the few entertainers that actually made Josh angry. But the panel of guests included the irrepressible Joel Wombaker, and the Smithsonian's Biblical archeologist, Andy Henderson, in addition to an American starlet named Sandee McClusky and the ever-grouchy atheist, David Hubbard. This ought to be interesting, Joshua thought. The program was just beginning, and the *Testimonium* was the topic.

"Now let's just suppose," said Mayor, "that this papyrus really is two thousand years old, and was really written by Pontius Pilate. Does that prove that the Christians have been right this whole time about their magical Jewish carpenter being the Son of God? I vote no, but since we have a certified fundamentalist idiot here, I'll let him speak first. Pastor Wombaker, let's get your take on this!" He rolled his eyes as he looked down the table at the evangelical preacher.

Wombaker simply flashed his famous smile at the cable TV icon. "Well, Will, I'm just blessed to be here tonight, and I know that, for someone like you who has based his whole life on the proposition that God is NOT real, this must be a really tough time! So you can keep right on calling me an idiot, because I am a fool for Christ through and through!"

Mayor laughed. "Well, on that at least we can agree!" he said.

Wombaker went on. "I remember you bluntly asserting in your little mockumentary about religion a few years ago that—and I quote—'the Gospels aren't eyewitness testimony!' And I also noticed you did not give the token Bible scholar you were interviewing any time to respond to that blanket assertion. So I am going to respond right here and now. We have now found eyewitness testimony, sir, and it confirms the Gospel accounts to a degree that we never even hoped for! So it is in a spirit of Christian charity that I offer, here and now, a washcloth for you to wipe that egg off your face." He produced a white cloth from his suit pocket and offered it to the talk show host, and the studio audience roared with laughter. Josh smiled. This was too good to miss!

Mayor, meantime, looked as if he had taken a bite out of a green persimmon. But, not willing to be upstaged, he smiled and felt around his mouth. "No egg here, pastor!" he said. "You still haven't proven that this mystery papyrus is the real deal, and even if you do, it just means that the folktales the Gospels were based on might have gotten a few details correct."

Wombaker shook his head. "You, my friend, are living in an Egyptian river if you believe that! First of all, the discovery and excavation of the *Testimonium Pilatus* was painstakingly recorded, and the preliminary tests of the dust and pollen from the chamber show that it originated in the first century AD. Even though many of the samples were destroyed, the scroll itself has been preserved, and the media told us this morning that some other relics from the chamber have also been recovered. If the dust is two thousand years old, and the artifacts in the chamber are two thousand years old, and the scroll itself dates back two thousand years, then what we have is historical confirmation of the most important claim of the Christian faith—that Jesus of Nazareth rose from the dead, which in turn proves that He was who He claimed to be all along!"

"Oh, please!" snapped Hubbard. "What a crock of bull! You know and I know, pastor, that we live in a day and age in which digital media can be manipulated and faked more easily and with less chance of detection than ever before. With much of the physical evidence conveniently destroyed, all the claims that this Dr. Parker and Father MacDonald and their cohorts are making will boil down to the tests on the papyrus itself. And I imagine that it may be two thousand years old—that doesn't mean the writing on it is! I also have no doubt that this hoax was years, maybe a century or more, in the planning. Recover an old piece of papyrus from some ancient document at the Vatican, use an ancient ink formula to do the writing on it, and plant it at Capri to be found. And then, hey presto! Here we have proof that the great fraud of the ages, organized religion, is no fraud at all!"

Mayor smiled. "That certainly would make a great plot for a novel," he said. "Dr. Henderson, you have handled papyrus documents all your life, and you are leaving for Italy tomorrow to examine this papyrus yourself. Would you be able to detect a fake such as my pal Hubbard here has described?"

Henderson was a dark-haired, rather intense Californian whose reputation in the world of classical archeology was legend. He had spent ten years examining the vast collection of ancient documents at Qumran, and had also assisted in analyzing a more recent cache of Gnostic material found in the deserts of Egypt in 2009. Josh had read his work on that discovery with great interest, and met the man personally on a couple of occasions.

"Well, Will, first of all, it would be pretty easy to detect modern writing on an ancient papyrus. Virtually all ancient inks used some form of charcoal for coloring, and charcoal is easily datable. There were only two or three varieties of ink available during the first century, all of which are easy to date using C-14. If the ink is not right, the writing is probably faked. But I will say, based on what I have seen so far—and I have viewed all the video and photographs of the excavations at Capri— that I have seen nothing which indicates any fraud, recent or otherwise, associated with the discovery of the chamber. Now I am no Christian, but as a historian and archeologist I will say that your dismissal of the Gospel accounts is a bit cavalier. They may not be eyewitness testimony, but they certainly could be! The Synoptic Gospels were all most likely completed within forty years of the time of Christ—some, like Pastor Wombaker here, can make an argument for an even earlier date—and even John's Gospel was still written at the end of the first century. If the early accounts of the Apostle John living to a great old age were true, then that Gospel could certainly have its roots in his testimony about Jesus. I have worked with the Gnostic Gospels extensively in the last decade, and I can say with some authority that none of them date to within a century of the actual lifetime of Jesus of Nazareth, and many of them were written two or three hundred years later. Does that automatically mean the Biblical Gospel accounts are true? No—but this latest discovery, if it is authentic, will show that they are far more accurate than critics like you have been willing to acknowledge."

Mayor obviously didn't care for the direction this conversation was taking. "Well," he finally conceded, "even if Pilate wrote this thing, I think it is worth recording that he never claims to have personally seen what happened at the tomb that morning. Everything he records is second-hand testimony from a band of ignorant and frightened soldiers who were obviously shaken up by something. But who knows what it really was? Maybe aliens kidnapped the body of Jesus!"

The pretty young starlet had been waiting for a chance to jump in. "Aliens!" she said. "That would certainly explain all those weird miracles stories, wouldn't it? I think the topic of Jesus and space aliens could make a really good movie!"

Wombaker interjected: "That would make more sense than an archeological find of this magnitude being a plant! But, Will, you are truly a jewel of denial tonight! Maybe they should make a movie about you!" The audience laughed again, and Mayor muttered an obscenity under his breath.

Hubbard jumped into the gap. "You know, Will, I would be more willing to believe that Jesus of Nazareth was a space alien than I would to think that he might be the Son of a fictitious God. At least science is friendly to the possibility of alien life!"

Now it was Henderson's turn to roll his eyes, and Wombaker tried to cut in again, but Mayor interrupted both of them. "Well, with that, folks, looks like time for this segment is up. Next up: the governor of California and Texas Congressman Rick Roberts on the topic of welfare reform. Thank you, Dr. Hubbard, Pastor Wombaker, and Dr. Henderson for your time."

Josh turned off the TV with a yawn. It was nearly midnight, and he was exhausted. His bruises and abrasions still ached a little, but he decided to forego the pain meds and see how he did without them. He was dreading the next two days—he hated funerals, and saying goodbye to Simone and Giuseppe was going to be very hard. He took his well-worn travel Bible off of the desk and read a couple of Psalms before bed, taking comfort in the three-thousand-year-old words of a shepherd boy named David. Then he said a prayer—for the souls of his departed friends, for their grieving families, and for Isabella—especially for Isabella. He had never wanted anything in the world as much as he wanted to make her his wife, but he wanted her to belong fully to God before she came to belong with him. He reflected on the verse he had just read from Psalm 37: "Delight thyself also in the Lord, and He will give thee the desires of thy heart." For the first time in his life he really knew what his chief desire was.

<<<TRANSCRIPT OF A PHONE CONVERSATION BETWEEN DR. BENITO CASTOLFO AND POLICE CHIEF ALESSANDRO ZADORA, APRIL 24, 20**>>>

CASTOLFO: Good evening, Chief Zadora.

ZADORA: Dr. Castolfo! I am afraid there is nothing new in the investigation of the bombing, but we are keeping security around the museum as tight as we can.

CASTOLFO: Your efforts are much appreciated, sir. I am sure you will find any accomplices that Ali bin-Hassan may have had very soon. But that is not why I called you tonight.

ZADORA: What else is going on, Benito?

CASTOLFO: I am concerned about transporting the scroll to Rome Friday. If Hassan has any accomplices out there, that would be the time for them to strike again and try to finish what he started. I think we will need massive security when we move the scroll.

ZADORA: Agreed. A full police escort, perhaps an armored car and even air support might be in order.

CASTOLFO: I was afraid you might think I was being paranoid.

ZADORA: These animals already blew up a research lab in the heart of a major Italian city in order to destroy one two-thousand-year-old piece of paper. It is obvious they will stop at nothing. I am not a religious man, but that Testimonium is a national treasure of the Italian people. Those bastards will not destroy it on my watch!

CASTOLFO: That is a great relief, Chief Zadora. I have to bury two dear comrades this week. I do not want to attend any further funerals anytime soon.

ZADORA: I will do my best to see to it you do not. Good night, Benito.

CASTOLFO: Good night, Chief!

CHAPTER TWENTY-FOUR

Josh woke the next morning surprisingly rested. His bruises still ached, but less than they had since the day after the blast. He looked at the clock in his room and saw that it was 6:30, so he decided to see if his battered body could still do a few laps in the pool. He slid into his trunks and T-shirt, grabbed a towel and his room key, and headed downstairs. He had the large, heated pool to himself, and the water felt wonderful as he stroked back and forth. He could feel the knots in his back and limbs unkinking as he swam.

He swam back and forth for about twenty minutes, then looked up and saw, to his surprise, that his dad was standing beside the pool watching. Josh climbed out and grabbed his towel.

"A long way from Lake Hugo, isn't it, son?" his dad asked.

"Sure is, Pop," he said. "But for all the sadness of the last few days, I wouldn't have missed it for the world."

"Why don't you join your mother and I for breakfast?" Brother Ben asked. "We found an American restaurant not far from here, and I sure would enjoy some old-fashioned pancakes or biscuits and gravy!"

"I'd love to," Josh said, "but I need to run out and buy a suit and tie this morning for the funeral, and I don't know how long that will take."

His dad smiled. "Son, you are selling your mother and I short! As soon as we heard the news, and then got word that you were OK, we knew that you would be attending your friends' funerals. So we brought both your suits, several dress shirts, and a selection of ties for you."

Josh embraced his father. "You never quit looking out for me, do you, Dad?" he asked.

"Of course not!" Ben Parker replied. "That's my job—at least, until it's your turn to look after me!" He looked at his son with great affection. "I hope you know that my heart sunk in my chest when I saw the news of the attack. Your mother and I were sure we had lost you."

"If Isabella and I had walked out of the building a few seconds later, you would have!" Josh said. "I thought I was a goner when that blast picked me up and tossed me into the side of the museum. But we Parkers are made of pretty tough stuff, I guess."

"That Isabella is a real beauty," his dad said. "And she has a sense of humor, too. Your mother and I are quite taken with her."

"Not half as taken as I am," Josh said. "I really think she may be the one, Dad. So please tell Mom not to scare her off!"

His dad chuckled. "I don't think you have much to worry about there," he said. "I don't believe Dr. Sforza scares too easily."

"You've got that right," Josh said. "She does scare me a little, sometimes. I don't ever want to be on her bad side. But she is just— well, what can I say? I find her amazing, fascinating, and completely awesome!"

Ben Parker laughed out loud. "You've got it bad, boy!" he said. "But, all joking aside, after over forty years together, your mother still takes my breath away every time I wake up and see her by my side. The world may see a graying senior citizen, but I still see the black-haired beauty that caught my eye at the County Fair in 1968."

Josh rolled his eyes, but in his heart he adored his parents' incredible love story. He never doubted his own place in their affections, but when they looked at each other he knew that the bond between them was something unique, and he had prayed for years that God would send him someone that he could share that same incredible closeness with. Now he hoped that his prayer had been answered.

He wondered if Isabella had read the Gospel as he asked her too. He wanted to guide her toward the same bright faith that had burned in his heart since he was a child, but he also knew that he could never push another person into a saving relationship with Christ. In the end, all he could do was model that relationship and try to nudge her toward it. But his heart ached with the knowledge that she had not yet made that personal commitment. When they were one in the Lord, they could be one with each other, and he could imagine no greater joy. Give me patience, Lord, he prayed. Let me be a stepping stone under her feet and not a millstone around her neck.

Suddenly he realized that his dad was speaking to him again. "I'm sorry," he said. "I was a million miles away for a minute there."

His dad grinned at him. "I think I know what country you were visiting," he said. "But what I was telling you was that I don't think the restaurant will let you in wearing swim trunks and a towel!"

Josh looked down and realized that he had walked to the elevators without even putting his T-shirt on. He shook his head, shrugged it on, and punched the button. "You're right," he said. "Give me a few minutes to get changed, and I'll meet you in the lobby."

"Sure thing," his dad said. "And feel free to call your lovely Italian friend and invite her along. I'd enjoy spending some more time with her."

"Only if you tell Mom to quit being such a walking cliché!" Josh said over his shoulder.

Back in his room, he grabbed his cell and dialed Isabella's number. She answered on the second ring.

"Hello, love!" he said, amazed at how naturally the word rolled off his tongue.

"Good morning, Josh!" she replied. "How are you feeling?"

"Tons better," he replied. "I don't think I am going to need these pain pills any more. I took a nice swim and worked my muscles out, and it's amazing what a little exercise did! Listen, I am going to breakfast with my mom and mad. Would you like to come with us?"

"Yes, I would," she replied. "It's going to be a long, sad couple of days, and I would like to start it doing something happy. Your folks make me smile."

"They have that effect on me, too," Josh said. "We are heading out in a half hour, if that is not too soon for you."

"Not at all," she said. "I woke about an hour ago, showered, and dressed. I will see you in the hotel lobby shortly. And Josh—"

"Yes, Isabella?" he asked.

"I read four chapters last night. I really didn't want to start, but I decided I would just read a few verses so I could say I kept my promise—and kept going! I must admit, John paints a compelling picture of Jesus," she said.

"Wonderful!" he replied. "The story just gets better as it goes along. Maybe we will have time to talk about it soon."

* * *

On the other side of Naples, Ibrahim Abbasside was listening to a conversation recorded the previous evening. The president of the Bureau of Antiquities was speaking to the Naples police chief, asking for armed escort when the scroll was transported. He was not surprised, since Hassan's failed attack had alerted the world that the soldiers of Islam wanted to destroy this accursed document. But the Italians would soon see what kind of firepower Allah's jihadi could bring to bear. He had already alerted the two sleeper cells in Southern Italy that he might require their services, but it was time to make sure they were properly equipped.

He picked up his secure cell phone and called a number he had committed to memory before leaving Libya.

"Ali's African Pets," said a voice on the other end in heavily accented Italian.

"Hello, Ali, my old friend!" he said in Arabic. "Do you still have those gerbils ready for Suleiman to pick up?"

"Two cages full!" said the voice on the other end. His name was not actually Ali, of course, but Ismael Falladah, a former Red Brigade member who had embraced the Religion of Truth after the end of the Cold War. Ibrahim had recruited him fifteen years before and sent him into Italy with a small, dedicated team of fanatical jihadists. All of them spoke passable Italian, and had acquired jobs, families, and cover stories that masked their actual purpose. The second "cage" was another cell, led by a portly restaurateur who went by the name Achmed, although his real name was Muhammad Sharif. He was a vicious killer whose plump build and deep laugh masked a truly psychotic nature that sometimes even frightened Abbasside. The two cell leaders were acquainted, but the members were all completely ignorant of each other's existence.

"Excellent!" Abbasside continued. "I need you to deliver them Friday, and I think we need a complete shipment of accessories to go with them. Food, cage litter, exercise wheels, and anything else you have available."

"They will be ready for delivery," said Ali. "Just name the place and we will deliver the animals and their supplies."

"I seem to have lost the address," said Abbasside. "But I will call you with it by Thursday morning at the latest. I'll talk to you then," he said before hanging up.

The simple code system had been worked out years before. The "supplies" were a huge cache of weapons, some smuggled in from North Africa, but most left over from the Red Brigade cell that Ali had once belonged to. RPG launchers, AK-47s, and even a surface-to-air missile launcher! That would take care of the police chopper that would escort the convoy. Abbasside already had the device he would use to destroy the papyrus scroll—a small flamethrower in the shape of an aerosol can that could shoot a jet of intense flame three meters' distance.

He had only used it once before, on a captured CIA agent, and barbecued the man's face from across the room in a matter of seconds. The memory of the screams made him feel warm inside. Perhaps, he thought, if there was enough juice left after the scroll was ash, he might use the flamethrower on the American infidel and his Italian whore. The thought only made his heart warmer.

* * *

Josh came down to the lobby about twenty minutes after getting off the phone with Isabella, dressed in a pair of cotton slacks and a polo shirt. His parents were waiting for him, and as he greeted his mother with a hug and a peck on the cheek, he saw Isabella over her shoulder, entering the hotel. He greeted her with a more enthusiastic hug.

"Thank you so much for inviting me along," Isabella said.

"Don't mention it, dear!" his mother replied. "As long as you are part of our Joshua's life, you will be a part of ours too."

"Then I hope to be a part of your life for years to come!" she said, hugging Joshua. "Now, where are we going for breakfast?"

"I found an American-style restaurant not far from here," said Josh's mother. "They say they have Southern-style cooking!"

Isabella looked interested. "I have only been to New York," she said. "But I have heard food in the South is very different!"

Josh laughed. "As long as you like bacon grease, you should be fine!" he said.

"That and fried chicken!" Ben Parker added.

"For breakfast?" the Italian asked in horror.

"No better breakfast when you are up early and in a hurry than cold fried chicken from the night before!' Josh said.

Isabella rolled her eyes. "Lead on," she said. "But tonight I take you lovely people out for a proper Italian meal!"

The four of them headed for the door. The press was still camped outside the hotel, waiting to photograph Josh and Isabella together.

"Dr. Parker!" shouted one florid Englishman. "Any thoughts on today's funeral service?"

"Yes!" Josh answered. "I wish it were unnecessary!"

"Are these your parents from America?" the man persisted.

363

"Yes, and they are hungry!" Josh replied. "Now please excuse us while we go get breakfast!"

With that they climbed into a waiting cab and drove off.

The restaurant was appropriately named Uncle Sam's Southern Cuisine, and was doing good business on this Monday morning. The waitress, wearing blue jeans and a Western-style shirt, greeted them with a heavily accented "Howdy, y'all!" that set Josh and his parents to giggling. Josh was delighted to see Dr Pepper on the beverage list and ordered one, while his dad got coffee and his mom requested iced tea.

"I guess I will try the iced tea, also," said Isabella.

Their drinks arrived moments later and the waitress handed them the breakfast menu. Josh thought for a few minutes, and then decided to order the biscuits and cream gravy, with some bacon and toast on the side. His dad got the same, while his mom ordered a stack of pancakes with scrambled eggs and sausage. Josh looked over at Isabella, who seemed rather puzzled.

"What do you recommend, Joshua?" she finally asked. "Aren't pancakes somewhat like crepes?"

"They are, but a little bit thicker and differently flavored. Personally, I think that biscuits and gravy are about as good as breakfast can get," he said.

"Then I suppose I shall try them," she said.

The waitress took their orders and their menus and headed off to the kitchen.

Ben Parker looked across the table at his son. "Well, Josh," he said, "are you ready for this afternoon?"

"I guess I am as ready as I can be," he said. "I hate funerals so much! And poor Giuseppe was such a good friend. Dad, how many funerals have you spoken at?"

"Nearly eleven hundred," his father said.

"How do you keep from tearing up?" Josh asked. "Every time I try to say out loud the things that I have written about Giuseppe, I can't stop myself from crying."

"I don't even try," his dad said. "If I am speaking about someone that I knew and loved, I just cry a little bit and go on. No one will be offended, I promise you that. If anything, just the opposite. It shows the family and friends that you are feeling this loss just the same as they are.

One thing forty years in the pulpit has taught me is that it never hurts to remind the church that the pastor is a human being, too."

Josh nodded, but it was Isabella who spoke up.

"That is so different from the way our churches work," she said. "As a little girl I learned to show great respect for our priest, because he was supposed to be a holy man—someone to be looked up to."

Brother Ben nodded. "Understand, my dear girl, I am not saying that those who dedicate their lives to serving God and the church do not deserve respect!" he said. "But, at the same time, when pastors and priests are idolized and put up on a pedestal, and then make a mistake, or get trapped into sin, it devastates the faith of those who think of them as holy men! I cannot tell you how many times I have dealt with people who abandoned God and the church because they saw their pastor do something wrong. I am not apologizing for or excusing men of the cloth who forget themselves, especially if they hurt someone else in the process—but everyone has bad moments. Even my sweet son here has been known to swear in Latin when a big fish gets away!"

Everyone at the table chuckled, and Josh's mom spoke up. "Now, Isabella," she said, "are you going to be all right today? I know you are speaking at Dr. Rossini's funeral as well, and you knew him much longer than our Joshua did."

Isabella smiled wistfully. "Giuseppe was like a second father to me," she said. "Today is going to be very hard. Fortunately I am not scheduled to speak for long. I know there will be tears, but I will finish anyway. It is the least I can do for him! He was so kind to me when I lost my own dear papa, and my husband, Marc."

Josh's dad nodded. "He sounds like a kind and good man," he said. "I would have enjoyed meeting him. Louise and I will be among the congregation, and we will be praying for both of you."

Isabella looked at him quizzically. "How does that work?" she said. "Praying for someone, I mean. If God knows someone's need, why do we have to ask Him to help them?"

Ben looked at her gravely. "That is an excellent question, and you are not the first person to ask me that. You see, as Christians we have a relationship with God. Every good relationship depends on communication. We talk to God about our needs, our hurts, and our lives not because He is unaware of them, but because He is our friend and guide. He wants to hear from us, just as any parent wants to hear

365

from their child on a regular basis. And I do believe that prayer works. I have seen more healing, more spiritual renewal, and more miracles wrought because God's people joined together in prayer than I could begin to tell you about!"

"Fascinating," said Isabella.

About that time their food arrived, still steaming hot from the kitchen. The waitress placed their plates before them and whisked off to refill their tea glasses. Isabella started to pick up her fork, but Josh took her hand. "Dad," he said, "would you say grace for us?"

"Gladly," he said. Parker took his wife's hand and reached across the table to take Isabella's, while Josh reached across to link hands with his mother. "Dear Father," Ben began, "thank you for this delicious taste of home in a faraway land. Thank you for keeping our son and his lady safe through this dangerous ordeal, and thank you for the remarkable discovery they made! We lift up the souls of those who perished, and the hearts of their loved ones, for your eternal comfort and love. Be with Joshua and Isabella as they speak today at the funeral of their dear friend. Continue to be our friend and guide, and bless this food to our bodies, and our bodies to your service, Amen."

After the blessing, they picked up their forks and dove in. Josh was pleasantly surprised to find that the food really did taste like what he would get at a typical roadside café in Oklahoma or Texas. He had worked up a good appetite by swimming, and tucked in with a vengeance. Isabella sniffed the gravy suspiciously, then carefully cut a small piece of the smothered biscuit off with her fork and popped it in her mouth. Her eyes widened as she chewed.

"Josh! This is delicious!" she said. "What is this gravy made from?"

"Flour, milk, bacon grease, and black pepper," said Louise. "It's a simple enough recipe, but if you get the proportions wrong, it can come out pretty awful. How does it taste, Josh?" she asked.

"Not as good as yours, Mom," he said. "But not half bad either!"

"I must admit I am surprised," Isabella said. "But it is a good surprise!"

After breakfast they returned to the hotel, and Josh called Father MacDonald.

"Hello, lad!" the Scottish antiquarian greeted him. "Are you ready for today's sad duties?"

"As ready as one can be for something like this," Joshua said. "When and where do you want us to meet?"

"Come on over to the museum's boardroom about noon," said MacDonald. "The two of you can ride with me to meet the family. Also, we need to speak with Drs. Guioccini and Castolfo about the rest of the week. Dr. Henderson will be arriving this afternoon in Rome, and will be here tomorrow morning for his first look at the *Testimonium*. Also, Simone Apriceno's family has arrived, and I thought you might like to meet them as well."

"That sounds good," Josh said. "I'll run up to my room and change into my suit and see you around noon. I am nervous about this, Father Duncan, but I am glad you will be there to help shepherd me through."

"Commemorating the departed is never an easy task, lad," said the priest. "And it is all the harder when you are speaking about someone you cared for. But Giuseppe was a good man whose life enriched all who knew him. Not only that—you and I both know that he died in a state of grace and now rests with the Father and his holy angels. That is a source of great comfort and strength."

"You sound like my dad sometimes, Father," said Josh.

"I shall take that as a compliment, lad!" the Scotsman replied. "I shall see you in an hour or so."

Josh changed clothes and combed his unruly hair, looking at himself in the mirror as he did. He was not a vain man, but not guilty of phony humility either. He was generally satisfied with the way he looked, although at times he wished his face was less angular and his nose a tad smaller. He had dropped weight since coming to Italy, although he was not sure how. The food here was wonderful, and he had always had an enthusiasm for eating. All in all, he felt at least that he was not embarrassing to Isabella when they went out in public. He wondered if she looked at herself in the mirror and nit-picked her figure flaws. Probably not, he thought, since she had none.

Several blocks away, Isabella was looking at herself in the mirror at the same time before dressing for the funeral. She was generally pleased with her appearance, although she could tell that her face had a few more lines on it than it once did, and the occasional gray hair showed up in her dark locks. But she still thought her figure was decent, although she sometimes wished she were a little more long-waisted and a bit smaller up top. She wondered if Josh ever thought about how he looked in the mirror, and shook her head. She doubted it. Men never worried over their looks.

They met at the museum at noon, skirting around the crowd of protestors that had gathered outside. They were fewer in number than on Sunday, but the same three groups still clustered together—the Christians, the Muslims, and the atheists waving their signs at each other. There were a few journalists as well, but the mob of reporters had shrunk considerably—world events were moving on, and the revelation of Pilate's report was now general knowledge, more to be debated by pundits and theologians than to be covered by newscasters. Josh was frankly relieved.

Father MacDonald was waiting for them in the now familiar boardroom, wearing his formal black frock and clerical collar, his gray-white hair impeccably combed and groomed, and a copy of the Bible in his hand. Castolfo and Guioccini were also there, as well as the Rossini siblings, Andrea and Guillermo. They shook hands and exchanged somber greetings. Josh was glad to see Giuseppe's children, although he knew how hard this moment must be for them. He spoke for a few moments, offering condolences, and then joined Isabella with the two members of the Antiquities Board.

Castolfo greeted him. "You look quite distinguished today, Joshua. I am sorry it is for such a regrettable occasion."

"I only clean up when I absolutely have to, sir!" Josh said. "Field khakis are my favorite attire."

"Spoken like a true archeologist!" said Bernardo Guioccini. "You're a credit to our discipline, young man. One of your colleagues from America will be arriving later today in Rome—have you met Dr. Henderson before?"

"Yes," Josh said, "I sat in on a couple of seminars he taught at a Classical Archeology workshop a few years back. The man has an impressive reputation, and the expertise to back it up."

"We have suspended work on the *Testimonium* today and tomorrow in order to pay our respects to the memories of those we lost Friday," said Castolfo, "but Dr. Henderson does want to take a peek at what we have been laboring on, so he will be coming down tomorrow morning at ten for a first look. Dr. Apriceno's funeral is not until three, but I will be attending the funeral of our fallen security guard at ten AM. His own parish priest will be conducting the service, so I was wondering if you and Isabella and Father MacDonald would be willing to meet Dr. Henderson here and show him your find? I am sure that he has many questions for you."

"I would be glad to," said Joshua. "Two funerals in two days are more than enough for me."

"I agree," said Isabella. "I sent some flowers to the family of Signor Luccatori, but I think it would be disrespectful to intrude on his family and friends when I did not really know the man very well. I have never met Dr. Henderson, and would like very much to do so."

"Count me in," said MacDonald. "I have to conduct Simone's services as well, but I can be here for an hour or so."

"Excellent!" said Castolfo. "By the way, here comes Dr. Apriceno's family now." He nodded to the rear of the room, where a middle-aged man and a teenaged girl were entering. He crossed over to meet them.

"Signor Apriceno, I am sorry to see you again under such terrible circumstances!" he said, taking the man by the hand.

"Thank you, Dr. Castolfo. Simone always spoke very highly of you," he said.

"Is this her daughter?" asked the board president.

"Yes, sir, this is Lucretia," replied Simone's ex-husband.

"You look much like your mother," Isabella cut in. "I didn't know her for very long, but we became quite close in that time. I am so sorry for your loss."

The young Italian woman nodded gratefully. She was much like her mother, somewhat stout in build, but with a pretty, honest face. When she smiled, Josh was strikingly reminded of Simone. "Thank you, Dr. Sforza," she said. "The last time we spoke, my mother told me you were the kind of woman she hoped I would be when I finished university."

"That was sweet of her, but I think you would do better to imitate your mother. She was one of the hardest working and most dedicated scientists I have ever known," replied Isabella.

"That she was," said Ricardo Apriceno. "The stupidest thing I ever did was leaving her. I hoped that someday, we could be reconciled, but we were both too busy—and now it is too late."

"She still wore the ring you gave her—the one made from a Roman coin," said Isabella. "She was wearing it the day she died."

Apriceno smiled. "That does give me some comfort," he said. "Thank you for letting me know."

For a moment, Isabella relived that horrible moment in the parking lot, when she saw the smoking, severed hand with the ring still on it, lying on the asphalt. That was one detail she would never speak about. She nodded to Signor Apriceno and then headed back over to visit with Giuseppe's children. She was far more comfortable with them, having known them for several years.

The group visited for a while, various individuals rotating from one conversation to another, until Father MacDonald called for everyone's attention. "All those attending Giuseppe's service, there are three limos waiting to take us to the church," he said. "Family will go in the first car, museum and team colleagues in the second, and all other guests in the third. We will leave in a few moments."

He turned to Josh and Isabella. "I will be riding with the family," he said, "but I will wait for you on the steps of the church when we arrive."

The cathedral was about a mile away, through fairly thick traffic, but they left in plenty of time and arrived at about ten minutes till two. The body was already prepped and lying in state at the front of the church, which Josh thought more efficient than the American tradition of a long funeral procession that blocked up traffic and left the mourners waiting for the body to be carried into the church. The first limo discharged its passengers. Andrea and Guillermo and their spouses got out and headed up the stairs into the church, while Father MacDonald waited for them to get out and meet him.

"There is a small side pew reserved for those who are speaking," he said. "Follow me in and have a seat. I will get up and speak the eulogy after the organ finishes playing, then Isabella, and finally Joshua. Then I will conduct the funeral mass."

"Will there be a graveside service?" Josh asked.

"That will be conducted at sunset, and it is a private service for the family," said MacDonald.

Josh nodded in agreement and they headed up the steps. The cathedral was gorgeous, with five-hundred-year-old stained glass windows and a magnificent altar at the head of the long aisle. The people of Naples still referred to it as the "new cathedral," since it had not been built until 1519. He smiled inwardly as he thought of how proud his hometown in Oklahoma had been that there was a log cabin there built in 1840!

Within a few moments they were seated next to Father MacDonald up next to the altar, as the organ swelled and the choir joined in the beautiful introductory notes of Giuseppe Verdi's *Requiem*. The casket was open, and Rossini's face was calm and serene in death. The mortician had done a masterful job, not only of concealing the damage wrought by the blast, but also of giving the old archeologist a natural expression, with the subtlest hint of a smile playing about his lips. Josh thought his friend looked to be merely sleeping.

When the music fell silent, Father MacDonald rose and greeted the audience in English and then in Italian. He blessed them and thanked them for coming, and then spoke the eulogy he had been practicing.

"Friends and family," he said. "Giuseppe Anton Rossini was born in Capua in the year 1950. He was the child of Hermon Rossini and his wife Andrea, both now deceased. Raised as the son of an Army officer whose sense of justice saw him jailed for opposing Mussolini, and of a local farmer's daughter who married his father after the war, Giuseppe grew up to be one of the foremost archeologists of our time. He married Maria, the love of his life, in 1972, and they enjoyed thirty years of blissful marriage together before her passing ten years ago. Together they raised their children, Major Guillermo Rossini and his sister Andrea, to be respectable and solid citizens, children any father could be proud of. Until his devastating injury fifteen years ago, he was one of the most renowned field archeologists in the world. After he recovered, he told me his biggest regret was that his injury would keep him from fulfilling his secret dream—to make a find so significant that his name would never be forgotten!" MacDonald looked out at his audience. "It gives me some pleasure today to tell you that Giuseppe's prediction was wrong. Just weeks before his untimely end, he made the greatest discovery in the history of Biblical archeology! I imagine all of you have heard of the "Testimony of Pontius Pilate" by now. It was Giuseppe who discovered the chamber, and it was Giuseppe who discovered the letter from the Emperor Tiberius which was the first artifact recovered. And it was Giuseppe, together with myself and my colleagues, who found the scroll that has confirmed the teachings of the Church about Jesus of Nazareth before the whole world. It was a truth so big that the forces of evil had to try and destroy it, and although the *Testimonium* lives on, I am sad to say that Giuseppe fell victim to those who would keep its truth from being made known to the world."

Andrea was sobbing softly, and her husband took one of her hands while her brother grasped the other. "It is sad, dear child," said Father MacDonald. "It is always sad when good men are taken from us by those who have sold themselves to do evil. But we have a promise from on high that evil shall not endure. Our Lord founded a church and promised that the gates of hell should not prevail against it. He also promised that whosoever believed in him would have eternal life. I know that my friend Giuseppe believed. And because of that, I know that there will be a day when we will see him again."

He paused. "Giuseppe's children asked that those who knew him best during the last weeks of his life be allowed to stand and speak here today. Dr. Isabella Sforza was not only our team leader and colleague as we excavated Giuseppe's remarkable find, she also was a close friend and second daughter to him. She will now share her memories."

Isabella stood, the scar on her forehead from the blast still visible, and looked out at the cathedral. Several hundred people were there to pay their respects to one of Capri's most beloved residents, and one of Italian archeology's brightest stars. She cleared her throat and began to speak in Italian. Josh was able to follow most of what she said, although he did have to ask her about some of her remarks later.

"Giuseppe Rossini was my inspiration even before he was my friend," said Isabella. "When I was a schoolgirl he came and spoke about classical archeology at our school, and that day I found my vocation. When I went to college, he became my favorite teacher. I had the chance to work with him on one dig before his accident, while I was still an intern. He was kind, warm, and funny, and he and Maria would cook up the most wonderful dinners for all of us starving grad students. When I got my degree and began doing actual field work of my own, he was the one I called for advice and guidance. When he broke his leg, I came to see him in the hospital several times, and grieved with him when I realized that he would be handicapped for the rest of his life. When Maria died, I came to the funeral and he wept on my shoulder as if I were one of his own children. In turn, his kindness when my own husband passed five years ago, and again when I lost my dear papa not long afterwards, won him a place in my heart that no one else could hold."

There were tears streaming down her cheeks, but she swallowed hard and kept going. "Dr. Rossini was an archeologist through and through. Even with his limited mobility, he loved giving tours at Capri, identifying relics found by local children, teaching seminar classes in Naples every fall, and going to the primary school in Capri village and entertaining the children with his matchless stories about Caesar and Cato and Pompey the Great. I do not know how many young people he inspired to embrace the disciplines of history and archeology, but I know there are a dozen or more of them here today.

"Sharing those last weeks with him, as we uncovered the priceless artifacts from the chamber of Tiberius, was like seeing him turned young again. We laughed and celebrated, dug and catalogued, and even went out dancing the night after we returned to Naples with the wonderful artifacts we had recovered from the chamber. Giuseppe Rossini loved archeology, but more than that, he loved life. He loved people. He loved every member of our team. And it is my everlasting honor to say that he loved me too. Andrea, Guillermo, from this day forward I will consider you my siblings, if you will allow it. Because your father became a second father to me when my life was laid waste by grief. He helped me find the courage to keep on living, and he urged me to find love again before I grew too old to cherish it. He was the dearest friend I could have ever asked for." Overwhelmed with emotion, Isabella bowed her head and sobbed, then turned from the lectern and sat down next to Josh. He gave her hand a quick squeeze and stood.

His heart sunk. The church was more than a third full, a daunting prospect when you realized that it seated well over a thousand. The vast majority of them were Italian, and he had no idea if they would understand him or not. His prepared remarks suddenly seemed trite and feeble. But then he looked about a third of the way back and saw his mother and father, along with Luke and Alicia Martens. They were looking straight at him, and his father gave him a smile and a nod. Dr. Martens mouthed some words of encouragement. Suddenly Josh felt confident again.

"I came here from America two weeks ago," he said. "I was a last-minute replacement for a far more experienced archeologist, Dr. Martens, who was not able to travel at the time, although I am glad to see him here today. My job was to help with the excavation and translation of any ancient documents recovered at the Villa Jovis. One of the first people I met on Capri was Giuseppe Rossini. We hit it off

373

pretty quickly—at least, once he realized that I was not going to take advantage of his dear Isabella! We became good friends over the next two weeks. He was a tireless worker, a consummate professional, a fun-loving companion, and a steadfast friend. Although our acquaintance was very brief, I had already come to regard him as one of my best friends by the time last Friday's awful events happened. I helped rescue him from the rubble and was able to spend a few moments with him in the recovery room after he got out of surgery. When we heard that he had succumbed to his wounds, I wept for a brother I had barely come to know, but already treasured. You may find it odd that I refer to a man so much older than me as my brother, but I want to explain my choice of words."

He looked across the audience. Guillermo and Andrea were looking at him intently, with a kindness that touched him deeply. He cleared his throat and continued. "All of you know what we found—a first-hand account of the trial and execution of Jesus of Nazareth, and a direct reference to His resurrection from the dead. Some are saying that this is the first-ever eyewitness account of those events, but Giuseppe and I knew that was not true. All the *Testimonium* did was confirm what the Gospel writers told us long ago: that Jesus rose from the dead on the third day, in accordance with prophecy, triumphing over death and proving once and for all that what He said about Himself was true—that He really was the Son of God. Giuseppe and I had talked at length about what we might find, and what we did find, in that tiny hidden chamber. He was like many of you—he had been raised in the Church, but never gave a great deal of thought to his faith. In the wake of his wife's death, he had questioned God, but he had never abandoned Him. I have believed all my life that the Jesus of the Gospels is the Jesus of history—that He really was the Son of God, and that the New Testament does accurately record His teachings, and that of his disciples. What we found on Capri forced Giuseppe to reconsider his beliefs about the Gospels, and to rediscover his faith in Christ before the end. After Friday's horrible events, Guillermo found this Bible on his father's nightstand, open to the Gospel of John. This verse was underlined: *I am the resurrection and the life; he that believes in me, though he were dead, yet shall he live. And he that lives and believes in me shall never die. Believest thou this?* In the margin next to it, Giuseppe had written 'I do!' and underlined it."

Many of the audience were listening intently, and some of them were sobbing softly. Josh looked directly at them, and finished his statement. "I am here, like you, to mourn the loss of a friend. But I am also here to tell you that Giuseppe Rossini is not lost to us forever. He waits for us by the side of that same Jesus he believed in so fervently before the end. I can think of no finer tribute to this good man than each of you finding your way to the same faith that he found." By now his own voice was catching, and as he sat down his own tears finally came. He glanced through them and looked at the still figure in the coffin. *Goodbye, my friend*, he thought. *We shall meet again.* He watched as Father MacDonald got up and led the audience through the majestic cadences of the funeral mass, and Isabella caught his hand and held it tight as they bowed in prayer together.

* * *

The funeral service made the news all over Italy that night, and some of the remarks of all three team members were broadcast. Even the big news networks gave some time to Rossini's service on their international news segments. From his cheap hotel room, Ibrahim Abbasside watched with contempt as all three of the archeologists—the priest, the American fundamentalist, and the Italian harlot—wept over the coffin of the dead infidel. *Weaklings!* he thought. *In the end, that is why the forces of the Prophet would triumph. Westerners shrank from death, grieved at it, wept over it. The jihadi embraced it smiling, knowing that it was nothing more than a glorious transition to the ever-flowing streams of paradise, and the houris waiting to service the faithful for all eternity.* He knew that, one day, his own hour of martyrdom would come, and he hoped to face it bravely and resolutely.

Suddenly his cell phone rang. He was startled, as very few had his number.

"Yes?" he answered cautiously.

"This is Ali's pet store," said the voice on the other end. "I just wanted to let you know that the pet supplies are ready for delivery."

"You did not have to call to tell me that," he said in a deadly calm tone. *This had better be important*, he thought.

"Actually, I did," the voice said. "Someone tried to steal the supplies. An employee of mine, actually. But he failed, and is no longer working for the store."

375

Abbasside was shocked. An informant in the cell! He had picked most of these men himself! "This will not interfere with the timely delivery, will it?" he asked.

"Not at all," said Falladah. "He did not know the delivery address or the date yet, so your products should arrive safe and sound."

"Excellent!" said Abbasside. "I will call you Thursday to arrange pickup."

<<<TRANSCRIPT OF A PHONE CONVERSATION FROM THE CIA'S COUNTERTERRORISM OFFICE, APRIL 25, 20** BETWEEN COL. LINCOLN BERTRAND AND FIELD AGENT DOMINGO GARCIA>>>

GARCIA: Colonel, we have bad news!

BERTRAND: What is it, Dingo?

GARCIA: Remember I told you that two sleeper cells had been activated? Well, I had an inside man in one of them. Been in place five years, and never a hint he had been made. He told us there was a large cache of weapons at a storage facility south of Rome, and that his group was detailed to go pick them up for an impending big op. We were going to swoop in and nab them in the act, see if we could sweat a couple of them into giving up the Ethiopian. But it was a set-up!

BERTRAND: How bad?

GARCIA: Bad, boss. They cleaned out the weapons hours before we got there, and all we found was my agent with his head cut off and severe burns to his lower abdomen. I am guessing that they got everything he knew from him before he died. Not many people can keep mum when they have a blowtorch aimed at their crotch.

BERTRAND: Damn! That's about as bad as it can get. I am going to tell the Italians they will need massive security on that transport route. I am guessing they are going for the scroll and everyone associated with it.

GARCIA: I think you are right, boss, and we just lost our inside link. I am activating every asset and tapping every line I can, to see if I can figure out when and where. But if you have not warned the Italians yet, I think it's time.

BERTRAND: Agreed, Dingo. Stay on it, keep me informed.

GARCIA: Aye, sir. Garcia out.

CHAPTER TWENTY-FIVE

Josh slept soundly the night of the funeral, his dreams chasing each other through his head, until his wake-up call came at 6 AM. He rolled out of bed, splashed cold water in his face, and donned his trunks. He figured it was time to resume his normal routines as much as possible, so he went down to the pool, swimming a dozen laps or so. The aches and pains of the blast were fading away quickly as his body healed itself, and the water felt soothing to him, as it always did. He was out of the pool well before seven, and took a hot shower when he got back to his room. He grabbed a quick and light breakfast, and then called his mom and dad's room.

"Good morning, Dad!" he said. They had spent a good part of the evening together after supper, but it had been a subdued visit, everyone still recovering emotionally from the emotional service that afternoon. Isabella had been unusually quiet, and wound up heading back to her apartment early in the evening. Josh had also retired early.

"Hello, son!" his father said. "Did you rest well?"

"Slept like a log," Josh replied. "Have you and Mom thought about my invitation?" Josh had invited them to come to the museum with him that morning and see the Pilate scroll for themselves.

"I think we would enjoy it very much," his dad said. "We are finishing up breakfast, and can meet you in the lobby in about thirty minutes."

"See you there," Josh said. He sat down at his desk and used the next half hour to answer some of the letters from the massive stack he'd received over the weekend. They were still coming in, but the flood was starting to slow down some. Three-quarters of them were junk of one variety or another—hate mail, crackpot theories, and love letters from total strangers. But he still had a stack of over 100 that he had designated worthy of a reply. He had his laptop hooked up to a small printer, and was pretty fast on the keyboard. He managed to get about five letters written, printed, and addressed before heading downstairs to meet his folks at 8:00.

It was a gorgeous morning, and they walked the short distance to the museum, chatting about friends and family members back home. His dad had spent the evening emailing and calling friends back in Texas and Oklahoma, catching them up on events and touching base with his church. He had agreed to return home Friday, so as not to miss two Sundays in a row.

Once they got to the museum, Josh had to call Dr. Castolfo to get his parents cleared through security, and they took the elevator down to the lab. Father MacDonald and Isabella were already there when they arrived.

"Good morning, lad!" said the irrepressible Scot. "Reverend and Mrs. Parker, good to see you two again."

"Delighted to be here, Father," said Louise Parker. "Joshua promised us a quick peek at the Pilate scroll this morning."

"Well, here it is," said MacDonald. "Impressive, isn't it?"

It was indeed an impressive sight. The *Testimonium* was neatly placed on the center of a large, stainless steel table, covered with its clear plexiglass box, resting on a black plastic stand that had been specifically crafted over the last few days to hold it in position and display the ancient papyrus in a visually striking manner. The scroll appeared to float above the blackness of the stand, the ancient Latin letters leaping from the page in their clarity.

Josh's dad leaned forward, his nose inches from the glass as he studied the ancient papyrus. He studied it a long time in silence. "Amazing," he finally said. "Not just that it dates to the time of Jesus, but that it was actually written by the man who presided over his trial. You can even see the distinct handwriting changes where Pilate takes over for his scribe, and then down here where Tiberius added his comments. Oh, how I wish my Latin weren't so rusty! We studied it in high school when I was a kid, but in college and seminary I focused on Greek because that was the language of the New Testament."

Louise Parker was also studying the scroll. "Even having read the text and heard the tale of its discovery, it is still hard for me to believe that the writing is so crisp and clear after twenty centuries. It is such a shame that all the other artifacts from the chamber were destroyed!"

"We have recovered far more than we thought we might," said Dr. Castolfo. "The sword that belonged to Julius Caesar is still intact and in its scabbard, after being hurled aloft and coming down on the windshield of my car! We also recovered the original Tiberius letter, his signet ring, two unbroken pollen sample vials, and the pendant from the reliquary. The will of Augustus Caesar was burned pretty badly, but we did salvage about one-third of the scroll. The salvage workers have folders full of pictures of all the artifacts we recovered on Capri, and are watching for them as they clear the rubble from the site."

Josh smiled. "That is more than they had the last time we talked," he said. "I am excited that so much has been recovered."

His dad straightened and looked over his glasses at Josh. "Any way I could get a look at that sword, son?" he asked.

"I don't see why not," Josh said. "Dr. Castolfo?"

The president of the Antiquities Board nodded, and Josh opened the sealed cabinet where the sword was kept. Donning a pair of acid-free gloves, he carefully lifted the ancient blade out and pulled it from its scabbard.

Ben Parker gave a low whistle of amazement. "My word," he said, "it's not even rusted over! I've got hunting knives that are in worse shape than that!"

"That sword was really carried by Julius Caesar?" his mother asked.

"This inscription is from his mother." Josh pointed at the Latin words. "Aurelia Cotta dedicated it to her son, and said 'Wield it with honor.' Apparently he bequeathed it to Octavian, who gave it to his adopted son Tiberius."

She studied the ancient *gladius*. "I remember as a schoolgirl, my Latin teacher had us read *The Gallic Wars* in the original language. He would dress up in a toga and go on and on and on about Caesar, the greatest Roman of them all! He would just die if he knew that I was looking at Caesar's sword."

"Joshua," said his dad, "thank you for letting us come and take a look at your finds. I know you have a busy day ahead of you, and I don't want to use up any more of your time. Dear, let's get out of our son's way and let him get back to work."

"I'll walk you to the front," said Josh. He led his parents back to the elevator and they boarded together.

"Thank you son," said his dad. "That was something to see!"

"You can't imagine how exciting it was watching those things come out of the chamber," he said. "The sword was completely unexpected. It was buried in a thick layer of stone dust, and when Simone uncovered it we were all stunned!"

"I guess we will see you at Dr. Apriceno's funeral this afternoon," said his mom.

"I am not looking forward to it," said Josh, "But I'm not dreading it as much as I did Giuseppe's. Not that I didn't love Simone, but I haven't been asked to speak at her service, so I can just sit in the audience and cry with everyone else."

"You did very well yesterday, my boy," said his dad. "There is no such thing as an easy funeral, but you spoke very eloquently."

"I never met the man, but you made me wish I had," his mother said.

"I couldn't even open my mouth until I looked out there and saw you two," Josh said. "You have always been there for me, and words can't say how grateful I am."

"What else are parents for, dear?" Mrs. Parker asked.

Josh walked them to the door and saw them off, and then returned to the lab. Dr. Martens had arrived, and Isabella and Father MacDonald pulled some chairs around one of the extra tables. Castolfo and Guioccini joined them.

Guioccini spoke first. "Dr. Martens, you were my first choice to be a part of this team, but could not be here when the excavation began. Joshua has done an admirable job in your place, but since our numbers are cruelly reduced, would you consider stepping in as a fourth member of our group? Even though the excavation is complete, there is still much to do in curating and cataloguing the remaining artifacts, and any others that we may recover from the wreckage of our lab."

"I should be delighted, Bernardo, but as you can see by these crutches, I am still not fully mobile. I find myself depending on my wife's help to get around," said Martens. "But, if you would be willing to allow her full access to the lab to help me when I need her, I will accept your kind offer."

Guioccini looked over at Castolfo, who nodded. "Welcome aboard to you, and your lovely wife, old friend!" he said. "I look forward to getting to know her."

Castolfo spoke next. "We will be transporting the scroll to Rome for further testing on Friday, to be conducted by Dr. Henderson from the Smithsonian. I am very concerned that the terrorists who tried to destroy it before may strike again while we are in transit. We are arranging some very heavy security for the day—we do not want to risk the scroll's safety. The police and the army will be assisting."

"The army?" Josh asked. "Wow! That seems a little extreme—but, then again, so does blowing up a lab to destroy a two-thousand-year-old scroll!"

"We are dealing with extremists here, lad, no doubt about that," said MacDonald. "I just wonder how many, and how well organized, they are."

"I am amazed that any of the papyrus survived the blast at all," said Dr. Martens. "And we found pieces of two documents?"

Guioccini nodded. "The Tiberius scroll was fused to the top of that ancient writing desk," he said. "The desk was broken by the blast, but only the legs landed in the flames. The top of the desk, with the papyrus attached, came down in an area of rubble that never caught fire, thanks to the quick response of the local fire trucks, and the sprinkler system, which did function briefly in the area of the lab left standing. As for the will of Augustus, it was apparently blown into the air and set ablaze, but came down in a puddle of water which saved part of it."

"I must admit, although they were a pain to work with, I will miss not being able to piece together all those ancient documents that the rats had chewed," said Josh.

"Well," said Castolfo, "so far we have recovered none of the fragments. I think the drawer that they were in was completely consumed by the flames. But we will be able to digitally piece them together—the two graduate assistants Father MacDonald assigned had just finished photographing all of them shortly before the blast."

"Excellent!" said Josh. "We found a few fair-sized fragments that had interesting contents. It will be neat to see if we can piece together enough to make complete documents. There was so much potential for understanding Augustan Rome in those pages!"

"I'm sorry I didn't get to poke through those myself," said Martens. "The idea of reading the personal correspondence of Tiberius Caesar— it's a classical historian's dream!"

The phone in the corner rang, and Guioccini picked it up.

"Excellent!" he said in Italian. "I shall be right up to escort him here personally." He hung up and turned to the others. "Dr. Henderson is here," he said.

"I look forward to seeing him again," said Martens. "He and I had a fascinating conversation at the Smithsonian's annual ball last year that got interrupted. I'd enjoy finishing it."

Moments later, Guioccini returned with Dr. Henderson in tow. Behind them trailed two young college-aged men, dressed in khaki pants and polo shirts, each one carrying large briefcases and clipboards. The team rose, Josh helping Dr. Martens with his crutches. "Andy!" bellowed Martens. "How good to see you again!"

"Luke!" said the Smithsonian paleographer. "You look a bit the worse for wear, my old friend!"

"Occupational hazard of having a younger spouse, I suppose," replied Martens. "So who are these two youngsters?"

"These are my two lab assistants, Cameron Hargrove and Justin Arnold," said Henderson. "They will be helping me measure and photograph the scroll so that we can be ready for testing on Friday. I have brought some equipment with me, so that we can begin to do some preliminary work today."

"By all means," said Guioccini. "We want to confirm the authenticity of all the pieces we found, but this one above all because it is so important to so many people."

Henderson nodded to his assistants, and they placed their cases on the table on either side of the *Testimonium*, and began pulling out various pieces of equipment. Meanwhile Henderson reached into his pocket and pulled out an old, well-worn, 15x lighted loupe.

"Gadgets are great, but for my first look at an important manuscript, I always prefer to kick it old school," he said. "You would be amazed how many things you can spot with a simple old hand-held magnifier like this, especially when it has different lights attached."

"Different lights?" said Isabella.

"Watch," said the professor. He flicked a small thumb switch on the side of the loupe's handle, and a powerful beam of light emerged from just below the magnifying glass, illuminating whatever it was pointed at.

"I have seen that before," she said. "I have used them on occasion. But that is just plain old white light!"

"Not done yet!" he said. There was a small wheel switch just below the lens, and he rolled it with his thumb. Immediately the light switched to UV. He scrolled it again to get infrared, and then a strong, greenish beam. "Handiest thing in the world for checking fluorescent properties," he said. "Flint authenticators use them to look for modern tool marks on fake projectile points."

"You've been lurking on the dark side!" said Josh. "Not many archeologists will admit to even knowing a collector, much less a commercial authenticator!"

Henderson laughed. "I realized a few years ago that the average collector of flint points and knives knows far more about them than the average archeologist," he said. "We are big picture guys, and they focus exclusively on complete tool forms. In the process, some of them acquire a lot of expertise. I'm willing to poach knowledge wherever I can find it. Now, can we take that cover off the scroll?"

Josh grabbed one end and Guioccini grabbed the other, and they lifted the plexiglass cover off of the *Testimonium*. Henderson leaned in very close and inhaled deeply, careful to turn his head before exhaling. Then he straightened up and smiled.

"Your stabilizing solution does mask a lot of the aroma," he said to MacDonald. "But there is still no smell in the world like ancient papyrus. I find it more exciting than the sweetest cologne!"

He clicked the light on his loupe and began poring over the ancient scroll line by line, occasionally switching the color of the light to study the ink or some of the ancient spots of stain and discoloration. His two assistants assembled a small, rolling tripod and mounted a digital camera with an enormous lens on it, canted at a slight downward angle. Then one of them pulled out what appeared to be a large remote control and hit a couple of the buttons. A small motor whirred as the tripod rolled across the table toward the scroll for a few inches, and then stopped.

"What on earth is that?" Joshua asked.

One of them—Josh wasn't sure yet which was Cameron and which was Justin—turned and answered.

"A little device Dr. Henderson invented," he said. "The small servomotor moves the tripod smoothly, without any vibration. It will give us a clear, sharp video image, better than any handheld camera could manage."

"Impressive," said Isabella, coming up behind Josh and putting her hand on his shoulder. She stared at the ancient scroll that Dr. Henderson was studying so closely. "It's still hard to believe it all," she commented. "The chamber, the artifacts, the scroll and the story it tells, the deaths of our friends, the crazy publicity—every morning I wake up and wonder if it was all just a dream."

"Are you OK?" Josh asked. "You've been awfully quiet since the funeral."

She nodded toward the elevator, and he turned to Castolfo and Guioccini. "I imagine he is going to be awhile examining the scroll," said Josh. "I think we may head up to the cafeteria and get a bite to eat."

"Take your time, Josh," said Martens. "I'll text you when he is done."

The two of them got in the elevator and went to the third-floor cafeteria. Josh got a sweet roll and some cola, and Isabella ordered a small fruit salad. There were quite a few tourists coming and going, but they found a quiet corner and sat down facing each other.

"So tell me what is on your mind," he said to Isabella. "It hurts me to see you so quiet and sad."

"I guess I am just mourning for my friend," she said. "That's most of it."

"And the rest?" he asked gently.

"Well," she said, "after I listened to you at the funeral yesterday, I went back home and read the rest of John's Gospel. There was so much there that I had forgotten—or perhaps never even knew to begin with. I am wrestling with the whole concept of belief right now. John's claims about Jesus are so extraordinary, and yet the proofs he lays down are very convincing! I would reject it all as simply good propaganda, but the *Testimonium* confirms so many of the details of Jesus' trial, it makes it very hard for me to doubt the overall truth of the rest of the story. There is part of me that teeters on the brink of faith, wanting to go ahead and take the plunge and cry out 'I believe!' But something keeps holding me back."

"What is it?" he asked.

"Well," she went on, "some of it is just good old-fashioned scientific skepticism. That God should become a carpenter in a backwater province of the Empire two thousand years ago—ten years of higher education screams to reject such silliness! And yet that same education has forced me to accept that the *Testimonium* must be authentic. And, to be honest, some of it is personal. Belief demands action, doesn't it? Taking that step of faith will mean giving up control of my life. I have worked so hard to be independent; the idea of surrendering to anyone—even God—scares me to death! And so I sit here, miserable and conflicted, pulled in two directions and not sure which way to go."

Josh took her hand. "Do you trust me?" he asked.

"Of course!" she said. "How could I not, after all we have been through?"

"Think about it," he said. "Why do you trust me?"

"Because you saved my life at the risk of your own," she said. "Because you are good, and decent, and honorable. And, most of all, because I have fallen in love with you!"

"Isabella," he said, "I am not that good. Decent? My thoughts are as polluted as anyone's. I am one flawed, sinful, mortal human being. But I do love you, and I am flattered and astonished that you return my love, and that you are willing to trust me. But if you can trust me, and love me, a wicked, fallen, mortal creature, how can you not trust a loving and perfect God—who has no wickedness in Him, who loves you more perfectly than I ever possibly could?"

She sighed. "Because I don't know Him!" she wailed. "I know about Him, but I don't know Him like I know you! And I'm a little bit afraid of Him. He sent His own Son to the cross—what sacrifice might He require of me? I have lost so much already!"

"That's where faith comes in," said Josh. "At some point, you just have to put your trust in the goodness and love of God, and invite Him in."

She bowed her head, pressing his knuckles against her forehead. "I just wish it was that easy," she said softly.

Josh's cell phone chimed, and he looked at the incoming text. "Looks like Dr. Henderson has finished his initial examination of the text," he said. "Let's go hear what he thinks of our find."

They walked back to the elevator hand in hand, each one thinking about what the other had said. Josh was hoping that Isabella's doubts would give way at some point, that she would see a clear path to embracing the faith that was so important to him. Isabella was wondering if she could ever find the strength to do so.

They entered the lab with lighter hearts than they left with—each of them felt a measure of comfort and strength in confiding in the other. Alicia had joined her husband at the table, and Isabella took a long look at them as she and Josh sat down. How confident they seemed, in their love for each other and their love of God!

Dr. Henderson had been taking a last, long look at the *Testimonium*, but as they sat down he turned and faced the group. "Well," he said, "what I can tell you with confidence is this: we are either looking at an authentic papyrus manuscript from the first century, or else we are looking at the cleverest forgery I have ever seen."

Isabella bristled. "Don't tell me you think there is any credence to the venomous slurs that Tintoretto has been—" she began.

Henderson held up his hand. "Hundred-year-old Vatican conspiracy theories?" he said. "I seriously doubt it. I am familiar with Dr. Tintoretto and her anti-Church crusade. I know all of you by reputation at least, and several of you personally. I have no doubt of your professionalism, and I have watched the video footage of the excavation. I believe you! But, we are talking about a document that will have a powerful influence on the faith of over one billion human beings—perhaps more. What I believe is immaterial. What the tests will prove beyond all doubt is whether or not the *Testimonium* was in fact written in the first century AD. The papyrus looks right, the ink looks right, and the document gives every apparent, visible sign of great age. But C-14 dating will confirm the accuracy of our assessments, and prove beyond all doubt the antiquity of this remarkable manuscript." He paused and looked at the papyrus again. "Or it will prove we have been the victims of the hoax of the century!"

"Well, the reason we chose you to conduct these tests is because your expertise and integrity are above reproach," said Dr. Castolfo. "We will have the scroll in Rome first thing Friday morning so that you may begin the testing process. Is there anything else we can do while you are here?"

"Of course!" said the Smithsonian paleographer. "I want to see every scrap of papyrus that you still have from the excavation. The *Testimonium* is important, but that does not change the fact that you also uncovered the oldest extant writings of a Roman statesman. In fact, to the best of my knowledge, what you have are the only known handwriting samples of ANY Roman emperor—except for a few Byzantine letters dating from the Medieval era. And those rulers were Roman in name only. I want to see the other things you have found."

They spent the rest of the morning pulling out the items from the chamber on Capri one at a time. Henderson stared, examined, measured, and photographed artifacts for the next three hours, sometimes calling in his assistants to help him take close-up photographs and measurements. He seemed equally interested in everything—he used as much time to examine Caesar's sword as he did the letter from Tiberius. The signet ring he examined for a long time, and when he got to the beautiful cameo of Vipsania, he studied it with a fascination bordering on reverence. Last of all, he read and examined the remaining portion of the will of Caesar Augustus, shaking his head sadly at the burned edges.

The Capri team watched him with interest at first, and finally decided to leave him to it, sitting at the table and talking quietly as they waited, occasionally answering questions from the American or from his two grad students. Finally, Henderson finished examining every remaining artifact from the Villa Jovis chamber, and sat down at the table with them.

"So what do you think, old friend?" asked Luke Martens.

"You know, I have examined some remarkable artifacts in my time," said Henderson. "But I can honestly say that I have never wanted to be part of the original excavation team quite as much as I wish I could have been with you folks two weeks ago. This is truly an amazing discovery!"

"Any doubts, based on your initial examination of the artifacts?" asked Josh.

"Not really," said Henderson. "Granted, the naked eye can only detect and measure so much, but I see nothing here that is not one hundred percent consistent with an origin in the first century AD. What a shame so much was destroyed in the blast! Looking at the photographs, I could have spent months reassembling and restoring the shredded documents from the rat's nest!"

"Well, they are still sifting rubble out there," said Dr. Castolfo. "Perhaps they may yet find some of the remaining artifacts."

"I sincerely hope so," said Henderson. "In the meantime, I think my assistants and I are due to catch the evening train to Rome. I look forward to seeing you all in the new research lab there Friday morning."

"Allow us to escort you to the station," said Guioccini as he and Castolfo rose. "As for the rest of you, we will see you at the funeral in an hour."

* * *

Simone's service was a simple Catholic mass, followed by two touching eulogies, one from her daughter and one from her ex-husband, who seemed far and away the more grief-stricken of the two. For Josh and Isabella, seated in the audience with the board members and Dr. Martens, the sight of their raw pain was difficult to bear. Josh found tears running down his cheeks, and Isabella simply stared ahead, her gaze a mask of numbness. Josh could follow some of what Ricardo said, and Isabella later translated the rest for him. It was a deeply personal and very moving tribute.

"When I met Simone thirty years ago, she was a beautiful college student with a smile that lit up the room, and a laugh that seemed to make the stars themselves twinkle," he began. "She was also the most magnificent cook I ever met! How could any Italian man not want to make such an enchanting woman his own? We fell madly in love, but she made it clear from the beginning that her career was very important to her. I thought I would humor her, let her look at her silly ancient pollens for a while, until she realized that being home with me was much more fun than staring at ancient relics and taking samples back to the lab for testing. I was foolish. Her fascination with the past was not some schoolgirl fad, but a true vocation. I tried to tell myself that it was all right, but eventually I got jealous of her job, of her absences, of her constantly trying to tell me about her latest project, her latest dig. It was hardly fair—she had made it clear from the beginning that she wanted a career—but I began to resent her job as if it were a lover. And out of that resentment came anger, a desire to settle the score. I began to keep company with other women. She found out, we quarreled, and we split. It was the most petty and vile thing I ever did."

He broke down and sobbed a moment, then continued. "For a while I told myself I was happier this way; that my girlfriends were more fun than she ever had been; that they did not have careers that took them away from me for weeks at a time. But to tell you the truth, they were boring. Not a one of them had her smile, her brains, or her common sense. It did not take me long to realize what a precious jewel I had cast aside. So I tried to come back to her." He swallowed hard and looked at the closed casket. "But I had hurt her too deeply. She did not give her heart away lightly, and I had broken it. I kept telling myself that I could make amends, that I could make things right again. We talked on the phone every now and then, and I would beg her to trust me just a little bit. Over the last year, I began to think that the ice was melting. I dared to hope that we could be together again one day. She even called me when the group she was working with returned from Capri, to tell me how exciting the dig had been. I asked her if I could see her when it was done, and she said yes!"

He put his hands over his face, and his whole body was racked with sobs. His daughter came up to him and put her hands on his shoulders, and he looked up again. "But it was too late!" he said. "I lost the most precious thing I ever possessed—the trust of a woman who truly loved me. No, lost is too flimsy a word. I threw her trust away. I discarded it out of pure selfishness, and I never got it back. Oh, Simone, if you can hear me now, I hope you know just how sorry I truly am! I would pour my heart's blood out on this altar just to see you smile at me one more time!"

He suddenly looked up at the mourners in the church. Every eye was staring directly at him. He raised his head high and addressed them directly. "That is probably not the eulogy that you were expecting," he said. "But it is what is in my heart. My wife was the most beautiful woman I have ever known, inside and out, and I cast her aside. I would tell every man here—never make such a mistake! You will never find anything that will take the place of your first love."

With that he sat down heavily, and the air seemed to go out of him. Lucretia Apriceno patted him on the shoulder, and then took her own stand behind the pulpit.

"That was not exactly the kind of remarks that my father and I discussed beforehand!" she said. "But scripts are boring, my mother used to say. Life is far more bitter and sweet than anything we can dream up. I will say this about my mother and father both: they always loved me, even when they forgot, for a while, how much they loved each other. Mama taught me her love of the past, and her love of the kitchen, as well as her love of life itself. I was never bored when I stayed with her, because she taught me how to enjoy everything that she loved to do. When she was studying ancient pollens, she bought me a microscope and taught me how to tell them apart, and what distinguished them from modern ones. When she baked lasagna, she showed me every detail of the recipe, and served me the first slice. When I wanted to go to my first dance, she put on her cassettes and we spent an entire afternoon learning every possible step to every popular song, so that I would not feel awkward on the dance floor. I could not have asked for a better mother."

A single tear formed and slid down her cheek. "She called me right after the discoveries from Capri were made public. She told me that the contents of the Pilate scroll had removed the lingering doubts she had harbored about God for many years. And she said that if God could forgive a contrary old hen like herself, then she probably ought to find it in her heart to forgive my father, too. Just a few days later, I saw the blast on the news, and then got the call that she was one of the victims. I felt as if my heart had been ripped out and stomped upon, but as I have had time to reflect, and to talk with her friends, I can honestly say that I am glad she died without any bitterness in her heart. As much as I might wish that she and Papa had gotten back together and enjoyed the autumn of their lives as a couple, it comforts me to know that love between them never died completely. I will miss her, but I will do my best to honor her, every day of my life, by being the kind of woman she taught me to be—the kind of woman she was. I love you forever, Mama!"

With that her resolve gave way, and she sat down next to her father. The two of them clung to each other as the choir sang the requiem mass, and the pall bearers carried the casket out of the church. Josh and Isabella stood with the rest of the congregation as they walked by, leaning on each other. After the funeral procession left the cathedral, he looked down at the beautiful Italian who had stolen his heart.

"I can't promise you much," he said. "But I promise you this—I will never have to speak such words over you. You will always have my heart, and you will always have my promise to be true."

She smiled, though her face was still wet with tears. "Of course you will be true," she said. "You are not Italian!"

<<<TRANSCRIPT OF A PHONE CONVERSATION FROM THE CIA'S COUNTERTERRORISM OFFICE, APRIL 26, 20** BETWEEN COL. LINCOLN BERTRAND AND ITALIAN SECURITY AGENT ANTONIO LUCOCCINI>>>

BERTRAND: Good morning, Agent Lucoccini. I am Lincoln Bertrand, with the CIA's counter-terrorism office.

LUCOCCINI: Yes, Colonel, your reputation precedes you! May I presume this is not a social call?

BERTRAND: That is correct, sir. I need to pass on a warning, and I was told that you were more trustworthy than the Naples Police Department.

LUCOCCINI: That is a harsh assessment, but not inaccurate. Chief Zadora is a scrupulously honest policeman who has implemented many reforms, but corruption is an epidemic among the rank and file that it will take a generation to root out. Tell me your warning, and I will do my best to see it is acted upon.

BERTRAND: There are two jihadist sleeper cells in Italy that we have been watching for some time now. Both have been activated and have gone off the grid completely. Our inside man was brutally murdered yesterday. We have reason to believe that the master terrorist known as "the Ethiopian" is in Italy, and may now be the operational commander of these two cells.

LUCOCCINI: Merda! We have been trying to nail that bastardo ever since he killed several of our medical nuns in Somalia in the 1990s. Shot them in the back at point blank range and then urinated on their corpses! Help us nail him and the government of Italy will be very grateful!

BERTRAND: I wish we could be of more help, but all I can say for sure at this point is that we believe his target will be the scroll known as the Testimonium. For religious reasons, the jihadists are scared to death of this thing. I imagine they will also want to kill the scientists that excavated it.

LUCOCCINI: We have already figured that an attempt might be made on the scroll when it is transported to Rome for testing. We have arranged for full security—two armored personnel carriers, an armored car for the scroll and the scientists, and several police cars as well. They will have a full-scale battle on their hands if they decide to take us on!

BERTRAND: It is good to hear you take this threat so seriously, but I will remind you of two things. First of all, these jihadists will be very well armed. There was a large weapons cache in a storage unit south of Rome that is now gone. I imagine they will have at least one RPG launcher. And one more thing—

LUCOCCINI: Yes?

BERTRAND: In our experience, the Ethiopian is very good at thinking a step or two ahead of his competition. So—be careful out there!

LUCOCCINI: Good advice. Can you keep me apprised of any new intelligence that you develop?

BERTRAND: I have an agent on the ground monitoring the situation. He will contact you if there is anything further to share. He will identify himself only as "Dingo." I have given him your number.

LUCOCCINI: Will your country be interested in interviewing the Ethiopian if we can catch him alive?

BERTRAND: Yes indeed. He is one of the most highly placed Al Qaeda officers still at large, and we could probably get some very valuable information from him—and there is also the matter of at least three dead CIA agents that we can lay at his doorstep. One of them was a friend of mine. The Ethiopian barbecued his face at point blank range with a small flamethrower of some sort. So yes, we would be very interested in . . . interviewing him.

LUCOCCINI: I take a rather old-fashioned view of justice, my friend. You know Italy no longer has a death penalty.

BERTRAND: We do.

CHAPTER TWENTY-SIX

That evening Josh and Isabella had dinner with Dr. Martens and Alicia. Reverend and Mrs. Parker had decided to take the train up to Rome the day after the funeral and see the sights before heading home, so they had retired early to pack up and rest. The two couples sat in the penthouse restaurant of the hotel, having decided to enjoy more traditional Italian cuisine in place of sushi.

Josh took a bite of a hot bread roll dipped in olive oil. "I don't understand why you Italians aren't the most obese nation on earth, eating this many carbs with every meal!" he said.

Isabella smiled. "It's the olive oil," she said. "Cooking agent of the gods! One reason the Romans lived longer than the other races of antiquity was the huge amounts of this stuff they consumed—that, and the fact that they despised beef. Romans loved fish and seafood, poultry, and occasionally pork or other more exotic meats, but they consumed far more fruit and vegetables than they did red meat."

Josh nodded. "That may be, but a mere decade of mortality is a small price to pay for a well-cooked cheeseburger with bacon!"

She shook her head. "Americans!" she said.

"Don't knock it till you've tried it, Izza!" said Alicia. Somewhere over the last three days she had bestowed this nickname on Isabella, who seemed not to mind it at all. "A good bacon burger is pretty hard to beat!"

"Well, I think Dr. Henderson was pretty impressed with your discovery," said Martens.

"I don't see how anyone could review all the evidence and come to any other conclusion," said Isabella. "The discovery was in such obviously ancient context, there is no way any of the artifacts could have been planted!"

Martens nodded. "I will tell you something, Dr. Sforza," he said. "People who do not want to believe will find a reason not to. I had a co-worker a few years ago who used to ridicule me to no end for believing in Christ. He accused me of pimping out science to serve the interest of those he called 'brain dead fundamentalist yahoos'! I sat and talked till I was blue in the face about all the valid, historical reasons for accepting the New Testament as an authentic, eyewitness account of the life and ministry of Jesus. No matter how thoroughly I thought I had proved my case, he managed to poke holes in it, and question everything I believed in. Proof and evidence didn't matter—he had convinced himself the Gospels were fairy tales, and no amount of persuading would convince him otherwise. As I got to know him better, I found out that he was a compulsive womanizer—a true sex addict, in fact. He was terrified of religion, because he knew that believing in Christ would require him to change his lifestyle, or acknowledge the eternal consequences. So, for him, it was safer not to believe—even at the cost of complete cognitive dissonance!"

Isabella looked at him with interest. "You know, Josh and I have talked about this at some length," she said. "Why does God care who, or with how many partners, we choose to have sex? The drive is a natural part of our biological nature, so why should He punish us for engaging in it?"

Martens nodded. "It is probably the biggest single impediment to belief for young people in the Western world today," he said. "I remember a quip from some comedian I was listening to once, he said that 'if it weren't for that whole "thou shalt not commit adultery" thing, France would still be Christian today!' But honestly, God has never based His commandments and standards on what people enjoy the most, but rather on what is best for them. Is society best served by rampant promiscuity and unwed mothers? Any sociologist worth his salt will tell you that societies grow and thrive when the family unit is stable, and study after study has shown that children do best when raised in a home with both parents. Is any relationship ever improved by adultery? None that I have seen! Think about what Signor Apriceno said this afternoon. How much happier would he and Simone have been if he had never strayed! God guides us, not towards the short term thrill, but towards the long-term ideal. However, I have found that, in following His plan, the short-term can be pretty amazing too!" He leaned over and planted a kiss on his younger bride's cheek.

Alicia squeezed his hand and spoke up. "There is this, too," she said. "I was a virgin when Luke and I married. He is the best man I have ever known and the only man I've known in an intimate sense. For however many years God gives us together, I know that I won't be comparing my husband to all the other lovers I have ever had. He will always be my first and my best!"

Martens blushed. "Unfortunately, I cannot say that," he said. "My first wife, God rest her soul, was a very special woman, and I will always love her memory. But my love for Alicia is something new and different, and so far she has not minded sharing me with the memory of the woman I lost. God put us together for a reason—even if, so far, she's managed to nearly kill me on more than one occasion!"

Alicia swatted his shoulder gently. "Don't blame me if you can't handle the bunny slopes, old man!" she said with a laugh.

Josh was amused. Dr. Martens had seemed rather stiff and formal when they first met, but Alicia had brought him out of his shell and turned him into a fun-loving, adventurous soul who was a joy to be around. Now that Josh knew them both better, he realized that Luke had still been grieving his first wife's death when Josh had met him. It had taken Alicia's warm, adventure-loving heart to give the archeologist a reason to emerge from his shell again. Looking across the table at them, he was happy for them both. The fifteen-year age difference seemed a little smaller and less troublesome every time he saw them together.

"So are you going to come visit the States when all this is over with?" asked Alicia. "I'd love to take you diving with me sometime!"

"That sounds wonderful!" said Isabella. "I don't know what my future plans are right now, but I hope that we can do that. I have enjoyed getting to know you so much! Italian archeology is pretty much a boy's club, and I get so tired of having to constantly prove myself to these silly jocks with degrees. It is nice to spend time with another woman my age!"

They passed that Tuesday evening in great happiness, the grief of the double funerals ebbing from them as they enjoyed good food and good company. The shock of the ordeal they had been through that awful Friday was still in the back of their minds, and both of them missed their lost friends, but the healing process had begun. Luke and Alicia Martens, Josh realized, had become an important part of that process. He had come to regard the American professor as more than a professional mentor in the last week, instead seeing him as a close friend, perhaps even an older brother. Alicia and he had been chums since college, although he had never had any romantic feelings for her—in fact, he had been shocked to find out that she had once been interested in him! But that, too, had worked out for the best. Luke needed her far worse than he had, and Josh had found the love of his life in Isabella.

That was the other thing that their terrible ordeal had cemented into place. When he first saw Isabella, he had found her charming and irresistible, an exotic stranger with a face that made his heart skip. Certainly that physical fascination was still there, but something else had grown alongside it—a realization that this was the woman he had waited for all these years. Isabella felt it too, he knew. Their conversations were no longer centered on whether or not they could overcome their differing backgrounds and beliefs about God, but rather how long that process would take. He had quit pushing Isabella on the subject of faith, instead trusting that God would draw her to Himself when the time was right.

After a big meal and an hour-long conversation over glasses of wine and iced tea—Josh had no problem with drinking in moderation, but he honestly found most wines to be nasty-tasting—the two couples separated. Josh walked Isabella down to the lobby, holding her hand and enjoying her company.

"Your friends are such good people," she said. "When I look at them, I see what I hope you and I can be someday."

"I was just thinking the same thing," he said.

"Excuse me, Dr. Parker, Dr. Sforza," said a familiar voice. They turned to see Drew Eastwood, the reporter from Chicago.

"Well, hello there!" Josh said, holding out his hand. "You know, I wanted to congratulate you on the article you did about our interview. It was one of the most straightforward pieces I have read about our work since this whole thing started."

Eastwood grinned. "You guys made it pretty easy," he said. "You are ideal interview subjects! But I am glad you liked it, because I wanted to ask you a small favor."

"By all means," said Isabella. "You have earned our trust by the honesty with which you covered our story. So what can we do for you?"

"I've been contacted by one of the major news networks," he said. "They want me to conduct an exclusive interview with you two on film, to be aired as an hour-long special on a major American network! They'd like it to include a tour of the chamber on Capri and a look at the lab where the scroll is being analyzed. We'd like to have a peek at the other artifacts that have survived the blast, and do an in-depth analysis of the story from the beginning. I won't lie to you; this could be a huge break in my career—a move from the print media to television is something reporters dream about! But I hope you know that I am not planning any kind of ambush. I would just like to actually walk the cameras through every stage of the excavation and analysis thus far, so the world can see how careful and thorough you have been."

Josh and Isabella looked at one another. Finally she spoke. "I can't give a final OK to something this big," she said, "but I do think it is a good idea. I will recommend to Dr. Castolfo and Dr. Sinisi that we go ahead with it. It will be good publicity for the museum, and for Italy, and I believe that you will do it properly and with a due respect to our friends. When could you be ready?"

Eastwood laughed. "They already flew a film crew over," he said. "I didn't exactly promise them you would agree to it, but I strongly hinted that you might."

Josh laughed. "Initiative is a good thing," he said. "What if we had said no?"

Drew smiled. "Well, you would have gotten to see my impressive begging skills up close and personal!" he said. "I have got the puppy dog eyes down pat!" He shot them a sad, woebegone look with his eyebrows drooping and his lower lip quivering that set them both laughing out loud.

"Well," said Isabella, "I am glad we did not force you to break out your heavy artillery! Now, if you gentlemen will excuse me, it is late and tomorrow will be a full day. I will call my superiors when I get home, Mr. Eastwood, and I may have a reply for you tonight or first thing in the morning, so be ready!" She leaned up and gave Josh a kiss on the cheek, then walked out the door and into the night. He placed his hand where her lips had touched and stared after her a moment, and then turned and found Eastwood watching him with some amusement.

"What are you looking at?" he demanded in mock anger.

"If I am not mistaken, a man who is in love!" the reporter replied.

Josh rolled his eyes. "You got that right," he said. "Are you staying here?" He nodded at the hotel around them.

"Just moved in yesterday," said Eastwood. "These network folks spare no expense!"

"I'm going to swim some laps before bedtime," Josh told him. "Feel free to grab a pair of trunks and join me!"

* * *

399

The next morning, Isabella met Josh at the door of the museum. Father MacDonald was with her, looking tired but relieved, no doubt, to have two very difficult funerals over and done with.

"Castolfo wants to see us about the Eastwood interview," she said. "I think we are going to get a green light."

"Excellent!" said Josh. "I think that Mr. Eastwood is the best and brightest member of the press I have met. He would be preferable to any of the talking heads we have met in the last two weeks."

"I haven't had the pleasure of meeting him, other than taking his questions at our press conference," said MacDonald, "But I must say his writing is first rate."

"I couldn't agree more," said Vincent Sinisi as he rounded the corner. "His prose is excellent, and he believes in the authenticity of your discovery, but he does not let that interfere with his journalistic objectivity. I was a bit curious as to why you singled him out for your exclusive interview, but his article was so impressive, I think you made an excellent choice. Come, my intrepid scholars, the board is waiting!"

They walked up to the boardroom, where Castolfo and Guioccini were standing and talking. The entire board was not present, but Cardinal Raphael and Doctors Stefani and Castellani were there. They all stood as Josh, Father MacDonald, and Isabella entered the room, and then Castolfo invited them all to sit around the conference table together.

"This is strictly an informal session," said Castolfo, "but I wanted to have a quorum here because we may need to officially decide some things before we adjourn from this ad hoc session. Signor Gandolfo cannot be here in person, as he has been meeting with the Prime Minister in Rome, but has asked that we call him and give the details of our decisions to him. Dr. Parker, Dr. MacDonald, both of you may consider yourselves as honorary members of this board for the remainder of your time in Italy. Your services and sacrifice have earned you the right to deliberate at this table as equals, not as hired consultants."

Josh swallowed hard. An honorary member of Italy's Bureau of Antiquities! That was a development he never would have anticipated!

"First of all," said Castolfo, "Isabella and Bernardo have relayed to the board your desire to grant a televised interview to the American journalist named Eastwood. His writing about the discoveries has been first-rate, and we are inclined to grant the request—on one condition. This is an Italian discovery, after all, made on Italian soil. So we wish for an Italian journalist to film this interview as well, so that the broadcast may be made in both nations simultaneously. Dr. Sinisi has been on the phone with Eastwood's network, and they are willing to agree to this stipulation. Is there any Italian journalist you would prefer?"

Josh looked at Isabella. His Italian was getting a little better each day, but he could not distinguish good Italian journalism from bad. She shot him a quick smile and spoke up.

"I imagine that it will be hard to avoid offering the assignment to Antonio Ginovese," she said. "He is the most respected journalist in Italy, but he is also territorial—if we cut him out, he will do all he can to sabotage the project from the outside."

Sinisi nodded. "I couldn't have said it better," he said. "I'll contact them both and you can begin filming the interviews on Capri this afternoon. I imagine they will want all three surviving members of the original team available, so I will ask all of you to meet the TV crews. Dr. Martens and Bernardo can hold the fort down here. Is everyone agreed?" He looked up and down the table, and the board members nodded.

Guioccini now spoke up. "That brings us to the primary reason for this meeting," he said. "On Friday the *Testimonium* will be carbon dated at the National Archeological Laboratory in Rome by Dr. Henderson of the Smithsonian. Obviously, that means that the scroll will have to be transported to Rome. There has already been one attack made by jihadists attempting to destroy the scroll. The Naples Police and the National Security Forces are convinced that another attempt will be made during the move. Transporting it by air would be highly dangerous—a single rocket launcher could destroy an airplane, along with everyone aboard and whatever cargo it was carrying. So it has been decided that we will move the scroll in a heavily armed convoy. We will be escorted by a helicopter gunship, several APCs full of elite Italian Army Special Forces, and the scroll itself will be in an armored car to protect it from any potential attack. We will set out under cover of darkness Thursday evening and cover the distance from Naples to Rome as quickly as possible. Hopefully the massive show of force will deter an attack, but if they do come after us, there will be enough firepower in the motorcade to hold them off until reinforcements arrive. There will be over one thousand military and law enforcement officers on call if we need them. My hope is that none of them will be needed, but after last Friday, we cannot afford to take chances."

Josh spoke up. "I must admit, I am nervous about having a two-thousand-year-old scroll in the middle of a potential firefight. Even if we manage to defeat these terrorists and get through to Rome, I am afraid that the *Testimonium* could be damaged or destroyed in an attack."

Guioccini answered his concern. "We share the same apprehension," he said. "We have designed a carrying case for the scroll that is made to be bulletproof and fireproof. The scroll will arrive in Rome intact!"

Cardinal Raphael spoke up, his voice shaking with age. The events of the previous week, especially the death of his friend Cardinal Klein, had taken a heavy toll on the old man. "Let us beware the sin of hubris," he said. "What our friends found on Capri is a unique treasure, an affirmation of the dogmas the Church has taught for two thousand years. Such a spiritually significant find should be handled with profound reverence, and yet it has been rushed to the limelight in a most perfunctory and improper fashion. I am not sure but that we may have offended God by trumpeting this find to the world before we verified it. Please do not mistake me—I understand the reasons why you thought it was necessary to reveal the scroll so quickly—but events have made me nervous, and when you speak with such callous certainty, I am afraid."

Everyone listened to the ancient churchman with profound respect—his decades of scholarship were legend in Italy, and his personal piety had seen him survive the darkest days of the German occupation as a teen, hiding Jews and dissidents in his parents' barns and outbuildings.

MacDonald was the one who answered him. "Your Eminence," he said kindly, "perhaps we should say that, God willing, we shall get this scroll safely to Rome. It was God who saw it preserved miraculously for twenty centuries, and it was God who revealed it on Easter Sunday morning. I believe that this scroll was discovered for a reason, and if God wants its authenticity verified, then no power on earth can stop it. If He does not, then no power on earth can get it to that lab safely. So it is up to us all to be the best stewards of this precious find that we can be, and that means careful planning and the best security we can provide."

The old Cardinal nodded. "I pray that you are right, Brother. But the events of the last week have left me sad and tired. I too want this scroll to be confirmed as authentic, so that the whole world may know that what we have taught for all these years is the truth. But a voice within whispers: 'If truth can be proven, what need is there of faith?' And that fills me with foreboding."

There was some desultory conversation after that, but with the issue of transporting the scroll on the table, and the old Cardinal's warning echoing in their ear, no one was in the mood for small talk. Once the meeting broke up, Josh, Isabella, and Father MacDonald joined Luke Martens and Alicia down in the lab. She was staring at the *Testimonium* with great interest. They greeted one another and sat down for a few moments.

Josh looked across the table at Duncan MacDonald. "One thing that I am curious about, Father," he said. "How big is this bulletproof case? I mean, the scroll is six feet long, and you have unrolled it and stiffened it in that open position. Can it be rolled up again without damage? Or are we going to be carrying a very large case around for the next few days?"

The Scottish antiquarian laughed. "I've made a refinement to my stabilizing formula since I last wrote about it, laddie," he said. "Essentially, my formula uses a stiff, wax-like polymer that adheres to the exterior of the papyrus and holds it in position. Unlike the stabilizing element, this polymer does not penetrate; it coats the outside in a very thin and rigid layer that also helps protect the papyrus from UV light. However, I recently came up with a compound that causes the polymer to unbind and evaporate on contact. When I spray the *Testimonium* with my unbinding compound, it will turn as supple as the day it was made. We have already designed an acrylic tube that will hold the entire papyrus, and then slide neatly inside this heavily armored carrying case. When we get to Rome, we can open it, unroll it, hit it with another layer of my original formula, and it will stay open for as long as we want it to. The beauty of it is that the unbinding compound causes the exterior polymer to evaporate completely, so you can use the process on ancient documents as many times as you need to without damaging them!"

"That is truly amazing!" said Josh. "You must have gotten a chemistry set as a kid and never quit playing with it!"

MacDonald laughed. "My parents were too poor for that sort of thing," he said. "But I did manage to blow up the science lab at my parochial school—twice!" He launched into an involved tale involving homemade gunpowder, white phosphorous, and an attempt to create fireworks for his classmates that ended up with the lab in flames and his teacher's eyebrows singed off. For some reason, Isabella found the story particularly hilarious, laughing so hard that tears streamed down her cheeks. Josh wasn't too far behind her—the Scottish priest was an excellent storyteller, and his account of the punishment meted out by the angry nuns was incredibly comical.

"So," the priest concluded, "we never were quite able to extinguish the phosphorus—it had burned through the lab table, through the floor tiles, and was eating through the building's foundation! We quickly spackled over the hole, once the fires in the lab were put out. But if a volcano ever erupts under the site of St. Matthew's Parochial School in Edinburgh, well—I did that!"

That story led Josh to share an account of a prank he had pulled on a high school classmate, and for the next half hour the team swapped stories around the table, chuckling and giggling together. For the first time since the horrible blast had shattered their world the previous Friday, the three survivors felt like a complete team again. Dr. Martens and Alicia fit in naturally, each bringing their own personalities and talents to the table. It was a pleasant interlude after the grim note the board meeting had ended on, and when the original team members left the lab, their hearts were light once more. The memory of sorrow still lingered among them, but it was losing its power.

They took a cab to the ferry station and caught the noon boat for Capri, watching over the sides as the beautiful waters of the Bay of Naples slid by them. Seagulls dove into the boat's wake, searching for fish, while dolphins jumped across the bow waves. They didn't say much; it was simply too beautiful a sight for words. When they arrived at the dock, they found Chief Rosario waiting for them in his police car.

"Greetings, friends!" he said. "It is good to see you on a better occasion than the last! But I want to thank each of you for giving my friend Giuseppe such a wonderful memorial. You said everything that I felt about him, far better than I could have! From now on, anytime you are here, you are my guests and my family. Anyone gives you trouble, you tell me!"

They thanked him for his courtesy and chatted as he drove them up to the base of the Via Tiberio, but his talk about Rossini threw a bit of a damper on the good cheer they had enjoyed that morning. Once the chief dropped them off, they walked up the ancient trail with a sense of relief. It wasn't that they wanted to forget Giuseppe, Josh thought as they neared the old ruins. They just were tired of hurting all the time over his loss.

The film crew was already waiting for them at the top of the bluff, and Josh saw the familiar face of Drew Eastwood talking with a cameraman.

"Dr. Parker and company!" he exclaimed. "So glad you could join us!"

"Wouldn't miss it for the world," said Josh. "So where is Ginovese?"

"He is interviewing the monks from the old church above the Villa Jovis," said the American. "I tried to follow along, but the old fellows don't speak a word of English, so I gave up on it. He's been pretty cool so far, though, considering I am a total rookie at this TV stuff."

"Well, do you want us to start talking you through what we found here?" Josh asked. "Or do you want to wait for him?"

"I promised to include him and his crew on every shot, and we will take turns asking the questions," said Eastwood.

"All right, then," said Josh. "While you are waiting, I want to walk over and take a look at the chamber." It was his first time to set foot on the island since they had left it ten days ago—how much longer it seemed! The Capri Historical Society had been busy at work. A bronze plaque stood on an upright wooden beam outside the chamber door, describing in Italian and English what had been found there. The bricks that had once concealed the chamber's entrance were all removed and neatly stacked to one side, exposing the original doorway in its entirety. A plexiglass barrier had been carefully placed over the entrance and a single floodlight inside illuminated the inside of the chamber. A replica of the writing desk and curule chair had been placed where the originals had sat for twenty centuries.

In a way, it was interesting to be able to look inside and see what the chamber had looked like when it was in use so long ago, but on the other hand, Josh felt as if much of the mystery had been sucked out of it. It looked like any number of other historical sites he had been to in his life—it gave the impression of a movie set rather than one of genuine antiquity. Eastwood joined him and stared into the ancient writing room.

"I bet it's nothing like it was when you saw it the first time," he said.

"Not at all," said Josh. "For one thing, you have to imagine a layer of stone dust about two inches thick over everything in there! You couldn't move without stirring the stuff up—I had black boogers for a week afterward!"

"Too much information there, Dr. Parker!" laughed the young reporter.

"Sorry—I thought you wanted it up close and personal!" Josh replied. Isabella shot him a glare, and moments later, the tall, impressive figure of Signore Antonio Ginovese swept into view. He greeted Isabella profusely in Italian, and then turned to Joshua and Eastwood.

"We meet again, Dr. Parker," he said. "You have earned a great deal of respect from the Italian archeological community in your short time here, and I am looking forward to our interview. Mr. Eastwood, I normally do not enjoy sharing camera time with a novice, but since it is your relationship with these scholars that has allowed me to be included, I must give you my thanks as well." He shook both their hands, and then turned to the camera crews.

The interview was awkward at times, with Josh answering questions from Eastwood in English and Isabella giving answers to Ginovese in Italian. Sometimes the tall European journalist would ask Joshua pointed questions in English as well, and Eastwood tried to give Isabella equal attention from the cameras. Father MacDonald was not questioned quite as much, but when matters relating to his expertise were brought up, both journalists asked him questions and listened to his answers respectfully. After they got used to the round-robin format, the team members warmed to the narrative and gave a colorful, blow-by-blow account of the discovery. All told, they spoke for almost two hours, from the moment of the chamber's discovery until the final removal of the artifacts from the island, and their going away dinner down at Rossini's house.

Once they were finished filming on Capri, Ginovese offered to fly the three archeologists back to Naples aboard the Italian network helicopter. However, it was a bit cramped when all three of them tried to join him, so Josh agreed to fly back with Andrew Eastwood in the American network's chopper. The afternoon was fading, and the westering sun over the Bay of Naples turned the sky's light clouds to streaks of stationary flame.

"Great sky!" commented the journalist.

"Sure is," Josh said. "I have never understood how people can look at the senseless beauty of the world and not acknowledge the genius of our creator. Water molecules refracting light should not move our hearts—but they do!"

"I never thought about it that way," said Eastwood. "But I sure see your point. When I turned my back on God in college, I thought science and Darwin could explain absolutely everything. But since I became a believer, just a few days ago, I am continually amazed at how many things I was blind to before! Nature should evolve to be efficient. But why should it evolve to be beautiful? I look at the world around me, and I suddenly see God's signature everywhere."

"Skeptics say that faith enslaves us," said Josh. "But I believe it is the only thing that truly makes us free."

With that they fell silent and watched as the city of Naples unfolded below them. There was a helo pad behind the museum, but it was still partly covered by debris from the blast, so the chopper landed a few blocks away, at a police station's helo deck. The network vans were waiting to transfer them to the museum. They got out in front and posed on the steps as the two networks set up their cameras again. Museum security kept the protestors that lingered in front of the building at bay. Once both sets of cameras were trained upon them, Andrew spoke to Joshua first. "Tell us what happened when you and the others arrived here," he said.

"Well, it was a weekend," Josh said, "so we were told to take a day to rest and adjust. Isabella here gave me a tour of the museum, and then we both went out to the museum's lab where the artifacts were to be examined." He then walked up the steps and led the cameras to the back lot, where the lab had once stood. The heaviness that had lifted from him earlier in the day returned as he saw the wreckage left by the blast, over half cleared by now, but still an ugly reminder of the power of fanaticism. As briefly as he could, he described the initial work that was done in the lab, and then the horror of that Friday morning when the terror attack had destroyed the lab and nearly killed him and Isabella.

Finally, they walked the camera crews down to the old lab facility where the artifacts were being analyzed. They exhibited and discussed all the surviving relics from the chamber, noting that the ancient bronze lamp had been recovered and brought down to the lab since that morning. Eastwood and Ginovese still peppered them with occasional questions, but both of them were more content now to let the three antiquarians tell their story without interruptions.

Last of all, they took the camera crews to the *Testimonium* itself. Josh described the moment when he first saw the Latin letters on the outside of the scroll and realized what he was holding. MacDonald described the opening of the ancient scroll and the tense moments as he and Joshua translated it together, and the decision to share its contents with the world despite the deadly jihadist attack. Last of all, the three team members discussed the implications of the scroll on modern Biblical scholarship, and its potential effect on a skeptical world.

"In the end," Josh said, "no one should be surprised that Pilate's testimony confirms the Gospel accounts. After all, they were composed from eyewitness testimony a very short time after the events happened. Only in recent years has it become fashionable to call every detail of the gospel narrative into question. That being said, the *Testimonium* does not 'prove' anything conclusively. It is simply one more piece of evidence that shows that the Gospels recorded actual events. But the substance of the Gospel claims—the divinity of Jesus Christ—is still a matter for individual faith to decide. God did not abrogate free will with the discovery of a piece of papyrus!"

"But would it not be safe to say that this does refute many of the explanations that have been offered about the events of the Passion Week?" asked Ginovese.

"On that count, I would agree," said Josh. "Many of those explanations have been debunked by scholars years ago, but they have persisted because hostility to Christianity has become so fashionable in recent years. But I do think that many of the more persistent myths—that there was never a tomb at all, that Jesus swooned on the Cross and somehow revived, or that the disciples stole the body—can now be put to rest."

Isabella and Father MacDonald each made their last statements, and that was the end of the shoot. Both journalists shook the hands of the team members and thanked them profusely, and then the cameras and lights were packed up. Within a half hour of the last recorded statements, the three team members had the lab to themselves again. They looked at one another, and Josh let out a long sigh.

"Well, that went well, I think!" he said.

"It did, laddie. You two are such naturals in front of the camera I felt like a stunt double!" exclaimed MacDonald.

"I don't know, Father," said Isabella. "I think your Scottish burr nicely rounds out my fluent Italian and Josh's incurable Southern drawl!"

"Hey, my drawl is just fine!" said Josh with a laugh. "But right now, I am ready for some supper!"

"Come to think of it," Isabella said, "we never did eat lunch, did we?"

Chatting among themselves, the three team members took the elevator to the first floor of the museum and caught a cab to a nearby restaurant. Their sorrows behind them for the moment, they laughed, talked, and reminisced throughout the rich supper. It was the last meal they would share together before Josh died.

<<<TRANSCRIPT OF A PHONE CONVERSATION FROM THE NATIONAL ARCHEOLOGICAL MUSEUM IN NAPLES, 11:30 PM, APRIL 28, 20** BETWEEN DR. BENITO CASTOLFO AND ITALIAN SECURITY AGENT ANTONIO LUCOCCINI>>>

CASTOLFO: I am still concerned about the transport of the scroll tomorrow evening, Antonio.

LUCOCCINI: What worries you, Doctor?

CASTOLFO: The near certainty of a terrorist attack is a bit unsettling, to tell you the truth! If they have rocket launchers, I am afraid that even the armored travel case we will be using will not be sufficient to protect the scroll from damage.

LUCOCCINI: Do you have a better plan?

CASTOLFO: I have been thinking. The convoy is a brilliant idea, in that it is big and conspicuous and sure to draw enemy fire. I am thinking that it should set out just as we planned, with enough museum personnel on board to look convincing, carrying a duplicate of the case we are using to transport the scroll. Meanwhile, I will wait with the rest of the team—we will tell the press that they are flying to Rome the next morning, or something. Once the convoy comes under enemy fire, I will take the two of them, and the scroll, in my personal auto, and leave for Rome by an alternate route. While all the security forces in Italy descend on the jihadists, we will be safely delivering the scroll to Rome on a completely different road!"

LUCOCCINI: That is quite brilliant, Doctor! If you ever decide to leave the field of Antiquities, we could use you in the Security Department!

CASTOLFO: Then you approve my plan?

LUCOCCINI: Yes, but stay in touch via cell phone. Don't leave the museum until we know for sure that the terrorists have attacked the convoy."

CHAPTER TWENTY-SEVEN

Josh slept soundly that night and woke up at six, a few minutes before his alarm. He pulled on his trunks, brushed his teeth, and headed down to the pool, swimming his usual twenty laps. Returning to his room, he showered, shaved, and dressed, then called up his parents.

"Good morning, son!" his father boomed upon hearing his voice.

"Hey, Dad, how was Rome?" Josh replied.

His father sighed. "Crowded, smelly, loud, and breathtakingly beautiful!" he said. "I was overwhelmed by the history all around me. I'll be honest, son, I want to go back and live there for the rest of my days, just so I can take it all in. I've been to the Holy Land twice, and did a tour in Vietnam when I was in the Army, but Italy is the most incredible land I have ever seen. But, since your mother spent most of our retirement savings yesterday, I imagine this visit will have to be it!"

"Ben, you TOLD me to buy some new outfits!" He heard his mother's voice in the background. "And don't get me started on all those silly old coins you bought from that shady antique dealer!"

"Now Louise, this is not about me, it's about you!" the pastor replied.

Josh chuckled. "Well," he said, "how about if I buy you two bankrupt tourists your breakfast?"

"That sounds lovely," said his father. "I'll see if I can get this wild woman tamed down enough to be presentable." He hung up after that, but not before Josh caught his mother's voice replying in mock outrage. He smiled fondly—his parents rarely ever fought, but they kept that kind of playful banter going almost constantly. He met them at their room a few moments later, and they chatted for an hour over coffee and breakfast rolls in the hotel's restaurant. It was not a deep theological or historical conversation, just memories of good times and old friends, and an account of the things his parents had seen in Rome the previous day.

When the meal was done, Josh and his folks went their separate ways. He made sure they had their tickets for their flight back home, and promised to call them before he left for Rome that night, and again when he safely arrived. He also paused a moment for a private word with his mother.

After that he set out for the museum, where he found Isabella arriving just as he did. He greeted her warmly with a kiss, and they headed down to the lab. Castolfo and Guioccini were waiting for them, and Father MacDonald joined them shortly thereafter. Once they were all there, the president of the Antiquities Bureau began to speak.

"After we met yesterday, I became increasingly concerned about the safety of the scroll during tonight's drive to Rome," he said. "Even though the travel case we have devised is supposed to be bulletproof and fireproof, I am still worried that it could be damaged in a determined assault—especially if the jihadists have got ahold of some serious firepower. So I had a long conversation with a senior agent at the Security Ministry late last night, and we have come up with a plan. It will involve some subterfuge, which is why I am informing the three of you now. There is potential danger in it, but I do think it offers the best chance to get the scroll to Rome undamaged."

The three team members looked at one another, then at the board president. Josh spoke up first. "Well, what are you proposing?" he asked.

"The convoy will leave as planned. One of you will carry a decoy case that looks exactly like the one we made for the scroll into the armored car, which will set out exactly as we have scheduled, about an hour after dark. The convoy will travel northward along this route "—he unrolled a road map of Italy—"going from Caserta to Tivoli, then eastward into Rome itself. It is two hundred twenty-seven kilometers, so roughly a four-hour drive late at night moving at top speed. I will wait here at the museum with the remainder of the team and the actual scroll, secure in its case. I'll be in contact with the police escort, and when the convoy is engaged by the jihadists, we will take the scroll and depart the museum and travel northward by the coast road, going through Formia and Latina. It's a longer route, but we will avoid the ambush altogether and be safely in Rome long before dawn on Friday. Our enemies will be striking a heavily armed target and taking mass casualties in order to destroy an empty briefcase!"

Josh looked at the map carefully. "Sounds pretty ingenious to me," he said. "I can travel with the convoy and carry the decoy case."

Father MacDonald spoke up firmly. "No, laddie!" he said. "I'll take that duty. No one will miss an old Scottish priest, but you and Isabella have a chance at a bright future together. I would never forgive myself if something happened to you when I could have stood in your place and given you two a chance to be happy!"

Josh and Isabella looked at each other, then at their friend. She spoke first: "That is beyond kindness, Father. How could we ask you to do such a thing?"

"You didn't, lass, I volunteered!" he answered. "It is the most Christian thing I could think of."

Josh nodded. "You can say that again," he said. "Thank you for your willingness to put yourself in harm's way for us."

Castolfo laughed grimly. "I doubt he will be in much danger," said the board's president. "These jihadists will be sticking their fist into a hornet's nest if they attack that convoy!"

"I am a bit uncertain, though, taking the scroll up that coastal road unaccompanied," said Josh.

"I'll have my cell phone open and active the whole time. I don't see any way that the terrorists could possibly get wind of our little deception, but if we run into trouble, well—my BMW can outrun just about any car on the road, and we'll be on the line calling for help," Castolfo explained.

"It does sound like a good plan," said Isabella. "We'll just need to make sure not one word of it leaks out of this room."

"Nothing to fear there," said Castolfo. "The only other person who knows about it is Agent Lucoccini. Even Chief Zadora thinks that the scroll will be with the convoy."

They discussed the plans a bit further, and then Father MacDonald stood up. "I suppose it would not hurt to get the scroll ready for transport," he said.

Josh stood too. "I want to see this new compound you were describing," he said. "I still can't believe it works so easily."

The priest smiled. "I'm a constant source of wonder to those who know me, laddie!" he quipped. "Dr. Castolfo, do you have two of the plexiglass carrying tubes as well as two briefcases?"

"Indeed, we have several of them in our collections inventory," said the board president. "What have you got in mind?"

"If we are going to play bait and switch, let's make the bait look as good as we can," replied the priest. "Joshua, be a good lad and go up to the gift shop for me. We'll need a poster that is roughly the same size and shape as the *Testimonium*."

Josh headed upstairs, and Isabella tagged along behind. "I swear he got this idea from watching *National Treasure!*" Josh exclaimed.

"You know, I bet you're right!" Isabella said.

When they arrived at the gift shop they had to look at each other and laugh. Right behind the cash register was a life-sized facsimile of the *Testimonium* hanging on the wall, and there were about twenty more of them rolled up in a tray beneath it. Josh looked at the price tag and whistled as he did the mental conversion from Euros to dollars. "Wow! They wasted no time cashing in on our find, did they?"

"For a capitalist, you are awfully cheap!" laughed Isabella. "Here, let me use my ID card and get us the museum employee's discount."

They purchased the fake scroll and headed downstairs with it. When they arrived, MacDonald was just getting set up. Two identical steel cases were on the table, both opened to reveal their heavily foam padded interiors. Next to them were two plexiglass tubes with metal ends—one end on each tube was hinged to swing open. They looked like a slightly larger version of the pneumatic tubes banks used to make drive-through deposits. Josh handed the facsimile scroll to MacDonald, who looked at it and laughed.

"We should be getting some kind of royalties off of these," he said. "Well, it will just make the decoy that much more realistic!" He deftly rolled up the facsimile scroll and stuffed it into one of the tubes, then closed and latched the metal cap into place. He set the tube into the foam padding and shut the case on it, then twirled the tumblers to deploy the combination lock.

"Excellent!" said Castolfo. "Now that is Case B, and the combination is thirteen-twelve-sixty-three—my wife's birthday. Father, if you are committed to traveling with the convoy, you might write that down somewhere. That way if you are asked to open the case and retrieve the decoy scroll, you will be able to."

The priest rolled up one of his sleeves and jotted the numbers on the inside of his wrist with a Sharpie. Then he took the case from the table and set it next to one of the filing cabinets. "I'm not even going to close the other case yet," he said, "so that there is zero chance of confusing the two. But I do want to go ahead and prepare the scroll for transport. Josh, Bernardo, Isabella—you all will want to watch this, I think," he said.

"So tell me, Father," said Isabella, "How many times have you used this compound?"

"About forty times so far," he said. "Of course, those were lab tests on papyrus and parchment samples. This will be my first actual field use on an ancient document."

Guioccini swallowed hard. "I think I might be a bit more confident if I had not heard that," he said.

MacDonald laughed. "Do you think that I would dare apply this compound to the *Testimonium* if I thought there was the slightest chance of damaging it?" he asked.

That pretty well shut them all up, and they watched as MacDonald carefully lifted the cover off of the plastic stand and metal tray that the ancient scroll rested upon. The ancient papyrus lay open and flat, to all appearances as stiff as a board. The Scot reached into his satchel and produced a spray bottle with a label that simply said UNBINDER in neatly printed letters. He started at one end of the scroll and began to spray the surface of it, working his way from top to bottom on each squeeze of the trigger, and then going over the same area again. The surface of the scroll darkened for just a moment, and then lightened again. A faint smell of paraffin and alcohol pervaded the air in the lab. By the time a foot of the scroll had been sprayed, the end he had started on began to curl up of its own accord. The team watched in astonishment as the ancient papyrus slowly rolled up behind the hand of Father MacDonald while he worked the spray down the length of the scroll. It took him about five minutes to cover the entire six-foot length, taking great care not to miss a single square inch of the surface. By the time he was done, the papyrus had rolled up into a loose scroll about six inches in diameter.

"I wouldn't have believed it!" Josh said. "That is truly an amazing technical achievement!"

The priest executed a mock bow, and then donned a pair of acid-free gloves in order to handle the scroll. He rolled it up a bit tighter, till it was small enough slide into the plexiglass cylinder, although it was still not as tightly rolled as it had been at the Villa Jovis when they found it. He snapped the lid of the cylinder into place once the scroll was inside, and then reverently laid the cylinder in its cushioned cavity, but left the lid of the carrying case open.

"There it is, laddie," he said. "Just snap it shut and spin the dials this evening, and hightail it for Rome!"

"Sounds like a plan," Josh said. "By the way, Dr. Castolfo, what is the combination on this case?"

"Well, I will be traveling with you," said the Italian, "but it would be bad if I had a heart attack or something and you didn't know how to open the case! The combination is four-eleven-eighty-one. That is my son's birthday."

Josh wrote the number on a slip of paper and slid it in his wallet, then jotted it on the back of his hand just to be safe. "Well, I guess that's about it, then, as far as getting ready goes," he said.

Castolfo nodded. "I could ask you to spend some time going through the items recovered from the wreckage of the lab," he said, "but frankly none of those things are as urgent as this. I'll be arranging our escort vehicles this afternoon, and I don't really need the three of you for that. You may take off until four PM if you like. That is when we will begin preparing for the evening's subterfuge in earnest."

"Father, would you like to join Isabella and me?" Josh asked.

"I think I will pass, my lad," said the priest. "I want to talk to Dr. Henderson and the other folk at the lab in Rome, and then I really need to speak to the Vatican. I will be spending the afternoon on the phone. Besides, when young folks get a chance to spend some time together, there are few worse third wheels to have along than a priest!"

Isabella laughed as she and Joshua walked toward the elevator. "So what would you like to do?" she asked.

He thought for a moment. "You know," he said, "we have not had a true American date yet. How about lunch and a movie? Normally it would be dinner and a movie, but our evening is already booked up."

Her eyes widened. "You know, I watch some films on my computer or TV at home," she said, "but I have not been to the cinema in ages! There is a theater not far from here that shows American hits. Let's go!"

They paused at a sidewalk café for a quick lunch and made it to the theater by 1 PM, just a few moments before the feature started. The movie was *The Avengers*, which Josh had seen when it came out the previous year. He loved the big-screen comic book characters, although

418

Isabella was a bit confused by the plot at first. After a half hour or so, however, she was able to follow it well enough to quit asking him who was who and simply enjoy the film. They stuffed themselves with popcorn and soft drinks, and applauded at the end, when the credits began to roll. Josh made sure they stayed until the little teaser popped up after the credits, and then walked her out onto the street.

"Now, I have never been on an American-style date before," she said. "But is it not traditional to now park our car in an isolated location and make out?"

Josh blushed. "You are right about that," he said, "but it is broad daylight, and that takes all the fun out of it. However, I do have something to make up for the loss a bit."

"What is that?" she asked.

He dropped to one knee in the middle of the sidewalk and pulled a small box out of his pocket. "Isabella Sforza," he said, "will you marry me?"

She stared in disbelief at the beautiful gold ring with its gleaming diamond solitaire. "Where—how?" she asked.

"The ring?" Josh said. "It was my grandmother's. My mom actually brought it over from the States when she saw that I finally had a girlfriend. Dad thought that she was being hopelessly optimistic, but you should have seen his face when I asked her for it this morning."

She took him by the hands and lifted him from his knees. "You know that I have not yet believed in your God the way you want me to," she said, looking into his eyes.

He nodded. "I have prayed about this since I met you," he said, "and God has given me peace about it. You will find your way to Him in your own time, and I will be there to rejoice in the moment. But something told me that today was the day I should ask you. So, how about it? Will you be Mrs. Parker?"

She threw her arms around his neck and kissed him enthusiastically. "Yes!" she said gleefully. "A thousand times yes! Oh, Josh, I am so glad that God brought you into my life! You have given me more joy than I thought I would ever feel again!"

They kissed again, and the small crowd of onlookers that had paused to take in the moment began to applaud. Josh looked at them and grinned. "THIS WOMAN IS GOING TO BE MY WIFE!" he shouted at the top of his lungs. Isabella elbowed him in the ribs, but the onlookers applauded even louder. The two of them collapsed in laughter, and then caught a cab back to the museum.

* * *

Ibrahim Abbasside had been a busy man. In the last forty-eight hours, he had met with both his cell leaders, purchased a swift automobile, and monitored the communications coming from the museum and the police department. Everything looked to be in order. The convoy escorting the scroll would leave the museum that evening, and his men would be waiting to intercept it. The escort was heavy, but not heavy enough. His men had two RPGs with multiple rounds of ammunition, and a SAM launcher. He decided to let the convoy cover just over half the distance to Rome—far enough down the road to lull them into a false sense of security—before striking. The first round would knock the helicopter out of the sky, while the RPG would cripple the lead vehicle. The jihadists would lay down a withering fire, killing as many of the escorting soldiers and policemen in the opening moments of the ambush as they could. As for Abbasside, he would be trailing the convoy in his sports car, armed with two pistols, a fifty-caliber sniper rifle with a tripod, and his pocket torch. He would take out the remainder of the convoy from the rear as they tried to withdraw from the ambush, and block their escape. He had already donned a Kevlar vest, and had the helmet in the floorboard of his auto. He was not averse to giving his life in glorious jihad against the infidel, but he did not want a stray round bringing him down before he completed his mission.

He had rented a small apartment overlooking the front of the museum from a few blocks away, and would be waiting and watching as the convoy departed. Since he knew their route from intercepted communications, he did even not have to tail them visibly. He could take his time, slowly bringing up the rear, not even getting them in view until they were well away from Naples. All he had to do was keep their distant tail lights in his sights intermittently, to make sure they did not deviate from the planned route.

On the seat next to him was a laptop computer, plugged into his email. The sheer bulk of communications coming from the museum was pretty overwhelming, but he had isolated the numbers that had most to do with planning the convoy and checked those intercepts every few hours. The Spider had been as good as his word. He would take the laptop with him when he left the dingy little apartment that evening, so that he could monitor any further communications.

As the time for his afternoon prayers approached, he unrolled his ornately inscribed rug and knelt, touching his nose to the ground three times as Islamic tradition required, and then mouthed the ancient words of the Quran. He could feel the righteousness of his cause in every word that he spoke, and knew that Allah was merciful. He would not suffer his faithful servant to fail.

* * *

Joshua and Isabella got back to the museum a little later than they had planned. There was a small knot of reporters near the entrance, no doubt there to cover the convoy's departure, which had been judiciously leaked by the police department.

"Dr. Parker!" shouted an English journalist. "Will you and Dr. Sforza be accompanying the scroll when it leaves the museum?"

Josh paused. "We have been asked to remain here until tomorrow morning," he said, "when we will catch a helicopter flight to Rome. Several artifacts we've recovered from the ruins of the lab are in precarious condition, and Isabella and I will be working most of the night trying to stabilize them. Two-thousand-year-old papyri and high explosives are a bad combination!"

The American correspondent Cynthia Brown cut in. "Dr. Parker, are you worried about what the carbon dating of the *Testimonium* might reveal?"

Josh flashed a huge smile at them. "Not in the least!" he said. "I was there when the scroll was found, and there is not a shred of doubt in my mind that the testing will confirm its authenticity. I feel kind of sorry for the skeptics who are trying so hard to debunk this find, if you want to know the truth. Once these tests are done, they will not have a leg to stand on."

One of the reporters had a cell phone jammed to his ear, and he put it down long enough to call out his question. "Dr. Parker, what is this I am hearing about a scene outside a nearby movie theater moments ago?" he asked.

"You guys don't miss a beat, do you?" Josh said. "All right, then, if you must know, I have asked Dr. Sforza here to become my wife, and

421

she has accepted!" He held up her hand to the reporters, showing off his grandmother's engagement ring. The journalists gave the two a good-natured round of applause.

"No more questions!" Isabella shouted as the two of them turned and darted into the museum.

Castolfo and MacDonald were waiting for them in the lab. "A bit late, aren't we?" asked the Bureau's president.

Josh grinned ruefully. "Sorry, sir," he said. "We lost track of time, and then got ambushed by the press at the door. We stuck to our cover story, though, and gave them something else to talk about!"

MacDonald suddenly spotted the gleaming diamond on Isabella's finger. "By God!" he said. "You actually did it! Congratulations, laddie! And you too, my girl!"

Castolfo took in the ring and Isabella's radiant face. His stern expression broke into a huge grin. "How delightful!" he said. "Congratulations to you both! Now, Parker, you are going to have to come and live here in Italy. I do not want to lose this valued member of our profession to some backwater Indian excavation on the American frontier!"

Isabella wrinkled her nose at him. "And what if I told you it was my career ambition to excavate Clovis sites in Oklahoma?" she asked.

"I would know you were lying!" said Castolfo. "But I wish you both the very best wherever you settle. I just don't want to lose you. There are not enough women in archeology as it is, and you have become an inspiration to all the girls in Italy!"

"Joshua, I realize that we come from different churches, but if you did want to have some wee input from across the denominational aisle, I would be honored to have a part in the service," said Father MacDonald.

"I would not dream of a wedding without you in it!" said Isabella.

"I think you and my dad could do a great service together," said Josh.

They chatted for a few moments, and then Castolfo answered the phone and spoke softly for a few moments. When he hung up, he faced the group with a stern face. "Well, our escort is here!" he said. "It won't be dark for a while yet, but perhaps you would like to go introduce yourselves?"

The three team members followed him and Guioccini to the entrance of the museum. Two large APCs were pulled up to the curb with an armored car in between them, and three police cars bringing up the rear. All of them were parked in front of the museum, drawing quite a curious crowd of onlookers. An Italian officer stepped to the front, and Josh recognized him immediately. It was Guillermo Rossini!

"We meet again, Dr. Parker!" said the Giuseppe's son. "It is good to see you!"

"I am glad to see you again, too!" said Josh. "Now I know that Father MacDonald and the scroll will be safe."

Major Rossini nodded. "And I am delighted to get a crack at the animals that murdered my father," he said. "If they touch this convoy, it will be the last thing they ever do!"

Castolfo looked skyward, and Rossini laughed. "Our air support is coming, don't worry!" he said. "We won't be leaving for another hour at least, and they will pick us up right at the edge of the city. This scroll will not have been guarded so well since it had Praetorians protecting it in old Tiberius' time!"

A tall police officer in a lavishly decorated uniform stepped forward. "Alessandro Zadora, Police Chief of Naples," he said, shaking hands with the team members. "My men are most anxious to see you safely to Rome, after the tragic events of last week. Who will actually be carrying and escorting the scroll?"

"That would be me and Dr. Guioccini," said Father MacDonald.

"I have a little something for each of you!" said the Chief. He reached into his patrol car and pulled out two Kevlar vests. "I doubt you will need them, but it never hurts to be safe."

* * *

Several blocks away, Abbasside watched the convoy parked outside the museum. He had watched the news coverage of the American archeologist and the Italian harlot with a sneer of anger, upset that they would not be in the convoy. How it would have pleased Allah to wipe the sinful joy right off of their infidel faces! But, he thought, at least his men would get a clear shot at the priest and one of the Italian archeologists. He watched the handoff of the Kevlar vests and took note that his men would need to be aiming for the head.

The light was fading fast, and he knew that they would be leaving the museum soon. He opened his laptop and went to his email, looking at the many intercepts that had been sent to him since that morning. He scrolled through them in chronological order, noting with pleasure that the Spider had actually flagged the ones that were most likely to be of interest to him. There was one from late the night before from the director's office to a number he did not recognize. He opened it and played the audio file. He heard the deep voice of the president of the Antiquities Board, Castolfo, speaking to someone he did not know.

"I am very concerned about the transport of the scroll tomorrow evening, Antonio," it said. He sat straight up and listened very closely. When the brief conversation ended, he was shaking with rage.

Cursed infidels, they were clever!! Had it not been for the Spider's ability to tap into their communications, he and his men might have thrown their lives away for nothing! But he smiled now. The scroll would be traveling unescorted, taking the coast road toward Rome. The infidels' cleverness would be their undoing—his sports car could overtake anything on the road, and there were many lonely stretches where he could have his way with them, far from any reinforcement.

But he would have no reinforcements either. Apparently the scroll would not even leave Rome until the attack on the convoy began, so he would have to allow his men to walk into a trap. He felt no regret for their deaths—martyrdom was the highest honor any Muslim could aspire to, and Allah would welcome them into paradise as honored jihadists. He debated on telling them that their attack was diversionary, but decided against it. They would spend themselves more freely if they believed that they were going to destroy a valuable target, and an all-out attack would be more convincing to the Italians. That meant, however, that the sole responsibility for the destruction of the scroll would rest upon his shoulders. However, he thought, at least there was the consolation that he would be able to kill the infidel couple after all. The thought brought a smile to his face. The future they imagined together would never be realized!

He watched carefully as the sky grew darker, and about an hour after he read the intercepted message, he saw the priest and the Italian archeologist from the museum carry a metallic briefcase down the steps and into the armored car. Headlights came on and engines roared as the massive vehicles and the smaller police cars started up and pulled away from the curb. As they disappeared around the block, he heard a helicopter swoop overhead and take its station above them. Its lights remained visible long after the buildings of Naples blocked the convoy from view. Abbasside closed his drapes and placed a call to Ismael Falladah.

"God is Great!" said the jihadist when he picked up the phone. The time for subterfuge and code names was over.

"They have left Naples," said Abbasside. "Be ready. The convoy must not get through! Destroy the scroll at all costs."

"It will be done!" said the sleeper cell commander. "We have chosen our spot well. They will never know what hit them."

"Allah is merciful," said Abbasside. "Strike hard! Call me when you see the helicopter approaching, so that I may catch up and join the holy assault!"

"Yes, sheik!" said the jihadist, and hung up.

Abbasside went through the apartment for the next half hour, clearing out all his possessions and wiping the room clean of his fingerprints. Everything fit into one small suitcase, which packed quickly. His room was paid for, and he left the key card on the table before heading to his car. The authorities had never gotten an image of his face yet, and he was determined to leave them no trace by which to identify him. He closed the door behind him and carried his case down to the car, and then drove it to a parallel slot a block from the museum. The parking lot only had two outlets, and both opened onto this street. He would see the president's BMW when it left. He settled into his seat and watched the street, patient as a cat watching a mouse hole. Sooner or later, his quarry would emerge. And he would be waiting.

* * *

Josh paced back and forth. The convoy had been gone for nearly two hours, and should be at least halfway to Rome by now. The case with the real *Testimonium* inside it was sealed and waiting; Dr. Castolfo's BMW was fueled up and parked in the side lot, and all of them had eaten some stale sandwiches from the museum's café for supper.

"Joshua, it would be a true shame for me to have to kill you on the day we became engaged," said Isabella. She was smiling, but there was some real irritation in her voice, so Josh sat down and took a sip of lukewarm Coke. He shook his head.

"I swear, this has been the longest two hours of my entire life!" he commented.

Castolfo nodded. "I must agree, my young friend," he said. "Perhaps our escort was so strong the enemy had second thoughts?"

"I would be very surprised at that," said Joshua. The words were no sooner out of his mouth when the ringing of the phone startled them all. Castolfo answered immediately.

"Is the convoy under attack?" he asked.

Guioccini answered: "Heavily! They just blew the chopper out of the air and crippled one of the APCs! Bullets are flying everywhere!"

"Stay safe, old friend!" said Castolfo. He switched the cell phone off and turned to the others. "Let's go!" he said.

Josh grabbed the case and they took the elevator up to the first floor. A security guard let them out the side door, and the three of them slid into the waiting BMW. Josh rode shotgun, while Isabella sat in the back seat with the *Testimonium* in her lap. The president of the Bureau started his car, jammed it into gear, and goosed the accelerator. They shot out into the street, took a hard right, and headed east toward the coast road. None of them saw the sports car two blocks behind them that slowly eased out of its parking space and began to follow.

* * *

Abbasside's heart raced as he moved into position behind the speeding BMW. He was an expert driver and had tailed vehicles before, but never with so much at stake. He could not follow too closely without alerting his quarry, but he only had the vaguest idea of their route, so he could not let them out of his sight either. He had received the call about five minutes before the BMW had come rocketing out onto the street. Falladah and his men had spotted the chopper approaching several miles off. They had chosen their spot well, just north of the town of Cassino, where the road wound between two fairly steep hills. He advised them to open up on the chopper and the lead APC at point blank range, to maximize damage and casualties, and then hung up. The true quarry was here in front of him, not in those distant hills, and he could not afford to lose it.

They reached the outskirts of Naples quickly, turning northward just before Bacoli. He dropped back a few hundred yards—the coast road was a straight shot all the way up to Pomezia, several hours away, and he

426

doubted they would stray from it. He was already plotting his intercept point. Between Mondragone and Minturno was a fairly long straightaway with no large towns, where his car's powerful engine would enable him to catch up to the German sedan. He unholstered one of his guns and chambered a round. One way or another, he would bring them to a stop!

* * *

Josh was nervous. He had spotted headlights in the distance behind them two or three times now, never closing in, but never turning off either. He looked across the seat at Castolfo, whose eyes never left the road ahead.

"Are you thinking what I am thinking?" he asked.

"I am not sure if he is following us or not," replied the board president. "He is certainly keeping his distance, but I am not comfortable with the fact that he has yet to turn off. I need to find out what is going on!"

He pulled out his cell phone, scrolled through some recent calls, and punched a button to call Antonio Lucoccini. Moments later the Italian agent's voice came on the line.

"Castolfo!" he said. "Are you safely underway?"

"We just passed Castel Volturno," said the president. "How is the convoy?"

"The army men in the APC suffered heavy losses, but they have the terrorists pinned down with reinforcements coming in. It's a heavy firefight, and a lot of good men are down. So unless something is really amiss, I need to let you go," said Lucoccini.

"We've had a single set of headlights following us since we left Naples," said Castolfo. "They're staying about a kilometer or two behind us, but they haven't turned off yet. It's making us nervous."

"I have a unit at Formia," said the Italian Security Agent. "I will order them south to meet you."

"Thanks," said Castolfo. "Try to keep our friends safe!" He hung up the phone and looked over at Joshua. "The cavalry is on the way!" he said with a smile.

Josh nodded, and looked in the back seat at Isabella. She looked nervous, so he took her hand in his and gave it a reassuring squeeze. "We will be eating breakfast in Rome before you know it," he said.

They had just passed the small town of Mondragone when the headlights behind them suddenly began catching up quickly. Castolfo punched it, but the mysterious vehicle was closing the gap rapidly.

"This is NOT good!" Josh said. As he watched the headlights get closer, he saw a small orange flash of light above and to the left of them. He barely had time to register it before the back windshield shattered into a thousand tiny shards of glass, and a bullet whizzed past him and through the front windshield. "Get down, Isabella!" he shouted.

Without asking permission, he grabbed Castolfo's cell phone and redialed the most recent call. "This is Lucoccini!" came the voice on the other end.

"We are being shot at!" Josh said. "How far off are your men?"

"Ten minutes," said the agent.

"That may be too long!" Josh snapped. There was another flash of light, and he heard the impact of a bullet on the car's rear bumper. "I think he is shooting at our tires!"

Castolfo tried to swerve, but the next round blew out one of the side windows. The Italian was flooring the accelerator, but the pursuing car was faster. The headlights were now only about twenty meters behind them.

"Josh!" the bureau's president said. "Under my coat, in a shoulder holster, there is—" He never finished the sentence. A bullet found its mark, and the back tire blew out. The BMW slowed, and the headlights pulled even closer. Castolfo cut hard to the right, trying to force their tormentor off the road, but before the two vehicles met, another shot was fired, and the right front tire blew. The BMW spun to a stop in the middle of the road.

Castolfo lunged out of the car, pulling a Beretta from a shoulder holster. Three barking reports sounded, and the Italian antiquarian crumpled, blooms of red spreading across the front of his shirt. He tried to lift his pistol to fire a shot at their pursuer, but a final report sounded, and the top of his head exploded in a cloud of blood. His body crumpled lifeless to the pavement.

"Come out, Dr. Parker, and bring the scroll and the girl with you. One bit of foolishness and she dies," came a voice out of the darkness behind the headlights. It was a deep baritone, with a slight African accent.

"No matter what happens, remember I love you!" whispered Josh to Isabella. He helped her out of the car, grabbed the metal case, and put himself between the shadowy figure and her. "What do you want?" he asked.

"Open the case and show me the scroll," the voice demanded. Its owner now stepped in front of the lights, and Josh could see that he was a tall, swarthy individual, but his face was still too strongly backlit for them to see.

"I don't understand," Josh said. "Why do you want it so badly?"

"Do not play games with me, Dr. Parker. I am a serious man. You know the scroll will do great damage to the religion of truth, while promoting your infidel heresies. Now open . . . the . . . case!" the voice snapped.

"No!" Josh said.

The sound of the pistol was deafening at close range. Josh looked down in astonishment at the hole in the front of his khaki shirt. The edges of the hole smoked for a second where the bullet had singed the fabric in its passage, but then the spark was extinguished by a sudden flow of blood from his abdomen. He felt his legs give way under him, and he crumpled to his knees. He would have fallen backwards had Isabella not supported him.

"Infidel whore!" snapped the figure. "Open the case, or the next round goes between his eyes!"

Blinded by tears, Isabella gently lowered Josh to the ground and picked up the case. She could not think of the numbers, so she began to lift up Josh's limp arm.

"What are you doing?" the voice snapped, and a pistol round passed through the air an inch above her head.

"I am looking for the combination," she said. "He wrote it on the back of the hand in case he forgot it!" The numbers were still there, and she lifted the case into her lap and began to twirl the dials.

"Isabella . . . no!" Josh pleaded, his voice a hoarse whisper.

She looked at him in fury. "Your life is worth more than a million scrolls to me!" she snapped, and opened the case. She lifted the clear tube out.

"Now take the document out of that sleeve, and lay it on the ground between us!" snapped the terrorist.

She took the scroll from its protective sleeve and laid it on the road, unrolling it and weighing down its edges with small rocks. In the glare of the stranger's headlights, she saw the clear, strong Latin hand one last time.

"Excellent!" the voice said. "Now get back!"

The tall figure stepped forward, and Isabella scuttled back, taking Josh in her arms again. He lifted his hand to place it over hers, and she saw that his face was a mask of pain and loss. Meanwhile, the terrorist— Isabella could now see that he was a black man, perhaps fifty years of age—reached into his pocket with his left hand and pulled out a small metal tube with some sort of trigger and nozzle on top. He aimed the nozzle at the *Testimonium* and pulled the trigger. A gout of flame shot out and hit the ancient papyrus dead center. The official report to Rome by Proconsul Pontius Pilate caught fire immediately and burned very quickly. The man directed the fiery spray back and forth, even kicking aside the small rocks that held the scroll down; making sure that every last scrap of papyrus was consumed. When he was done, he slid the mini-flamethrower back into his pocket and turned to Isabella, leveling his pistol at her.

"And now, Doctor Sforza, you will die!" he said, pulling the trigger. The hammer fell on an empty chamber. He scowled, and then lifted his head. The sound of sirens was growing in the distance, and a pair of headlights topped a hill a couple of kilometers away. He holstered the gun and pulled the flamethrower out again, aiming it at her and pulling the trigger. She flinched, but only a small flicker of fire emerged— apparently his thoroughness in destroying the scroll had consumed all its fuel.

Rage twisted his dark features for a moment, and then a look of serenity returned. "Allah is merciful, whore!" he said. "You are allowed to keep your infidel life—for now!"

He turned on his heel and climbed back into the sports car, and with a screech of tires and a shower of gravel sped back down the road toward Naples.

Isabella cradled Josh in her arms. With one hand, she tried to stem the flow of blood from his wound, but she could feel his life ebbing between her fingers. In the absence of the headlights, the half-moon gave scant illumination. His breath was weak and labored.

"Isabella?" he whispered.

"Shhhh!" she said. "Don't try to talk. Help is coming."

"I'm so sorry," he said.

"You have nothing to apologize for," she sobbed through her tears.

"I'm sorry we won't grow old together," he said. "I was . . . looking forward to being your husband so much. . . please, Izza. Please don't blame God. He didn't do this . . ." His voice trailed off, and his eyes closed.

She cupped his face in her hands and wept. Sobs racked her body, and in her grief, something else surfaced—rage! A white hot anger that surprised her with its intensity. She turned her eyes to the starry Italian sky above her. All the anguish of her soul came out in her next words.

"Why shouldn't I blame you?" she asked the Almighty. "What kind of God are you, anyway? How could you allow this? Why would you let the kindest, most loving and decent man I have ever met die like a dog in the middle of the road? Josh was innocent!!" The last word left her mouth in an audible howl.

Where the answering voice came from she did not know. It was not from Josh, who lay unconscious and dying in her arms. It was not booming down from the sky above. It seemed to come from within, from the deepest coils of her mind, and yet it reverberated gently in the air around her.

Was my Son any less innocent? it asked.

She thought of the suffering Jesus that Pilate had written about in his *Testimonium*, and of the compassionate Jesus hanging on the cross, praying for those who drove the nails in His hands. She thought of the shamed woman, taken in the act of adultery, that he had treated with gentleness and compassion. Then, in her mind's eye, she saw the full horror of the cross as if for the first time. She hung her head, and the voice that came from her next was as soft as a little girl's.

"I'm sorry, God," she sobbed. "Please, Lord—please don't take this good man from me! I will believe! I will serve You! I will love You forever, if You will just give Josh back to me. I can't stand to lose anyone else!"

But then her cool, rational mind scolded her. Was this the best she could do? Bargaining with God, like a fishwife in the marketplace? Do this for me, and I will do that for You? How did that honor the life that Josh had lived before her every moment she knew him? Her body racked with sobs as she bowed her head again.

"That's not right," she said. "Josh is Yours, God, not mine. I love him so much, but he belongs to You, and he is in Your hands. Thank You for sharing him with me for a while. You showed me Your love every time he looked at me, and I was too foolish to see it. I trust You now, Lord, to do what is best for him, but if You take him home, I will miss him so much. I cannot bear to think I might never see him again. But there is a way I can, isn't there? You showed us that way!" The realization swept over her, hard and sudden.

"Oh God, I love You! I am Yours! Please, Jesus! Save me!" The words tore out of her, hard to say but impossible not to say. When they finally escaped her lips, she felt something she had never felt before, never even dreamed of. It was the love of God, washing through her like a strong wave, cleansing every dark stain from her soul. Her grief and anger remained, but they were purified and tempered by a depth of compassion and love that drowned out the old Isabella and raised a new, clean, and shining self in her place.

Suddenly three sets of headlights came swooping in from the north, topped by flashing police lamps. A door slammed, and a voice called out.

"Are you all right, ma'am?" it asked.

"I am unhurt, but my fiancée has been shot," she said. "And Dr. Castolfo is dead."

"There is an ambulance right behind us," the officer replied. "Who did this?"

"A tall black man in a sports car," she said. "He has an African accent!"

The policeman sprinted back to his car, barking orders into his radio while the other two cars drove past her on the shoulder, taking off after the terrorist. She watched them go without a word, focusing instead on the ebbing life of her love, dying in her arms. His eyes were closed, but his breath still came feebly. She leaned forward and kissed him on the forehead, wanting him to know just how much he was loved in the last moments of his life.

A few seconds later an ambulance pulled up, and two medics rushed to her side with a stretcher. They lifted Josh out of her arms, and she tried to rise as they placed him on the stretcher. Her legs would not cooperate, but a policeman came to her side and lifted her to her feet. She staggered toward the ambulance, and one of the medics helped her climb in behind Josh. The second one had a stethoscope to his chest.

"I've got no pulse!" he shouted. "Get the paddles ready!"

Then the ambulance doors slammed shut, and it carried Joshua and Isabella away into the night.

* * *

Father MacDonald moved from one fallen soldier to the next, administering the last rites to them one by one. The firefight had been horrific, and over half of the escorting force had been killed or wounded before the last of the terrorists had fallen. The burning helicopter, crashed in a field next to the road, cast an eerie glare over the scene of the firefight. A second chopper had landed moments earlier on the other side of the road.

Through the confusion, a middle-aged Italian man in a dark suit approached. He had not been part of the escort, and Father MacDonald did not recognize him.

"Are you Father Duncan MacDonald?" he asked.

"That I am," said the priest.

"I need you to come with me," the man said. "I am Antonio Lucoccini, Italian State Security."

MacDonald glared at him. "These men need my priestly offices!" he snapped. "You will just have to wait!"

"Father, I have something to tell you," the agent said. Something in his voice sent a chill through MacDonald's soul, and he rose to face the man.

"What is it?" he demanded.

"Somehow the terrorist who masterminded this attack found out that the scroll was being taken up the coast road," explained Lucoccini. "He caught up with Dr. Castolfo and forced the car off the road. The Pontius Pilate scroll has been destroyed."

433

MacDonald looked at him in amazement. "Bugger the stinkin' papyrus, lad!" he snapped. "What of the people? Are Joshua, and Isabella, and Dr. Castolfo all right?"

Lucoccini hung his head. "Castolfo is dead," he said. "The woman is all right, but the American has been shot. I just heard over the radio that he has no pulse. They are rushing him to a hospital in Cassino."

MacDonald hung his head for a moment, and let out a stifled sob. Then he grabbed the Italian by the arm. "What are you waiting for, then?" he snapped. "Take me to them now!"

The helicopter delivered them to the emergency room only a few moments after Joshua had arrived. MacDonald found Isabella in the waiting room, and she rushed into his arms. She was covered with Joshua's blood.

"There, there, lass," the priest said as she buried her head on his shoulder. "I am sure they are doing all they can!"

She shook her head. "His heart stopped three times on the way here," she said. "Oh, Duncan! There was so much blood!"

He saw the hospital's tiny chapel off to one side of the ER waiting room. "Let us pray, lass," he said, guiding her toward it. And pray they did, as they waited for someone to emerge from the operating room and tell them the inevitable news.

* * *

Joshua Parker opened one eye, then the other. Every muscle in his body screamed in protest, and the pain radiating from his abdomen was incredible. Harsh fluorescent lights made him squint, but then something came between his face and their glare. In a dim haze he saw Isabella's face looking down at him.

"Am I still in heaven?" he asked faintly.

Through her tears, a smile touched the edges of her mouth. "No," she said. She took his hand and squeezed it. "But now I am."

She leaned down and gently kissed his forehead. He turned and saw his father's tall frame filling the doorway.

"What happened?" he asked.

"You died, my boy," his father said. "Three times in the ambulance and once on the operating table. You were gone for over ten minutes that last time; the surgeon said that he was about to cover you up when your heart started again. That bullet did a quite a bit of damage."

Josh's eyes widened as his memories returned. "The scroll!" he said.

"It's gone," said Isabella. "But you know that God did not live in that scroll. He lives in our hearts, just as He always has."

Josh furrowed his brow. "Our hearts?" he asked.

"That's right!" said Isabella, her smile widening even further. "Mine too! Now you will never go where I cannot follow!"

Josh closed his eyes, his pain forgotten as tears of joy ran down his face. He faded off for what seemed like a little bit, but when he opened his eyes the room was dark and his father was gone. Isabella still sat by the bed, however, and she came to his side the minute she saw his eyes open.

"What happened to the man who shot us?" he asked, which was going to be his next question before he passed out.

"The Italian police caught him as he tried to re-enter Naples," she said. "And, according to Police Chief Zadora, not long after that, a helicopter lifted off the roof of the American embassy. No one knows where he is now."

"That's not entirely true," said a voice from the doorway. A tall American with short cropped hair and a military bearing entered the room. He looked down at Josh and took him by the hand.

"I am Colonel Lincoln Bertrand, with the CIA," he said. "The man who tried to kill you is Ibrahim Abbasside, an Al Qaeda agent that we have wanted to get our hands on for a very long time. Officially, we don't 'have' him, if you know what I mean—but we know very well where he is. And I am about to go have a long and heartfelt conversation with him when I leave here. Any message you want me to convey?"

Joshua shook his head, but Isabella spoke.

"Tell him," she said, "that God is indeed merciful. But He is also just!"

The CIA officer smiled grimly, nodded, and then turned and left the room.

Joshua looked at the face of the most beautiful woman he had ever known, and smiled at her.

"How long was I out?" he asked.

"Three days," she said. "And most of this afternoon and evening."

"Well," he replied, "I think you and I have some wedding plans to make."

She kissed his lips very gently. "Get well first," she said. "And then we will have all the time in the world . . . and whatever time comes after."

EPILOGUE

Joshua Parker and Isabella Sforza were actually married twice—once in Italy, in the presence of all her friends, extended family, and co-workers; then again, two weeks later, back in Oklahoma at Reverend Parker's church. Both weddings took place in October, six months after the discovery of the chamber on Capri and its remarkable contents. At the time of this writing, they are excavating a Clovis culture site in West Texas, and planning to return to Italy in the spring. They just found out that Isabella will be bringing their first child into the world next fall. The baby's gender is not yet known, but if it is a boy, it will be named Giuseppe.

Reverend Parker and Father MacDonald co-officiated at both weddings. The lanky Texan pastor and the gray-bearded Scottish priest had become close friends, and while they continued to re-fight the battles of the Protestant Reformation in their lengthy conversations and emails, they did so in a way that honored St. Augustine's ancient dictum: *"In the essentials, unity; in the non-essentials, liberty; and in everything, charity."* Father MacDonald's parishioners commented that his homilies sounded increasingly Protestant, while some of Reverend Parker's more conservative church members groused that he was starting to sound like a "dad gum priest."

The destruction of the *Testimonium* made any final pronunciation on its authenticity impossible. Father MacDonald managed to locate a few tiny fragments of ash by the roadside, and they carbon dated to 2,000 years, with a 115-year margin of error. Critics were quick to point out that all that really proved was that the document had been written on ancient paper.

That fall, Maria Tintoretto and David Hubbard co-authored a book attempting to debunk the entire discovery at Capri. Entitled *The Grand Deception: How the Church Engineered the Discovery of Pilate's Testimony*, it claimed that the chamber on Capri had actually been discovered by priests in the late 1700s, and that the Pope had ordered the *Testimonium* to be forged on an ancient papyrus sheet and planted in the cabinet to be discovered at some later date. Other than the fact that there had been a similar earthquake on Capri during that timeframe, the duo was able to present very little in the way of proof of their hypothesis. That did not keep the book from quickly rising to the top of the bestseller lists.

But the general public was more sympathetic to the claims put forward by the Capri team. Every other artifact in the chamber had been dated to the first century, and the evidence that the chamber had never been disturbed was overwhelming, even though most of the dust samples had perished in the museum attack. Pastors around the world shared and discussed the contents of the *Testimonium* with their congregations, and some new study Bibles were already including its text as an appendix to the New Testament. Church attendance in America increased markedly, and the number of citizens identifying themselves as atheists or agnostics began to decline for the first time in two decades. Even in jaded, cynical Europe, the moribund Protestant and Catholic Churches showed signs of revival. The *Testimonium* had everyone talking about Jesus again.

As for Ibrahim Abbasside, no official record of his arrest exists, and the U.S. Government denies having him in custody. However, in the months since the death of Dr. Castolfo and the destruction of the *Testimonium*, nineteen senior terror leaders have been killed or captured, and numerous sleeper cells taken into custody. The Italian Security Agency, with the aid of a sixteen-year-old hacker from London, finally traced the source of the intercepts found on Abbasside's computer, and "the Spider" was arrested two months ago.

About a month after they were married, Josh and Isabella agreed to appear on the Will Mayor show, opposite Dr. Tintoretto and David Hubbard. Even with the host joining the two atheists in questioning the *Testimonium's* authenticity, the newlyweds handled themselves quite well. The parting exchange illustrates the whole tone of the debate:

> **Tintoretto:** *Surely you must agree, Dr. Parker, that the destruction of the scroll on the eve of its most rigorous testing is awfully convenient for those who want to proclaim its authenticity!*

> **Parker:** *Actually, ma'am, being shot through the stomach and having one of my kidneys destroyed was a considerable inconvenience! The only way that it would have been 'convenient,' as you put it, was if the scroll was faked and we were aware of that fact. But the scroll was real and ancient, as all of us who discovered it knew from the beginning, so its destruction was a real shame, as the testing would have borne out our claims completely.*

> **Hubbard:** *But now the only real proof of your god is a little pile of ashes!*

Parker: *(laughs for several seconds) That is the saddest thing I have ever heard anyone say! The real proof of God is all around us every day. It is in the love we feel for each other, our capacity for compassion, in the wondrous complexity of the cosmos, and most of all in the historical record of the Gospels. We don't need some carbon-14 date to "prove" that God is real. All we need is the evidence of our own heart. After all, that is what faith is all about, isn't it?"*

36780920R00254

Made in the USA
Charleston, SC
18 December 2014